Another Man

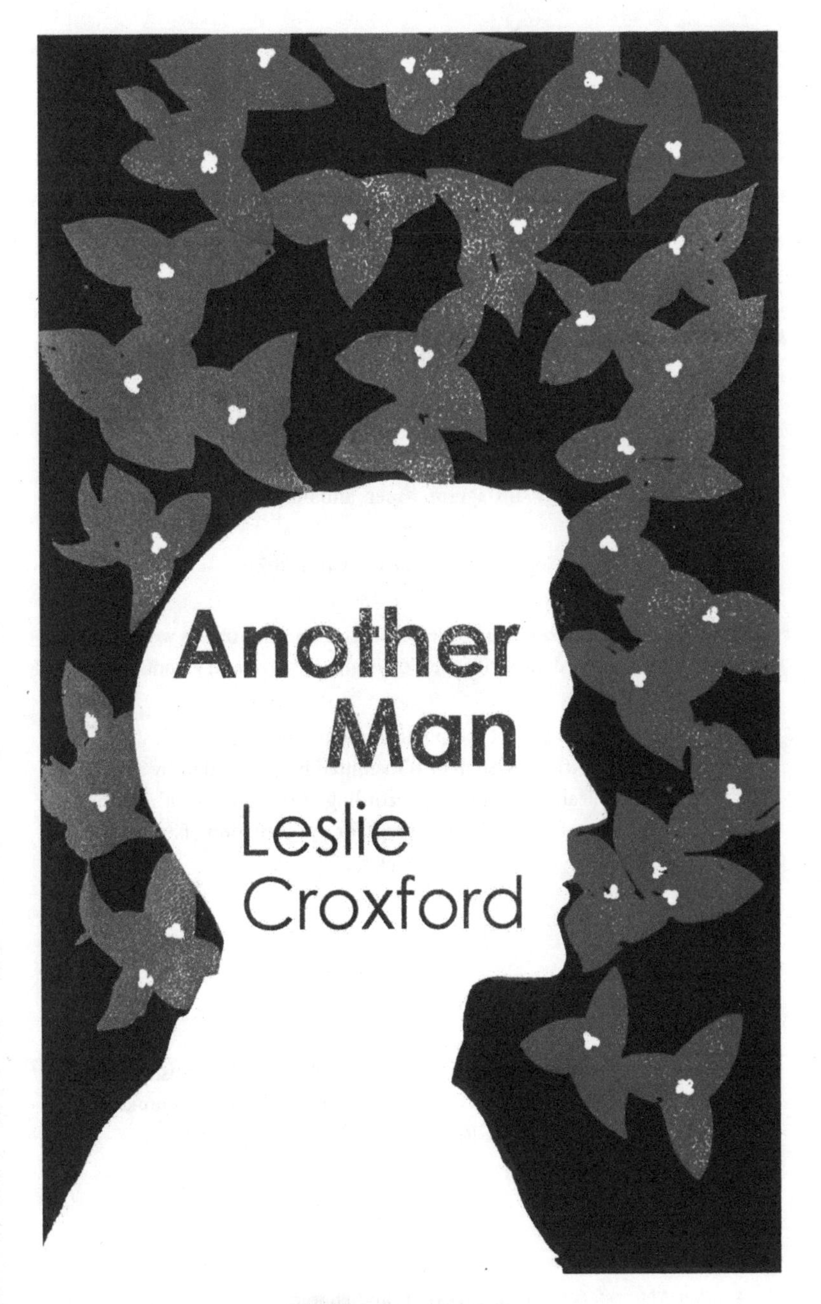
Another
Man
Leslie
Croxford

PAPER
+ INK

Another Man by Leslie Croxford

This edition has been published in 2021
in the United Kingdom by Paper + Ink.

www.paperand.ink
Twitter: @paper_andink
Instagram: paper_and.ink

1 2 3 4 5 6 7 8 9 10

ISBN 9781911475477

A CIP catalogue record for this book is available from the British Library.
Jacket design by James Nunn: www.jamesnunn.co.uk | @Gnunkse
Printed and bound by CPI Group (UK) Ltd, Croydon CRO 4YY

Another Man refers to historical events and characters sometimes extended into new situations. These are for entirely fictional purposes, and are not proposed as fact. Beyond Albert Speer and his associates, no portrayals of actual people are intended unless specified.

It takes a great deal of history to produce a little literature.

Henry James, *Hawthorne*

BOOK ONE

Part I

1

The beach is deserted this early in the morning. No one else is in the sea. Waves lap in the clear Mediterranean sunlight. Small fishes dart, silver, in transparent water. A conical stone watchtower stands on a nearby rock promontory.

I am coming out of the water, salt rivulets streaming from my hair, down my chest and arms, my loins. I make for the granite shelf where I left my clothes. I thought it was this one – or was it that one? I cannot find my trousers, which contain my wallet. I just sit on the rock without my towel.

The sun soon dries me. People have started coming onto the beach, families with small children and coloured umbrellas. They are talking. I do not hear them for the soft thudding of the tide. They skirt me, in my cocoon of still silence, stealing glances at someone sitting naked on a rock.

Policemen wander over to me from their car parked on the beachside road.

"What are you doing here?"

"Swimming, but my clothes were stolen. They had my money and identification."

"Who are you?"

I can be anyone I want now, can't I?

I hover in this rare freedom of being no one. Who – what *– do I want to be?*

The man wakes. He realises he has been dreaming, though he has not recalled anything from sleep for years. Sitting up, noticing *The Costa Times* newspaper on the floor, he again takes in the front-page story:

> A man was washed up yesterday on the coast of Almería in the south of Spain. Tourists found him drowned on the beach beneath the village where Albert Speer's chauffeur had

convalesced after his release from long-term imprisonment as a POW in Russia.

The British family discovering the body alerted the Guardia Civil. The police are trying to determine the man's identity. But they told reporters they also want to establish the current whereabouts of the man who once drove Speer, an infamous war criminal and Hitler's friend, popularly known as 'the Good Nazi'.

The man recognises the connection with his dream. He lies down again, intending to return to sleep, yet he remains awake for a few moments, thinking about Speer. 'The Good Nazi' has fascinated him for years. What can have happened for his chauffeur to go missing from this *pueblo*, from which he himself has been absent for over a decade?

I never expected to return. But I have awarded myself a month's vacation for having finally finished my book on late medieval history. The moment the printed pages came into my hands, between their hard covers and the dust jacket, I felt a burst of pride. My study is firmly based on the archives, resisting the siren calls of those new forms of historical interpretation. From the outset, I intended it as a polemic in favour of objective evidence, albeit in the neglected field of late fifteenth-century administrative history. So, whatever the reviewers may say, I am well satisfied, not to say delighted, at finally being released from the labour of so many years. I deserve this holiday.

It proved difficult to arrange, however, so far into the summer. The desirable destinations were fully booked. Nothing much seemed to remain except this primitive Andalusian village, of all places, hours from the airport across a volcanic moonscape.

The crumbling coastal road curved back on itself in repeated oxbows as we pursued it yesterday at dizzying heights. I sweated as we turned inland through a blinding grey blur of flat terrain, nauseous from the smell of the jerky old taxi's engine. Then, after crossing the parched plain for hours, overlooked by dark hills, we came out to a beach of rock and black sand. Its private coves, I know from my previous visit, can only be discovered after a long, hot climb over that promontory with its watchtower. To the other side a mound rises, skirted by new hotels and surmounted by white, Arab-style houses.

We chugged up to them, passing donkeys drinking at the *pueblo's* watering place, then an orange grove. And I was delivered to the *pensión*. Opened since my last visit, it is tasteful. Yet, arriving last night, as the terrace garden became a restaurant, I found few other diners, just a painter and his friends.

I ate alone – virtually unprecedented for me in the *pueblo*, I realised, casting my mind back to my previous visit here. I took refuge in reading *The Costa Times* and took it to my room.

2

The *pensión's* new guest, an Englishman, is unexpectedly wakened again from his snooze, this time by an old-fashioned radio alarm; the room's previous occupant had, apparently, left it on.

"Imagine the gates," a sepulchral voice says. "They are tall, many times a man's height. They are made of bronze so heavy that, when open but set moving on their rollers, it is impossible to stop them closing. Take heed, then: they are closing now. Slowly at first, so gradually as to be unnoticed, yet with increasing speed, they are heading for each other. They will never reopen. No human force could prise them apart.

"Still, there is time: just enough. We have been left exactly the time required; a human lifetime; the part, the last, intense part, of a lifetime that *is* our life. Even now, as we ourselves are slower, as time moves faster, there remains precisely the time necessary for each of us to do what specifically is required of us: to pass – to squeeze – through those shutting gates, leaving behind our unfulfilled pasts and their detritus; abandoning all those left out to their eternity of empty chaos; of dread nothingness. But we must decide; submit now, without delay, while there is still –"

Static sweeps over the believer's voice, obliterating it in a fierce roar. The guest switches off the alarm, finally getting out of bed. He goes across to the window and widens the wooden shutters to look down from the *pueblo*, atop its mound, at the Mediterranean.

He breathes the salt air, drinking it in. Unlike the previous foreign occupant, setting the alarm to an English programme so early on holiday, he feels no need for a clarion call. Here, seemingly randomly, for his first vacation in years, he is free: free both to clear his mind after recent scholarly exertions and as a reprieve from embarking yet on another research project. He can lounge as he pleases. There is surely nothing to prevent him idling sleepily by the window, alone as he is this summer, scarcely considering what might distract him during his otherwise empty days here.

He lingers, too blank to take in fully an urge growing upon him to step away from the view. It is an impulse drawing him from the brilliantly sunlit room much as dark currents claim swimmers in the sea down there. Something he barely senses is tugging him inwardly down a deep, silent path, into the village where a chapter from his past was ended; in which a brief affair was let go altogether, as he has assumed since, in London, over the years.

He is being wrested blindly back to that previous visit here, which he never expected to repeat. Not that he is merely poised nostalgically to set foot again in those narrow streets. Rather, he is a sleepwalker heading back into the month he once spent in the *pueblo*, in a foreign country, before having inevitably turned away from it to embark on another life with its academic goals. Half-roused now, he is re-entering a period sealed off in his mind, which remains to be reckoned with. There is unfinished business, he starts to feel in his bones.

Soon he is out in the *pueblo*. In his wide-brimmed straw hat and sunglasses, the man is walking both now and then. Effaced, he might be anyone with squinting eyes taking refuge from dazzling cotton sheets billowing on that roof. The maid will soon take them down, dry after only a brief time in this summer heat.

The villa ahead has no washing – except that, for him, there hangs the searing white laundry supplied by his memory, quarantining what's stored within him. Tiles on the villa's flat roof will, he knows from having lain there before, remain warm well into brilliantly starlit night.

Bougainvillea crowds the front of the villa. Pausing there, he finds it covering the white walls and street-level window panes. Supposing he was inside again, would it still be possible, he wonders, to see through the dense growth, from this *pueblo* on its high perch, down one kilometre to the blue haze that is the sea?

Soon the bougainvillea will have covered the upper stories of the villa, too. Yet the first-floor bedroom terrace is still open. All that space, that light before it, remains unobscured. Though the plant must already be intruding, he supposes, on the flat, tiled roof.

The sun is pitiless. It peels paint, splintering wood in this villa as in the others. It invades the slightest space, leaving it bone-dry, as he passes on through the *pueblo*. For it is noon, reminding him of that time when he had found the sun especially fearsome. The hour is shunned by all except women in black, scurrying along knife-edges of shadow in the alleys, survivors of husbands but also of the catastrophe he now feels, inexplicably, imminent in the region's geology.

A strange restlessness drives him round the circumference of this peak. He might be an unsighted man ritually repeating a route bringing him again and again to see-but-not-see his implicit destination: this Mediterranean-facing villa.

Circling the *pueblo*, he has the increasing sense of being here and now as he was years ago – but without the one in the villa.

He is alone, as he has been ever since leaving her in the *pueblo* over a decade ago.

3

Landward, there is a *mirador* beside the main plaza. Fredrik Solem, a resident, leans against its wrought iron, waist-high fence, gazing over hills such as this on which the *pueblo* is built. They rise from a dusty plain.

Solem, a Scandinavian archaeologist, wears khaki shorts but no shirt, and open sandals. With his moustache and perpetual cigarette, he's a parody of an RAF officer. In fact, they say he did do something or other in the war – the same *they* who named him "Bog Man": a *they* with no identifiable individual.

Solem and his past have fallen as deeply into this nickname as nameless men in northern parts once did into prehistoric peat bogs. Yet he is unexhumed, outside anything remembered here; he gives no hint of whether or not an occurrence in the Norwegian fjords during the war brought him to live in Spain for so long thereafter.

Versions vary. But it is the only thing he never mentions. Speaking English with a perfection of grammar and accent – albeit with a pitch declaring him a foreigner – he prefers to tell all and sundry over drinks in the plaza's open-air café about his excavations of Palaeolithic dwellings and burial sites hereabouts. Man-made mounds are full of the dead. You hear endlessly about his pursuit of long-concealed subterranean chambers.

It has been going on for years, this tunnelling into darkness that he seems to bring out with him, sitting here each evening in shadow, with the peaked plain spreading away below. And nocturnal, that vista, unacknowledged as dreams from deep sleep by those chattering over their drinks, is as obscure as everything lying long-silenced beneath it. Buried or exposed, there is no difference now, with this invisible current cooling the day's heat.

Bog Man, archaeologist, is also a self-declared expert on the *pueblo*. Daily he tells tourists sitting with him on the plaza that there was a small Jewish quarter – the Judería. A trace remains: he leads groups over to the scarcely legible stone surround of the gate.

There is another historical remnant: the local women, wearing black, hold a corner of their headscarves between their teeth. It's a continuation of the veil worn during the time of the occupation – "the Arab occupation", he adds. The stone tower down on the beach, built as a lighthouse and lookout point, is a further reminder of the centuries the Moors were here. All the country round about was irrigated by them. The hills were terraced, verdant.

These days, agriculture is either a matter of the villagers' few rocky plots in the dusty valley, or a city of polythene tents providing fruit and vegetables for Northern Europe. But that is further along the coast, near the airport. The poor roads, the rocky terrain, have long secluded this *pueblo*, this beach, from the intrusions of commerce and tourism. Until recently, visitors were few and select: cultivated travellers drawn by the rugged natural beauty of this largely undiscovered spot by the Mediterranean. They were not, Bog Man continues in a swipe at his audience, the sort now packing the bars and nightclubs of the beach hotels. Real development is finally taking place, he laments, overheard by the *pensión's* new arrival.

The new arrival has not joined Bog Man's audience. He continues to walk around the *pueblo* on his first full day back, hearing only commonplaces any resident might express – the lowest common denominator, what everyone here knows, they come from outside the range of personal impressions, of individual memory, as he knows from his previous summer here.

Pacing on, he remembers overhearing the painter at dinner last night, who comes every year and was about to leave the following day. The painter told the rest of the table how productive he had found this season; but then, his summers always were. *The light here is exhilarating. There's a thrilling sense of space. Nothing can ever change that. It is the visionary freedom Spanish artists found all the way along this Mediterranean coast in canvases no less important than those by their French contemporaries, the Impressionists, if only people recognised it.*

The newcomer is left to match the painter's words to his own view of the place. But his memory of the *pueblo* as it was keeps surfacing, with the few – the one –he'd known here. It invades his perception of the visual surface he's admittedly seeing simultaneously through the painter's eyes: a serene, luminous, natural scene. It influences all he takes in, as if he were still here years ago, somehow unreasoningly, almost unknowingly, awaiting a deferred outcome of that time, rendering him and all he views nervously expectant.

Bog Man's lecture tour ends. People escape the heat. Only the *pensión's* newcomer idles on the *mirador*. He gazes at the dark hills in the abandoned afternoon. Barren once more, long-dormant, they have lost their Arab accretions; subsequent centuries of peasant excrescences from their sphinx sides. They have settled back into stillness: inanimate for this long-held moment. Nothing grows on them these days but parched everlasting flowers, spindly century plants, cacti. The sole fruit is that savagely spiked wild Barbary fig with seeds on which he remembers you can break your teeth.

The hills, the plain, the dried riverbed have apparently returned to that immemorial sterility into which an ever-churning earth once settled them. They are one with the desert he imagines far further south, across the sea, beyond cities, rural vestiges of civilisation. They are of a kind with northern wastes a virtual continent away: vast steppes; solitudes of snow; ice-hardened seas. Static, the hills have been travelling silently back to exist as always; to go on existing until – unless – convulsed again by the same energy with which an ever-revolving world gave them this form in a cataclysm of which they have no memory.

Later, the *pensión's* new arrival, returning to the *mirador* on his continuing walk around the *pueblo*, sees the fierce sun set over those parched, grained shanks. The light mutes, turning scarlet, pink: it fades. Out on that plain he sees the electric glow of a house, then of another. They seem incongruous, like the fires of primitive dwellers huddled in the dimness of the prehistory in which these hills were formed. Looming in the eventual moonlight, huge, the mounds are somnolent forms arrested in an inconceivably distant past. They only require some flicker of the Earth's unimaginably huge energy to return them to being. Dead, they live imperceptibly for the moment, these prehistoric forms.

The man crosses the darkened plaza and makes again for the seaward side of the *pueblo*. He is drawn back to the villa. Blinding sun is eclipsed for night. It is barely possible to see beyond this wiry bougainvillea wreathing the window. Electricity hereabouts is dim, fluctuating, reduced almost to nothing. Is there a light within? It is a guess at best, or some remembered image transposed onto a moonlit patch of the glass pane: features from the past, somehow entered to stare back at him.

Is it a shadow he all but glimpses moving inside the villa? Leaving the bedroom, it might be crossing the hall with its marble staircase, its Middle Eastern plates set in a row on a white, distempered wall, that perforated brass lamp hanging with coloured glass panels. And isn't *she* now climbing up the terrace, with its rustling beneath the stars? Well, it has to be, doesn't it? For he is taking it in doubly, then and now.

The guest, about to return at last to his *pensión*, smells charred meat drifting through the evening's balmy sea air. It sets the dogs off barking, as they did when ancient Greeks visited from the other end of the Mediterranean. Merchants, their spits on the beach, presented offerings, smoking like incense, to the gods – just as their ancestors raised semi-divine humans to heroic status. Immortal, they lodged perpetually in memory, those finally accomplished beings memorialised in funeral barrows. And on this beach, mongrels had yapped like jackals for gobbets that will not now, millennia later, be thrown here in the *pueblo* to these dogs.

Some other sense the visitor possesses conjures up fumes on the roof of the villa. He sees no fire there. It is too high to make anything out. But that is where it must come from, as it always has, together with bygone barbecues, invisible to him here, though rousing the dogs. He, too, is swallowing, his mouth watering, among furious barking by long denied dogs.

Somewhere a piano is playing. Passages of Chopin sound in the evening through the *pueblo's* alleys and streets. He hears phrases repeated. Again and again those invisible hands, that unidentified mind, returns to them, never released from the haunting, obsessing bars. Phrases, passages remain stubbornly short-circuited, never able to realise themselves in a melody. On and on they return, the notes, the keys, sticking in the humidity. Then silence, heavy, unfulfilling, stifles them for the rest of the night.

4

Sitting on the terrace of the *pensión* with another cup of breakfast coffee, I await the peace of mind for which I am vacationing here. But my return to the *pueblo* is clouding any such blissful vacancy, casting me back to a time in my life over and done with; it weighs on me as it did yesterday while I sauntered through these streets. Shadows of that past keep darkening my mood.

I was a fresh graduate that previous summer, unable to visualise how I would come into my own as an historian. But now, perched atop this hill, the Mediterranean and Africa before me, my book finally published, unexpectedly I see myself as I was during my years of work on the project. I am sure that I could no more have imagined bringing it to a successful conclusion then than had the new graduate.

Unreal, that endlessly far off date meant, I had unknowingly presumed, that I would never cease travelling the length of the London Underground to archives with rats' skeletons falling out of uncatalogued parchment rolls. I could not have envisaged a time when I need no longer read in a library the windows of which dim early in London's fading daylight, or continue writing during evenings stretching on in the green glow of my banker's lamp. With my head down, thrust into my task, I was frankly unaware of myself or anything else.

The nearer I came to finishing, the slower my progress. I spent an inordinate amount of time on details. It might have been fear of how the book would be received by academic colleagues with their lethal scholarly standards. Though detached up here, I suppose it was also implicit recognition that this was a craft keeping me afloat on the uncharted sea of life; a vessel I held to with ever increasing scrupulousness about quotations, footnotes, references.

How long I demurred about the final form of the author's name! Should it be traditional and impersonal, with initials, or "Frank"? In the end I was F. J. WARD – and the book is out.

Satisfaction at completion: that is what authors feel. Besides, what is at last in print can finally be left behind, like insecurities and painful memories; all those mistakes, hurts and failures of nerve. It is too late now for regrets, second thoughts, fussy perfectionism. Nothing can draw one back. So there is a sense of freedom, levitation surely, with such release – precisely the peace of mind for which I have come here.

But it is evasive. Not least because there is also a feeling of lowness; a heaviness of spirit. Surely that is predictable, and no more lasting than after coitus. After all, my study of administration in an early modern state stands, along with the method I deploy. There is no reason for me to feel like a monk who, having given up love, intimacy, sex for the religious life, finally finds himself defrauded with dullness, repetition, nothing – and despair of ever reclaiming all he had once surrendered.

Breakfast over, Frank returns to his room. Gazing distractedly down at the sea, he again sees an image in the window of a shop near the British Museum specialising in lavish art books. It was in his first year of research. The volume on display reproduced some artist's self-portrait. It showed him before a full-length mirror, taking himself in, naked, at middle age. The artist presented his entire body for a total impression that facial features alone cannot convey. In fact, his expression was not clear. There was no attempt at mere likeness, let alone a mood, in the paint-splattered mirror, the painted reflection of which showed through Frank's own features in the bookshop's vitrine.

He does not remember the artist's name. Has he ever known the one presenting an image of himself, here looking out the window? For years, it has been an anonymity in the mirror's mercury; that glass. He hovers still before Frank in those greys and whites of an extensive membrane, self-encased like a chrysalis waiting to open.

Immediately after that first summer in the *pueblo*, I began graduate work. I moved to London to work in its libraries and archives, returning to the university every month for my professor's seminar. Yet during lunch hours, after work, and at weekends, I was distracted from the rigours of research by the capital's plentiful bookshops. I rummaged through stock on mobile shelves on the pavement, as well as in bargain basements.

That reference to Speer in *The Costa Times* reminds me of the paperbacks pouring out about the Second World War. They were dangerous diversions, I know, sinking onto my bed after a drawn-out breakfast, the sun now too strong to go down to the beach. I have long been captivated by a war to which my father – a veteran of El Alamein – often refers, leaving my mother glassy-eyed. My fascination with it continued in London *sub rosa*. Discreetly absorbed, as if by pornography, I stood at a book stall reading the autobiography of Speer, Hitler's closest associate and friend. Widely acclaimed, it allegedly led one for the first time inside the Third Reich. Together with the author's prison diaries and admission of general guilt for crimes of which he nonetheless claimed he had had no specific knowledge, it had increased his moral credibility – and so that of many Germans with him.

I could not prise myself away from Speer's bestsellers, so different from the documents I picked through for my research, with their required knowledge of late Latin, palaeography and scholarly sources. They overcame me with the thrill of Speer's story and its exhilarating risks; of the voice telling it and the man himself. And in addition to their many sensational revelations, I learnt, day after day, of how, according to Speer, Hitler – his Mephistopheles – had increasingly claimed him. With an uncanny scrupulousness I wished I could have displayed in my work, I retained every detail of how he had become enthralled to him.

Then I found Speer reduced to lying low in forest ditches as planes bombed the road on which he raced to rescue what he could from the Allies and Hitler's scorched-earth decree. Everything was falling into ruins, all he had built for the man he finally saw as his false master, in that early part of what eventually proved a long life. What could he be thinking and feeling, trapped with his subaltern and driver on damp forest ferns and pine needles, in darkness whose limits he could not know?

There would have been a pool of drivers. Assuming this was the one who had come to the *pueblo* to recuperate from his years as a Russian prisoner of war, some (besides the police, I suppose) might wish to find him. They would surely seek to discover what light he could shed on Speer, especially now that his name has been darkened by new evidence emerging since the publication of his memoirs and *Secret Diaries*.

For myself, I recall an encounter with the man. It was shortly after I moved into a large Victorian house on the Bakerloo Line, converted into flats and bedsits. Other residents, spending Sunday afternoon in the overgrown garden they considered bucolic, in English sunshine too weak except to provoke allergies, hailed from deckchairs. They invited me to share cheesecake: I have always found it too dry.

Politely declining from my upstairs window, I returned to my room. It was curtained for me to work undisturbed, yet also disguised me doing the forbidden: idly reading the papers. "Forbidden" because, although I had finished my doctorate some time ago, my position as an archivist, which allowed me time off from regular duties, specifically required me to advance my research and publish. Despite which, scanning the press, I lighted on a German prisoner of war recently discovered in a Russian psychiatric hospital, having forgotten who he was. I was curious: what possible existence could he have had in all those years?

Now, here in the *pensión*, I stretch out on my bed. Again I take in a man in an unacknowledged coma, in the shadows of a London bedsitting room.

Unwittingly, Frank enters a twilight state, experiencing burial within his own body. He drifts, desiring details of how self-discovery is achieved, finally, here in the *pueblo*. Later, he rouses, once more, from a hovering dream. It is still the one in which he emerges from the sea: naked, as whomever he wishes to be.

PART II

1

As each afternoon wears on, and the weakening light slants, the glinting increases from the hill opposite – not one of those in the plain behind the *pueblo*, but standing to the side, forming a pair with this hill. Over there, the day's sun finally catches on shards of glass from broken windowpanes in collapsed shacks. For villagers had fled the *pueblo* during the Civil War, upon hearing rumours of advancing Republicans killing priests, raping nuns and looting property. Worse, there was a bloodletting locally, having nothing to do with politics: a settling of old scores over water rights, land claims, immemorial family feuds. People took refuge inland as far as the mountains, or just on the rough, scattered parcels of land they farmed. Then, when the war ended, they re-emerged; but not to the derelict *pueblo*. They formed a haphazard colony on that glittering hill opposite.

Bog Man has been sitting again through the sunset at a café table out on the plaza telling these people how the abandoned *pueblo* revived. In addition to tourists, his audiences contain some foreigners who had come to live here: *pieds noirs* and Germans arriving in the province since '45. But I have no need of his explanation. Leaving the *mirador* to walk back to the *pensión* once more, I remember hearing it from my friend Juan twenty years ago.

Juan, calling me from my suburban London habitat to this other reality, invited me to spend the summer of our graduation here with him. His father had been sent to the province several years earlier to survey it for a place to build the local airport. He met the mayor: "You know what you should do? Give people land in the *pueblo* to build houses. It will create employment, and you'll attract only the kind of outsiders with enough money to pay the construction costs."

The house Juan's father built is further up the hill than the *pensión*. When I next walk round the *pueblo*, all these years later, I pursue an alley up from the plaza, past the church, then the mayor's office. I must take a turn – though is it this one? Strange, that I can lose myself in such a small place, where I once repeatedly made my way to the house. But then I lost contact with Juan too, after that summer. He went to work in his maternal family's wine business in Madrid, his English education over. I devoted myself to research with Professor Keller.

The house, now I'm in front of it, looks smaller, with its unadorned stone exterior. A jeep with a Netherlands licence plate is parked in a widening of the alley beside it. There is sudden banging. One of the fierce sea winds has suddenly gusted through, slamming a door. Large fragments of plaster fall from the recently finished walls, powdering the floor tiles.

"I don't think I could bear this for long," Juan's mother would say.

Now, through the open window, there's the clogged, adenoidal exclamation of the Dutch owner.

Driving along the coast, one sometimes still sees a family restaurant advertising couscous. In summer, the smell of kebab might continue to drift even from the new beach bars. A camping site, set in a palm grove, retains the original French proprietor's name.

These small businesses were established by *pieds noirs* unable to afford life in a France now foreign to them after generations in Algeria. Doubtless, too, there were those for whom it was dangerous to return to Paris, say, because the security services might take too much of an interest in their past associations with the treasonous OAS. Better to lose themselves in this southern Spanish province where the landscape, climate and pace are similar to what they had so reluctantly left behind.

It offered the chance to start a new life for a man Juan's father knew. With the money from selling his two furniture stores in Algiers, he had been negotiating to buy a small hotel on the coast between here and the provincial capital. But first he built a home for his family in the *pueblo*, on land the mayor gave him.

The house is on the village's seaward slope, and therefore on three levels: the entrance hall with bedrooms and bathroom; the living room, with another bedroom, complete with terrace giving onto the Mediterranean; and the dining room and kitchen, with a staircase leading up to the flat roof. The villa still smelled of paint when Juan's parents went with their son and his friend to visit the man's family in a social round the outsiders – the builders – maintained throughout that hot summer.

The man is telling Juan's father about the football they used to play in those days, as I remember it. His wife is Spanish, from Oran. She and Juan's mother drink Málaga Dulce, exchanging tales of the slovenly unreliability of the local women as servants. They criticise the food here: so much pork, everything fried, no wonder they're all so fat.

Now everyone is discussing the recent news of village boys killed while climbing in a local cave. I hear how deep such caverns are in those mounds beyond the *mirador*, inwardly shrinking from pursuing the daredevils into that awful chasm. I'm hanging back, paralysed, losing my foothold, only to find the terrifyingly precipitous space swallowing me up, as our host says:

"Parents can't be too careful, looking after their children".

His daughter, Esther, is sitting before me, listening. She's several years older than Juan and me. She's more assured, as if she knows things we don't. She has a good figure. Her features are attractive, if severe. She's detached to the point of boredom: waiting, just waiting there, perhaps even after we've left.

She's out of the question for me. I know that. She's put herself out of bounds, hasn't she? Certainly I've put her there, this being outside my reality. I don't look at her. I don't bother to feel for her whatever I feel for her. No, she isn't looking at me: she's barely looking at me: that can't really be her looking at me – can it? – as she springs up and suggests that Juan and I take in the view from the roof terrace with her.

We follow her up the narrow, curving staircase, past the kitchen, still hearing the conversation below about how the bougainvillea her parents are planting is indestructible, though it's mainly a reminder of their garden in Algiers; and about how the local bureaucracy is keeping them going to the provincial capital to complete the purchase of the hotel.

We walk through a door: surprising silence, starlit night.

Juan is confident with girls. Unlike me, he has sisters, female cousins. His Catholic boys' boarding school in England, to which the sons of his Anglo-Spanish family have been sent for generations, was only a fraction of what he'd come to know. School excursions into the local town served as excuses for meeting girls. He had no nervousness about pressing his claim on them. He has always been matter-of-fact about his interest in women, never mystifying it with abstract terms, remotely sacred feelings.

These days Maruja has claimed his attention – or, rather, her large breasts: "They're heavy! So heavy, in this heat!" Thus *la bruja*, the sorceress, tells him. That's how Maruja, the daughter of a lawyer from Barcelona, is known throughout the *pueblo*.

Juan is helping her relieve her load.

But now Juan's official girlfriend is arriving from Madrid. We drive to the provincial capital to meet the train. She is nice, this elegant, self-possessed young woman whom Juan's family expects him to marry.

"We must find an attractive girl for *you*," he says, as I unload Maruja's suitcase from the car, arriving back in the *pueblo*.

We are on the roof terrace again. The maid and her teenage son are barbecuing meat for us, this group of friends whom Esther has invited this weekend while her parents are away. Someone produces a camera with a flash. There is a photo of that evening with young people lightly dressed in the summer heat. There are photographs of the even more primitive *pueblo* we all went to, further up in the mountains, with its stone grinder for olive oil dating from Arab times; snapshots of our day in a nearby small town in which a horse-drawn carriage led us past some bronze grandee in a rotunda of geraniums to the harbour. There we had lunch from whatever fish the boats did not send to the big tourist hotels further up the coast.

I am rarely photographed these days, a decade and half on. I use an electric shaver; I do not see myself in the mirror. Only in passports, official documents, does my face look back at me – as unremarkable, I suppose, as any man's in a crowd.

Yet the picture of the barbecue, the mountain *pueblo*, the waterside lunch, may still exist. The people in it must still be alive somewhere, somehow. But the image of that nocturnal terrace where the two of us lay alone on warm, moonlit tiles, of just myself with you then: it's lost to me.

This is the photograph never taken; never developed. It stands in the darkroom of the years, of forgetfulness, soaking away in the unacknowledged emulsion of my mind. It is the escaped image I am finding indelibly imprinted on my retinas as I walk round the *pueblo* again, after all this time, at the villa's obscuring bougainvillea.

I wonder how it happened, her taking me up to the terrace alone like that. Was it stage-managed, by her, by me, the two of us, climbing to the moonlit roof? I am having to stage-manage it even now, though I am hardly aware of doing so in lapses of attention, distracted moments, back here a decade or more later. For what happened – but surely can't have – is still happening, as somewhere my mind rehearses what has to be taking place again for the first time.

Like the photos that always exist, although lost; like my image of the climb, not brought into being, but there, it did happen. It is always happening, her impossible leading me up to the terrace. She, beautiful in that somehow Oriental way acquired through generations of her European family settled in North Africa; she, exotic, distant, beyond my grasp, is leading me by the hand from the sitting room up the narrow passage that smelled of local volcanic rock, as if we are tunnelling out of one of these hills to the stars.

For I, wandering the *pueblo* at dusk, while Juan spends more and more time alone with his girlfriend from Madrid, have encountered her coming out of the shop where she has just bought lapis lazuli earrings. She invites me for a drink at the villa. She would welcome the company, she tells me, passing newly planted bougainvillea by the entrance. Her parents are away on business.

We are in the sitting room, drinking her father's Ricard *pastis*, on chairs still sheathed in plastic to protect them from legs in shorts, sweaty with suntan lotion, or from the ubiquitous sand. She is saying she has heard Englishmen are very romantic.

I suppose I should take it as a jest; playful friction intended to set a conversation going with someone she has never previously addressed directly. At the barbecue, though friendly to the group, she'd spoken to no one in particular.

Yet, an instant ago, the very first moment I heard what she said, I did not consider it a tease. She looked at me with an expression I cannot fully make out in the light draining into the sea framed by the window. But I am inexperienced, too much at a loss to dare take the words seriously.

The plastic on my chair is hot and sticky now. I am tongue-tied at the prospect of being the subject of even her joking interest. Without knowing it, I am aware that I have nothing to say for myself. Have I even existed so far, unformed, unexceptional, in a cloudy, predictable English world conventional to the point of banality compared with the violent upheaval, the wrenching exile, in her scorching Mediterranean reality? I doubt if I have the strength of personality to hold her, to sustain her; to be such as she's looking for.

"Who are you, really?" she says in the same baffling vein. I'm struggling. Is there anything to know of me? I've lived so far but acquired no history. "Maybe you don't need to answer."

It's dark now. We're shadows to each other.

"Don't say anything." She's touched me on the arm. "Let's go up on the roof."

Coming up the narrow, musty stairwell, she has taken my hand as if to guide me through a dark tunnel. She is still holding it as we come upon the stars. Lounging on the warm tiles, gazing upward, she tells me she has decided not to accompany her parents on their trips to the provincial capital. They say it is for business, but they always meet other *pieds noirs* there. They spend their time remembering. It is morbid. One cannot keep holding onto what has been. One must let things go; move on with life; forget. Resentment's an unproductive emotion.

Her face is ghostly in the moonlight. Her eyes are glittering sockets, with no trace of recognition I can see, as she goes on that some make a profession out of being an exile. But doesn't the future hold out hope to us, if we grasp it? She is squeezing my hand, talking distantly of what matters to her. Yet she is lost to me, following her train of thought. It is as if she is not taking me in at all, still staring out, apart. She might be talking to herself of such as means nothing except to her, elsewhere; matters making scant sense to me, from a reality unconnected to mine.

Then she does turn to me; I can barely see her shoulders, her head, in the night – the face that hardly sees me. Dense silence leaks out between us. She touches me on the arm, drawing it down, drawing both of us onto the floor. We are kissing, stretched out.

Instantly aroused, I find there is no question but that she should set the pace. Nervous with the novelty of what is happening as she unbuttons me, releasing herself, I let her pursue matters at her tempo. She determines the phases, this obscure being who, as though materialising from earliest, dimmest dreams, has always, since long ago, imperceptibly been making love with me.

I am not confident enough to take the initiative as her hands, her mouth, plane over me, seeking. She is staring into shadows that are my limbs, my torso, my sex. She is trying, by dint of the patient, relentless searching of her palms, her tongue, her tight nipples, by this repeated motion of her thighs, so soft, silky, viscous, to discover what her distracted expression reveals she has yet to find.

But now I am restless. A reflex movement shifts my leg, turning numb. It brings her to. It is as if her mind is no longer elsewhere. It is on nothing at all. It is as if this is nothing at all, even as she says *go on, go on* – till a spasm ends it for her with me, almost matter of fact, seemingly as casual as our encounter, as the seeming accident of our being up here together like this on the roof.

We are still lying here. She turns on her side and looks at me, as if only now awakening to my presence. She is talking to me of myself. Why should I be surprised? Why should it seem strange on all these other occasions, following our lovemaking on succeeding days, that she should finally turn to me to say my hair is nice; that I have nice eyes; that I could look nice in a year or two when I have filled out; that, eventually, I might be quite handsome? I am surprised to hear that I am intelligent; that I speak well. seem lively.

Up to now I have had no idea of the impression I make on others. It has hardly occurred to me to think of it. It pleases me, this account of me, arousing a wish to hear more, a desire for much more of what I have always wanted without realising it: this interest of hers, miraculous, almost, but a miracle I know I have been awaiting all along yet could never have known I was expecting till it happened – because, in the nature of the case, it is inconceivable. I am yearning for more, for *her* – who, again and again, I find has now turned silent beneath the stars.

Juan and his girlfriend are never to be seen. They are, perhaps, out in the brilliant sunshine, in another of the secret coves to which, on the occasion when Esther's parents return for a time, she and I go. We climb over the high promontory with its Arab watchtower, down the steep precipice to those sandy bays bowered by limpet-encrusted caves tirelessly reclaimed and released by the tide. Maybe Juan and his girlfriend have come down like us from a particularly hot, windless day in the *pueblo*, to the wide, moonlit beach.

There I emerge from the rhythmic pull and push of sea, where I have been washing off her blood as she lies after love on our towel. I am encountering things I have never known before when we are disturbed by yellow headlights. The police, seeking smugglers, may have cautioned Juan and his girlfriend, naked too, in this era of puritanical dictatorship.

Has my absentee host found a space to retreat to in the *pueblo*, away from his parents? We do, when Esther's leave again for the provincial capital where they are spending more and more time.

We have taken over the roof terrace; made it ours, the two of us. It is sheltered by high bamboo screens, a trellis on which creepers are just taking hold. We cannot see the pigeons, the doves next door: they coo with unbearable tenderness. The sides the neighbours do not overlook face the inland plain here, and there the sea.

Sometimes, drawing apart from me for a distracted moment, she looks aside from the coast and gazes down beyond her breasts, her sex, to the hills; to prehistoric man's mounds beyond. She is staring in this silence coming upon us; sifting, perhaps, the volcanic ash covering domes like skin; seeking, I sense what lies within: that centre of energy once producing forms again liable to shift violently when they burst once more from concealment into being.

Yet something is now happening on these warm tiles, in this lunar light. It is advancing, invisible, hitherto unnoticed, but certain as a chemical transformation. The atmosphere is ever more concentrated, leaving us to intense wordlessness among mute mounds, inaudible sea, with no coherent sense of what is taking place.

Like the shadows, our silence is continuing to deepen, remote from the sounds of the *pueblo*, of holidaymakers surging downhill to the beach. The neighbours' pigeons and doves are asleep; they don't exist. We are behind glass, in an aquarium, in the ocean, into which our lovemaking has been imperceptibly lowering us at depths where there is no sound. We are regaining the medium we shared from the start, cohabiting aeons ago, before emerging for the long, diverging crawl now bringing us together on this warmth-flooded bed of tiles.

I do not ask her anything in our vibrating speechlessness. It is not shyness, or tact. She is withdrawn: she is not there to question, as we hold each other. Not that anything about her life occurs to me to ask of one whose only reality is that with me here, now. She is without past, without history, the woman I have joined. And I am nobody except this self: touching, holding, making love without which nothing can be, can ever be, has ever been. This love, this silent loving that does not have anything to recall, to discuss, is all there is. Without it, nothing.

Deeper, we are drawn into it. But what is it that is pulling her down? It is the deep dream within which she kisses me, laying her head on my groin, lips wet, hair scattered across my legs, all with soundless solicitude, as if I might be injured. There is an entranced drawing of her eyes away to somewhere inside her, as they continue to be heavily focused on a torso, a face, far beyond them.

It feels almost morbid, this lostness to her immediate self with me here. She is outside my reality, she who is my reality here, whose reality I finally know, now I am with her, that I had been awaiting, I had seen, before she existed. And here, making love in the blanching moonlight, making love to a phantom, some form stealing in on our silence, she is clasping now, scratching, as if in pain; in the torturing agony of love in our desperate shadow play.

She cries out. She howls, at last letting out – what?

"What d'you feel?"

Nothing, is what she says. A look has come over her face, filled with whatever is within her but remains beyond me in this eerie light.

Time is unreal. It has evaporated in our eternal present with no conceivable ending. It is only ever punctuated by the periodic, brief appearances of her parents. We hear them arriving again as we drink this morning's coffee. Esther's father, having parked his Renault in the garage beneath her bedroom and studio veranda, walks up the few stone steps to the front door, beside the bougainvillea cutting. He is followed by his wife, trailing the concentrated fragrance of orange blossom favoured by European women who have spent their lives in North Africa, with its oil-based Arab perfumes.

Strangely, she has suddenly disappeared, leaving me to wonder, naïvely, what the man standing before us knows about me and his daughter. His jaw is blue, no matter how closely he shaves; his expression, always dark, is especially gloomy today. Even more curt to me than usual, his few words are for Esther in French. They're spoken seriously, in a heavy accent with the rolled Mediterranean *r*. I take them as my cue to leave, as I have upon his other arrivals during the course of the summer. I suppose it is disapproval of a situation he must consider has lasted too long: the absurdity of her, a mature woman, with a mere youth.

It brings me back to myself with a jolt, realising that my summer with Juan has all but gone; that our – my – eternal present is finally revealed in its true colours: passing. Tactfully I leave; tactful to the point of non-existence for them there in the tiled kitchen with its coffee bowls, open to the day's hazy sea.

I hardly exist to myself, leaving her; leaving us; leaving who I am with her; the one I have become, noiselessly treading the marble floors in these rope *alpargatas* the locals wear, through the sitting room, past the bedrooms, down the front steps beside the bougainvillea – at which point I hear her shriek. Wild, terrified, terrifying. I am paralysed here, by the parked car – then by her father's gruff voice, low, indistinct.

He must be rebuking her for her affair with me. What can I do? She is sobbing above me, this woman who has been suspended in our silence for so long, revealing nothing. Finally, she is releasing sound, as the once-inert volcanoes might.

I walk away in the brilliant sunlight, fleeing the blinding white villa with its bougainvillea and concealed roof terrace, leaving behind me the stricken woman, my lover. Then I wander at dusk – alone, since Juan is gone somewhere with his girlfriend.

I can face no other parents; not his. I am tracing through dark alleys, a lost soul, now the sun has set; passing Maruja *la bruja* trudging slowly, with all that weight, on her own. Sightless, I circle the *pueblo* again and again.

The following day, the car has left the villa's open garage beneath the bedroom and first-floor bedroom veranda. Finally, the bougainvillea loses the mauve of its flowers, the green of its foliage. It is obscure against rosy walls. It is dusk again as I go in.

She takes off her dark glasses. There are discoloured pouches under her inflamed eyes. Her expression is heavy with something unbearable she cannot let go of, cannot begin to express. There is no point, surely, in trying to make the polite young Englishman – with whom she has passed several weeks now, coming to like him – appreciate his company. That lack of intrusiveness prevents him from asking why she has chosen him. No, there is no question of making him, whom she has loved, understand. How could he comprehend, even if she were to know where to begin, how to open up on it, thereby utterly changing the way the two of them have come to be together, suspended and floating like the unborn, in the solution of their silence? She cannot, in any case, talk. Her gorge is silted up, as if closed off by choking ash from some violent eruption of which only these late, mute signs remain. She does the only thing she can, the one thing that comes naturally to her: she hugs him. She is being held. It is what she wanted – needed.

I find I am supporting her until, by unspoken consent, we move through the dim, musty tunnel of stairs to the view of the hills in fierce sunset. Now we are making love as always, but as never before. There is desperation in this holding, this shadow-boxing with what is undeclared, in one another's arms. More than ever, there is something morbid about the sheer passion with which she wrestles with what she is holding … not releasing. More tormented than before, she enters the agony of our lovemaking. It is the fullest expression she has ever given it. She is crying, sobbing at the paroxysm of her climax. The agony *is* – finally – her climax. It leads her to this thrilling savagery.

Sunset has bled away. It is dark, a night with no moon. An unaccountable breeze in this season feels cold, detoxifying the narcotic of this latest lovemaking. It is the last time we shall make love to one another. Do we yet know it?

Our limbs, lapsed into stillness: *they* know it, now stirred, shivering restlessly. Does something in her know too, sitting up and drawing her knees to her breasts, arms around them, to clear her throat and speak?

"Tomorrow I'm going to Paris – for good. Come with me. We'll live together." She must know that I will inevitably say I have to continue my studies. I have a scholarship I cannot let go of. It's an honour. No, she can't take me on her escape.

The night, the silence that once held us together as an unacknowledged but palpable medium of our own, now yields to this chill. It makes our shadows detach, drawing into itself. Then she pulls over us one of the rustic covers they make here from scraps of coloured rags. It does not stretch fully. Half of me, half of her, is unprotected from the air. Yet she is asleep almost immediately. She is dead to the agony her day has brought, and whatever it meant; to her exhaustion; to this terrace and what it contains. She has fallen into a well of insensibility.

I continue beside her, lost to me, cold, she who had shared our atmosphere. I lie there for long while: it is growing light, revealing the sea, those inland hills. Her eyelids flutter open – to the ghastly realisation of day. She looks at me.

"My father will be back here soon, from the hotel. He's taking me to the airport."

I remain there, scarcely covered, empty moments longer. The pigeons, the doves are cooing on the neighbour's roof: unseen, unsettled, they're the palpitations of a stricken heart. They bring back, unbearably, a time when tenderness could express itself forever. I reach out to her: I, with whom she had always taken the initiative. We hold hands, tightly now, in the merest fraction of all that has passed between us; as a memory of it; a farewell; an admission of what cannot be acknowledged: that it remains permanently but will never continue or come back. Then – however it happens – I am suddenly up.

For the rest of my life, I shall never know how I am off the roof, down the stairs, through the living room, out the door. It is the last time I will be in the villa with her on warm tiles, beneath an infinity of stars. Never again will I climb those few stone steps by the recently planted bougainvillea I am passing, seeing the car now. No more will she be waiting for me behind those white walls, on marble floors, as, returning here after finishing my book, completing my next walk round the circumference of the *pueblo*, I approach to find the garage door beneath the bedroom terrace closed. And in the painful sunlight the bougainvillea is ready now to grow over many years, until it must virtually block out the sea view from the downstairs bedroom window as I pass, covering the front door that does not open to reveal North African ornamental brass plates in the entrance hall, with its brightly coloured glass lantern.

2

Juan's girlfriend is returning to Madrid. He and I are seeing her off at the railway station. I am struck by the matter-of-fact way, the self-possession, with which they kiss. Saying goodbye might be the most natural thing in the world. They will see one another again, of course. Or, if not, another as good. If ever the one should lose the other, it would not be the loss of love itself for them, these easygoing people. So I think, dazed as she hugs me breezily, as if these past weeks that have barely brought us together were just a holiday, a diverting period of which there will be many more – not the indelible month, the unsuspected reality it has been for me, now standing on the baking platform, awkward, *de trop*, as she prepares to enter her air-conditioned compartment.

Driving back to the *pueblo* beside Juan, with whom my own time is fast fading, I find him asking how my summer has been. It is only now everything is over that we, barely having seen each other during his parents' absences, are talking about it.

I have no idea how to begin. I am back for an instant in the exclusive silence we had shared, she and I – till Juan, outside it, hands on the wheel, breaks in with: "Will you be seeing each other again?"

"She asked me to go to Paris with her."

"Will you?"

"But forever."

"And?" The scorching breeze continues rushing in from the volcanic landscape. My arm is raw against the window frame. "You did right," Juan eventually says quietly, with comradely sympathy. "How could you turn up the honour of doing research with Professor Keller? Not many people are offered that chance. And what have you in common with her? Your backgrounds are completely different. With her past and extreme personality, it would have been totally impractical. You'd always regret it. No, you were right, whatever you may be feeling now."

Juan's father met Esther's this morning in the provincial capital, he tells us at dinner, our last. Tomorrow I shall return to England. I am listening as Juan's mother serves us from a porcelain tureen. I am trying to decide if she or her husband know about Esther and me; if it is for my benefit that he is recounting her father telling him she had been engaged to a French army officer in Algiers, but that they'd broken it off for whatever reason – painfully. It was said that he was an interrogator during the independence struggle. He'd supposedly used torture. Last weekend his body was found dumped in bushes in the Bois de Boulogne. His genitals had been cut off.

Unable to touch my gazpacho, I see I have never known her. I never knew she was keeping the torturer there with us: how would I have recognised him? But he it was who hooded her eyelids, weighed down her stare, made her remote, unknown to me. It was over between them. It was never over. It is never over. Love that had ended has not ended. The knife ending it, those terrible wounds, could not end it. The torturer was the heavy burden in her mind while making love to me. He was what she was remembering, the one she was clasping, entering the torturing agony of love with me, his spectre.

It is her love with him that she has desperately acted out in our shadowplay, the dumbshow whose muteness provides that silence in which no voice can distract from the sound of his. What he had meant to her, what he means, what they were together: it is the heavy dream, the trance, from within which she has kissed me, touched every part of me, loved me. It is that, and the pain of losing it, that has made her howl out; wanting me, wanting me to join her in order to keep him, to stop feeling the agony of knowing she has lost him, now he is severed, gone.

Making love to me the last time is the agony of trying to keep the one she has lost now, of having him die again in me whom she knows can never accept her impossible summons to remain with her in a Paris in whose Bois he is always bleeding to death. Only here, now, at the dinner table with Juan's parents, do I begin to find her mystery revealed: the relationship between pain and pleasure in her body, making love to me, the exquisite torture of her climaxes, the agonising paroxysms of her final one – and why she wanted me to go up those stairs to a starlit roof terrace.

For I, a young man, inexperienced, shy, bearing no freight from a past of his own, am the *tabula rasa* through whom she can be with her beloved. She rejoins him, whose absence tortures her, whose love and all her impossible feelings have tortured her, the ecstasy of whose physical passion tortured her, whose death tortures her, except as he exists in me – whose refusal to journey on with her, to *be* with her, tortures her ... me.

I am wounded, mortified, intolerable hurt welling up, hearing my spoon clank down into the gazpacho. I am deceived. But I know she never told me anything untrue; that she promised nothing; that nobody truly knows another's feelings or reality; that it takes no time at all in life for there to be a precedent, an inescapable forebear for the other; that such a one is actually eternal, outside time, preceding that first appearance even.

Now I know it, revisiting the *pueblo*, with that far-off summer welling out of me like magma in lava flows. Idling in the *pensión*, on the plaza, at night, I suddenly do not even know if I resent her exploiting me anymore, using me for other than whatever I am. Wouldn't I have paid any price to have been with her at that time, like that, to have entered upon the quality of silence, the special atmosphere, exclusive to our loving selves, surely to have found some particle of her feeling, for me, myself, unique to me, and not for some other seen through the medium of her random, chance encounter with me?

Maybe I, too, have stayed with her over the years. Might she not have come to think of me as I am, over the decades, as I have perhaps separated in her thoughts and feelings from the one I stood in for, from the purpose I disastrously served? But how dare I imagine it! There would be no way to know, lost as she now is to me in France, back in Africa, even. What difference would it make? Who sees the other as the other is? Could she know me any more than I knew her? What makes me suppose I knew her, at the core, in our silence, beyond detail, events, circumstance, having come through that tunnel of volcanic rock, a narrow staircase, onto a warm roof terrace and sudden burst of stars?

It is finished between us, something in me is saying as I take in the Mediterranean again from the terrace of this *pensión* over a decade later. But it continues forever, our impossible loving. I cannot let go now of what I had abandoned, but the grasp has been killing me. It has been wearing me down, feeding off me, an incubus leaving me wasted across the years. Lethargic, wanting, I have been emotionally famished to the point of nausea so constant as to continue unrecognised. For there is no end to it for me, a phantom, a ghost for her, through the phantoms of her, her ghosts for me, in affair after affair.

I have already come too late for her, a decade and more ago. Her invitation to me to go to Paris with her is escapism, denial of her suffering with the young officer twice lost to her. It is an illusion, not a summons to me at all. I was right to refuse, to deliver myself to Professor Keller and survival through researching with him, without her. It was inevitable. What choice did I have? But doing the right thing can be wrong, too. It can damage. It isn't right.

From then on, knowing it or not, my mute voice continues to say, all my relationships have been attempts to connect with, to rediscover her, lost to me through her fault, through my fault, our most grievous fault. They are the only way at my disposal to touch her, departed: through ghosts. And each time I meet someone, later, there is a momentary yearning for the novelty of the original experience with her; its dooming mystery. Yet instantly there is no such thing. I know it even before I recognise it. I have found it finished between us before it has started. There is just the disordered tangle of feelings, of difficult circumstances, which she, the other now, seeks to throw over me like a net, drawing me in, struggling. And I am silent.

It is the detached silence I sensed when we were on the villa's roof: the muteness of one already not there; one elsewhere, with the other who is not there; of Esther, absent too on the *pensión's* terrace, in a dreaming part of me. It is the all-embracing silence we had shared; our private atmosphere from which I have been excluded all these years in London streets where I have travelled every day from my rented rooms to old books, old documents – always back.

Gradually, increasingly, I have done it without any other, not even ghosts. Apparently I have forgotten the ever-fainter presence of her for whom I was a ghost – until now, my book finished. Whereupon, seeking a change of scene, of air, I find myself returned to the *pueblo*, seeing from my *pensión's* terrace the villa whose blocking bougainvillea summons me back to the year a sapling was planted.

Part III

1

I am the only person staying in Pensión Amalia: the painter and his friends left after my first evening. This morning I have again come to sit on the terrace, looking out to sea, alone except for Isabel, the local girl who serves me breakfast. Now, only three days later, though it feels longer, she volunteers in conversation – a succession of monologues – over coffee, strong and bitter as a purge, that Amalia herself has been visiting her family in Granada. She will be back soon.

Isabel is clearly bored, having little to do this late in the season. She is gossipy in the way of her *pueblo*. She would stand there talking for hours to the mute foreigner with his schoolboy Spanish, explaining that Amalia is divorced, was married to a German and that they have a daughter, Heidi, who teaches at university in Berlin. But I also feel her circling around me conversationally too, like one of these wasps she keeps waving away from the butter and apricot jam on the small wrought-iron table where I am sitting.

I do not ask Isabel to join me. I let her continue standing to ask where I am from, if I like it here, if I have a family, why not. Yet I am taking her in, with her unruly mop of frizzy hair, long nose and flat chest. She does not arouse me. Doubtless she expects to, as she would from *amour propre* with any man. That is surely why she is beside me.

Isabel is called inside by the telephone. Frank is alone on the terrace with the white cockatoo in its ornamental cage spattering out words that are obscene except when incomprehensible. He moves from his place, with wasps circling the uncleared breakfast, to another table further along the terrace. It is at the far end, almost out of sight, beneath a bamboo canopy thick with jasmine, wisteria and honeysuckle. There is still a view of the sea.

Frank closes his eyes to summon up a still centre without images: a blank slate surely launching him at last into an unencumbered future. But realising instead just how long it has been since he has felt sexual desire, or allowed himself to, memories surface of how hard he had found it, returning from that previous summer here, to forget Esther and their nights on her terrace.

He wanted to write to her, pouring out his heart, although, for all the emotion, he wondered exactly what his feelings were. He would lament not joining her in Paris, but lamely, pathetically, as he knew he would not have acted any differently now. So, never finding exactly what to say, Frank did not finally write to the woman he had never actually known, except, at best, in arrears. She had moved on from motives not involving him to a life in which he could clearly never have played a part. The letter floated off, an unrealised intention, leaving him to his sole alternative: buckling down to research.

Professor Keller held a seminar once a month for his graduate students. Reliving it on the terrace, Frank recollects knowing nobody from his undergraduate days. Most are Americans: it is getting harder to attract British students, already familiar with what they regard as a dryly impersonal, constitutional approach to their national history from school and university. For although Keller maintains that he is interested, above all, in the human beings who make up the past, he does so to oppose Marxist and social history rather than to commend biography or the role of the emotions. Not that Americans have much appreciation of what makes Professor Keller passionate about his approach. They are drawn less to his values than to his fame, which they hope will one day reflect on them when seeking employment.

This is admitted with surprising frankness by a young woman as ill at ease in the presence of the great man as the rest of us. She has been increasingly, defensively, attaching herself to me after the last couple of seminars. I have made no resistance to her or her naïve honesty. She is scarcely more than a girl, I suppose, wiping away her blood in her room in the student residence. We have gone there from the stilted Christmas reception to which Professor Keller genially invited us all.

"Did it hurt?" I feel like a torturer.

"No."

"I didn't realise."

"I was waiting," she says. "You're so silent; still. I wanted someone deep."

But the second, the third time we meet, I find *her* becoming still and silent. She just wants to be with me, to curl up beside me. She is remembering how we first met – so short a time ago; my seriousness in the chair apart from Professor Keller; my habit of looking unflinchingly, eyes as dark as my hair. She has already ritualised all that I am, her first lover, whom she's always known, who is all she will ever know, of whom all others are ghosts: I, for whom she, a shadow, does not exist; for whom she cannot be.

I am the torturer whom she tortures with the reminder of that absence, that vacancy where she is, that she is. Only my courtesy, good manners, prevent me from casting her off directly as an increasing irrelevance, a heavy burden, a reawakening of pain that I, her torturer, inflict on her with my callously withering internal shrug.

I go to an historical researchers' common room for tea. A ginger-haired man from Yorkshire, stirring his cup with white, freckled fingers, laments the way in which documents have a bad habit of stopping short precisely at the point one really wants to know about.

"Characters from the past always seem out of earshot."

"It's only a problem for history based on personalities," someone else says.

"But it does leave one wondering if one has any recourse."

"Does it?" the other man says, overcoming any impulse to be helpful. He focuses instead on his planned trip to Paris the following day to research French demographic history.

The flight, I know, will be short. Within an hour, he will be a universe away: in France with its abandoned provinces, deserted villages, empty fields. Where are all the people? I can't get the thought out my mind. It stays with me that night, waking from a dream of stalking the demographer to see what he might find in Paris.

Her, perhaps, I belatedly realise in the *pensión*. But he would never see her as I did; as I still do – but lost in whatever teeming quarter of that denied city no researcher will ever visit.

The archive is closed today. I consider returning to the researchers' common room, but the tea tastes of washing-up liquid and upsets my stomach. I drift instead down a street of bookshops. Yet the sky is overcast, and in this painfully luminous greyness I find it difficult to see the second-hand stock set out on the pavement in front. Minuscule writing on parchment, faded, in artificial light, is taking its toll. Finding the window display unclear too, I face the glass as if in an aquarium, whether visitor or creature. The world beyond is unreal. I float on.

I find a couple holding hands ahead of me on Oxford Street. Without realising it, I traipse after them into Selfridges. I have nothing to buy. I barely take in what I see, passing between brilliantly lit, overheated counters. There is no reason for me to be at this perfume section with its poster of a seeming Mediterranean beauty. She is looking across the flat roofs of a tier of whitewashed village houses to glittering sea. Then it is as if the stopper has just been removed from the perfume advertised. The store's artificial air is all at once filled with another atmosphere: salty, citrus, volcanic, borne on a breeze.

I am inhaling the *pueblo*; drinking in her fragrance. My chest expands instantly, holding her, loving her, back in each other's arms so unexpectedly that my eyes are now brimming with the shock of it in this distracted, devastating moment from which I emerge achingly bereft.

I will never be back.

It is much later, buying a notebook in a stationery shop by the archive, that I meet the Portuguese woman. She works there, but it is a long journey for her. She explains it in her good English, loquacious, longing to know people in this foreign country.

"And where do you live? … What a coincidence! We're neighbours."

We have exchanged addresses and telephone numbers almost before realising it – against my better judgment. So now I am in her room one Saturday while the landlady is away for the weekend. The curtains are drawn against afternoon light as we lie on the single bed that hardly holds us both, still dressed. I am just hugging her, motionless, looking at the poster of a sandy beach in the Algarve while hearing the repeated roar of planes taking off from Heathrow airport nearby.

Every two minutes people are being propelled into another world. The further one travels from the centre, I am thinking, the closer one moves to other hubs.

"You alright?" she says, as I continue lying there, still, making no move, not even kissing. "Is there someone else? There is, isn't there? It's alright, you know."

Then, beyond my silence, in that distance where she is turned away from me now, against her back, to face the room, I hear her remembering her lover in Lisbon: her first, the one she has never been able to forget. He is always there at the back of her mind, even when he seems not to be, that one whose ghost I apparently am.

"Other people get over these things," she goes on, sensitive, vulnerable despite her garrulousness. "They get married; settle down. Though for people like us, it isn't an option, God only knows why. Our lover is holding us back. Will we ever get over it?"

Will we ever give ourselves permission to do so? I wonder, still out here on the terrace. But then, wouldn't we run the risk of feeling nothing?

I do not see the Portuguese woman again. I do not even go to the stationery shop in the years after she must have stopped working there. Throughout the rest of the time I am completing my research, I resolve to stop seeking ghosts, no matter how fleshly, attractive, uniquely themselves at the outset. Despite the perfect features, the trim figure, flowing hair, finely manicured nails, gleaming teeth, soft eyes, I have increasingly perceived from the first such as overshadows them. I have foreseen each new arrival, robbed of her animating bloom, her fresh complexion, by the usurper in what invariably turns out to be an emotional *cul de sac*. She is dead on arrival, each and every one.

No, I do not go to the stationery shop from which the Portuguese woman has moved into whatever unfulfilling sameness might stretch before her. And the man she had invited to her rented room near the airport? He, as I now view him from the high terrace of this *pueblo*, having busied himself exclusively with mere archives and booksellers for years to come, no longer indulged a wild longing for the life-giving embrace, the life raft, of another. He quelled the desire, the sexual feeling, the long absence of which he has just been reminded by the Pension Amalia's unkempt waitress.

2

Isabel returns to the terrace, setting off the cockatoo, thrashing around with a black tongue in its white cage. It sounds like static on the radio alarm, blocking transmission. But it is as hard to unscramble as for Frank to order his thoughts in this cacophony, with so many thoughts and memories swarming in his mind. Once more seeking mental calm, he assures Isabel that he wishes to order nothing more, not even a cold beer. Turning his back on the terrace, *pensión* and then *pueblo*, Frank begins walking the kilometre and half downhill to the sea.

Sweat pours down his cheeks beneath a straw hat defending him from the sun. It is British, old-fashioned. And repeatedly, passing century plants growing on the crumbling reddish slope, he is brought up short by realising he cannot remember his progress along the last part of the road.

I will try, I think. But I simply cannot recall it. My awareness of my surroundings flickers as unreliably as the *pueblo's* lights with its unstable electrical current. Yet I keep taking account of my lapses into unconsciousness; these submergences of my self. It is the state I have been striving for, that I have relied on such a strenuous walk in the day's heat to produce. Though rather than the clear mental slate I desire, this is insensibility.

Even so, the self, the past it embodies and imports into the present, has apparently not gone into abeyance, merely underground. For my footsteps, I find, are leading me a considerable distance over the beach. They have taken me up to the Moorish watchtower before I know it. By now it has become inevitable for me to climb down to the cove, sufficiently inaccessible for us – for you and me, the me I am finding again – to swim naked.

We make love, I feel; swim again; then sit in silence. We listen to waves encroach till the sun loses force and the sky reddens.

The light has failed when he finally abandons the scene. He turns his back on her anew, but still as this rediscovered person he had been all that time ago. Only in darkness, leaving the beach and laboriously returning to the *pueblo*, does that twenty-years-previous self dwindle. It is Frank as he now is who walks into his *pensión*. He is exhausted, drenched, so much less energetic than when he had stayed in the *pueblo* with Juan.

He goes to his room. sensing, nonetheless, continuing reverberations of a past summer. Almost aware of them as a live presence beneath this parched surface, among seemingly extinct mounds, he hopes that despite local shortages there will be sufficient water for a shower.

There is, although it is warm from having stood in the metal tank all day, absorbing heat. Saline, undrinkable, it comes from wells in the vicinity of the *pueblo*, not from the underground rivers formed by ice melting in the Pyrenees. They gush below the Earth's crust all the way through Spain; beneath the nearby mountains of Granada, adding their melting winter snow; under the Mediterranean, into North Africa, slowing en route to the Sahara.

The *pueblo* has been hoping to tap into these subterranean currents; that dark flow, unseen, inaudible, seemingly absent though undoubtedly there. Strain as the mayor might, for all his political skills and contacts with the provincial governor, he has not yet been able to effect a connection with that life force. He, like the rest of the *pueblo*, is waiting; waiting to be visited by more than the shallow trickle the *pensión's* guest now feels dripping onto his head, too stunned by the day to admit conscious thought.

Emerging from my shower, I find Bog Man at Pensión Amalia's bar. He is smoking, talking to Isabel, in shorts but no shirt. His long, lean body is brown and bone dry. He has lived here so many years that he knows never to exert himself except when absolutely necessary. He is expert at hiding from the light of day, this lizard. His gnarled feet, for years not having known shoes, wear the dusty leather sandals in which he creeps in underground passages. How much time has he spent in their enclosed, musty air, the used atmosphere of the primitive – some say barbaric? He does not seek to tell me in conversation, which I cannot politely avoid.

I understand his reluctance: I no more wish to dwell on my book, my life. But, as my day's excursion suggests, there are aspects of the past, *my* past, me myself, that, while displaced by my historical research, I apparently cannot resist exploring.

What has happened to the original owners of Juan's house, of the villa?

"You're talking about prehistory. Both are long gone. Others have come in their place. And others yet have displaced *them*. Different groups come here at different times: the British, the Dutch, the Scandinavians and," – eyes glinting – "the Germans … "

"Pieds noirs."

He ignores the impertinence of my interruption. "It's a movement of tribes. What drives one on the heels of the other? Are they sun-seekers? Who knows? It's hardly worth asking, is it?" Bog Man draws musingly on his cigarette. Impenetrably vague eyes watch its smoke unfurl, disappearing into nothingness.

This evening I am too tired to walk in the *pueblo*. In any case, what would be the point? Nobody I know, who means anything to me, is in the villa. But then I have been solitary for years. It is no different now, except that I am no longer protected by a routine of work. That defence peeled away like shed skin when I finished my book. So here I am exposed, flesh painfully raw after my hours alone in the sun. I need to settle on a new project, despite the beguiling illusion of finding each other as before on our beach cove.

I must seriously consider the subject for a new book, dismissing my impossible longing as do the local inhabitants who just ignore me. They are quite untouched by my fated search for one long gone, by the bizarre melodrama I now see I have been acting out to myself. They mock at most, with a backward glance, the surely demented man walking round the *pueblo's* alleys like some prisoner inwardly circling the world over the years of his solitary confinement. Except tonight, as I hear that invisible pianist struggle yet repeatedly fail to break out of a few blocking bars on this terrace where I remain for dinner.

3

It is noon. I have gone down to one of the beachside hotels catering for British tourists to buy *The Costa Times*. I am curious to see if there is further news of Speer's driver, rehabilitated in the *pueblo*. There is not. I toss the flimsy pages onto a table, barely avoiding a spilled coffee cup. The deserted foyer is heavy with the cloying odour of scented sun cream: most residents are on the beach at this hour.

I continue sitting here for no reason, my hand encountering the worn imitation silk on the arm of the sofa. I really must be moving on, as I clearly realised the previous night. There is no reason for me to distract myself from research as, I only now realise, I have again been doing, coming down from the *pueblo* for details of Speer's driver as I used to seek out his master. I can rightly be proud of my book, summoning me, all modesty aside, to further success in late medieval studies.

But Speer himself, not just his driver, comes back to mind, for I cannot deny a long-standing interest in twentieth-century German history such as my contemporary Peter Freeman has pursued. With his award-winning publications on the Second World War, he is already in the public eye. But I remember Professor Keller saying that the war does not justify serious study, especially not by apprentice historians for whom he would never countenance contemporary history. Training in the use of evidence requires well-established national archives. They document the major political events, the true focus of historical enquiry, but at a sufficient distance to allow objectivity.

From the outset I have known that there are, of course, other, less political aspects of the war. My extracurricular reading has fully borne this out. They include epic military engagements, gruesome personalities and unspeakable crimes. There were also newly emerging moral issues, such as the Allied carpet-bombing of Dresden and the failure of the Royal Air Force to pinpoint the railway lines to concentration camps. Yet to study the period, no matter how intriguing the subject, I would have had to learn German.

"Not an easy language for one as weak as yourself in Latin," Professor Keller added as a further disincentive, in his vestigial Sudeten accent.

Leaving the hotel and sitting in this bus, chugging up hill to the *pueblo*, I think about Professor Keller and his contempt for all who study history differently. Such acrimony disconcerted the Jewish scholar's British colleagues when he joined their department during the war. Their retaliation was characteristically English: caustic wit at the spectacle of such emotion; distaste for a personal investment so foreign to Anglo-Saxon reserve; a superior air of boredom when confronted with indigestibly narrow constitutional studies; and belittling accusations of naïvety when he affirmed the possibility, centrality even, of scholarly objectivity.

Yet I doubt that Professor Keller's colleagues ever understood how their criticisms touched him. It would have been impossible without recognising his personal motivation for his work. They would have needed to know that he, like his forebears, was trained as a classical historian. The late-nineteenth and early-twentieth century German scholars he read were drawn to the study of ancient Greece and Rome by the seeming parallel rise of their own nation, and its desire to unify in a single state. Their academic approach resonated for the young Emil Keller, if only in terms of consolidating the weak Czechoslovakia to which his family had moved in his parents' generation. From this it was but a short step, when Keller necessarily came with his family to Britain, taking up the study of history there, to seek the origin of the modern state in fifteenth- and sixteenth-century government and its administration. Whenever his approach was questioned, the challenger was Hitler invading, or one of those detestable European statesmen seeking to appease the dictator by sacrificing Germany's weaker neighbour.

Given this basis for Professor Keller's own work, I realise, as the bus comes to a halt, he too was obsessed with a war in which he disavowed interest.

Walking absently from the bus stop by the *pueblo's* watering place towards Pensión Amalia, Frank again feels the force of Keller's personality. "Dr Keller" he had been, with that vestige of a German accent, when he taught Frank as an undergraduate; he became "Professor Sir Emil" within two years once he had adopted Frank as a promising graduate student.

Keller – short, his dark hair thinning, with a black moustache and pink cheeks – is a charged individual as Frank takes him in now. It strikes Frank instantly, this impression of pent-up physical energy. He has a panther's eyes: dangerous, unnaturally still before pouncing. The impact is of mental power, too. There is total mastery of his subject; the vast range of knowledge beyond it that is his to command; that potent instrument, his intelligence. It all comes into play through his polite, if serious, even stern, manner. Here is someone certain of his outlook; utterly confident of himself; not to be trifled with. There is an almost religious devotion in his approach to what his students study with him. He might be a zealot, expecting equal commitment from these devotees.

They are bewildered that such material can provoke this kind of interest. Unaware of whence the man's passion springs, they will never determine the source of this concentrated energy continuously welling up. Still, they capitulate to him, swept away by his force of personality, as well as by the opportunities studying with this "name" offers.

He takes one over, unless one were unusually sure of oneself, Frank thinks, now knowingly approaching the *pensión* in this enervating midday sun. It suddenly feels that there is no alternative to him, to his vision, no matter how little you plumb what really drives it.

I cannot imagine an interview in which, standing up to such a powerful personality, I might have declined the effective decree to do research with Keller, this internationally celebrated scholar. It was, of course, an honour to be invited, as Juan said at the time. But honour or not, I am not sure I could ultimately explain to anyone who was not there why I succumbed to Keller. Certainly not to Esther, assuming I myself know exactly how I came to cross my Rubicon.

Professor Sir Emil Keller and his wife were famously devoted to each other for over half a century. Their closeness was reinforced by the zealous historical positivism that separated them from most of their colleagues. Chain-smoking, whisky-drinking, they were virtual alcoholics by the end. Back in my room, sheltered from the glare, I lie on my bed and remember the last time I saw the couple. It was with a handful of other ex-pupils, all that visited them by then. The Glenfiddich was flowing by three o'clock in the afternoon against a metallic English sky. Professor Keller was in a wheelchair, and his most brilliant student knelt beside it, begging forgiveness for a savagely critical article, witheringly mocking of his supervisor's methods, assumptions and conclusions. The apology had to be false, just an attempt to mollify for a brief remaining period the badly wounded, thunderously angry old man. The student was far too aware of the attacks by the rest of the profession, too canny in expecting others to see through his remorse not to be positioning himself advantageously for a forthcoming career among his professor's critics in the last days of Keller.

Several more years were to pass before I finished my book. Now that it is published, I should like to appear with it in the hallway leading to Professor Keller's office. A potted plant grows there, although I do not know its name. I no more spared it a thought until this moment, than have the rest of Professor Keller's students – mostly university lecturers – even now. Yet, overlooked in an atmosphere of technical historical discussion, clouded by cigarettes, the butts of which are deposited in its bin, I realise the plant has survived; something has been at work. It has gone on growing from the cutting first set into this caked earth. Unobserved, it has never stopped foliating, spreading, rising. Throughout the decade and more I have been researching, even on late afternoons, evenings or during long weekends when the building is locked and the corridor has effectively ceased to exist for me, it has continued to be there: green, responsive in myriad unimagined ways to whatever unseen elements sustain it.

It is there this very instant. But I am robbed of the opportunity to walk past it, book in hand, to meet Sir Emil in the office whose new occupant, his successor, is his merest shadow. I shall not see him receive the volume, although he has just begun to do so in my mind.

Keller is turning a page or two until, frowning sceptically, he stops with rigid intensity at some paragraph. He smooths his small moustache with thumb and forefinger, facing me with that odour of eau de cologne and spiced tobacco proclaiming him Central European despite his avowed love of cricket and British ale in *Who's Who*. Then he greets my book as he had hailed me on my undergraduate degree: with "modified congratulations".

Or I fear he does, perhaps finding it restricted, lacking breadth and vision. For the mere following of his party line was never enough for him. He always wanted the increased range and depth he knew none could provide except for the one now, in any case, no longer available: himself.

I must face the unwelcome fact that the endorsement I realise I want for my orphaned book's "onlie begetter" is at once unavailable and unforthcoming. But without it, I am finally recognising too, here in Pensión Amalia, I have shied away from embarking on its sequel.

Lying on my bed, I nonetheless imagine myself picking up my book and holding it in my hands. Its mere weight, its very existence, prove that it stands of itself surely. Though before I can again summon up my author's pride, especially for the book's brave championing of a controversial historical method, I hear voices: they are raised in protest.

I find it increasingly difficult to ward off the critics' presumed attacks. They challenge my academic stance and self-confidence, destroying precisely the mental calm to which I have felt the work entitled me. For the likes of Peter Freeman, my contemporary, say I am tarred with my Professor's brush. It undermines the liberal basis of our historical profession.

Worse, Freeman effectively says that my book is, as it has always been, simply my Professor's project. The history of government and the governed; the records of institutions; the creation of the state: these are all his impersonal political themes. Even so, I fight Freeman's implication that I, together with the other graduate students under Keller's aegis in a field he has made so magisterially his own, am the great man's agent. Now dead, he survives through me, among others. He lives on with the procedures of his school applied by proxies, rather than independent historians, in books laid as offerings at his feet.

Not that I deny these elements are badly out of fashion, even reviled, when set against the study of societies, beliefs, personalities, discourse – not to mention the role of mere accident. They are defunct; as dead as Sir Emil exiting in spirit at his memorial service through the Great Gate of Kiev played in Ravel's orchestral version of Mussorgsky's *Pictures at an Exhibition*. But it is an approach I might as well admit to myself, now my book is out, that I have always felt, in my bones, to be severely restricted. It curtails access to history's – to life's – fuller reality. Yet failing to research into my preference, modern German history, unlike the strikingly bold Peter Freeman (beside whom I must confess a previously unavowed if stinging sense of inferiority), I did not study the war. I, with my lesser linguistic capacities, pledged myself to one who became my scholarly compass. I had no option. I see it now. There was no choice except to pursue this track – an academic one – back in Britain after my Spanish summer and aborted loving.

It was my only way of existing then. Without it, there would have been, well, nothing.

Frank has not expected that, celebrating his publication, he would find, instead of peace of mind after his decade and more of strenuous work, something conspiring within him to question his achievement. It is casting a pall over his view of who he has been while writing the book. For, leaving the shuttered room, longed for after his exhausting mid-morning trip to the beachside hotel, and now sitting on the terrace for lunch, an image returns to him from the reverie into which he finally fell on the bed.

He, an automaton more than a researcher, numbers among the other mute humanoids uncommunicatively handling parchment in artificially lit basements. Responding to an unseen outside stimulus, he moves every day mechanically to the archive from increasingly far out on the Tube.

As in the dream, Frank sees the map of the London Underground. Subterranean, its lines are a complex of long nerves, resembling the primitive nervous system of the most archaic forms of life still in existence. Its main function is protective; to carry one into an ever-deeper recess, with consciousness – pain - muted, remote from all that might alarm.

Later, the worst of the day's heat over, Frank watches the sun set. From up here on the *mirador*, it troubles him to see, his book out, what his life – he himself – has been; to foresee what might be. At this very moment, here in this place, he finds himself empty-handed: unable to summon up the ghost, let alone the flesh-and-blood lover, of a season past, but failing equally to enjoy a sense of achieved being over his years since. He feels a stab of panic, having no idea how he will fill his time here – a whole month – as irrepressible self-questioning subverts any chance of mental calm.

I did not have a good night. I spent the dark hours, between sleep and waking, fruitlessly trying to advance some ghostly enterprise. But awakening, determined by contrast to be decisive even before getting up, I elect to focus on my next historical project. It will serve the much-needed double purpose of occupying me right now and in future.

It should not be daunting to identify a subject. After my years of working with Professor Keller, I am fully familiar with late medieval studies, specifically the areas calling for further attention. I know well the relevant archival collections. My scholarly habits are ingrained. Once I choose a topic, the rest will fall into place inevitably, faultlessly, as any piece of heavy equipment does in an engineering project. It will determine the organisation of my day, repeated over months and years, in the library, records office and my bedsit.

Yet it will, of course, return me to my previous existence, head down, undertaking research as for my first book. Hence, with a backward glance, having finally accumulated by the green of my lamp another stack of pages ready for publication, I will recognise how in that moment of decision the exhilarating idleness for which I have supposedly come to this Mediterranean village, how the flickering sensation of life beckoning in these few uncommitted days, dimmed the instant I stepped across the threshold of another all-encompassing project.

I recoil, still lying here in my bed in Pensión Amalia. Although I know that, evading a new research subject, I am neither hereby ushering in peace of mind nor the promise of future freshness. This is vacancy, mere emptiness that I feel, noticing the radio alarm beside me.

I switch it off before it can sound. Even so, during my solitary breakfast, I have the sensation that it is broadcasting. It does so more and more insistently, far into the morning. By noon, returning from my walk in this straw hat and sunglasses, sodden with sweat, I have received its urgent message: new life awaits behind relentlessly closing brass gates.

How enticing! How simple! But I cannot help weighing the resolve necessary to pick oneself up and approach the narrowing entry, the sheer willpower required to keep open the tightening aperture, to pass through it.

I am brought face to face again with the man in my London bedsit, curtained for me to find, apart from neighbours eating dry cheesecake, the ghost of Speer's driver. Not just the curiosity he had seemed at first, I find him eerily fascinating. I now want to know how it is possible for one, having lost track of who he is, to come to himself in this primitive Andalusian *pueblo*.

Part IV

1

Amalia has returned from Granada. She sweeps in from her car, chattering, trailing magnolia perfume. Now she stands before me, buxom, energetic, smiling as she recommends the swordfish kebab for dinner: "I know you'll like it."

And I do – as I like her, with her face still attractive despite being filled out; that plunging neckline; those breasts I know are disturbingly naked, ample, beneath the printed cotton. I have not expected to be so aroused.

Amalia and I chat for some time: there is only one other table occupied, by a man and woman. Amalia, who speaks reasonable English, is patient with my Spanish, (which survives from my last summer here), and she is not too inquisitive. Before I know it, given the naturalness of our conversation, I have volunteered that I am here to revisit a previous vacation, just over ten years earlier, one in which I knew the first owners of the villa at the far end of the street opposite.

"You mean Villa Bougainvillea."

"That's right," I say, half-struck by how Amalia's warmth has taken me out of myself, so solitary since the day I arrived, and by the way in which I have just explained my reason for being here. It is the first time I have explained it like that, I think, noticing "Villa Bougainvillea" echoed by the other table. They must have heard the name in Amalia's reply to me – the cue, it seems, to whatever the couple are beginning to discuss.

"My daughter knows the owners," Amalia says. "You'll meet her. She's on holiday from Germany."

"Ah!" I say, with a further pang of, well, physical interest.

Then I wonder, in this balmy, nocturnal air, what it would be like to make love again – back here alone in this *pueblo*, of all places. Though it is just a fugitive thought, as my realistic self acknowledges, watching Amalia return to the kitchen with those thick peasant's calves, enslaved to the restaurant.

I am sitting at my table. I have finished the watermelon but am slow in draining my wine. Amalia has gone inside again: she is speaking to the cook. I suppose I should leave, but I am slothful. I will get up when the piano plays. It should have done so by now. I wait, overhearing the conversation of the man and woman over there by the side of the terrace, as I have intermittently during Amalia's absences.

The woman is matchstick-thin and has been saying, in her exaggerated upper-class English, how little she relishes coming to the *pueblo*. Her speech is theatrical in its precision, like her erect posture. It is as if she is deliberately holding herself apart from everything she so dislikes out here. "Of course, I'm really only doing it for Paloma's sake. She should know she has a mother as well as a father."

"Naturally. Naturally," he says with heavy sarcasm, this short, balding man, in slow, singsong Spanish, sounding somehow Italian.

"I'm not well pleased by the kind of people she meets here. Not at all. This isn't a civilised atmosphere. I can't imagine why *you* stay here. Just think of that archaeologist –"

"*El Hombre de la Ciénaga.*"

"– offering her drinks half-naked, not to mention the man over in Villa Whatd'youcallit …?"

"Bougainvillea."

"… with Lord only knows what past. I was *always* against him."

"Me too. But he's gone. So is Paloma. Which makes me wonder why you bother to come here now, Magda. You know she's not joining us till later."

"Dear Bruno, always the gallant gentleman."

Later, too, Villa Bougainvillea crops up in their conversation, though I am too drawn by Amalia and her own mention of it to be aware of the context. Only now, as I sit alone, finishing my wine, am I actually listening to the man. I am afraid he might notice me and speak to me directly.

"He was completely under his spell. It offered him opportunities many would envy: a ready-made life for all those years. It was what passed for his reality. Anything else would have seemed unimaginable to him."

"But he must have known the damage it was doing," the woman says.

"He said he did finally break away. And he expressed remorse."

"Remorse! Does it change anything? … Like that dancer we had at the Rambert."

"I know the story, Magda," he says, sighing wearily. "Remember, it was all going on when we had the flat in Little Venice."

"How could I forget?" she says with prim coldness.

The silence of unhappy memory slices them apart again like a steel knife.

"Who knows if he was even capable of feeling real remorse, a man who'd behaved like that for so long?" she says, looking at him. "Although he certainly should have been, Bruno, with blood on his hands."

"So you say, though he always denied specific guilt. And he never flinched from contact with those who'd suffered."

Magda does not reply yet. She's looking into the glass bowl round their lighted candle, seeing a trapped creature winging ever more violently towards its inescapable fate. "But Bruno, I simply can't see how a show of remorse can help anyone in whatever time's left. I mean, they both must have been quite old when they met – *if* they met, which I really can't bring myself to believe."

"Why shouldn't they have? He eventually became friends with some rabbi, didn't he? And in any case, it was reported to me by someone who'd heard it from an eyewitness in Marbella."

I am getting up to go. Amalia emerges from the kitchen to thank me, and the couple, whom I find are right behind, leaving too.

"I wanted to offer you all a *copita*," she says by way of introducing us.

"How kind!" says Magda. "But I just arrived today. Travelling exhausts me."

"He comes from London too," Amalia says, smiling at me. "He's staying here."

"London. Really! Whereabouts?"

"Near the Gloucester Road," I lie, ashamed of how far I have strayed from Kensington, the centre of Magda's undoubted social map. We introduce ourselves.

"Well, you must come and see us, mustn't he, Bruno?"

"Of course," he says with toneless courtesy.

"There's so little civilised society here. So why not tomorrow, for a drink – at, say, eight?"

My acceptance is assumed – and given without ado to people such as I would never normally agree to visit, having neither research nor, I find, anything else to restrain me, left now with only time on my hands.

"You can't miss us," Magda goes on. "We're at El Castillo, at the top of the *pueblo*. And if you can't see it, you'll hear it." Bruno looks at her dourly. Magda ignores it, with: "How's Heidi, Amalia?"

"Fine. Looking forward to seeing Paloma. How is she?"

"Well enough," Bruno says in a studiedly matter of fact voice. "Working in Madrid. It's done her good to get away from ..." He's waving his hand dismissively. "So she'll be here sometime later."

Magda turns to shake my hand. But I say: "I'll walk out with you, if you don't mind. I'd like to stretch my legs."

"Why not?" Bruno says as Amalia kisses us all.

The night is clear and cooler now. Somewhere a guitar is playing. There is a staccato clatter of heels and frenzied clapping: flamenco. Voices bray with cheap wine in a bar. Bruno does not hear it, walking apart from the woman incomprehensibly, inevitably, still with him, this lost husband of hers. For she has been invisibly holding his hand throughout, while he has long ago let go of hers, which could never now still appeal with the heavy veining, wrinkling and blotching of a retired ballerina.

Bruno tolerates her sullen, inexpressible love. He is shouldering its burden, hidden behind her proudly composed, unvaryingly correct, brittle exterior. He is doing so by detaching inwardly from its weight to lose himself in evidently all-consuming silent striving.

The Englishman, walking with the self-absorbed pair up the lane from the *pensión*, now holds back. Calling goodnight as the others continue on, he focuses intently on a bank of dark foliage; dense bougainvillea growing over the entrance of the villa. He could not help listening, even if he wanted, for an echo deep inside – inside *him*; longing to make of it his present reality.

2

Frank wakes to learn that a gypsy has been murdered. He is standing in the narrow shade of the mayor's office on the square beside the plaza. There, by a dribbling fountain, the man lies covered by a tarpaulin. Just beyond the dark patch that has formed on the paving stones stands a member of the Guardia Civil in his green uniform and shiny black tricorn hat dating from Napoleon's occupation of Spain. A scorching sun, presiding over this death, reflects in the hat's black patent leather sides as the policeman wearily turns away from village onlookers asking questions. This might as well happen every morning.

Bog Man is inevitably there to "explain" the death. Most *pueblos*, he says, will not allow gypsies to live in them. But one, a couple of kilometres inland, baking behind the hills that deprive it of sea breezes, has permitted a gypsy quarter to grow up beside it. Its menfolk, cheap day labourers in the vineyards and orchards, sometimes come here to drink, as last night in a flamenco bar, with the result that there was a knife fight over a woman and the predictable consequence the tourists can see stretched out before them.

Bog Man rounds off his account by flicking the match he has used to light his cigarette onto the paving. It lands in the pool of blood already reduced by the heat to a sticky trace. Yet Frank finds in it the shadow of a man who has bled for his woman. For he is imagining how popular lore will explain what has happened.

He had absorbed by osmosis a decade ago what the local mores assumed in such matters. And Frank senses within him again his unformed self now conveying it. So, distracted by the glaring sun, there wells up in him certainty that the man here was destined one day, suddenly, fully to come to himself with his lover. All in a terrible moment, which can happen at any time, he sacrifices himself for her – but not by leaking away silently, invisibly, merely anaemic, without vigour or ardour. He dies with a love of her passionately acknowledged from the first instant; defended to the death in a confused, accidental flash. It is always going to occur in a second that is precisely the whole of his short life, without which he will never have lived, passing only from day to day in extended survival.

A moment it is, Frank thinks, dying for his love of her, that is as unique as when this gypsy, this dancer, this man, had arisen from the others seated round the flamenco *tablao*; from all those who themselves, at some point, suddenly separate individually from the rest as the most recent of immemorial generations to do so. Unique is the instant when he had suddenly surged up in furious solitude, to rouse her and dance in their ecstasy of rhythm. Yes, unique he was, the lover, stretched invisibly beneath an enveloping, stifling tarpaulin this blazing summer morning; matchless, beloved, mourned so hysterically that the woman's own life might be sharply ebbing too in an encampment smelling of pigs and carnations.

"No, there's nothing romantic about gypsies," Bog Man says. "That's a silly, common misconception. Their behaviour follows a predictable, sordid pattern."

No, it is all too easy to misunderstand them – the gypsy, to be lowered into the ground for his love against a flaming sky; to be shrouded and embraced by the earth before sunset. Bog Man is gazing through depersonalising sunglasses beyond hills to mounds containing desiccated human remains in the prehistoric charnel house he seeks.

The piano is playing as I wander the narrow streets and alleys leading up the *pueblo* in this weakening afternoon light. It is not the usual musical passage, with bars like gates past which it is impossible to burst. It is an earlier section of the same piece, run over in a desultory manner.

The music grows closer. At El Castillo I am received by Magda, who takes me towards the patio. But behind the plate glass of a room we pass, I find Bruno at his piano. Without rising to greet me, he continues screwing up his eyes to read the score through thick glasses that reflect the lamp. Then, returning his hands to the keyboard, he runs lightly through some phrases.

I watch from my wicker chair on the patio. Pink oleander bushes and orange bird-of- paradise flowers surround this miracle of a lawn in such dry, rocky earth. Magda serves me white wine from a cooler on the drinks tray, asking me what I do. She wants to know about my book, and if I, an historian, am discovering anything amazing.

The present continuous reminds me that I have effectively suspended rather than resolved any decision about my next project – recalling, in its wake, that I am constantly being disturbed by memories, by my sense of myself. I put such thoughts at the back of my mind. Continuing to peer beyond the pantiles of the garden's terracotta wall, I say it is the best view I have found hereabouts of the sea, that immense emptiness.

"Yes, and we're also completely secluded here. Bruno never goes out unless he absolutely has to. He can practise in peace – can't you, Bruno?" Magda says, not turning to look at him, but loudly enough for him to hear.

He is approaching the dangerous section, the one halting him night after night. It is as if Magda knows it and, solicitous of him after all, throws him a social lifeline – one that he, steeling himself with an intake of breath, though instantly sighing, still not ready to renew his attempt, decides to grasp. He gets up, muttering more to himself than to those on the patio:

"I played it in my concert in Marbella."

"That was so long ago. When *did* you last give a concert? Maybe you've just forgotten it."

"How could I? I even dream it; daydream it, too ... But it isn't just a matter of recalling it. It has to be reinvented, as if it's occurring for the first time, then and there. The pianist has to play as if he's composing it *now* – the way Rubinstein did."

"Rubinstein again," Magda says, eyes uplifted.

So that was who they were discussing last night, I realise.

"He insists that he met Albert Speer. And I was saying I simply can't believe it," she tells me.

"And *I do*."

Bruno's engaged. He explains: Arthur Rubinstein was giving a concert in Marbella. Speer had been invited to stay by some Germans living nearby, after his decades of imprisonment in Spandau and following the publication of his bestselling autobiography. It was a period when he received all who wished to interview him, and travelled to meet anyone who would listen to his confessions of general – rather than specific – Nazi guilt. And what could be more natural than for him to come to Spain, where Franco had provided a safe haven for many members of the Reich since the war? Germans continue to live here, even in this *pueblo*. Speer's own driver spent those months in the Villa Bougainvillea.

"Well, Speer's hosts were going to Rubinstein's concert," I hear Bruno say. "The Nazis, especially Speer, had a great appreciation for music."

By now his words are a voiceover for scenes I am inspired to project in my mind's eye: the tall, elderly but still handsome former Minister of the Reich, isolated to the point of loneliness; Hitler's friend, stiffly courteous, with that melancholy charm, walking into the celebrated old Polish Jew's dressing room after Chopin's *Preludes*.

What has he come for, with these congratulations? Does he find it in the artist's sharp instant of recognition? Is there the least acceptance by one artist, a pianist, of another, an architect, with all his public avowals of contrition in books, the press, on television? Is there a flicker of approval for these shows of reparation, such as this risky intrusion itself? Is there licence for him, finally, to let a door close on the past, allowing him to emerge in the brief time left him? Or is there to be no reaction, the instant drawing of an inner blind against such unimaginable chutzpah, a visit that could not be less welcome, from one damned beyond salvation in the worthless remains of his days?

Bruno's source, his alleged eyewitness, provides no evidence. He was not in the dressing room. Magda repeats her doubt that the incident ever happened: the eyewitness has always been a teller of tall stories, and would be prepared to say anything that made for a striking anecdote.

"In any case, Bruno, I don't see that there can be any question of believing Speer when he says he knew nothing of Nazi crimes. How can one possibly credit a man who" – she turns to me – "used slave labour, earning him his twenty-year prison sentence at Nuremberg?" Magda returns to him. "No, you give him far too much benefit of the doubt, Bruno … and certainly too much attention, with all those books you keep reading about him."

"They were bestsellers. Everyone was reading them."

"So you say. But all this comes of you being Argentinean. You've become used to the kind of Germans who went there after '45. You're far too relaxed about their ethics."

"But I'm a pianist. I'm also surrounded by Jewish musicians, close friends. They came over in the war, too. Simply being in the profession in Buenos Aires means having to rub shoulders with Germans of all types, accepting them as they are, or want to appear, often not quite knowing what's really the case but wondering – as you seem to complain I do."

"Speer claimed Jewish friends," she says dryly. Whereupon, suddenly turning to me, she asks: "But what does a *real* historian think of it all?"

I shrug my shoulders, half-smiling, as if to say I won't blunder into a dispute between a couple, that it is all very complicated … yet not quite daring to admit, for some reason, that I am not that kind of historian. Archivally speaking, I am just a technician, if not even that on this subject of which I am no more than a furtive pavement reader of bestselling paperbacks – though long absorbed by Speer, in whom I now find myself jolted back into as much overt interest as in his driver. My gesture seems enough. Bruno is not waiting for more. He has just got up, irritable, and stepped inside.

"So Speer's driver lived in Villa Bougainvillea, did he?" I say. This time it is I who receive no answer. Bruno has put on a recording. We hear, as he must do habitually in his silences, the piece he is practising, performed now by Arthur Rubinstein. Chopin's *Last Prelude* cascades, its painful beauty streaming through the evening air.

Part V

1

A new person has appeared on the terrace at breakfast. She sits apart from me. We nod a courteous 'good morning' to each other, but do not speak. She is self-contained, this woman in her late thirties, with short blonde hair. Nor do I intrude. My own habitual reserve apart, it is perhaps because, suspecting who she is but, observing that she is thin, her skin white, her face full-jawed in a Nordic way, I find her less beautiful than I realise I had expected – or hoped – so as to carry through feelings I had unexpectedly encountered with her mother. Though possibly I am relieved, too, at the simplicity of not having to experience desire and all the feelings, the thoughts, it churns up.

She does indeed turn out to be Heidi, whom Amalia, now strolling out, chattering in her easy way, introduces. Obviously the young woman takes after her German father, with whom she lives, unmarried, in Berlin. We talk for a few minutes, long enough for her to discover I am a late medieval historian making his living as an archivist, while she tells me she is a university professor teaching Political Science.

Amalia, no academic, is visibly at sea with her daughter, whose interests and personality are so foreign to her. She says she will leave the two of us to talk, but Heidi, saying she must be getting on too, picks up the book she was reading and, rather than kissing as the locals do even on first meeting, shakes hands, wishing me a pleasant stay.

Surely I have no right to be disturbed by an evident lack of interest in me by one in whom I myself have no interest. But then maybe my expectation of Amalia's daughter has awakened wishes in me that survive the arrival of Heidi herself. Not that I shall ever meet the woman again in this small *pueblo*, invisibly cocooned in that reserve of hers: a protective sheath I realise I, too, have employed ever since my last summer here.

Later, they encounter each other on the plaza's *mirador*. They are both staring beyond the railings, down at the hills in the plain. He sees her – himself reflected – in sunglasses beneath a straw hat. But for the missing veils, they are beekeepers, gingerly handling swarming trays.

They hear Bog Man discoursing at a café table laden with apéritifs for holidaymakers committed to having a riotously good time.

"So he's still at it, the old bore!" Heidi whispers. They laugh, enough to set them at ease with each other in a camaraderie that disregards attraction and the need to defend against it. "How are you finding your stay here?" she says.

He tells her about his invitation to a drink at El Castillo, and the interesting story Bruno told Magda and him about Rubinstein meeting Albert Speer.

"Oh yes!" Heidi says. "They'd be very aware of Speer. One of his drivers stayed at Villa Bougainvillea. Their daughter Paloma knew him for a while."

"I believe they're looking for him now," Frank says, recalling the newspaper report.

Heidi does not answer. Inwardly, she turns away to the plain. She takes in the hills.

They both stare at them in silence.

"She's coming back this summer," Heidi says vaguely. "Paloma ... I expected she'd have been here by now." Another minute passes. "It's getting hot," Heidi says. "Let's go back to the *pensión*."

Heidi must be having lunch with her mother elsewhere in the *pensión*. Her dinner, too. Nevertheless, Frank encounters her again the following day, on the terrace for coffee and again in the plaza. They sit, chatting casually. But, academic colleagues as they surely are, the tone is detached even when desultory conversation touches on the personal.

Heidi's father, she says, is in the German diplomatic corps. That is how her parents met: he was posted to the embassy in Madrid. When he went back, he was involved in repatriating German prisoners of war from Russia after the end of the Cold War. Virtually all were supposed to have been returned by '59. He dealt with the few remaining, difficult cases.

One presented a real problem. His papers were lost. So was his memory. He could not recall who he was. Forbidden to speak his native German, he did not communicate in Russian either, having entirely lost the power of speech. Only little by little did his language, his memory, return.

It emerged that he had been Speer's driver on occasion. But he had no close family, or even distant relatives, and certainly no friends. When Heidi's father repatriated him, she says, he arranged with colleagues – the German owners of Villa Bougainvillea, as it happened – to let the man recuperate here. So he did, accompanied by Paloma.

"Till he suddenly left," Heidi adds.

I hear more of the man, of his story, next day. It is Heidi who broaches it. She has forsaken her earlier reticence so that Amalia, not knowing what we are discussing, assumes she is witnessing a budding romance with her daughter. She leaves us ostentatiously alone, allowing space for matters to develop.

Amalia, good mother, with her instinctive human responses, is too temperamentally remote from the young woman to see our conversation for what it is. Heidi, an academic researcher, and I, a detached archivist, having no personal interest in one another, can feel at ease in each other's company, unthreatened by it, dispassionately considering something objective.

Frank continues listening to Heidi out of politeness. He lets her talk without disclosing how much he is aware of Speer, or even his driver, whom it is hardly surprising for him to be encountering here where he had recuperated. Certainly, it is better than thinking up a new project that, while propitiating the exacting spirit of Professor Keller, can only disturb, as he has seen, the relaxed mental state he seeks on this vacation. Then, too, something must fill the next three weeks, occupying his otherwise bewilderingly blank hours here. The case of Speer's driver, pressed by Heidi as if on her father's behalf, more than serves for the time being.

Insofar as it touches on Speer it interests Frank, although he finds his fascination with Speer has changed. Once he had been drawn by the fame of Hitler's architect and Armaments Minister, faded by twenty years in Spandau prison then revived by the sensation this 'good Nazi's' memoir caused. That had been at university; now, quite apart from the interest of the man's glory days or even in what he really knew of the regime's crimes, there is, with new revelations, what one historian has termed "the Speer mystery": that intriguing opaqueness of character seeing him triumphant right up to his very nearly sticky end.

The chauffeur is, of course, a different matter. Lacking not just a personality but a self, this is a nobody. Frank, moodily deflated, finds, back here by the Mediterranean, that less than an oddity, even the intriguing one it has started seeming since London, this now touches a nerve: the unknowing sense of having lacked a vital self of his own, toiling daily among other myopic drones in dim archives. More than passively hearing news about a nonentity, he actually listens to something apparently mattering to him.

From this personal vantage point he learns from Heidi of a German submerged in his Russian twilight zone without identity, memory or anyone close. And Frank, surfacing in the *pueblo* too, is invaded by a feeling of returning to gather up scattered pieces of himself in Villa Bougainvillea.

Heidi drives us inland in her mother's car to a large gulley thickly overgrown with wild capers, thyme and mimosa. There we sit, her voice strangely clear and loud in the stillness of this natural auditorium beneath which the seemingly non-existent Rio Aguas will one day revive. First a dampening of the ground, then a trickle, a flow, a flash flood, it will rage back to life, triumphantly justifying its name.

In the drowsiness of the gulley an absence comes upon me: a time during which, I rouse to realise, I was *not*. Silence continues reverberating when a thought enters my mind, seated beside Heidi on this rock: the idea of somebody not being anyone. Absurd! Such a thing could not be.

But then I am not even aware now, with Heidi brushing an ant from her arm during this pause in speaking, whether or not it would actually be possible to know you are no one. Or perhaps being no one robs you of the self-consciousness to realise you have no self to be aware of lacking.

The thought of Speer's driver instantly comes back to me. He had slipped to the back of my mind, unbeknown to me, this cypher.

Though the idea of him evokes the man, here in the gulley – as when a medium holds a button, a watch, a photograph, anything belonging to the departed so as to summon up his voice, his very self, and to be taken over by him.

His loss of self-awareness is mine.

Yet I wonder if Heidi is aware that I am assigning her the role of clairvoyant, also my own, in an impromptu alfresco séance. Surely she does not sense why she is being encouraged to report on a temporary occupant of Villa Bougainvillea.

2

My mind wanders to the house where I lived when I began my research. The first of several, reaching progressively far into the suburbs, it is central enough – in Bina Gardens, just off the Gloucester Road. I know nobody in the other rooms. They must leave for work before me; I have no idea when they return. Their only trace is a pubic hair in the washbasin below a sign faded from steam, asking residents to leave the bathroom as they would like to find it.

This has been put up by Mrs Cragge, the landlady. I never see her either, now that our arrangements are complete. I just leave the rent on Saturdays on the sideboard by the stairs leading to the basement, home to this reserved woman with unruly white hair and flushed cheeks.

Only my sheets remind me of her, as I awaken to a name tape for the laundry: V. D. CRAGGE. That, and what happens on Thursdays, although it is not every week. Yet, with the time of my return, I miss those climbing the stairs in the late afternoon, past disturbingly lurid amateur paintings of Jesus in his final agony, to Mrs Cragge's séances.

In some upper room I do not know, gloomy London light is blocked out as this ordinary woman becomes a medium for strangers. I imagine her breathing, while her awareness of her surroundings, of the present, is reduced, then eclipsed. Something flickers within her:

she is awakening at a level unbeknown to her. The departed are being summoned up above me for those believing it possible in sessions I instinctively feel too hectically superstitious to ever attend.

Something catches my eye in a bookshop where I rummage through basement stock during my lunch hour. Gingerly skimming a thriller in which I seek not to become engrossed, I notice a character lives in my street, Bina Gardens. He is in the Foreign Office, specifically the grey world of intelligence work. Anonymous, a hermit crab, there is something equivocal about him. I consider buying the book, but guiltily feel it a distraction from that single-minded dedication to research Professor Keller so insists upon. I read it standing in the bookshop over the next week. The man in a Bina Gardens bedsit turns out to be more and less than he seems: a double agent, a traitor to all that is held most dear.

I mention the book to someone I knew at university. I tell him he might like to read about the man at what is about to become his new address, now I am moving out of my room. Not that he seems interested in the story of someone remaining obscure here. Outward going, he tells me with a chuckle that Mrs Cragge, arranging in her basement for him to occupy the vacated room, could not even remember my name. She called me the "perfect tenant". I am very quiet. She has barely seen me, including at weekends, and never in the evening. I am a ghost, slipping in and out unnoticed. But for my regular deposits, I do not exist.

3

"How much inkling could he have had that he'd become no one?" Frank breaks the heavy afternoon silence in the gulley to ask Heidi. "And what robbed Speer's driver of the sense of who he was? Something so personally annihilating surely that it also deprived him of the memory necessary to knowing how it had deserted him …

"However was it that he," Frank goes on, "unlike all the other prisoners of war, came to lose his personal coordinates, dissolving into nothing among so many other nobodies in psychiatric institutions, none of whom knew him or each other?"

"He was trapped," Heidi says, "behind the Iron Curtain in a Soviet psychiatric ward."

She tells Frank of interminably long, empty years in the vastness of the USSR. Forbidden to speak his native language, he had lost his use of it, and forfeited such Russian as he had initially acquired, too – and then his very power of speech, sitting in dark, overcrowded silence with nothing finally to communicate.

Lost in his thoughts, Frank supposes, in a place he was no longer aware of, he had eventually come to lose thought itself, staring vacantly, with memories, fragments of memory, the entire faculty of memory drifting away from him towards some diverging shore; out of sight, out of mind.

"And what was it," Frank asks, "that made him, unlike all the other prisoners of war released years earlier, manifest the symptoms interning him in a psychiatric institution?"

"My father thought it must have been some constitutional weakness," Heidi says. "A temperamental feebleness unravelled the man's sense of himself, converting him into a mental patient. So he was shipped to one of those hospitals set up across the USSR and used to incarcerate political dissidents as psychiatric patients in the 1970s."

Heidi continues to describe how the Soviets had fought that undeclared war, as she and Frank get up to leave the gulley. Yet, as she talks, driving back to the *pueblo*, her passenger is silent. Drowsy in the heat, he appears to doze. For mentally he has somehow remained with that man in his peeling ward identical, doubtless, with all the others throughout Russia.

The sensation stays with Frank. It is there even when, discovering Heidi with a glass of iced mineral water in the cool of the late evening, he sits with her in Amalia's dim, closed restaurant. Then, going to bed, his dark room feels to him crowded with stunned, silent men. He cannot see them, but knows they are breathing.

The man is sitting on a shared bunk, or lying on a bed narrow as this, lost in Soviet vastness. He continues in cotton pyjamas with others, never fully rousing from their perpetual light, dreamless doze, even once night has turned to day's perpetual gloom. They are waiting, without hope of release, in a quasi-convict state.

4

Music wakes me from a night-long dream, struggling to free myself from a distempered ward. Switching off the radio before another hectoring religious broadcast, I sense the brass gates closing, but just go on lying here. It is an instant of paralysis as in dreams where one cannot shout for help or find the strength to defend oneself. And I have a sensation of cold dampness as on a dark forest bed. I am lost in a disabling moment. Consciousness is draining away …

I come to. I have awakened. I leave my room and stand on the terrace, lightheaded, unsure whether or not I am out of sorts. It is as though it is my body, my self, that I have left on the bed. Insubstantial, the least that I am, I seem to be levitating.

But then, taking my place for breakfast, looking beyond the geraniums and oleander, I take in the *pueblo's* sweeping Mediterranean vista. The sun is not yet oppressive. I smell sea lapping the beach down there, half-expecting to feel I am coming out of water running salty from my hair, my shoulders, over my torso, my naked body. And I might be sitting on a rock on a deserted beach: I, now anybody, or no one.

For I have dreamt of being a new man – unlike last night when I was overcome by an empty self, not a new one. But this is not being confined to a specific self: it is unencumbered, cleansed of the silt of previous, unrealised half-persons, fragments of less than a life. It brings freshness to the early morning. And finding myself alone, apart from the still-reticent cockatoo and irksome recent probing of non-existence, I wonder how I might be such a man.

I am perplexed by how one might ever attain to such an ideal self. It bemuses me – until I feel there is really no reason on such a glorious day to consider anybody lacking a solid core, a barely human transparency without a nucleus.

Then, when a sleepy Isabel finally approaches with my coffee, I remind myself, sipping, that I can at least take some pride in having completed my research project. I have successfully published the book as Professor Keller expected of me on that distant afternoon in his study when he proposed the topic. But then again, there is nothing to stop me from finding a worthy sequel after all; neither dispiriting lethargy nor, as I have been recognising, any need to kotow exclusively to Keller's historical approach.

"Good morning." It is Heidi. "D'you mind me joining you? Seems I'm interrupting your writing."

"My *not* writing, you mean." Frank looks up from the blank notebook and pen he has brought out, gesturing to the wicker chair before him.

The page is virgin even now, he explains, as Heidi sits and gestures for her own breakfast, because he is still seeking whatever subject for a book leads most naturally from the theme of his last one: the late medieval roots of the state. He goes on to describe to Heidi the argument, the evidence. For won't ensuing discussion help Frank stumble on what keeps evading him, despite this morning's good intentions: his new topic?

No. Within minutes conversation has moved to the modern state: the USSR. Though, to be precise, it is a monologue by Heidi – again. For she has soon shifted the agenda, almost as if she has one of her own, talking of how someone who was nobody came back to himself with the collapse of the Soviet Union.

Frank is not surprised that Heidi is pursuing the case of Speer's driver so intensively. Her father had a prominent role in the man's rehabilitation; she coincided with him in the *pueblo*; and the press has now raised the question of his current whereabouts.

Frank anticipates Heidi asking what interest he, for his part, has in the man. Although she, a reserved, flat-chested academic woman, is actually unlikely to be so personal. Only for a fleeting moment does Frank imagine answering that *The Costa Times* has made him curious. He barely considers mentioning the private sense of attachment that has stealthily come upon him to one seeming to embody, and express for him, a deficient personality.

Frank scarcely admits, even to himself, that he has started feeling strangely haunted, if not possessed, by him, whether dreaming or waking. Virtually hallucinatory it had been in the gulley of Rio Aguas, forgetting, but remembering, his self through him.

So Frank, knowingly or not, is committed on his own behalf, as much as for the driver, to follow all the man has gone through, from start to finish, finally to stand and present himself on the threshold of Villa Bougainvillea, with all that might become of him there.

5

Heidi is talking about what the breakup of the Soviet Union meant to the man.

"No one predicted it," she says. "Not even Kissinger. But as monumental as the USSR seemed, it did suddenly fail. The Iron Curtain collapsed. And with Germany reunified, as an unintended consequence, its few, final prisoners of war from the ex-Soviet Union were repatriated."

Instinctively, however, Frank supposes that, despite Heidi's emphasis on the fall of the Soviet Union, the man who was *not* remained unaware of world-shaking changes. He doubts that it is the big events, the violent ruptures, that people most feel. The decline and fall of empire, Frank finds from his reading of history, occurs imperceptibly, over great periods of time. In this case, it took place in measurelessly distant cities on a continent stretching from the Atlantic to the Pacific.

Frank struggles to imagine the sheer extent of that landmass, half-listening to Heidi as the terrace grows hotter. It breaks his concentration. Moments later, summoned back from dark lostness by dazzling sunlight, he shifts his chair further into the shade of the umbrella, sensing something unbeknown to the man.

Neither he nor any other psychiatric patient is heeding what has started impinging on him from the far-off changes. Some extra person is now appearing in every bunk; greater crowding has begun at some indeterminate point. Patients have not noticed the fewer nurses, or the longer intervals between their appearances, so Frank finds in this visionary moment. Meanwhile, assistants – no longer wearing white coats – walk between rows of bunks to pick up this or that which might have been someone's personal possession had there been persons, rather than ghosts, to own them.

Yet patients cannot know, Frank thinks, that these intruders are not members of a staff long vanished since salaries have not been paid for months, then years. They are locals, as though at some unrecorded time barbarians, entering the great spaces from the periphery, have occupied the crumbling places of civilisation, displacing its officers, becoming its natural inhabitants, now society's previous structures have collapsed.

The inmates do not realise that far, far away, crowds have gathered. Masses have cried out and walls have crumbled. Peoples have swarmed across borders; governments have been toppled. An empire has broken apart.

"The changes were monumental," Heidi is saying.

But no, the patients have had no awareness of them, Frank senses. Disoriented creatures, they have not registered the slightest recognition of such developments in psychiatric institutions once imprisoning them but now serving for them to huddle in. They are nobodies, just surviving, yet merely more chaotically.

Isabel has arrived to clear their breakfast plates. Heidi watches her, though with inward eyes still registering what she has been saying about the collapse of the Iron Curtain. So important was this period she studies professionally, taking her cue from her father, that Frank supposes Heidi cannot but assume it is this epoch-making development that took a nobody and released him to become a somebody with an identity.

Frank continues to see the matter quite differently. He imagines, rather, that the Russian state, binding its empire together with its oppressive identity, faltered, too. It caused different, less visible but equally far-reaching change.

The state's previously tight control was, for a few crucial years, loosened. Psychiatric hospitals opened, releasing some inmates. Frank, silently reflecting on what Heidi, still across from him at the breakfast table, has claimed, presumes other denizens were shunted from one locale to another as lack of funds forced some institutions to close. In the resulting reduction and overcrowding, patients, oblivious to the changes, might have been repeatedly moved from one hospital to another, unaccompanied by papers outlining their case histories, reason for being admitted and trajectories.

These documents, Frank thinks, like others being made public only now, belonged to the national archive. They were part of the memory of the state. Yet just as the state failed to maintain its original identity, Frank supposes it lost its memory, too. Papers were misplaced, stolen and destroyed. Some were shunted around like the psychiatric patients themselves. Inmates were unremembered, such as this man with no memory, not even of himself – with no official documents to say how he had come to be lost and who he was.

The sea is glaring now. It is mid-morning. Isabel, who has cleared away not only breakfast but the pair's coffee cups some time ago, throws back her frizzy hair in irritation at them remaining here so long, or maybe from feeling ignored.

Heidi gets up. Doubtless she assumes that, as a serious academic, she is rightly using the fall of the Iron Curtain, an incontestable fact, to explain how a nobody finally recovered himself. Frank himself, Dr F. J. Ward the scrupulous archivist and objective historian, regretfully picks up his notebook. It is still blank. Speer's driver has subverted discussion of his new project. Taking it to his room with a mute sigh, Frank is suddenly halted in its salty mustiness. Standing there, motionless, he finally glimpses why, historian or not, he could never believe it needs the fall of empire to bring a man to who he is in a remote Spanish *pueblo*.

How might he become himself in such a place?

6

Frank has lunch alone. New arrivals sit at a table further down the terrace: a woman smoking a pipe with a man holding a restless chihuahua under his arm throughout the meal. Somewhere in the *pensión* there is a loud exchange: mother and daughter. Amalia emerges with an uncharacteristically pained frown. She manages a stoic smile while serving Frank, who has not previously heard Heidi's voice raised to such a pitch.

Lunch over, Frank does something that would never occur to him in gloomy Britain with its scant lunchbreaks: he takes a siesta. But lying on his bed in the dim room, about to fall asleep, he cannot stop thinking about what lately he has found dominating his thoughts: a lost man coming to himself – barely paces away where Frank, on repeated walks round the *pueblo*, chases memories of his first summer here.

He is drifting into a hinterland between waking and sleep. An image faces him. It, he, is a wandering psychic – not water – diviner. A cleft stick twitches repeatedly before Villa Bougainvillea. There he summons up a man thirteen years' previously: the fresh English graduate still to embark on his own search for how to come to himself. Then the dreamer is his current self. The vacationing youth's uninitiated quest is now his own late hunt – instantly merged with the hitherto deflecting question of how somebody, once a German driver, then nobody, had become himself in Villa Bougainvillea.

I awaken later, thinking about how the man achieved it. It haunts me without Heidi's prompting. Alone, pacing out of the *pensión*, I start sensing what happened, though without evidence – certainly not such as Professor Keller would demand for his categories of politics and the state. It invades me impressionistically.

Slowing down before the seaward houses, their whitewashed walls especially pale in this weakening light, I have an image of the man existing merely among peeling distemper. It is in the latest overcrowded

Russian hospital ward to which he has been moved. Looking up at the window on a villa here in the *pueblo*, I visualise a sole pane too small and high to admit sufficient air to all its mindless inmates.

Suddenly there seems even less oxygen than ever. He feels a desperate need to breathe. His lungs will explode if he does not satisfy this painful requirement for, yes, life – reminding him that he does exist after all.

He presses among the others who, until now, have also been sitting stupefied on shared bunks, but unexpectedly find this moment to respond to the urgent summons of even so faint a breeze drawing them away from the benighted mass of remaining inmates. They breathe in gasps, seeking to climb, one upon another, to that blurred source of light and air. Then, seizing the chance to raise himself several notches above the rest, he grasps at a space at the window. He drinks in the current playing before the grille.

Stopped here, I all but see the face hard against the imprisoning pane. Chalk-white, like his thinning hair, it quivers from the effort of holding himself up this far with arms puny from age and lack of exercise. His nose, dry from the inner airlessness, draws deeply where smeared glass is lowered a crack. Eyes stare intently into what locked him out. Taking in their reflection, he gazes on as if to recall more of himself.

Frank continues staring at the villa's window, its frame encircled by dense growth with purple flowers rising from beside the entrance to the weathered villa. Absentee German owners he does not know have, in the missing decades during which he has been numbed to what happened there, to who he was then, to what he has – or has not – been since, have given the plant's name to the building. It is only right. Its coils, wiry despite green tendrils, have tightly confined the place throughout that entire period of Frank's last thirteen years.

They refuse his eye passage through the window; they wreath shutters denying access on the first-floor terrace. The creeper continues climbing the outer wall, and Frank imagines grasping it, raising himself. Then he is released onto the roof, where the plant grows as luxuriantly as in the decades he has been absent; a seeming lifetime of unacknowledged longing to renounce faded manuscripts in favour of freedom that had lain before him up in efflorescent Villa Bougainvillea.

7

Heidi is absent at breakfast this morning. "She went to the beach," Amalia tells me. "She should. The days are passing. She must enjoy them before they've gone, not just sit around waiting for other people."

Then, flatly: "The one renting Villa Bougainvillea last summer isn't coming back. Who knows if anyone else will, finally? Even so, the owners will have to renovate the place. They ought to return more often from Germany. Villas deteriorate quickly if they're not occupied, especially in this sea air. Wooden frames rot; the metal hinges rust and paint peels. The building is starting to look as if it has leprosy.

"The problem is they're absentees. They don't give Villa Bougainvillea a thought. But it is theirs. They can't disown it, even if they find it more convenient to forget."

Amalia sighs, beckoning Isabel to bring me coffee. Then I am left alone to stare out on the sunlit terrace.

Heidi eventually reappears. Having risen with the sun itself, profiting from the calm of the early sea, she appears fresh, renewed. She seems to have been consciously composing herself in solitude after whatever irked her yesterday. Breezily, she suggests another drive.

"Let's go to the gypsy village. My mother has offered us her car again."

I accept readily. It will be a welcome break from the terrace and what has become an unexpectedly narrow theme: the dark matter of Speer's driver; a man lost to himself.

Setting out, one of the *pensión's* used guidebooks in hand, I am happy to see even this parched scenery. I tell Heidi about the gypsy who left his *pueblo*, fast approaching, to lie dead one blinding morning, his blood spread, viscous, from that tarpaulin laid out in a small plaza. Now there is no trace of him in front of our mayor's office.

We arrive and cross the village square. Plastic bouquets, like those found on the altars of Andalusian churches, lie at the foot of its memorial to the fallen in a forgotten colonial war. Walking into the gypsy outskirts of the *pueblo* with Heidi, I am struck by the fresh flowers as I think of the man surging up out of the darkness. Roses and carnations stand in tin cans of earth on the window ledges of whitewashed shacks.

I share with Heidi the popular view of him passionately affirming himself against whichever of his fellows. Yes, all at once, with the glint of a knife in the bar's gloom, he has risen to full stature. And coming to the very point giving value to his entire life, to the instant in which he finally achieves his entire being, he can die.

"What provoked the fight?" Heidi says.

"A woman – what else? Love."

"Fancy that!"

Her tone begrudges admiration. She sneers at gypsies as much as Bog Man did on that painfully brilliant morning beside the perfected man's remains. Yet there is surely envy also in her implied judgment on this romantic ideal of Romany perfectibility. For she says, with words carried on a sigh: "If only things were that simple."

From which I take it that she, in what might look like a lovers' stroll to anyone not knowing we are unattached; she, the plain woman sauntering at arm's length from her withdrawn acquaintance, feels love cannot be relied on to give you the chance to come conclusively to who you are. Then I imagine she aches for – dreads – a climactic situation without which life will never be life and one cannot be oneself. It breaks out of what she surely feels is habitual dullness; a burst of painful longing ripping right through.

They return to the *pueblo* proper. It has had, according to the guidebook, a presence of some kind since Neolithic times. There are Roman and Islamic remains. Though not till the nineteenth century, well after the Christian Reconquest, did a boom in mining here (as in much of Andalusia) put the *pueblo* on the map in its own small way. It employed not only locals but also gypsies as day labourers.

Yet the excavations were limited. Technical problems led to the flooding of galleries. In the twentieth century, competition from the

United States in mining silver and lead created a crisis in this local industry. It was closed down, scattering inhabitants, sharecroppers really, back to their smallholdings. The *pueblo* was depopulated. Hence this deserted air the two foreigners take in, walking its deserted streets. Few but the gypsies remain.

Frank senses Heidi is turning her back on the gypsies. She has dismissed all thought of the murdered man coming to himself through love, thinking instead of that shadow emerging from the frigid Russian wastes. Not that Frank is surprised, as they walk two abreast in this dim lane smelling of drains. For Heidi, losing that lightness of spirit, natural or – as now appears – contrived, with which she had emerged from the beach that morning, apparently cannot help reverting to the countryman her father had repatriated. Nor, truth to tell, does Frank find it strange that he, too, should revert to considering the virtual spectre they initially came upon. There is now no denying the echo, even reverberation, he finds in him.

Then Frank wonders what the German authorities were actually given access to when the USSR collapsed, the moment Heidi stresses. It must have been some holding centre where, now that all other POWs had been released, a lone nobody faced simply existing – as Frank had the previous night imagined him doing at a scarcely reflecting window. And how might the inmate, raising himself up there, go on to achieve the gypsy's human stature?

But Frank assumes Heidi is not concerned now with any such elevated comparison, or even with how the man came to be identified as Albert Speer's driver, as he is presumed to be hereabouts. She stops a moment, drawn instead to the *ex*-driver, the elapsed person as he had originally been presented to her father. Then Heidi, considering the agonisingly slow way in which the catatonic prisoner came to, starts walking with Frank again.

They emerge from the alley. Sitting on a stone bench between dusty fig trees, they blink at an open vista. An unexpected expression of civic pride for such a remote *pueblo*, the garden provides a landward vantage point for taking in the hills.

Frank notices traces of mining as Heidi describes the work the German repatriation team did in recovering their countryman. She emphasises her father's difficulty in helping the man recover who he had been. His lack of memory, his inarticulacy, drastically limited the number of clues. What was left? A muttered phrase; words ending in an uncompleted gesture; a partial thought. Only after frustratingly long, finally inconclusive interpretation could her father tentatively claim to construe muttered remarks as references to a given place, to some specific person or to an actual event.

Frank listens, sighing before the disfigured vista. It is the heat. Or maybe he also regrets that Heidi's excursion, originally welcome, far from allowing him respite from Speer's driver in Pensión Amalia, thereby denies him both repose and the dream of a new life. But it is not just Heidi, Frank knows, who draws him on, pursuing her quarry. Promptings of his own have been leading him on this invisible itinerary, step by step, through each of the painful stages by which Heidi's father summoned the POW into possession of himself. He is following it no less than the tourist does this battered guide round the *pueblo's* historical remains.

Heidi continues rehearsing the work her father did in restoring the man. Frank notices her earnestness. Something must be driving her fully to encounter the one finally alone with a woman in Villa Bougainvillea. Even so, he inwardly takes over her account. He reviews it, probes it, as if the least lapse of logic, or missing detail, might omit something essential to a being resurfacing in the *pueblo*.

Frank wants to know if the guttering speech and spastic movements scarring the POW's muteness were thrust up from beneath. Properly understood, they may have established a submerged past; primordial dramas. Perhaps something fundamental, an irreducible self, survived even in this primitive husk of him.

What Heidi does not consider, Frank finds, is that the man's words, his movements, might all have resulted from purely haphazard contacts in his current situation. Unchosen, it put him in touch with other inmates in the psychiatric ward, as well as with Heidi's father from the world outside. For the German had hurtled in with intimations of another sphere, a different ambience, a foreign character, providing what did not exist within their empty patient – soft wax to his impress.

There was no deciding which had scratched the surface – pressures from within or without, Frank supposes, staring from the bench beside Heidi at the noiseless view. Or if both, in what combination? Perhaps no one knew, for all the attention devoted to it, whether or not the mumbling, in a context of lost German and unlearned Russian, was even in the language presumed. Fractured utterances, strange sounds, responses to what lay outside or in: they might ultimately seem Delphic. It required interpretation by someone familiar enough with the effort to exist to have empathy, it is clear to Frank – no mere eavesdropper.

The visitors leave their bench among the fig trees. They turn into a dark street, on their way to the *pueblo's* archaeological remains. Coming out of it, dazzled by the light, Frank is struck by the distance between *realising* that one is and *knowing* who one is.

Heidi's father and his psychiatric and social consultants had worked to establish the man's identity, she says. But Frank, waiting for Heidi to continue, supposes somebody may have overheard or even recognised him. Maybe the team showed him photographs of people, places, as spurs to memory. A laconic nod, an absence of "no", might have served as affirmation.

Frank is reminded of the Yorkshireman with ginger hair in the researchers' tea room in London. He lamented that historians are frequently deprived of what they most want to know. Yet informed speculation, even trained imagination, can supply the rest, Frank thinks, going on from where Heidi's account has strangely faltered.

"Might it have started in a dream?" he asks her. "Perhaps the clue to the man came from the place where he continued to speak a language he had forgotten but would remember; where he unexpectedly retained the power of speech.

"Possibly his words muttered in sleep were overheard by another inmate wakening to himself in the psychiatric ward; say, a second prisoner of war who had somehow come to be trapped there. Or they could have been picked up by a nurse, or an orderly."

They have stopped at an abandoned chapel. It was built, Frank reads in the guidebook, on a now-indistinguishable mosque. Then he adds: "Of course, whatever the man said might also have been caught by one of your father's team to start the identification and repatriation. But is it clear which, if any of them, suddenly took in a mumbled snatch about driving Speer – if that's what it was? For what, finally, could be known about him? It isn't even certain whether or not some such thing had been heard well before the Soviet Union collapsed."

Frank looks meaningfully at Heidi. Yet she does not insist as previously that it was the end of communism specifically that had roused the man to himself. Preoccupied, she is silent. Frank mentions something Heidi has failed to touch on: why the man had not been repatriated with even the second, supposedly final batch of German prisoners of war, before the fall of the USSR. "In the chaos ensuing from the Soviet demise," he says, "with papers and patients misplaced from filing cabinets and wards, his identity as Speer's driver might well have been lost again, only to be found once more, only much later."

We are passing the remains of a Moorish reservoir. It is made from the local mountain stone, largely shattered, leaving little to see. But then we barely look at it, minds elsewhere.

Not that Heidi comments on my imagined account. She has withdrawn from discussion. Though there is no reason why she should consider on my terms, mutely overlaying her words, the man in Villa Bougainvillea whom she has been so keen to scrutinise up to now. There is not a shred of evidence that a neighbour had ascribed an identity to a man without memory on the basis of something overheard in a dream. No matter; as a dutiful academic, I am implicitly telling myself it is "a working hypothesis" – although it has occurred to me instinctively.

Speculation is doubtless meaningless for Heidi. Never improvising, she does not speculate on how, after all, one might establish contact with what is long unrecoverable. In fact, for some reason I simply cannot fathom, she is not talking at all now. At first moody, she has become inward to the point of remoteness.

Further on, Heidi pauses beside me in the *pueblo's* musty sixteenth-century church. She hardly takes in the Mudejar décor, "fine" according to the tourist guidebook. She is petering out.

They leave the church. The street widens as it leads up to the plaza. The pair enter it alone, except for stray mongrels. Overlooked by shuttered first-floor windows, they sit at an open-air table in front of the bar and order mineral water.

Neither speaks in a late afternoon that glows with the Mediterranean barely four kilometres away. Frank puts the guidebook on the table, inwardly also ending a lost man's trajectory to his self. He muses further on the stages through which the man and the increasingly silent Heidi have just drawn him. Yet it occurs to Frank that the man on whose account this journey has increasingly haunted, even implicated, him is not at all the one in whom he is most interested. That is still Albert Speer. For Speer, always so dominant, self-possessed, the matter is quite different, Frank supposes. It is not how he found his self: it is *who* that self was.

If, in the case of the ghostly creature sighted in a bedsit, it is now finally possible, after Frank has seen his case through, to say that he *is*, the question is *who* he too is. To answer, which Frank has vainly sifted through information and contexts a dolefully uncommunicative Heidi, sipping from her glass here beside him, has provided in discussions, he wonders if they will ever resume. Now reflecting on the subject for himself, he finds the most that is available is what is ascribed to the man. He is Albert Speer's driver – as Frank is an historian schooled by Professor Keller.

Eventually, Frank breaks the stillness of the plaza. He says to Heidi: "I don't think it's hard to see why Germany wanted him to have the identity they released him with." Surely not, he supposes, instantly recalling browsing among the master's bestsellers during London lunch hours. And how it suddenly comes back to him, the sensation of standing outside bookshops with the rattle and dust of heavy traffic, killing time by reading at random from their pavement shelves pages secretly written in Spandau! That was when Speer, released from twenty years of imprisonment, had become a public personality with his widely respected admission of general guilt for Hitler's crimes. For did he not, in creating the possibility of an honest, "good" Nazi, thereby also implicitly elevate millions of his wartime countrymen?

"Latterly Speer's claim that he'd been ignorant of the atrocities had come under increasing scrutiny," Frank says, barely seeing Heidi, a shadow against the light. "Then he died. So what could be more welcome in Germany, engaged in a battle with its own conscience, than a close witness who might have evidence bearing on the veracity of Speer's account? Might no less a person than the driver of Hitler's minister share what he'd overheard from the man whom he'd taken to Mauthausen, where Speer was photographed with prisoners early in '43? Or did he have something to report from journeys in '45, when Speer defied the Führer's so-called Nero Decree, that scorched-earth policy, driving him at dusk to factories along roads where, evading the enemy's ground-attack aircraft, they spent hours under cover in deep forest?

"Of course, the Russians had their reasons too," Frank goes on. His voice is successfully testing the plaza's acoustics. "If the KGB could produce someone identified as Speer's driver, it would expect him to paint the man blacker than the whitewashed, contrite version of himself he presented at his Nuremberg trial, then in his books.

"Although we can't say whether, by the time the Cold War ended, the KGB had lighted on the supposed driver but failed to make him say what it wanted, or simply hadn't yet completed the process of announcing he was there and bringing him to the fore. Maybe he hadn't come to its attention at all. But whatever political form Russia was to take, with the KGB just reverting into its intelligence function, the country must have continued to feel keen antipathy for the German Minister of Armaments and Munitions. Speer had been zealous in the role, extending the war by eighteen months and costing the vengeful Soviets millions of dead.

"Even after the Cold War," Frank says, "the Russians, no less than the Germans, would have been profoundly interested in Speer's driver. He might testify to the falseness of his superior's self-serving assertions. So the Russians, too, wanted to display the man who'd lost his memory as that chauffeur. And if he'd revealed it as his identity in a dream, it was the Russians' dream too.

"Hadn't there been a tug of war," Frank asks Heidi, "between the Russians wanting to detain the man able to testify against a leading Nazi, and the Germans seeking to repatriate someone shedding light on Speer the supposed apolitical technocrat standing for a nation misled by Hitler, now absolved? Was this why his release had taken so long, finally occurring only years into the post-Soviet era? For that was when Russia was in such disarray that its officials had the greater priority of rescuing it from chaos – or grabbing what they could of previously state-owned property. Distracted from preventing it, had they simply let the man elude them?"

He has not escaped Frank, still seated beside Heidi, their mineral water drained. Heidi is not answering. Frank, hardly aware of the coffee machine hissing behind them in the bar, or the dogs beyond on the square, recognises once more that this excursion has failed to divert him from discussing Speer's driver. The man, his predicament, has proved inescapable. Frank has even usurped Heidi's role in explaining, on her father's authority, the delay in his repatriation. Maybe she resents this, masking it with unnatural quietness.

Then Frank, feeling the silence resonating in the emptiness of the *pueblo*, recognises something else. Visiting the gypsy village, with Heidi's snatches of information, her lapsing exchanges, his own musings, he has surely not only been glimpsing a nonentity, lost to himself. Nor, taking up Heidi's original theme himself, has he simply followed the man, merely coincidentally recovering his self from Frank's London bedsit to a villa in this *pueblo* where either finds himself. Frank, rather than abstractly anatomising, if with mounting fascination, how he has come into possession of it, now knows he has been pursuing him as closely as one would one's own shadow. Increasingly insinuated into a stranger's awakening mind, he has found it implicitly also serving as his own.

It is a strain. Wearied too by the summer heat, he feels light-headed, standing up from the table – with Albert Speer entering his mind. It brings back turning from the archives to bestsellers featuring the Führer's protégé, his one friend. Though does it still offer, with Heidi also rising, what Frank finally recognises as relief at losing himself in the spectacle of a poised, indomitable sense of self?

The visitors leave the plaza and make for the car, still in the silence that has come upon them. They drive in light remaining, here by the Mediterranean, till late in summer. But the sun is setting. This is a bloodletting. Mute drama plays out in the sky.

Frank, looking towards the heavens, half-wonders whether or not the Nazis were *Übermenschen* after all. Perhaps Albert Speer, Reichsminister, resembled heroes of the Greeks who had visited this beach they are now passing: offspring of execrably behaved gods from on high. For he was effectively the son, if ever there was one, of Adolf Hitler, Father of the *Vaterland*. He was the favourite of Germany's Angel of Providence. And through his intimacy with the Führer, the near-divine blood of Destiny, of History, streamed through his veins. So, like the tragically flawed Hellenic demigods, Speer – the terrible story that *was* Speer – was a larger-than-life exemplum of forces at work in life for ordinary beings.

Despite his attraction, the magnetism of one standing so confidently, so firm, given all the mighty things he had been and done, his foundations were flawed. His persona, his personality, he himself was the flaw. In which case, true to the Greeks, a clairvoyant might from some inner awareness, however acquired, perceive what inevitably lay in store for him – for who he might turn out to be.

Perhaps.

The idea slips from Frank's thoughts. Gazing beyond the hills, he finds their outlines growing indistinct. Massive, motionless, they betray no sign of what is within; something beneath the Earth's crust, deep in its core.

It is working all the time, as for untold eons, he supposes. It will erupt again, without warning, as it did once in that eternity without sentient being, the mere suggestion of which catches Frank trembling as though it is cold in this summer darkness where, round some blind bend, still awaits the *pueblo* of his distant youth.

8

Getting up naked after a stifling night, Frank catches a reflection in his bedroom window. Modestly closing the shutters, blocking out the rest of the *pensión* and sunlit sea, he inwardly glimpses again a painter's self-portrait. It is the one he had seen displayed in London, in the Museum Street bookshop. But Frank, only just graduated, had barely considered what the naked image, no idealised nude, signified about the man in middle age. And he had not stopped to take it in, a decade or so later, on first arriving back at the *pueblo*. Though now, days later, following his excursion to the gypsy *pueblo*, it holds him on his way to the bathroom.

Frank momentarily sees that the emphasis on an entire body rather than on a flat, facial still life, even one concentrating on a specific feature or expression, conveys a picture by this stage of the man's life of a whole being. Yet he does not linger long enough specifically to ask what has now come to animate this full self. Despite which there remains at the back of Frank's mind the undeclared if nagging question of what finally gives the man his achieved human reality.

Something of it exudes from the painted exterior: the brazen, disturbingly animal vitality of the one choosing such a form of self-presentation. While for Frank, always physically prudish behind his straw hat and sunglasses, not to mention with the impassive mask of his Englishman's face, there is also the issue of who, finally, if anyone, he has become.

An observer, if bothering to glance at the seemingly conventional guest idling away the hours on the *pensión's* terrace, might never guess that the calm he seeks here is constantly disrupted. The search for a new project is invaded by suddenly surfacing quests. Overtaken by them, driven hither and thither, he pursues memories of his past in the *pueblo*, shadowing a resurfacing German POW here. The searches coalesce, merging confusingly. And Frank, now seeing himself in the mirror above the washbasin, the painting fading from his mind, cannot help wondering what is to be made of him. Who in sum would anybody find in the face staring back?

Sitting again over breakfast, he plays a game of blind-man's-buff. Sightless, he reaches for the man, Speer's driver. *I won't, he thinks – I* can't *stop trying to feel him out; no, not until I have finally made contact with him in this* pueblo. *Because although I stalked him in the gypsy village, rising with him out of my researcher's stupor pace by pace, the place where a mere self will be recognised fully to find himself is precisely in that villa with a woman.*

So I tell myself, barely taking in Heidi's voice while she sits before me over coffee, as I suppose the woman, Paloma, scarcely heard his in

Villa Bougainvillea. For regardless of how Heidi is somehow talking again about the prisoner of war, I now find myself viewing him as no mere psychiatric patient. A case history does him scant justice. I suppose they may not even have talked at all, Paloma and he.

I feel the silence spreading between them. If she sensed him, it was porously, admitting what his stillness conveyed, being filled with it. But had it given access, that proximity, even if not to the circumstances at least to a precipitate, the essence, of the shadow-self nearby?

Then again, it might easily have been nothing but self-reflection; illusory.

No, I am scarcely aware of Heidi speaking. It might not even be she, with the silence of the villa continuing within me, whose skin cream I am scenting, she whose tiny hairs I am now conscious of on the back of an arm. Were I to move a fraction of an inch, they would touch mine. Her bosom is rising and falling; through a slight opening in the blouse, I glimpse a bra. But what I am seeing, feeling, are the breasts of she who would never wear one in this heat. With a deep intake of breath, I know again I am not interested in Heidi. I am attracted to the one in Villa Bougainvillea for whom I am apparently still searching. I watch Heidi tensely adjust the button of her blouse, displacing the half-focused image I realise has been surfacing in my mind's eye.

"Do you think the driver *did* reveal anything?" Heidi asks. But she might as well never have surprised me by resuming conversation. For she does not wait for me to supply an answer she knows I could not possess, although it seems that she cannot help posing her question.

Her eyes glint. They are fixed on mine. A taut white band spreads across the bridge of her nose. Then Heidi says quietly: "Who knows what to make of that time in the villa?" She pauses, adding, as if sharing something dangerously confidential: "Someone could … But what's to be done except hope, when – *if* – she finally arrives, that the whole affair will break open." Whereupon, wearied perhaps from talking on a bright new day, Heidi turns her head. It droops. She fades into dimness.

Alone at a terrace table later, I seek to answer for myself what that source of information about Albert Speer might reveal. But it is no use. I never saw anything in my illicit skimming of the press. And anyone can see that just as the Russians were unlikely to concentrate on him with the collapse of the Soviet state, their historic empire, Germans were distracted by the fall of the Berlin Wall and reunification.

There were more pressing concerns for those two dramatically transforming nations than Albert Speer. Although he apparently remains a matter of intense speculation in this remote Spanish *pueblo*. Something of the man seems to survive here in Andalusia, where he had supposedly visited German friends just up the coast.

Despite which I still cannot help wondering which revelations about Speer might be significant for those now interested in him here. Yet I ask myself how informative the man coming back into existence as Albert Speer's driver could be. The Reichsminister had been driven long ago, in the war. But Speer was soon sentenced to twenty years in Spandau, far out of range of his driver – himself imprisoned on the Russian steppes, in Siberia, by an ice-bound sea, till confronted by himself (I have supposed) in a high pane giving onto vastness. Speer had died by the time the POW was belatedly released to face quite another question: what became of him, of who he was, in Villa Bougainvillea?

The following day, Heidi asks again what the driver knew in Villa Bougainvillea. She does so haltingly, as if experiencing emotionally the effect of a disagreeably humid, sandy front now overshadowing the *pueblo*. It is the remains of a Saharan wind that has lost force travelling over North Africa and the Mediterranean.

The morning after, even when she keeps to the terrace, Heidi resumes her practice of bringing books, her manuscript, to the table as she once had on days of bright sunshine. She does not take breaks with me. She suggests no further excursions. Our drive to the gypsy *pueblo* was four days ago. But she does not even accompany me anymore to our landward lookout over the hills.

Heidi sits with a studiousness barely masking broody remoteness. I attribute it to her time of the month, preferring not to consider whether or not I have done anything to change her attitude to me. She cannot believe, surely, that I am seeking to come threateningly close.

Heidi never comes to the terrace now. It halts even desultory conversation with someone in whom she obviously barely has interest. But then it would not serve further to consider Speer's driver. I could hardly discuss with her the issue of who he had been among a villa's climbing plants, overlooking the Mediterranean; of who exactly it was who peered down at that boundless marine shadow from a starlit roof with its jasmine-heavy trellis. For she, unaware of the answer, is professionally unused to, if not personally contemptuous of, so intimate a question. Heidi has done well to remove herself permanently to her room.

Of course, no one is indispensable. Yet I still cannot help wondering why Heidi seems finally to have gone to ground. What is this greater dejection, or unexplained resentment, that, increasingly stealing over her, has at last claimed her entirely, perhaps concealing her even from herself while she supposedly retires to work more intensively on her book? It leaves me supposing once more, sitting alone with the cockatoo, squawking with its leathery black tongue, that I, too, should begin a new project. Best to be productive rather than expose myself to distracting queries into how a mere self could become somebody. And in time, when the cockatoo has grown silent, its cage covered for the night, I abandon the terrace. I wander the streets as, I recall, I had done near the British Museum.

My mind conjures up the unruly nineteenth-century figure with his haystack of grey hair walking that way after hours beneath the glass dome of the Reading Room. He is unknown, Marx, just as decades later in another capital of empire, Vienna, a puny youth, Hitler, drifts anonymously on the pavements, painting and scavenging among ideas of the commonest currency. The fullest expression of their thoughts is still to come. Nor is it only their writings that are to have an explosive impact. Something of *themselves* will shake their worlds to the very foundations. Yes, soon, very soon, improbable as it seems, each wandering soul will come fully into who he truly is.

9

Frank imagines himself approaching Professor Keller's office. But he is not taking with him the idea for his next book. He has leapfrogged over his failure to find it this week. For although he has not discovered its theme, he has, strangely, acquired a sense of what it will be like. In fact, it is as if it is ready, miraculously completed within him, though without a subject and not a single word written. It is just waiting to surface.

Less impersonal and analytical than Frank's last book, it has somehow been loosened in his mind from the static sense of a single, dominating issue. Yes, liberated for whatever reason from a constraining central idea, its focus can still allow the free flow of narrative and character, with the natural influence of time. But Frank wonders if he is really offering this to that fearful ghost of a man. It is both too little and too much, he thinks, approaching Professor Keller's office. Still, he hovers by the open door of the dark, vacant room – only now realising he is once more standing by that bin with its neglected plant.

Despite dusty leaves, he notices it is straining towards the light. Its tendrils strive. They have green points, new shoots, a bud unobserved by those speaking of a dead man's fading legacy. It grows heedless of opinions on matters it oppresses Frank even to recall, this apparent cutting from a jungle. And it displays the pullulating resistance of Amazonian flora, surviving the abuse of cigarette butts in its dry earth, the gloom of a frequently unpeopled passageway such as these Frank has been crossing in the *pueblo*.

Frank sits on the terrace again, with its nocturnal fragrance of climbing plants. Their flowers have opened on the trellis overhead: jasmine, honeysuckle, Dama de noche, Copa de oro. He is drinking them all in as Amalia comes to take his order for dinner.

It seems that she is using a magnolia perfume on her smooth, still-attractive face and all that is exposed by this low-cut dress. He imagines it smeared across those breasts he is again disturbingly aware are naked beneath cotton worn by the warm, pleasant woman of whom he takes in more now that Heidi is absent.

But she would surely be nonplussed by an advance from a man she assumes is interested in her daughter, an Englishman in his thirties with the identity of an archivist. Although based on experience, the Mediterranean woman might well suppose there is more to a foreigner coming to the *pueblo* than meets the eye.

It is true. Frank is aroused more strongly than ever before in Amalia's presence. How inconvenient, this sharp access of passion! It is unsettling of his sense of himself; of what is possible for him. What meaning can it possibly have for him since whoever, whatever, he might be can have no more to do with Amalia than with absent Heidi? Hardly expecting her to return, as he takes his place on the terrace he senses, without specific evidence, that she is responding to the summons of a personal destiny.

No, it is not for her that he goes on dining beneath this trellis. It is not even for her mother, whose attractiveness serves to call him less to Amalia herself, were he to know it, than to such as might lie unsuspectedly ahead.

Nor is it to await the idea for a book, pleasing to Professor Keller, that Frank lingers here over dinner. His imagined visit to the great man's office has transported him beyond it, focusing instead on green shoots in a wooden plant pot.

Rather, Frank is detained here on the terrace, in the *pueblo*, beneath a southern constellation, by such as something within him is unknowingly reaching out to. It is straining. He is near to touching …

Dinner over, I am drawn back to the streets. Abandoned to these alleys, I feel more alone than ever, haunting repeated passageways.

That is a cul-de-sac, with the glow of a small flamenco bar at the end. Within, there is exploratory strumming. It will continue, desultory, endless – till the abrupt appearance of what is solely able to turn the guitar fierce, the heels ferocious.

But the dancer will burst out. He must, I know, as that gypsy flared up one night from beneath the olive oil company's calendar, with its almost Oriental Cordovan beauty, over the bar where I order red wine.

It had to be here, didn't it, that he finally exploded into his life? He did so, I am certain, exactly where I stand, propelling him into those ultimate moments before the woman with her slender arms and legs, long, dark hair and almond eyes. It is the ideal of beauty implanted by women arriving from North Africa.

The *pueblo's* dogs bark wildly tonight. They give vent to such agony that nothing exhausts them. They cannot stop. What is stirring them, Frank wonders, exciting them to this frenzied distraction? There are no Greeks on the beach sacrificing to their gods. No priests have interpreted for them the oracles, deriving from fractured utterances what the Hellenic mariners and traders must resolve with bonfires and roasts on spits. There are no barbecues this evening, not a whiff of one, he is certain, on the roofs of vacationers' villas like that one, from sea air so fresh now that several days' mistiness has cleared.

The dogs' olfactory senses are picking up something unknown to others, but precise and powerful enough to set them off. It is as if they are nosing out a hidden timing device, ticking in readiness to detonate some unimaginable explosion. They are the deafening signal, he imagines, that what others are not aware of awaiting is coming.

I move round the *pueblo*. My legs carry me automatically. I want to be free from this repeated circuiting, succumbing to the insistent question of how – of whether – a 'no one' found himself. For decades he had been lost, beyond recall. What would it take to recover memory, I ask myself – but truly to open it up to oneself, not just to onlookers, reanimating the lost part of one? Once more sighting the bougainvillea-constricted villa ahead, I suppose it first requires penetrating the scar tissue concealing the wound that is the past.

I am brought up short at Villa Bougainvillea. Is a light on? My chest tightens. I fight to breathe. My mouth is bone dry.

It is dread.

I realise the light has always had to be on. I recognise now that I must really have known all along that it has to be showing just past the front door, barely ajar. Its perforated brass lamp must be scattering luminous coloured discs across the hall wall as it has done throughout the time the house has been in utter darkness. An extinction so total it is that it even smothers awareness of itself, together with memory of the light that is on, that has been on, that will be on all the time, cast over burnished brass plates from Algeria. They shine before my benighted eyes near the Gloucester Road, off Leicester Square, in Paddington and even far out beneath the roar of air traffic over Heathrow Airport.

This is the light that suddenly must be on in the villa where it has been off during each of my days, my nights, at Pensión Amalia, off during years unimaginable as the eons mutely withstood by nearby prehistoric shanks always about to shudder and move cataclysmically. Once-inhabited mounds, these necropoleis, wait to be laid open and revealed.

A light it is always on, I recognise, where a man, a foreigner, a stranger to himself, now finally returned from exile, recovered his sense of being, of being throughout, for all the identity dreamed up and ascribed to him.

It is the light I shall see walking past tonight, tomorrow, each evening after that, seeking myself where I have always been with the climbing plant at that wall, beyond the front doorstep and half-open door, where there must be the soft echo of a woman's voice. I am straining to catch phrases whispered below the threshold of hearing, where I know them, can never forget them, keep hearing them again for the first time, but find myself night after night passing the phantom light, while actually hearing an invisible piano playing the same piece again and again.

The pianist started from the beginning as always. He continues towards the demanding final passage. There the piece fragments. He repeats the marred bars endlessly, becomes mired, breaks down. And he returns to the start, carefully replaying sequence after sequence, as if by dissecting the piece like this, Frank thinks, seeing and not seeing the light on tonight in Villa Bougainvillea, he might finally achieve the understanding, the momentum, to carry through to what he longs for.

Maybe he will liberate himself from what has long tied him down, rediscovering the *Prelude* – the last in the sequence. Perhaps he will render the full, spontaneous performance always in his inner ear, never entirely silenced throughout the many discordant months in which it has kept eluding him. At long last, he might come into his own through it, the composer's medium, giving himself thrillingly free flight through this night air to what has always been here – and then?

PART VI

1

It is Sunday, the day on which the local market, circulating from one village to another, comes to the *pueblo*. "It's done so forever," Amalia tells me. "You should go. You never know who you might meet there."

It is noon by the time I come upon the noisy stalls with their produce from *fincas* hereabouts: fresh cheeses, honey, earthenware jars and jewellery made from the province's semi-precious stones.

Halted in the *pueblo's* blazing sunlight, I fan streaming cheeks with my sunhat by the old woman trying to sell me onions; she has brought them from her patch of land in the hills on the mule quivering beside her. I am trying to recall if I had previously known the market existed. Yet what the place was like, the atmosphere all those years ago, who I was: it all evades me among these flies the donkey vainly seeks to shudder from its flanks.

Of course, the location of the market has changed. It has been moved downhill for easy access to the new car park. Not that I am remotely interested in developers' attempts to attract tourists. I prefer the reality that was, even if only as a sepia memory like the framed photos hanging in the café on the plaza. Expressionless men with big moustaches and waistcoats stand eternally holding billiard cues years before the eruptions of the Civil War.

Suddenly, a female shadow is ahead of me. I blink absently at the woman I have all but forgotten. Then Heidi emerges in full focus from the glowing silhouette. She is talking to Magda, who is out shopping with her maid.

Magda breaks off from their earnest conversation to greet me. "We *did* enjoy having you over the other day. Bruno doesn't have much intelligent company. He's become a recluse. All he does is play the piano. I left him doing that just now. 'You'd be happy in prison,' I tell him, 'as long as you had your Steinway.' But I suppose he has to be alone all this time to practise, doesn't he? The piano is his life."

Magda returns to whatever she was discussing when I arrived. I, too, register the tense way Heidi has clearly been waiting for the interruption – me – to yield. "So just to finish what I was saying, she's doing much better now. Nothing dramatic of course, but calmer. Yet peacefulness is what really counts, isn't it?"

"When's she coming here?" Heidi asks. Her tone sounds especially direct.

"Well, this summer," Magda says, with flickering eyelids and a vague inclination of her well-coiffed head.

"But we're well into it. Isn't there a specific date?"

"Soon," Magda says flatly.

Heidi just looks at her. Her eyes, the set of her mouth, are hard. "Soon?"

"We don't want to press her for too many details, her father and I. She needs time, space, for herself."

"I know she'll want to see her friends: the people who *really* care about her. And she'll certainly realise they want to see her."

"I expect she'll get in touch with you, Heidi – eventually. One way or the other."

Heidi does not answer. Not for the first time, I see a white band appearing across the bridge of her nose.

Magda has simply turned away to affect amazement at the quality of embroidery on some Andalusian shawl.

Suddenly Heidi discovers it is hot. She feels the onset of a headache. She is sorry, but she really must go back immediately to her mother's *pensión*. She absolutely has to lie down.

"She's very high-strung," Magda says refusing to turn a hair. She has resumed her shopping, the maid at her side. "She's always been difficult," she's telling me. "I've known her and her mother since she was a child … Be careful."

Magda bends to choose orange-streaked peppers from the frugal pile set out on a raffia tray. Putting them on the metal pan of the storekeeper's hand-held balance, she adds, as an aside: "She certainly didn't do us any favours arranging for Paloma to look after that driver – if that's what he was. Imagine! Putting her in touch with someone working for a war criminal. We were beside ourselves, her father and I."

The peppers are dropped onto the rest of the vegetables in the maid's basket. "And our idyllic Mediterranean calm has been ruined with these constant discussions of Albert Speer. We've come to know far more about him than we ever wanted."

At which point the maid is dispatched with her load up to El Castillo. Magda turns to me with: "You don't have to run off too, I trust."

"Not at all. There's not a thing on my agenda. I'm on holiday, aren't I?"

We stop in the plaza for lemonade. They boil the peel as well as the flesh from the local fruit. I taste it, sweet yet tart, as Magda says: "I hope you didn't mind my argument with Bruno about Speer the other night. But does anyone still seriously believe what he said to his daughter: 'as for the horrors, I knew nothing'? And I doubt the sincerity of his remorse. It was all window dressing.

"Bruno can't understand there's a huge problem of credibility. Or he doesn't want to. As he says, he's from Buenos Aires, with its postwar German immigrants, especially in the arts. Everyone has a past. It's inconvenient to probe. Take people at face value. Let sleeping dogs lie.

"But I feel there's part of Bruno that can't bear to accept that Speer's twenty lost years in Spandau are simply the beginning and end of the story. I actually think his mind keeps coming back to it during all those hours he spends at the piano."

Savouring my fragrant lemonade while listening to the onetime pianist's ex-wife (as Amalia has referred to her), I see the man haunted by the thought while practising the Chopin he once discharged brilliantly, but doing so now, during presumably damp winters, quite alone here, on long, chill nights. All but hearing his inconclusive pursuit of the *Prelude* he had originally played to such acclaim, I somehow know the solitary being cannot imagine how everything achieved by an ambitious young man without a trace of self-doubt can have merely disappeared. Won't the chances originally coming so easily somehow return? And maybe it is impossible to believe one can be withdrawn from life for an eternity without eventually recovering one's sense of self-value.

"Yes," I say, my glass clinking as I put it down on the cracked marble tabletop before Magda. "It sounds like an aspect of Speer somebody might well be interested in. I mean how one comes back to oneself, re-establishing one's worth."

"Assuming Speer did."

Which Magda obviously does not. But she foregos expanding on her view. It is hot even under this sunshade. Besides, she is feeling the strain of trying to understand a man who does not exactly invite an ex-wife into his thoughts. Still yearning, despite her proud self, to be one with him, though denied openness, she has been diverting, divulging, her insights to a stranger – only to find herself garrulous. It makes this controlled, soignée older woman apologetic a second time.

I shrug my shoulders at the self-abasing words, implying no pardon is necessary. Swiftly, I move us away from momentary embarrassment by widening the scope of conversation beyond Bruno's focus of interest. "Did the driver shed any light on Speer?" I say.

Like sargasso, a patch of shadow appears to float across the sun's harshness. Within too, in my mind's eye, there is darkness – and cold damp; a mouldy smell of pine. It is a forest where the men had to lie, with Speer blindly faced by the destruction of everything he had built.

"I hardly met the man," Magda says. "He made no impression on me." She pauses and then mutters, almost irritated, as if to internal hearers: "And I simply can't understand how he did on anyone else. He was ordinary; depressingly ordinary, like Eichmann, with barely a trace of personality."

"Maybe he talked to others."

"Why bother them?" Magda says tartly. "What d'you expect to find? Who is ever understood by someone else? Besides, do you even need to know?"

Do I? What's Speer to me? Frank's mute question holds in his mind as he says goodbye to Magda, traipsing back to Pensión Amalia. Of course the driver, and what *he* means to Frank, has also dominated his thoughts recently; thoughts that Frank supposes he should rather focus on finding his next academic project. Yet, arriving on the terrace, he feels too drained by the heat to consider future research or either Nazi. He cannot think. Frank heads straight to his room, where it seems he repeatedly takes refuge these days. He throws his sunhat on the bed like a lifebuoy, as if to help consciousness keep afloat.

Now, sinking heavily onto the cotton coverlet, Frank's mind is extinguished. It is blank through lunchtime this afternoon, which he finally awakens to find he has largely slept through. Later, sitting out on the terrace alone after a snack of cheese instead of dinner, with his late-night glass of cold mineral water, his thoughts return. But what would it take to respond to them? It rankles to know he will just have to wait for such as must finally come to him. He will remain expectantly in the *pueblo*, no less in the dark than that covered cockatoo.

The thought of having two more weeks to kill here makes me want to cut my vacation short. I see myself packing in readiness for a taxi to take me through chill dawn to the airport. Even so, I lounge lazily, simply sampling, on succeeding nights, the silver moonlight. But I also feel something magnetising me to the place. I am not free to move.

Once more, I cannot bear the idea of returning to my shadow life of many years. I have found its grey reality exposed, on surfacing here with the publication of the book which I, Professor Keller's constant student, researched there. Again I recoil from the subterranean archive's rows of mouldering documents. It is a bunker in which time is eked out to evade some irrationally sensed foreboding overhead.

I could not, of course, reappear there without a project to lend a modicum of meaning to my otherwise aimless cataloguing. Returning empty-handed to daily dullness, to blankness, would stealthily make me – this very self of mine – part of the void I shall enter. The prospect holds me here, endlessly seeking a purposely elusive subject.

"My subject": but what is it, really? It merges inescapably with what else tugs on my mind in the *pueblo*. I am wondering how someone, albeit returned to his self, can, more than merely existing, avoid being empty; becoming, instead, fully who he is. That is what Speer represents for me, finally answering the question Magda left me with. It applies no less to his driver. Though to see how – if – such being can actually be achieved, I know I must wait in the *pueblo* until the arrival of the woman spending time with a man in Villa Bougainvillea.

2

Magda has decided to invite some people to El Castillo. She is a social being. A ballerina, she sees life as formations of people. Certainly, she cannot understand her husband's preference for being alone with his piano, playing the music in which he keeps losing himself.

It was not always so. Originally, he had many mistresses. They surrounded him. It was a keen, painful need. "There are days when all women look attractive," Bruno would say.

Yet once married, his sole affair, making him break up with Magda, soon guttered. He was suddenly alone. Bruno fell back into the emotional vacancy from which all those liaisons had been distractions. He was lost, as if in a dark wood, turning to the piano to play his way out of it. But his bearings had apparently gone even in the pieces hitherto coming naturally to him. So, too, his self-confidence, beneath that veneer of dry irony that was actually lonely, courageous stoicism in the face of disturbing emptiness. The music, Chopin, is a bog sucking him in. The harder he plays, the more he is dragged into opacity; suffocating nothingness.

Bruno, despite his misanthropy in which he knows no one else can assist him in his impossible fight into the open, has reluctantly acceded to Magda's wish to have a group round for tapas and drinks tonight.

Heidi has reluctantly been persuaded to join her mother. They come upon the Englishman staying at Pensión Amalia. Heidi has not seen or at least talked to Frank Ward since the last few days of her withdrawal. More composed now, she takes him in as if it is their first meeting. He is in his early thirties, serious, his face made youngish by the clarity of his features.

Despite his social reserve, Frank grows steadily less tongue-tied as conversation turns from how much hotter it has been over the last few summers and whether or not the mayor, a butcher, can evade corruption charges being brought by the baker's family. For talk has now settled on a subject the hosts sometimes introduce when there are guests, a topic teasing enough to avoid the cocktail group failing to find anything interesting of itself: Albert Speer's alleged visit to Rubinstein in the Jewish pianist's dressing room in Marbella.

"Se non è vero è ben trovato," Bruno says, his Argentinean accent making Italian sound natural.

"D'you think it's likely?" Frank asks Heidi.

"Why me?" she says, rebuffing his politeness.

"It occurred to me you might know the, em, context," he says with hesitant reasonableness.

"What do *you* think?" Bruno asks Frank, ignoring whatever Heidi, the difficult lecturer, student of her modern Germany, might decide to take offence at. Plain as she is, he could never be interested in her as a woman.

"Of course, it's unknowable now if Speer saw Rubinstein," Frank says. "But regardless of whether or not the two men met in fact, I suppose it'd make a kind of sense if they had. I see what the pianist could have meant to Speer."

"Oh, really!" Bruno says, his interest piqued. "How so?"

"Well, I've been mulling over the idea of the encounter in Rubinstein's dressing room in Marbella you mentioned the last time I was here."

Frank speaks with what Heidi now finds an especially English academic accent, his words becoming increasingly clear in the evening. His voice is gaining in confidence, discussing the kind of historical conundrum she assumes is professionally natural to him. Not that his intelligence seems dry. It is engaged, even earnest, fully holding the attention of this gathering for tapas and drinks.

"I know it's tempting to suppose Speer sought forgiveness for war crimes from so universally respected a member of the race against which they'd been perpetrated. What's more natural than to think he wanted his contrition accepted by the great Rubinstein? But he never admitted real responsibility: nothing specific, not even for removing Jews from their housing in Berlin, although evidence had started surfacing about it shortly before he died.

"So if he wouldn't admit more than generic responsibility for the worst crimes, denying specific guilt except for the lesser charge of using the slave labour that cost him twenty years in prison, the forgiveness of even a Rubinstein would have been beside the point.

"Of course, he may have deluded himself during the decades granted him by his narrow escape from hanging at Nuremberg, both in Spandau and then after it. Yet did he really think contradictorily that he could be, that he *was*, both innocent and contrite? Whatever the case, I wonder if it wasn't art rather than politics that dominated his mind. Because his strategy for survival in prison was to transfer his focus to culture.

"Speer studied the history of architecture. He began books on the function of windows. Not that his own massive buildings lasted. The most that survives of his work is a few lampposts. Yet his artistic impulse did endure. That, surely, is what he wanted recognised. It was at play in his urge to write – though any real artistry surely came from his editor, making something compellingly readable from his turgid, impersonal prose."

Frank sees himself devouring page after page of the bestsellers in London bookshops during his lunch hours. Then he adds, as an aside, with a slight wave of his hand as if to an inner hearer: "After all, they do say that even the writing of history can be an art. Yet, what exactly was the artistic impulse he might have wished the great pianist to acknowledge in him, this once-acclaimed architect entering Rubinstein's dressing room? Wasn't it self-expression? The expression of a self thus affirmed, thereby confirming to Speer himself that he possessed it? For the reality – not just the existence – of that self, of his very being, was no foregone conclusion.

"What a struggle he'd had to maintain the sense of some such thing in Spandau. And didn't he need to overcome his personal void now that he, no longer the Führer's architect, Minister of Armaments, friend, was no one – simply nothing?"

Bruno is tracking back over what he has just heard: that the pianist might, through implicitly confirming Speer's artistic self-expression, endorse the highly self-aware Nazi's self that was in doubt – to lend support against his fear of non-being. He repeats the idea over and over, from different angles, in different ways, just as he plays, again and again, the emotive passages of that *Last Prelude* in which he finds the concentrated rendering of an entire life as it plunges into an abyss.

“So is that what you mean?” he says. “Speer sought out Rubinstein as if the mere contact, touching the hem of his garment, shaking the hand that released streams of life-affirming notes, would stop him being sucked into the vacuum he was at his centre?”

“Possibly – *if* they ever met.”

3

Bruno, a non-performing artist, was so taken by Frank’s observations on Speer and art that he invited him again. But as he did so in Magda’s hearing, she, the social animal, had, despite his usual reclusive reluctance to leave his studio, the library, his shell, reconvened the whole of the previous evening’s group for *paella* at Amalia’s restaurant.

The men talk over *pulpo* served first. Their discussion continues as they eat the main dish, washing it down with Jumilla, that strong red wine from the neighbouring province of Murcia. The women, or more exactly the mothers seated by an abstracted Heidi, discuss the plants in their gardens. Some grow here in pots on this heavily shaded terrace overlooking the Mediterranean. Others are up in El Castillo, screened by terracotta walls and bamboo. The women describe how they nurture those that are sickly, temperamental even, needing special care; tending fragrant, exotic ones which retract and seem as shrivelled in the morning as at season’s end. Some, they say, stray far off, ever climbing.

Now they are considering how unpredictable life can be for those we love. And you can never know what effect it will have on a child, regardless of what she has been like from infancy. *“Dans l’amour il y a toujours celui qui aime et celui qui donne la joue,”* Heidi contributes unexpectedly. Her eyes are gentle, vulnerable, without a hint of resentment. Yet an instant is all it is. She draws away, sighing from her deepest recesses. It is as if, half-suffocated, she is coming up for air out of the dark, unimaginably heavy depths of that sea glittering below. With the sternly chastened face of a slapped child, Heidi leans back in her chair, spine rigid. Her eyes are fixed on the long, pink langoustine from which she has been straining to release the flesh. But the tender lobe she is struggling to open up is suddenly flooded red. It is blood from the finger she jerks back, having just cut it on a sharp claw.

Heidi's mother spontaneously comes to the rescue. She instantly leads her daughter to the kitchen to dress the wound. For the cut is a gift to Amalia: it enables her to treat the child long passed from her hands as the infant for which her kind of affection is specifically suited.

"Cariño! Pobrecita!" The words reach down the long, shaded terrace, where Bruno is talking to the Englishman.

Reverting to his fond belief that Speer had sought out Rubinstein, Bruno seeks to make it plausible by detailing the man's strong interest in the arts. "There were occasions in Paris, arranged by the German ambassador and his French wife, when Speer met Cocteau and Vlaminck. Even at school music meant a lot to him according to his memoirs, *Inside the Third Reich* – ah! So you know it?"

Indeed, the Englishman does.

"Well, in that case you'll remember he heard the young Furtwängler in Mannheim. And then, in '44, Furtwängler invited Speer to his dressing room." Bruno says it meaningfully. "There, privately, he asked Hitler's minister, no less, if the war was lost. When Speer said the end was imminent, Furtwängler nodded. He'd come to the same conclusion. And Speer feared for him, knowing Bormann, Goebbels and Himmler had heard many of his frank remarks, including his defence of the blacklisted Hindemith."

"Who do you think Speer's favourite orchestral composer was?" Frank says. "It has to be Brückner, doesn't it?"

"But of course," Bruno says smiling expansively. "And he liked *The Romantic Symphony* in particular, with that architectonic final movement. It was played at the end, in April '45, by the Berlin Philharmonic. Because it was Speer who did all he could to prevent Goebbels from disbanding the orchestra and drafting its members into the Home Guard for a suicidal defence of the doomed capital. In fact, Speer ordered the electricity that was usually cut off to be switched on in the Philharmonic Hall. So although it was unheated, and they were all in overcoats, the concert could at least be lighted."

"I've read," Frank says, "that as the audience left they were offered cyanide capsules from baskets held by children wearing Hitler Youth uniforms."

"True," Bruno says dryly, taking several mouthfuls of the thick, dark wine. His face shows him following it down his gullet. He pauses, then comes back to himself with: "But don't forget Speer was also very fond of the piano – and pianists." He raises his emptied glass. He is peering, self-absorbed, through its purple-streaked curve, as if expecting to glimpse clearly what lies beyond such opacity. "He saw a lot of his friend Wilhelm Kempff in Berlin, in a circle of artists he preferred to the company of party members. And remember the idyllic account in his *Secret Diaries* of evenings at Coq Hardi, a famous restaurant in Bougival on the Seine. He dined there with what he describes as a 'loose group' of German officers and French artists, industrialists and aristocrats. They were served by Maître François himself. And he met Alfred Cortot.

"After dinner, Cortot would invite them to his small top-floor apartment. They would sit on his rolled-up rugs, because there weren't enough chairs. And they heard him play Chopin and Debussy … Imagine …" Bruno inhales deeply, drawing back from the table as a basket of figs is placed before him. He is living the scene, hearing Cortot play, staring unseeingly at the pianist. "Speer says he especially remembered Cortot's playing of *La Cathédrale Engloutie*. But just think of him calling it back to mind in his cell over the inconceivable ocean of time he spent in Spandau. That, surely, is when Speer relapses into emptiness. It feels to him as if he'll never surface. What could possibly draw him out of it?"

Him: who he really was, Frank thinks.

4

The last person I expect to see on the terrace the following morning is Heidi. Not to judge by those recent temperamental withdrawals of hers, especially after yesterday's incident with the langoustine. But now, far from keeping her distance from me, she walks right over to my breakfast table, raising a hand with its cut finger in greeting. Giving me a book with the other, she sits, explaining it was delivered to the *pensión* for me earlier that day. It came with a note.

Bruno writes that after our conversation yesterday he thought I would be interested in this biography. He has not read it yet himself, but he understands it is the last word on Speer. He looks forward to discussing it with me. Looking up from the scribbled page, I find Heidi looking at me with dark, yellowish rings around her eyes.

"So, what do you make of this Speer business?" she asks, as Isabel serves her coffee. It is the first time I have heard her forsake academic parlance in referring to it. Gone is her originally restrained, almost formal cordiality to me.

I demur, surprised.

"Somehow you're interested. I can tell," Heidi says, picking her wounded finger. Pained, she is inflicting more hurt on herself.

My delay in answering is also defensive, I suppose. For Heidi's tone feels strangely accusatory. While Albert Speer, hardly a subject of which Professor Keller would have approved, is even now a distraction from my true focus as an historian.

But I have no more time to plumb my reaction, let alone to expand on my greater avowed interest in late medieval studies. This sunlit Andalusian terrace has just filled with the voluptuous fragrance of magnolia-scented skin cream.

Heidi's mother comes up to us with her generous smile and "*Buenos dias*". Standing behind our chairs, a hand on each of us, she says: "How would the two of you like to take an excursion to Granada with me?"

Can Amalia really so misunderstand the situation between us? Thus her daughter's irked look seems to say. Does she seriously think the outing would cement our non-existent relationship? She twitches her shoulder away from her mother's hand and gets up, murmuring barely distinctly that she does not have all day to go on sitting here. She goes into the *pensión*.

Amalia remains half-smiling at me, the man assumed to be concerned for her daughter's welfare, with a look of: "Heidi's only being Heidi." Then she tells me just how beautiful her Granada is. Eyes still trailing towards the bedrooms, she says: "It's impossible for anyone to be unhappy there."

Frank is alone now at the terrace table. Amalia has cleared away the remains of breakfast before going in. Only his cup remains as he prepares to get up. Even the shade is oppressive by this late in the morning; the cockatoo is drowsy. Still, he lingers with a further sip of this bitter *café con leche*, musing further on Heidi's allegation that he is interested in Speer.

Heavily adrift in thought, he wonders if, by focusing on someone precisely calculated to subvert everything his esteemed Professor held dear, this is a final, guilty renunciation of his dependence on Keller. Worse still, if Speer is the case of an empty man challenged to become fully himself, fascination with his search for who he is must surely invite suspicion – no! the fact – of one's comparable deficiency. Which is, if anything, cause for defensiveness.

Later that afternoon, Heidi finds Frank still sitting on the terrace, engrossed in the book Bruno has lent him.

"Devastating!" she says, in mock echo of the judgement on the dust jacket.

"Yes, it's surprising that historians have anything left to say about Speer," Frank mutters, rousing himself.

"*Someone* would," Heidi says meaningfully. "We might be told what his driver said."

"Maybe," Frank says, hardly turning the matter over in his mind for the first time.

He does not invite Heidi to his table. Nor does she appear eager to join him. He is speaking to someone who, far from facing him, studies the scar on her finger as if seeing through it to some mesmerising wound throbbing invisibly within her.

"But what, in any case," Frank goes on, "could the driver tell us about the occasions we're likely to be most interested in – the ones when he was closest to Speer, hiding in the forest outside Berlin? They're early in '45 when Speer started leaving Berlin at dusk to reverse the Führer's scorched-earth policy ...

"Speer was repeatedly driven under cover of darkness," Frank continues, despite Heidi's self-absorption; she is finally perched beside him. "He headed for the Ruhr mining districts and other western regions to ensure continued industrial production and prevent extremist Gauleiters from implementing the Nero Order. During the day, the Allies' ground-attack aircraft forced Speer to waste hours at a time hiding in woodland or ditches. Though he was sometimes also brought to a standstill at night on roads badly congested by army vehicles, goods transports and refugees.

"But what did Speer feel, lying low like this in darkness by day, or stopped on blocked roads at night, beneath relentless bombing?"

The question is rhetorical. It expects no answer from Heidi, sullenly abstracting herself from a query that Frank, no less than she, is unexpectedly finding fully posed.

"How is the man experiencing these blackouts? Well, there's no question of the driver himself being able to provide significant information on occasions he was with the Minister, hiding from enemy planes. More particularly, one can't expect him to have been aware of his master's state of mind. For the drivers, a senior minister was no less than a god ... a god in an era as irrational as that of those ancient Greeks casting up on this shore. Not given Nazi beliefs in Providence and the *Übermensch*. And while Speer might have lain in the dark woodland, hiding from enemy bombs next to his liaison officer with the General Staff, the young Lieutenant-Colonel von Poser whom he liked and trusted, he would never have been close to the chauffeur."

Heidi appears not to be listening. She might not even have heard Frank citing what Speer's secretary, Frau Kempf, said after the war about the psychological gulf between them. A driver at the ministry had confessed to her much later that he had known what was happening in the death camps. "'Why didn't you tell me about it at the time?'" she asked him, whereupon, amazed, he replied: "'How could I, a mere lance corporal, have mentioned it to you and thus to the Führer's great Minister? Herr Speer would have had to make a report, and that could have caused him terrible trouble.'

"Speer's driver obviously has nothing to tell us," Frank says. "There is no point appealing to someone to share what there isn't." Heidi bridles at her table as he continues: "Which means we're still left with the question: what *did* these long periods of eclipse mean to Speer? Is it just a feeling of defeat?"

Yet, does Heidi wish to explore such an emotion? She might simply feel forced to remain on the terrace by the momentum of the monologue coming upon Frank, allowing her no interval for escape.

"No. I might have presumed he had a sense of nothingness until …" Frank says, fingering Speer's new biography. "But now I doubt that even at this late stage of the conflict, it's annihilation that he experiences. The scales haven't yet fallen from Speer's eyes. He still doesn't really see in the dark that each of his buildings, every city he's planned, is ruined; that the war he specifically helped extend as Minister of Armaments and Munitions is lost; that the Reich is fated; that the Führer to whom he's pledged his loyalty, if not love, and attached all his hopes and ambitions, is finished; that all he himself, Albert Speer, is and aspired to be has collapsed."

Then Frank tells Heidi that Speer had written that he simply ignored Goering's order, issued from his country estate Kerinhall, not to step out of one of those flak towers Hitler commissioned as defence against the RAF. They provided shelters for tens of thousands of people. On the roof during an Allied bombing raid, he is mesmerised by the night sky – which Frank discovers himself seeing in his mind's eye from Villa Bougainvillea's rooftop. It is a barely acknowledged image instantly overtaken again by that wartime sky before which Speer is thrilled by parachute flares, "Christmas trees" as Berliners called them. He is dazzled by flashing explosions attracting German searchlights. Flames plummet brilliantly from planes hit by anti-aircraft guns on the flak tower.

Speer is overawed by the apocalyptic spectacle. He is barely touched, Frank is telling, well, not Heidi, who is withdrawn, hugging her arms as if shivering in the summer morning. Yes, Speer is untouched by the grim reality behind this coldly beautiful appearance. Far from deepening his awareness of the wider situation, Frank says, the man's heartlessly aesthetic perception of the bombing, the destruction, the night, keeps him from recognising what he is actually seeing on the flak tower, no less than when hiding in a Berlin wood or beside moonlit roads.

There is a pause. Frank's nocturnal image reverberates in the still afternoon. Heidi gets up, unimpressed by how little she has heard can be gleaned of Speer's state of mind. She says stiffly that she really must go.

As she leaves, Frank is aware of how surprisingly easily the words have been coming to him. So fluent is he that they seem to be speaking themselves through him in fully formed paragraphs. Just as unthinkingly, he finds himself back atop the flak tower with Speer, viewing a scene from the "opera", as the man later called the end of the war. But once more, Frank also senses an under-image, this time quite aware of being mentally transported to the roof of Villa Bougainvillea.

He is with Esther years ago, witnessing the night sky. They are breathtakingly close, he and she, hearts beating and thudding as one as they take in the measureless glitter of heavenly bodies, shooting stars. They have opened up to this evening's liberating infinity coming at them in a sudden rush, breaking through whatever he senses might previously have restrained it.

How different, Frank feels, from that cold, heartless beauty bedazzling Speer! The illumined illusions crossing the night's surface prevent Speer from seeing the destruction, from facing the reality of that darkness. And for only an instant, the blink of an eye, Frank reassures himself that he is not mistaken in his own different view of such softly engulfing obscurity, so close to this shadowy, phantom woman. For silvery, pale, its flickering lights are runic signals, aren't they, to so much more than annihilating vacancy?

Now Frank is halted again, mindful of the discrepancy between what he and Speer see, marvelling, in the darkness. He considers the scale of the misalignment. Though finally getting up, setting aside the borrowed book with its new data, its damning portrait, he leaves the terrace wondering why he even cares.

Part VII

1

Bruno is always testy on awakening from his siesta. He feels weakened by the medication for his heart condition. But this afternoon he is even more irritable than usual. The water has been turned off again. He cannot douse his head beneath the tap, drowning the darkness carried out of sleep. There can be no washing away of irresolution, lending him the sense of a fresh start with which to return to the piano.

If only the mayor would speed up plans to link the *pueblo*, like the rest of the province, with that underground river surging away from the mountains. For now, increasingly for days on end, there is not a drop of water. The imported bluish grass, the tropical flowering shrubs, the entire garden will wilt, leaving only wiry bougainvillea to give colour to the adobe walls.

Bruno moves barefoot in the hall, his hair tousled and his badly shaven face gleaming with sweat, while a torrent gushes beneath him. He is denied access to its life-giving cascades by the cool marble, the Earth's crust. But he is prevented from complaining to Magda, approaching him.

She herself never takes a siesta. She hardly sleeps at all. Always tense in her endless waking, she is especially so this afternoon, with Bruno half-staggering towards her. For, covering his hoarse voice, she tells him that while he was resting, in one of his ever longer after-lunch sessions, their daughter called. She is catching the train in Madrid the following morning and will be with them by evening.

"At last," Bruno says as they diverge to sit together in the large living room, dim with its drawn shutters.

"You're not the only one who'll be saying that."

"Well, we have to accept it's not going to be easy for her to come back here."

"In which case we mustn't let people know she's arrived for a while. She'll need time to settle – without being harassed by questions about how much that awful driver said about Speer."

“What could the chauffeur have said?” Bruno says. “The usual stuff about how much the man did or didn’t know of Hitler’s horrors? But that was all in the war. He never saw Speer again. He was in Russia during the Spandau years – and after. But for Speer, that’s the period which actually matters.”

“How can you possibly mean that, Bruno?”

“Easily,” he taunts. “Just forget Hitler’s architect, Speer as Minister of Armaments, even Nuremberg. Think of him later, having lost everything. He’d fallen into an abyss. This is where the story really begins: how he came out of it.”

“If he ever did,” Magda says with distaste. “Not to judge by the lies he told to the end. Just think of what’s emerged since he died about his treatment of Berlin’s Jews. So, good riddance – to the driver too …”

She flicks the whole business aside – along with a mosquito.

2

Frank reads Bruno’s book during breakfast. Then, at a loose end, though too preoccupied to feel idle, he takes the walk round the *pueblo* always drawn to Villa Bougainvillea. Soon completed, it begins again beneath a sky blazing by this stage of the morning. But re-entering the plaza in straw hat and glasses, he finds a commotion on the *mirador*.

Tourists are crowding round a table on trestles, such as those displaying pottery and jewellery at the Sunday fair. But these are not handicrafts. The merchant is Bog Man; characteristically self-promoting, whether now lecturing or working, he is setting out archeological fragments.

Actually, these are bones, unearthed by Bog Man in a lifetime of successful excavation, as he proclaims. Frank, who would normally give him a wide berth, is unthinkingly drawn to this long table: a man is apparently being assembled there for close inspection. Pressing forward, he takes in Bog Man’s well-practised explanation of how he constructs someone like this, laid out on the canvas sheet.

"You start with a single bone, such as this femur," says the great palaeontologist. He holds it up as if having received an award. "Then, armed with my specialist knowledge and skill, I build up the rest as the pieces come to hand. Though when they don't, I'm experienced enough to fill in the gaps, grafting on the rest, either imaginatively or with copies from another man."

"Cannibalising!" a drunken British tourist shouts.

Bog Man simply ignores the heckler. Loftily stroking his RAF-style bomber's moustache, he says, triumphantly: "Behold, the result: an entire person, from head to toe! A human being just like us. Differences of time or place just don't matter."

"Brother Man," Frank murmurs as he turns back from the *mirador* with the rest of the slowly dispersing audience.

3

Frank paces the plaza, an alignment between Speer and his driver coming pat to his mind after Bog Man's words. Distracted, he does not, at first, see it is Bruno leaving the bank, looking warily aside, patting the top pocket of his shirt. But realising that this is the Englishman, despite – or because of – the straw hat and sunglasses, he greets him and suggests a coffee in the café.

They bypass tables crowded with loud Scandinavian tourists like sunburned albinos, who do not bother to ask for the café's umbrellas. Bruno leads the way inside, saying: "The place has filled up. It gets less peaceful every year. I hope you can still find whatever you're here for."

Frank inhales, readying himself to speak, as they sit in this fly-filled dimness among photographs of the *pueblo* before the Civil War. But he is relieved of having to search for the words as Bruno goes right on to say: "I missed you yesterday. I could have done with some support with Magda. We were talking about Speer."

Of course, Frank thinks. He is braced for this inevitable subject of discussion.

"I was saying," Bruno continues, "that the Speer story actually begins in Spandau. Because it really isn't about how privy he was to Nazi crimes."

"Or directly implicated in them?" Frank adds, turning over in his mind what he has been reading these days during breakfast.

Bruno goes on regardless: "It isn't even how he dealt with the destruction of everything he'd accomplished as Hitler's architect and Armaments Minister. It's later, during his twenty-year prison sentence, that Speer has to face his utter emptiness – and that's something his driver certainly can't tell us about. He wasn't even there to witness it."

But it is something Frank understands. Not that he would dream of comparing himself personally to Speer, so famous and infamous. Yet this is but one of the occasions on which he has recognised what it is like to feel a void engulfing one. Even so, all Frank says, drawing on his reading, is: "Speer tells us he felt dead on entering Spandau. 'What shall I do with all those years ahead?' he asked his wife. They were a permanent death sentence starting again every day, he says. In the past he'd always found an answer to the problems, the crises in his life, by undertaking some task. Now, for the first time, he was denied any such solution.

"He'd expected a key role in the reconstruction of Germany, if not Europe. Which is why he'd supplied detailed information about how Germany had survived Allied bombing to his American interrogators, Paul Nitze and John Kenneth Galbraith. In fact, they found him outstandingly forthcoming in their five days of intensive debriefing. It came as a great shock to him to be set aside, to find he was suddenly beside the point: Speer the great architect, the brilliant minister."

"Exactly," Bruno says wincing at the bitterness of the coffee, if not a mite peeved at having his view expressed for him by the Englishman. "Speer was empty. It's what Spandau meant to him: his challenge. In which respect his situation was very different from what the driver had to go through. That" – Bruno continues, seeking the conversational advantage – "was just to regain consciousness of himself. But for Speer, there was never any doubt that he existed …"

"Except perhaps during days without entries in his diaries," Frank says. "His personal black holes."

"Maybe," Bruno sniffs. "Nevertheless, he somehow always knowingly survived – if no more fully himself than was his rehabilitated driver in Villa Bougainvillea … Who knows," Bruno mutters pensively, "or cares what became of him once he abandoned the village – even the police?"

Sitting here in the dark, the men go on to consider techniques, amply described in Speer's bestselling memoirs, that Spandau Prisoner Number 5 developed to ensure a modicum of survival. With implicit competitiveness, each contributes to an account playing out as if in the gritty grey of a war newsreel seen not now in some cinema, but on that large café window lighted ahead like a screen.

There the man in his drab prison uniform, never seriously contemplating suicide, sits in his narrow cell, executing the painstaking writing tasks he sets himself. They will produce his celebrated memoirs and *Secret Diaries*. Besides which, he undertakes extensive reading and study regimes.

Now he is in the elaborate garden he has been building. It even has beehives. Although he is not allowed to eat his own strawberries, an obliging guard turns a blind eye as he tastes them.

Then he advances on his so-called walk around the world, undertaken in meticulously researched stages in the prison grounds. Hoping to be released early as a result of pleas by international figures responding positively to his celebrated contrition, he expects to halt at Calcutta. But in the face of opposition from Russia, one of the four powers controlling Spandau, he must overcome his bitter disappointment at finding China, Vladivostok, even the Americas beckoning. He eventually crosses into the unforgiving Mexican desert, his soles burning on the parched roads.

Disciplined activity might have helped distract. Yet according to the suave elder statesman Prisoner 5 apparently becomes on his release, no project could ever have fully protected him in Spandau from the despair in the one circle of Hell Dante omits: boredom. There were times when life just lost its appeal. The doldrums of prison life were simply too great.

"Doldrums." Which of them, Bruno or the Englishman, has ascribed the word to Speer? It must be Frank, remembering Professor

Keller using it to identify something his student soon found accurately describes what academic researchers intermittently suffer from, but must learn to overcome. During long hours in an archive's hypnotic atmosphere, one loses awareness of oneself, of existence itself, like Speer's driver, in an absence total as dreamless sleep. Though Frank, awakened these days in the *pueblo*, if too abstracted in this dark café to sweep away the fly barely felt on his hand, also finds himself imaginatively undergoing Prisoner 5's different doldrums: the consciousness of being inescapably where he is, but without knowing as who or what.

These doldrums, discussed with Bruno at this murky table, recall Frank to Mrs VD Cragge's Thursday séances in Bina Gardens. They would be in session when he arrived back from a dutiful day as Professor Keller's graduate student. Though climbing the unlighted stairs, Frank had not known, as he has lately been realising, how much more he had been in the dark than the spiritualists in their shuttered room behind the closed door he passed. Despite advancing his research, from routine and the lack of an alternative, Frank sees, now virtually psychic himself, that the doldrums he'd been in were a void.

His emptiness had, however, been hardly more apparent to him than he presumes it is for most people who realise at some time that they are experiencing a vague feeling of personal dissatisfaction. With sleepless nights, an indefinable malaise, one suspects there is something behind it one cannot quite put one's finger on. One has no idea how or when it all started.

"Of course, Speer's emptiness might have been there for much longer than suspected," Frank tells Bruno. "Sure, he was desolate, having to serve out his unimaginably long sentence in a cramped Spandau cell. But this wasn't just distress at being faced with enforced idleness. There was also the worthlessness of all his previous years to consider. Even his greatest achievements were hollow."

Frank says it with that book in mind – though not only the one Bruno lent him. Implicitly matching *his* doldrums – his vacuousness – with Speer's, Frank is also thinking of his own volume.

"Oh?" It holds, between a question and an objection, as Bruno starts drumming his fingers on the coffee table.

"Yes. Although Speer presents himself as an artist, with his architecture and friendship with Furtwängler and Wilhelm Kempff, it doesn't amount to much."

Frank says it in marked contrast to the lunchtime conversation in which he had agreed with Bruno about Speer's strong interest in music. And he shares what he has recently been reading about Speer's signal lack of creativity in arranging the very Nazi spectacles for which he is usually praised. He simply lifted from Max Reinhardt's theatre his staging for the mass rally in Berlin's Templehof Field on 1 May 1933, when Hitler became Chancellor. As for the 150 antiaircraft searchlights sending their columns into the night sky above the Nuremberg Rally in Speer's famous Cathedral of Light, well, of course it was all suggested by Leni Riefenstahl.

Bruno is listening, continuing to drum his fingers. Frank, not seeing the movement but feeling the rhythm, almost hears one of those acclaimed virtuoso concert performances Bruno gave until philandering spoiled his marriage and his music career faltered. It is as if Bruno is trying to cling on, through these wooden echoes of past piano notes, to that dazzling early achievement going to pieces in his hands.

Hasn't Bruno stopped drumming yet? Not as Frank expands on the sterile Neoclassical Reich Chancellery Speer converted – hardly in the record time he claimed – from Bismarck's so-called "cigar box", with a gallery twice as long as the Hall of Mirrors at Versailles. It is the sole building completed in the World Capital, Germania, that Speer planned for Hitler to rival the great cities of Antiquity with their Acropolis, Parthenon and Colosseum. But not even the Chancellery now remains from an inhuman project whose Great Hall could contain the Arc de Triomphe with a dome high as a New York skyscraper.

Speer himself, Frank continues to explain with newfound detail, failed ultimately to think of his architecture with pride. It reminded him of a Cecil B. DeMille set with that element of fantasy. He claimed, at least, that the buildings expressed cruelty, tyranny, as much as the rest of the regime of which he was a minister.

By now, Bruno has grown unnaturally still. He has heard more than enough of this record of flawed early achievement. Gulping, he puts a hand to his chest. Then he brings it to the table with a loud bang. "It's suffocating here. Just look at the fan. It's barely turning in this heat. I'll collapse if I'm stuck here any longer with these flies and that smell of lavatory."

Curtly, he shrugs off Frank, now fumbling with his wallet. Irritable, if not angry, he throws down a bill instead. Then he springs up, advancing through darkness to light framed by the café window.

4

Bruno barely mumbles goodbye, heading off alone for El Castillo. Frank is left to the plaza, emptying out now. Frowning, he reflects on how his words could have provoked the man's ire. But then, engrossed once more in his thoughts about Albert Speer, he fails to put on his hat and sunglasses. Lost in the sun, he carries them absentmindedly back to Pensión Amalia.

There he goes to his room, as he sometimes does in the day here, just as he used to return to his London bedsit from the archive, settling before the luminous arc of his green banker's lamp to make meticulous notes. Loath to forget any detail, he would commit information, as well as developing thoughts, in neat handwriting, to carefully stacked notebooks, even after the onset of computers.

In fact, Frank suspects that these retreats to his room in the *pensión* have been in response to the tug of his bedsit. He has, perhaps, still not been as liberated from it as he has thought here, with all his research, his writing, behind him. For though vacationing between the Mediterranean and the mountains, he has, far from facing wide expanses and panoramas, been inwardly constraining himself. The *pueblo* has been reduced to a circuit; an occasional lookout; a terrace; then, ultimately, to what was in London, and now is, his room.

Not so today, he feels. Lightheaded, with flecks of light swarming before his eyes from direct exposure to the sun, Frank kicks off his shoes and sinks deeply onto the welcoming white bedcover, shuttered against the day's heat. He has brought back from the café not only that subject of conversation clearly so offensive to Bruno – namely, Speer's supposed but blighted early triumphs. Nor is Frank simply importing his loss of purpose on finding his – actually Keller's – book finished, on looking over his shoulder at Spandau's once high-achieving Prisoner Number 5. He is, rather, transporting the café's imagined screen playing out visual embodiments of his thoughts.

Images intrude unbidden: clips from historic newsreels, but not viewed from without. Coursing past his mind's eye, they absorb him, half-aware, in a waking dream. Drawn into events, Frank is repeatedly part of them as they happen, though not in a room in a *pensión* or a bedsit, but wherever they take place in the world.

I have a spasm of nervousness – the same as I had on seeing Professor Keller, with his charged personality, German accent and uncompromising standards. I am answering with Speer an unexpected summons from Hitler.

We meet him at one o'clock in the afternoon on 8 February 1942, in Rastenburg, the Führer's headquarters in East Prussia. Hitler is tense following the morning news about Fritz Todt, his strong-minded Minister of Armaments. Todt had advised him, the previous night, to find a political solution to a war undoubtedly lost militarily now the Russian campaign is failing. It was fruitless. Hitler would not listen. Now Todt has died in a mysterious plane crash. Hitler, forsaking accustomed familiarity with Speer, brusquely appoints him Todt's successor.

What a success Speer appears to make of it! Soon enough, he assumes the bulk of Goering's portfolio. From being Minister for Armaments and Munitions, he becomes – in just a year and a half – Reichsminister for Armaments and War Production. No wonder Admiral Dönitz calls him "Europe's economic dictator", completing Hitler's political and social revolutions with an economic one. And Goebbels, in his microfilmed diary, transferred to the glass plates discovered in boxes by the Soviets at Potsdam, praises the young minister's ruthlessness in pressing for total war. Speer, with his administrative brilliance, his passion for work, his unlimited ambition, extends a war already lost by eighteen months.

Even Galbraith, always sceptical of Speer – and especially of his professed ignorance of Nazi crimes – considered him responsible for this "armaments miracle". Yet closer inspection proves this to be another of those myths that Speer, the arch-deceiver, created about himself.

The book I am reading details this and the rest of the charges. Todt laid the foundations; Speer doctored the figures. Production methods were unexceptional but for the scale of the labour, material and capital made available brutally from across Europe.

The "miracle" is a mirage, flawed – and fated, I see, discovering myself standing here in Berlin, the city reduced to rubble. There is a frantic bustle at the end of the last lines of resistance with motorcycle couriers, supply columns and troop movements. Bitterly cold people tramp senselessly past broken-down tanks on icy roads.

Speer is returning to the ruined capital in these last frantic days. The Russians are at the gates. His grandiose plans for Germania must be shelved till a victory never to materialise. But I wonder whether or not he recognises at last that the projects with which he will always be associated have failed. Worse, can he not finally see (as I explained in the café to Bruno), soon distraught, that all his past achievements were worthless from the outset? The value of everything Speer is and does was suspect from the start. He was compromised, empty, far before his intolerably empty Spandau days. Even when imprisoned, can he still not acknowledge what contaminated his every effort? Such was the appalling Nazi vision it advanced, springing from what made him personally subservient to Adolf Hitler.

What exactly did so, Frank wonders, supposing it is no more sufficient to make this sweeping claim about the nature of Speer's relationship with the Führer than it would be simply to say that he himself came under Emil Keller's influence. But there is scant evidence that historians understand it. Yet to do so is surely indispensable for identifying whatever weakness in Speer Frank wants to see if and how he will overcome.

Perhaps there is a way, after all, to chance upon that flaw. It is to watch their relationship play out, almost cinematically, in Frank's mind.

I am taken back to the moment when Speer, an architectural teaching assistant, is overwhelmed by first hearing Hitler. No matter that even this early point may not prove the absolute beginning. The speaker declaims with hypnotic power in what seems now, after everything, a surprisingly sober blue suit. But I don't need to open Bruno's biography of Speer, with its photographs, to visualise Hitler as he was in those early days. I all but see that potent figure here in Pensión Amalia. He is causing Speer to separate from his companions immediately after the initial encounter, to drive in his car to Berlin's Havel woods.

I, on my own too, lying on this bed, but in the researcher's solipsism (second nature to me since Professor Keller proposed – decreed – that I become his research student), find young Speer has now become site manager for restoration of the Chancellor's residence. He is unexpectedly invited by Hitler, visiting the work, to lunch. Hitler lends one of his jackets so that the handsome, talented, socially superior young man can sit at the table. And from that fateful hour, the Führer makes Speer both his alter ego and willing instrument. Chosen as Hitler's blank slate, Speer dreams – so he will write – Hitler's architectural dreams.

He is, in fact, Hitler's "unrequited love", as Speer's associate Karl Maria Hettlage calls him after an evening when Hitler pays him a visit at his studio. Speer also admits to his *Secret Diaries* that he wanted to show the older man his total veneration, but was never able to express his feelings freely.

Hitler has taken hold of Speer, and will never release him. Speer says it himself. But then this self-confident, mannerly, twenty-eight-year-old, so unlike the Führer's usual boorish sycophants, is hardly without ambition. Speer, canny as any architect, knows how consciously to anticipate and satisfy his client's wishes, even if it involves regularly extending the already monstrous scale of Hitler's projected buildings. And, scarcely naïve or detached from the Führer's worldview, he becomes a member both of the Nazi Party and the Sturmabteilung, if not as a passionate ideologue.

Does it suggest that Speer, far from an innocent enticed and subserviently caught up in an enchanter's web, is a willing collaborator after all? This is the damning case my breakfast reading advances. It is Speer's own flaws, hardly just Hitler's influence, which are at work. It leads not only to Speer's knowing acquiescence in the Nazi crimes of which he claimed to have been unaware. He is actively implicated in the horrors remorselessly detailed in this exhaustively researched book.

Despite the brusqueness with which Bruno had terminated their discussion, it pleases Frank to think through, or hallucinate, his own view of Speer, alone. It relieves him from taking account of perceived similarities with Bruno's defective achievements. On the contrary, Frank, no longer treating Speer merely from afar or as a diversion, has actually been finding himself increasingly implicated in him. And in this hiatus he freely challenges the biographer's view of his subject's fatal flaws.

Veering between visualising Speer and criticising the writer, both clairvoyant and reviewer, Frank doubts that it is vice, some deadly sin – be it ambition, greed, or a passion for self-promotion – that fundamentally blights the man. Frank focuses instead on the curious bond between Hitler and Speer in their photographed moments alone: mute on the terrace of Hitler's Berghof in the Obersalzberg, walking through snow towards a darkening sunset.

But they are not, Frank supposes, simply actors in an implicit drama recompensing them for childhoods similarly lacking in love and warmth, with equally unresponsive fathers. For, in the moment of each snapshot, these are not only an idealised parent and son – or even self. Nor, certainly, are the pair thrilling in these roles as when a preening Speer presents the jubilant Hitler with his absurdly inflated architectural plans. The men have, rather, lapsed separately but together into emotional inertness: a dead space where, Frank senses, each can just exist, with the other.

Neither ever really spoke about this link. Maybe that was beyond them. Yet everyone knew of it and some were envious, though Frank finds the biography touches on it only gingerly. It almost shuns it, leaving it intact. Starved of documentary evidence for it, barely probing any implication of homoeroticism, the tie and all it implies for Speer is overridden by the new damning view of him as the opportunistic impostor, which his lately exposed dissembling makes all too credible.

Still, the bond was real and needs probing, even if there was a time when one could well doubt it, along with whatever flaw one might suppose it entailed. For Speer had changes of heart, notably in March 1944, described by the book closed beside me on the bed.

The Hitler of that moment stares out at me as he is doing at Speer. There has been an estrangement, following a period in which Speer escapes power struggles around the Führer by spending Christmas in Lapland and the forests of the Arctic Circle. He falls ill, feeling Hitler has succumbed to the intrigues against his "friend", as Speer will one day refer to himself. Hitler is betraying him.

Speer recovers. But meeting Hitler again, he sees his face as never before. So do I, looking at it through Speer's eyes. For he is becoming much more for me than the subject for a biography.

A book like this is, in any case, a lesser form of historical study according to Professor Keller. He is critical of focusing myopically on any period from the perspective of a single individual. History, he repeats, views the major events of the state, using the full range of a nation's archive.

I have, rather, recurrently caught myself taking on the very existence of Speer, somehow inhabiting that other, darker self; experiencing what he was and did from within – as now I myself unexpectedly find Hitler's nose square, the shape common, his complexion pasty. The man is ugly, I find. His mask has dropped. The magic is over.

Just listening to Hitler, without speaking, there is a sense of futility. The "ash war", as Speer will later call it, is lost. His plans for buildings can only ever remain on paper. It is the overt start of disenchantment that has been there for some weeks. And Speer's detachment from Hitler eventually leads him to disobey the Führer's scorched earth decree, even planning his assassination.

In spite of which, Speer visits Hitler in the Reich Chancellery on 23 April 1945. It is the very end, and mad to return. Hitler believes, so Eva Braun confides to Speer, that he has betrayed him. This is in the lethally suspicious atmosphere of the bunker where an absent Goering, who asked if Hitler's suicidal decision to remain in Berlin activates the law on the Führer's succession, is dubbed a traitor on Bormann's prompting.

Why does Speer go? I mull over the question, staring from my damp pillow at the dark space where my inner eye repeatedly finds these events projected, drawing me in. I assume it is because the bond between the two men, and whatever it implies for Speer, has survived their rift. It is why Speer, whom I find saying goodbye to Hitler at his birthday party a few days before, returns.

Speer says, in furtherance of his wider claim that whatever evil he – innocent like Germany – had been party to was the result of Hitler's mesmerising influence. Hitler's personal power over him supposedly persists even now. Speer has lost all urge to continue his opposition. Once more, Hitler has succeeded in paralysing him psychically.

Yet this biography offers a quite different explanation. Speer expected Hitler to appoint him his successor. It is plausible enough. As early as '43 Speer had asked Hans Kehrl, who would assume major responsibilities in the Ministries of Armaments and Economics, if Hitler might think of him for the position. Perhaps Speer, throughout his disobedience of the Nero Decree, had started imagining for himself a leading role in a post war Europe.

I wonder, shadowing Speer as he arrives at daybreak for his meeting with Hitler. He is walking again through the dark Chancellery he himself designed. He is proceeding to the Mosaic Hall; the red marble has turned black. The glass ceiling is shattered and has crashed down, covering the floor with shards. Beyond, the Court of Honour is stacked with ammunition cases, boxes of tinned food and field kitchens.

Far from merely surveying the ruin, Speer spends these minutes supposing that, depending on what transpires in his final interview with Hitler, he may be returned here within an hour. He wonders, looking back from this top step of the main courtyard, what place the head of the firing squad will choose for his execution.

Maybe it is just melodrama, as an earlier biographer of Speer, his eventual editor, called it. Perhaps it enables Speer, the Führer's architect, to evade this concrete reality staring him in the face: the destruction of all he has built through prolonging, as Minister of Armaments and Munitions, a hopeless war.

I, in the moment too, also sense that this posturing, playacting, is intended by Speer to shield himself magically from the worst. To experience it as an illusion that he survives, shields him mentally against the prospect of having to submit to its reality. It implicitly reassures him that Hitler could never want to sentence to death his one friend to whom he had offered fabulous architectural commissions, putting the world at his feet. For, in reasserting the strange bond between them, Speer assumes feelings in Hitler such as he cannot shrug off when news of his suicide reduces him, famously unemotional, to tears.

Once in Spandau, Speer's thoughts about Hitler begin to lapse. The fatal link between the men breaks. Speer belittles Hitler for his ill-chosen neckties and excessive bouquets of flowers. There are his monstrous crimes. And a monster is all he really is, Speer writes.

Thought itself wilts, I think, as it must on killing time in a narrow room – such as mine – without a project and a vacant mind. It is a long period in which Speer, admired for his moral courage in admitting to general guilt for crimes committed whilst associated with Hitler, seems not to consider him at all. But then in 1952 he writes in his *Secret Diaries* that this is not the result of having exorcised him; he has merely evaded him. Speer knows he will never exist independently of Hitler.

I recall him protesting that the postwar picture of Hitler as a demon is too simplistic. It cannot be all that he was, or else he would never have captivated people as he did. Speer itemises his gifts: wit, intelligence, that Old World Viennese charm. Then there was his extraordinary energy. And where others think of him solely in abstract moral terms, Speer remembers a living human being and their car rides, picnics and architectural fantasies, as well as his friend's concern for people's families and apparent modesty.

Again and again Speer tries to assess Hitler, setting what he does not doubt must be the judgement of history against the man he knew. From what survives of their personal bond, locking Hitler in Speer's thoughts, I remember him seeking to modify even that inescapably terrible verdict of the future. As late as August 1960, furtively scribbling on scraps of paper on the bed in his Spandau cell, Speer asks himself, I reflect here, whether or not Hitler might experience the same as Napoleon: his nation regarding him as a hero a mere twenty years after his death. Hitler was, after all, no different from Napoleon, with his insatiable appetite for power provoking a bloodbath in Europe. And Hitler's misdeeds in pursuing and consolidating power, namely the murders of Röhm and the SA, the breaking of treaties, the war, the plan to dominate Europe – all these were within the tradition of European history. Even Nazi anti-Semitism was nothing new. The governments of nineteenth-century St Petersburg and Vienna provided examples, while in the heart of Western Europe was the Dreyfus Affair.

Only in his insane level of hatred of the Jews did Hitler go outside European norms. But at the time, Speer alleges, he and most others regarded the Führer's anti-Semitism as a somewhat vulgar incidental. And in those days, Speer later admits, he had believed morality was not applicable in politics. Feeling incompetent to judge in such a matter, he never questioned it.

What, Spandau Prisoner Number 5 wonders, might have been the historical outcome for Hitler without that incidental hangover from his early days in Vienna? Dare the Führer's friend believe that Hitler will be reinstated in only a few short decades more than it took for Napoleon – namely now, as I lie on a bed of my own in Pensión Amalia?

Evidently Speer wishes it. But this is not just some old comrade's undying support for Hitler's cause. Frank supposes it also betrays something in the bond between the two men, marring all Speer was and achieved in Hitler's name.

What exactly that was becomes apparent in a BBC interview, never broadcast, about which Frank has read. Recorded after Speer's release from Spandau, it is finally transmitted in Frank's mind.

Hugh Trevor-Roper, the historian, is on the panel. Speaking in his plummy don's voice, with that thatch of hair and tortoise-shell glasses, he prompts Frank finally to sit up and view Speer from without instead of losing himself intermittently in Speer's dark, ambiguous form.

What, Trevor-Roper asks, were Speer's unrealised plans early in the summer of 1945? Speer says he intended to take off with a couple of friends from the whole "mess" in Germany, as he calls it, to one of the quiet bays of Greenland. It was too remote in those days to be within range of air reconnaissance.

Medicines, books, a typewriter and boxes of paper were packed in a long-range, four-motored seaplane. For Speer planned to begin his memoirs at once. He also decided to take rifles, his faltboat, skis, tents, hand grenades for fishing and food.

–Yet what about the climate so far north?

–Greenland is simply wonderful in May and summer.

–But what would it be like in winter?

"Oh!" Speer says. He had intended to return to Germany in October. By then the war and the horrors would no longer be remembered. He would begin a new life, comfortable and safe, he said, in Heidelberg. Trevor-Roper is shocked that Speer comments no further on such a plan, even now all is known.

Frank suspects that Speer's reticence holds the key to his link with Hitler. Quite how, he will divulge to what is increasingly the lecture audience coming into his mind. But first, scrupulous historian that Keller made him, he cannot let Trevor-Roper's misapprehension stand. All was *not* known.

The Nazis' atrocities were. Yet the documents proving Speer's awareness of them did not fully emerge until after he died, rightly suspicious as many already were. Only more recently has there emerged the full list of his own crimes. Keenly recorded by this biography Frank has beside him on the bed, it is a terrible tally of all Speer did from allegiance to Hitler. Added to what is actually criminal: his monstrous architectural and administrative so-called achievements.

Nevertheless, even before the most disastrous revelations, Trevor-Roper is ultimately undeceived by Speer, who had been artfully hoodwinking him along with those at the Nuremburg Tribunal, so impressed by the accused's show of contrition that it spared him the death penalty.

Never mind that at the outset, the brilliant young Oxford historian, commissioned to write his scintillating report on how Hitler died, wolfed by Professor Keller's student, had been thoroughly taken in by the good-looking Speer. For how, when Trevor-Roper interviewed him at Kransberg Castle as he awaited trial at Nuremberg, he had stood out from the rest of the thuggish Nazi leadership with his intelligence, ability and social poise! But even then, Trevor-Roper had called Speer the true criminal of Hitler's regime, not least because so civilised. Though he had only accused him of *trahison des clercs*.

Later, however, Trevor-Roper considers he has finally found the key to the "Speer mystery". He is not corrupt, malicious, hard-hearted or base. He is something far worse, which will become even more evident once the full extent of Speer's complicity becomes incontestable after the historian's death. There is a void that Trevor-Roper feels opening up behind all the impressive mental sharpness and clarity. The man is morally and emotionally hollow.

Speer is deeply offended, Frank has read, when his editor Joachim Fest reports the judgement to him. Well, he might be. It is, as Frank knows, exactly what he deplores in Hitler. For Speer says there was an ultimate coldness about him, in his famous *Playboy* interview. He had never met anyone else with whom he had felt this sense of something missing; his impression was that at the core of Hitler's being there was deadness.

It is a characteristic Frank finds Speer mentioning again, when describing Hitler's daily Berghof circle at the Obersalzberg. His memories are of a strange emptiness, implicitly shrugged off by Speer in the way we criticise in others what we least approve in ourselves. Like attracts like, Frank reflects, sunk in these pervasive thoughts about Speer. Invisible as gravity, as dark matter, they draw one another in. Either is empty, open to the other. They are of themselves the space where each – alter ego and quasi-father – can exist.

Their bond, Frank concludes, is their emptiness.

Trevor-Roper once thought of writing Speer's biography, Frank has read. But maybe now, having supposedly seen through Speer, it is as much disillusion as age, the wish for a quiet life, that prevents him. Maybe he is instinctively prey to resentment, judging by all he will open himself up to in allowing the wool about Hitler's supposed diaries to be pulled over his eyes. Or perhaps he might simply be too disappointed in someone of whom he had once thought so much.

I wonder, impulsively casting aside the book, which is stylistically cruder than any Trevor-Roper would have written. I get up from my bed and open the door to stand with my back to this small room, a theatre for conjuring up my thoughts, now with a fleeting sense, too, of a Spandau cell.

I pause, unfocused. Vacant, I find myself awaiting the idea for a new project – but with no more relish than Trevor-Roper did the prospect of a book about Speer. Not that I should be too deflated I think, moments later, making my way to the covered terrace. My mute interaction with other academics, while a digression, may not have been meaningless. Decades of study, albeit of another period, have left a positive mark. The whole enterprise of my research with Professor Keller has enabled me, surely, to perceive more of the importance of that bond between Speer and Hitler.

Strange bond indeed! It results from their emptiness – abhorrent, I guess, to Bruno but fundamental to Speer even before meeting Hitler and undertaking the Führer's great works. Yet that is precisely what so disillusioned Trevor-Roper. The mere thought of it prevented him from writing his biography, I understand.

What good could ever come of one in such a void?

Then, consciously, I discard the idea of engaging with historians on an issue remote from my field; a survival technique of my own, I acknowledge, hovering here in the *pueblo*.

The thought holds as Frank weighs whether or not any remedy is possible for a personal flaw so radical as that on which he has been brooding. Concentration lapsing, he takes in sea and sky beside the noisy cockatoo. Its restlessness is infectious, setting off nervous inner fluttering as Frank glimpses, obliquely, unnaturally still, white villas.

Later, once the day's heat has passed, Frank walks into the dark *pueblo*. Once more he is stricken by this vague yet immobilising feeling of expectancy, approaching a lighted doorway surrounded by bougainvillea.

BOOK TWO

PART I

1

Paloma starts. Someone is out there, standing in the dark. She is just within the lighted entrance to the villa, its front door ajar in the heat.

It's a man, she thinks, silent as this cat I've been caressing and whispering to as it brushes its black fur against my bare leg on passing by me down into the dense bougainvillea with which the figure keeps merging. Yes, it must be that man again. A dream might as well be conjuring him up once more, as if tonight for the first time, in this perpetual moment in which he stands on the overgrown doorstep before me.

Should I be afraid? The *pueblo* is too small, too intimate, for the kind of savage crime I am constantly on my guard against in that little apartment in Madrid where I have lived for the last year. But I am jolted to find the man at the villa, beside the twisting foliage he seems part of. It just goes on growing in this spot, more and more rooted, higher and higher. And in this spell the reverie of memory casts over me, I am taken aback to find us again at Villa Bougainvillea, where we always are.

She remembers walking towards the villa one evening last summer. She relives herself glimpsing an inner light, from further down the narrow street fronting it, beside bougainvillea. There was a presence just within the door: a man – another one – drawing on a cigarette. Its orange glow palpitated with his breathing, his heartbeat, as he took in shimmering sea, black sky – and now me, the 'me' I felt incorporated by eyes no more than gleams in shadowy features. They gathered in, it seemed, through smoke unfurling from a spicy cigarette such as those in Eastern Europe, from which (it would emerge) he had lately come. Yes, they drew in a presence only gradually more visible before him.

We looked past what I sense he, too, overlooked: looks, to see what we saw on facing each other, as strangers across a doorstep, unseeingly as bats in the obscurity of a cave. Eyeless darkness it was, with a searching-out other than by sight.

Emotional radar registered our approaches above or below the threshold of usual activity. They were at work, summoning up the other; finding each out in such stealthy silence that neither of us was exactly aware of it at first in Villa Bougainvillea's barely lighted shadows.

That was last year, a summer unforgettable not only for Paloma but for Heidi, too. For she had asked her friend to look after the man, the shadow, to whom her father in Germany had arranged contacts there to rent their holiday villa.

Heidi has already known Paloma over many summers. In the Julys and Augusts they have both spent here, she has seen her younger friend grow more and more beautiful, passing from late childhood to adolescence and so early adulthood. She has noticed it in the shapely arms and legs, the waist bare beneath short T-shirts in this heat. But then she has found it too in the buttocks, the breasts, the tufted sex in a deserted cove where they've swum; where she's hugged her, kissed her, this young woman whom she has taken under her wing, for whom she has felt this surging tenderness and – yes! – love.

But what is it that, over the years, has remained remote, lost almost, in Paloma's perfect features, the almond eyes, straight nose, full lips, shawl of dark, shoulder-length hair? Something seems mutely resistant to Heidi's appreciation of looks she appears neither to value nor even notice, of affection by which she seems quite untouched.

Paloma is distant, her older friend senses, not only from the surface of her self and these passionate demands on it, but also from her *feeling* self. Recessed in some obscure inner part, airless and inert, she has yet to emerge and make contact with the rest of who she is and all that lies beyond.

Thus the young woman with what Heidi feels is a broken wing, the one to whom the older offers shelter under a wing – at a breast – of her own. She is the girl for whom Heidi, seeing her bored, withdrawn, vacant, could not stop feeling love even if she wanted to. No matter that it seems not to reach her. Heidi just goes on yearning to express it – expressing needs of her own, doubtless, that being the nature of love, isn't it?

Hence Heidi, finding Paloma at this loose end with no idea of what to do with her life, while living out the whole year here in the *pueblo* with her father, suggested she visit the stranger last year. She might look in on him from time to time in the remaining weeks of the summer, especially once Heidi returns to Berlin in September. After all, Paloma learned German at school in Buenos Aires.

Paloma took up Heidi's suggestion. It brought her, last summer, directly into contact with the man whose dark eye, overlooking dense bougainvillea, had already caught mine, Paloma recalls. And it drew some strange part of my self to the obscure presence setting foot out of the habitat where it awaited me on subsequent evenings as I passed the villa yielding up its dim light.

I took to visiting that shadow morning upon morning. And I find, reliving it this next summer, that last year's stranger has no conversation. He is an immense silence. So, as something to do, sitting with him in this living room during the hours of his speechless recuperation, I open art books I have brought down to the villa from El Castillo. They come from the well-stocked library in which my father buries himself when not lost to his piano and recordings. The stranger and I sit together on the sofa, still covered in plastic, turning the pages of a volume on Dutch landscapes.

I am beside him, drawn to flat land stretching far out to once-inundating sea. The terrain absorbs me imperceptibly. Without being aware of a specific moment of concentrated interest, I repeatedly find I am one with an atmosphere I realise, looking at the next colour plate, has strangely enough become the air both of us are now breathing. I am sharing his mood.

This has been no moment of sudden attraction. Here is no satyr like Bog Man. There has been no play for each other. It's a deep, calming inwardness that is drawing me in, I find, turning to a page with an estuary – an eye admitting all.

Here is a feeling of Low Countries: land recovered from sea; a world risen in eerie silence made yet more resonant by the cry, bark almost, of seagulls. Even so, it is not quite *terra firma*. It continues to carry something of its submerged character. Water shows through rich earth, verdant fields, in glistening irrigation channels. Pools reflect a greyish-white cloudscape far into a middle distance with its brilliant shafts of sunlight.

Isn't he glimpsing in it the mute surfacing he had experienced in some Siberian spring? And surely I, unsuspectingly ready for awakening myself, feel the pull of a body rising from a measureless expanse of frozen tundra, rivers and forests – I, who am barely aware that it was already starting in me through him?

Sea air merges indistinguishably with the heavy odour of black fields and sluggish canals. It is an infinitely wide, sodden terrain where roads, poplar-lined, answer to a beckoning distance. I, no longer observer, feel drawn along them with him by that sheer stillness of unpeopled space that is the atmosphere of us two.

I make coffee. Water bubbles, boiling on the stove before percolating down through the grounds, filling the kitchen with its aroma. The smell envelops us before Dutch scenes, morning after morning, as we silently sip from bowls left by some previous owner. It holds us in our soft serenity.

One day I arrive to find he has already made this coffee, its atmosphere embracing us. He had never had coffee in Russia, he says. But he used to drink it in Germany, I am surprised to find him telling me, this man who has not been speaking till now. It brings back that time to the silent man, morning after morning, as we drink in that vapour, that fragrance, enfolding us in shared moments, before remote yet vividly present scenes.

It is noon, and we have wandered into the village church. At least we have stretched our legs, even if some might think there is nothing much here except the single old villager in her black headscarf and dress among the plastic flowers, electric candle bulbs and a half-life-size effigy of the hectically suffering Mary. It will be loaded onto a garishly decorated Semana Santa float carried through the *pueblo* in unknowing perpetuation of late Roman superstition.

We sit beside each other in a centuries-worn pew, barely able, in this dimness, to make out Christ risen from beneath the grime on a faded painting by the confessional. It doesn't matter. We are just taking in the deep silence here with the odour of candle wax, old incense and mould. It is all-pervasive, this atmosphere in which we find ourselves at one with each other in a place too simple, remote, off the map, to cease celebrating a miraculous theology.

The privations of war; the years of imprisonment with an unvarying diet of watery cabbage soup, causing repeated bouts of dysentery: these have given him cravings for all he missed, especially sugar. He now has a very sweet tooth, he tells me, along with miscellaneous other things his memory is starting to throw up. They arise just as rocks, jets of molten lava, would spew from a suddenly active volcano, such as those hills might become on the landward side of the *pueblo* where we now sit in the plaza's café in late sunlight, just the two of us, for him to have ice cream.

Others sit at nearby tables. People mill about in the square, often going up to the *mirador* to lean over its metal railing and peer out at waning light softening those sphinxlike shanks. The afternoon is heavy with the odour of a Mediterranean summer: salt from sea air wafted up a kilometre to the *pueblo* on one side; dust from the bone-dry desert plain on the other.

We continue lounging here, breathing deepening; chests, breasts swelling, reducing, to expand again; outlines dissolving in shared twilit space where our figures eventually cease registering even as figments from our private dimension.

Away from this atmosphere of ours, could we survive any more than in the air of an unimaginably distant planet? For what we have come to breathe, inhaling this invisible mist, an unseen vapour, is ourselves. We are held, all that we are, together here that is everywhere for us, in our timeless stillness.

So much a part of each other after our mornings with books at the coffee table, noons in the church, late afternoons on the plaza, then sunset on a *mirador*, we eventually forsake the *pueblo* for the villa's roof. With night odours of jasmine from other terraces, orange and lemon blossom wafted up from the grove by the village well, moist lips come readily to receive. They draw in, uniting as ocean does, breaching dikes, surging onto the land. Separateness is dissolved. We are as indistinguishable as sea is from the water of canals, ditches, sodden fields.

Lying here, still now, on roof tiles beneath the stars, I smell the salt of the kilometre-distant Mediterranean; of our lovemaking, his semen. Only gradually do I realise I am becoming aware of the difference between seawater and freshwater. Within sight of each other, they are nonetheless kept apart where land surfaces. There are fields reclaimed to grow and yield harvests.

Isn't he living these images too, the man beside me on warm, dark roof tiles? For haven't the boundaries of our selves given themselves up to each other? Here our minds are porous, surely, to thoughts seeping from one to the other; here, where a man is so silent now that his breathing is barely audible. A nocturnal shadow, his features, torso, sex, are all but invisible. It's a being only just there as the faintest imprint of himself.

The beach is overcast this morning. But the oppressively grey sky does not make it any cooler. Amalia and her cousin are scrupulous in spreading suncream over their already well-tanned limbs and backs. They smear their ample middle-aged breasts too, despite the sand stinging in this hot wind. Teasingly, they encourage Heidi and me to swim topless also.

Heidi does not react. She simply goes on looking further down the beach towards the cove where we had once been naked together. It's severe, if not defiant, this staring out of the glare by a daughter always seeming to hold herself rigid to avoid falling between separated parents.

Heidi disdains these high-spirited distractions from being with me; I am no more inclined to strip and relax than she. I begrudge having been deliberately lured out of my life, as it has already come to feel, with the man in the khaki swimming costume that looks military, if not issued by a relief organisation. For when my mother told me Amalia had asked her to invite me to a picnic on the beach with her cousin visiting from Granada, I knew Heidi was behind it.

I realised how long it had been since we had been in touch: ten days barely connecting me with the person I had been before meeting Franz; ten days without contacting the stern, troubled Heidi, who cannot credit the speed with which her forlorn friend has fallen away from her for this equally lost man. I knew I could not avoid facing her and this bristling resentment. I have no wish to threaten the new life – the new me – I have discovered through this person beside me.

And yet he is not next to me. So I find, turning to see he has left the pair of us talking in Spanish, which he does not understand, while Amalia and her cousin stretch out on towels further off in sunlight finally breaking through. He is perched on a flat rock away from the testy question posed to me about him as if he were not actually present.

"Can you tell me what he's revealed about Speer in all those hours you're spending with him – if it's not too much for your best friend to ask, since, as you know, I'll be leaving for Berlin in just a few days?"

There is the rush of the sea. It mutes Amalia's laughter with her cousin. Again the tide crashes, half-drowning a car puttering on the road above. Only now do I hear my own voice saying, *it has never occurred to me to quiz the man.* I know too little about him or what he signifies to have much idea of what to ask. I understand virtually nothing of the situation to which he supposedly holds the key.

Heidi scolds me for sleepwalking with a being able to bring something so valuable to light, for remaining unaware of what – of who – he actually is. Surely he is no more real to me than a figment of my imagination.

What can I say, I wonder, turning round as if to invite a response from the rock – only to find it deserted except for the khaki swimming costume abandoned to its black, quartz-veined surface. It brings me up short. I stand to search the beach darkened by patches of tar; the water's foaming edge; the waves. Where is he, the man so near to me, slipped out of his last identifying article of clothing, out of my fingers and away before his significance has been established? He has dissolved, naked, without persona, into sunlight, sea. My eyes are scanning as far as the horizon – until I discover the man, who might never have been, dripping seawater, back beside me.

My father has gone. He left on personal business. Periodically he drives to Madrid in his decade-old Mercedes to dine with an ancient lawyer and whoever is from one of the families he knows and happens to be working at the moment at the Argentinean embassy. For years, he has been trying to resolve inheritance disputes over his grandfather's *estancia*.

"Just forget about it," my mother said over the phone from England. "It's useless."

She is irritated at his feeble ineffectiveness, the impossibility of the project. How could one expect success, operating at such a long distance? Though the estate, sultry hours from Buenos Aires, must seem remoter still, not worth a thought, to someone who can never now inherit it; one speaking from the London ballet school among whose rowdy *ingénues* she seeks to mute her undesired solitude, to distract herself from pained bitterness at this latest in his series of unrealisable enterprises.

From the first day my father is absent, I spend my nights in the villa. He is a magnet, the man drawing me there. Yet I am also fleeing Heidi, whose mother doubtless told her I am alone in El Castillo, misguidedly suggesting she look in on the lonely girl actually escaping her company.

Why, then, can't I leave Heidi behind? She stays in my mind, or at least her rebuke on the beach does. I resent the sting of her reproof, temporarily muting my more painful, spontaneously felt guilt for hurt I am causing a begrudged friend: hurt that she, too, used the very harshness of her chiding to efface.

It makes me listen more closely, but no more knowledgeably, to what I am hearing on the roof beneath clouds unusually frequent these last few days and nights. They block out the stars, obscuring sight of him by my side as we subside from our climax.

Words seep out of an unseen source, as though through a medium: "It brings me back to when I was in the dark – all that time."

"Where?"

A pause intervenes: searching, perhaps. "In the past."

"What were you doing?"

Another pause, ending with: "Lying there … with no idea when it would end."

Then he is saying nothing. A life is uncommunicated mental echoes in this deepening silence – till words resume from that unseen source. They enter my mind, making themselves felt in my thoughts as if I am a psychic.

These are memories of the lover who might not be there, from a being fading again, at last, into a long night's silence.

I am first roused at dawn, the time the slight movement of our mattress – the gentlest, most considerate sound of him getting up to go to the bathroom – usually stirs me. I slip back into that sleep from which I barely surfaced with him, only reopening my eyes much later to find he has not returned to our bed in a room scattered with sticks of sunlight fallen through the jalousies.

He has usually joined me again by now. He would only wake me fully when hauling himself up to sit on the edge of our bed a moment. Then he would walk naked over to the shutters, opening them up to sea, sky and all that can be seen from the bedroom terrace, well above the roofs of the village houses below.

The alarm clock reads nine. I have been left to sleep on undisturbed. He will be in the kitchen drinking coffee, or smoking a cigarette on its tiny patio.

"Franz!"

My mother always insists that I put on my *alpargatas*. Barefoot, I call over the tiles, across the hallway. The echo dies among brass wall plates; then again upstairs among plastic-covered sofas, coffee table books, a blank television. The reverberations continue beyond the dining table, before the stone kitchen sink, inert now in a silence deepening except for the tap dripping, dripping, dripping, as if measuring the moments between these abrupt surges of panic.

But how absurd! With me sleeping late, he's simply gone out, hasn't he, to buy cigarettes? It is what I am telling myself, abruptly breaking away to race up to the roof where, throwing open the door, I am ambushed by sun. I just stand there, blind, soaked, overwhelmed, setting off the neighbouring pigeons and doves into loud confusion as I call his name to a glassy sea.

Back inside, my hands tremble wildly, opening the shutters for something – anything – to do. The sunlight is angry. It hurts as I take in a paper serviette on the kitchen sideboard. It is marked with virtual runes by the blunt pencil we used for our shopping lists. This is what any foreigner, anybody at all, knows of the local language:

"Adios. Gracias."

Two words, a mere six syllables, four as pronounced, tip me into a well. I am hurtling down with no more warning than when the deep, airless crevices in those hills will start their violent shuddering. There's no bottom. Nothing to hold on to, nothing to stop me plummeting faster and faster now that the one I depend on has gone. He with whom I'm *me* is no more, leaving nothing: emptiness without end.

What is left in these heavily unmoving minutes? Drab clothes on the rocking chair; shaving tackle set out neatly, as in the army; this early morning's cigarette stub in the ashtray on the kitchen patio table: it is all he has shed here of whoever, whatever, he was with a young woman trembling deliriously, undone, in annihilating sunlight.

Morning has broken into the villa. It thrusts past brittle windowpanes, beyond frail wooden slats with peeling dull green paint, kept shut in summer against a painful brilliance that today nonetheless seems to search out every corner. Nothing remains hidden from this harsh intrusion: no crumple of the bedclothes, no drop of water remaining in the bath nor landed in the single coffee cup left in the kitchen sink, perhaps since dawn. Unsparing, it exposes the inertness of all these smooth stone surfaces, scorching underfoot without the fans turned on as usual to air deep shadow.

Sunlight has overwhelmed Villa Bougainvillea. It fills the place with an unsettling energy, making the atmosphere toxic, as if on an inhospitable planet, an unimaginably distant star. A reaction is already at work, depriving the blood of red corpuscles, the body of oxygen. It's impossible to breathe here. Deterioration is advancing rapidly. Movement is becoming virtually impossible.

I almost collapse on the sofa's scorching plastic. I must escape this increasing heat and light. Yet where?

2

I might have made for the dim, decaying church, or crossed the blistering beach to take refuge by a shaded cove in the Moorish lighthouse. But my feet have hurried me instead to the one place I have sought to abandon: El Castillo. Home. And these steps, rushing a fugitive from the midmorning through the plaza with its unreal festive clatter of solos and apéritifs, bring me face to face with the very person I have sought to avoid: Heidi.

Yet Heidi's appearance is deceptive. She gives no audible sigh of relief at the miraculously opportune departure of a man, a distracted driver, too many decades older than me. Heidi is gentle and kind, accompanying me – her distraught friend – up to El Castillo, its Venetian blinds all drawn.

She knows what it is to be abandoned, to feel so empty, deadened without appetite or desire, that others' voices and faces only emerge from a haze at a distance. I think she understands what it's like to lie for hours, unable to move, let alone respond to concerned people asking how one is, urging one to get up. She must have experienced the involuntary valve of feeling open again, allowing a disturbingly vivid image, a memory from life together, to flood beyond the inertia. She recognises, surely, the agonised realisation that this, embodying the very essence of living, will never come again; this, which it is therefore torture to feel but which goes on until the return to feelinglessness and voices saying, *snap out of it*.

So what if Heidi's sympathy is not principally directed to me, if she is really experiencing it for her own abandoned self? With that egoism they say is universal in love, her solicitude provides me comfort during these first moments after the earthquake ending life as I have come to know it. She has been close to me up at El Castillo over the last days of her summer holiday.

They have gone: he, Heidi, my father, mother. Things have changed so fast. The sun has lost its fury for most of the day.

Fig trees are heavy with fruit in the nearby *fincas*. Their large yellow leaves flutter to the ground. This year, the grapes are especially luscious in the vineyard my father owns down in the valley. Teresa, his youngish maid, suggests I go with her to harvest them. She tells me I am missing my father: he has rung to say he's been detained in Madrid. From the way she says it, I wonder if she is referring to more than the daughter moping about the house. I am suddenly sure that she herself, with her attractive looks, might be drawn to the older man as I, riding the *burro* beside hers, see her pull her skirt over her shapely calf.

We join others from the *finca* to pick huge bunches of black grapes. Children race between dense rows of vines, screaming with laughter. Basket in hand, I stray into another aisle, coming upon a couple holding each other. They are kissing passionately. I stare, mesmerised. The heat of a sun showing itself unexpectedly untamed suddenly falls upon my neck like a punishment. Memory erupts.

I run out, my basket falling to the ground. I, too, subside. Teresa sees me. She crouches, her own eyes brimming. She wipes my cheeks with the same part of her apron as she dabs her own eyes.

"He'll be back soon, *cariño*."

All that there is to look forward to here in winter is a cold, grey sea; deserted beaches; chilling mists; numbing nights. There is no one in the narrow streets after dark. Even the stray dogs avoid them, taking refuge by doorways that widows have abandoned to cook green peppers over charcoal inside.

The *pueblo's* flat roofs are deserted. The fêtes, the fun, the lovemaking, the seemingly endless futures on warm, starlit nights: they're gone. So are the people.. Summer is dead. All that is left is the eternal trembling of the pigeons and doves, the television aerials transmitting to darkness below inaccessible ghosts from other worlds.

Heidi must have been uncharacteristically forthcoming to her mother; certainly more than I would have liked. As it was not about her, but me, I suppose it came relatively easily to her. Though maybe it did benefit me after all. My father, on his return, heard from Amalia, without me having to be questioned, why his daughter is in such a state. Never at ease with emotional situations anyway, he doesn't ask why I am lying face-down on my bed without speaking in the mid-afternoon. An arm around my shoulder, he simply mutters:

"It had to happen, *hija*. It's for the best, you'll see."

The bulk of his talk is reserved for a half-heard telephone conversation with my mother, whose *I told you so!* I dread, given her loud displeasure at my association with a Nazi war criminal's driver. Heated, their discussion raises a vexed question: *what will she do now?* Ever since I left school in Madrid last year to live with my father, *faute de mieux*, the issue has been ignored like so much about me, the girl who has always seemed to have so little she is interested in, nothing she was passionate about – till now!

Painting, if anything, comes closest to what I like. Not that I have ever taken the plunge with oils. And timid, I have drawn only occasionally. Even so, my father, prompted by my mother – thinking conventionally of the restorative value of a change of scene, of meeting new people – arranges a job for me with an Argentinean friend who owns a Madrid art showroom.

3

The gallery is in Calle Ofelia, behind the British embassy. An entire morning often goes by without a single person coming in to see decorative canvases of Spanish landscapes imitative of the Impressionists. I have more than enough time alone, flinching from luminous Andalusian scenes, to brood on what has brought me to this point: to feel my feelinglessness.

It is a void the 'I' who is hardly me comes to know more and more. As I look at the contemporary art with which the owner is now beginning to vary the gallery's usual fare, my observing being reaches for some other self coming through like a fading echo of who I am on my mental radio. It is an impersonal, detached series of vibrations: the trace of that barely present self. Will I ever fully make contact with the stranger: me?

There are images of walls in a series the gallery exhibits one week. They are worn, with the impress of long-departed beings. Peeling plaster leaves only illegible signs of life long gone. And there are doors, even part of an actual one. Hinges, handles, knockers are heavily decorated but rusted from disuse. Do the keys even turn in the lock? Is there anything beyond?

The show is over. The doors have gone, unopened. Instead, there is a dark abstract. A roiled white turns to grey in a corner of the deserted gallery, merging into surrounding shadow. It is eclipsed, totally, as she stares with eyes so unfocused now, lost in it, that she, her self, dissolves, absorbed too in formless penumbra. Nothing in her withstands that cold blackness. She has no density; no centre. Inside, she is not. Wind blows through this vacancy: a freezing space where no strength of personality stops her diverging from what she is, to float far from her self in an infinite vacuum.

The few people who enter the art gallery barely notice the woman seated at the desk. It is easy for them to look straight through her. She is transparent. What is there of her to block the light?

I have felt, thought, done nothing.

Nothing has accumulated within her as a human nucleus. She isn't. So when she is asked for a catalogue, she cannot find a voice with which to reply, or even muscles to summon up a smile. Her hands are weirdly leaden, alien. Without a body, a place to repose the being she does not have, she does not exist, handing a catalogue to the man asking what time I finish work, if I would like to join him, a stranger, for a drink; asking where I live.

Where *does* she live in this city of classical gods bearing down from atop granite ministries, businesses and banks: severe stone presences from a legendary past overshadowing those presuming they have free passage below? It is not in acacia-lined roads like Calle Espronceda or Hermanos Becquer, named after nineteenth-century romantic poets. Yet it's somewhere, always in the same place actually – though not as her address. She is squatting in the house of her self.

It is a structure appearing like any other – if more attractively fronted than most, they say, especially her parents. But it's derelict. It is dark within, with that cold, unlighted air of abandoned buildings. It is not certain who owns it; unclear whther or not the owner may even recognise doing so. The absentee landlord accepts no responsibility for the property; it is someone who has disappeared long ago, leaving no trace. There is no forwarding address. The title holder is an unknown, unknowable entity; only pain results from seeking "The Owner", to whom mail piles up. No contact is possible.

Looking out from her squat, she sees no garden. It is a wilderness of weeds.

In the gallery where she has sat since the blazing morning Franz left, one picture has been hanging for some time: a businessman in an electric-blue suit without a defined face, his features a blur, slumps in a heap on his hotel-room carpet. An executive, he has lost the organisational capacity even to raise himself, to so much as to put one foot before the other. He can find no centre within himself to gather around. He cannot pick himself up and move purposefully on. What is his way ahead? He has no will power; no vision; no enthusiasm; not the slightest inner stimulus. Nothing holds his splaying limbs together. He has gone all to pieces in exactly the place where he is supposed to dress, plan and set off from, refreshed, making an impact, executing a plan, a strategy, tactic by tactic. She has seen, day after day, that there is no forward movement; no possibility of change, for that collapsed being in a picture still on the wall, although it is now next summer.

It has not stirred: it is hanging forever in Madrid, which I finally left to return to the *pueblo* a year later, for the long vacation. Here in El Castillo once more, I still seem to see the broken image in the art gallery where I was sent to recover myself from the collapse my parents recognised in their daughter.

I keep to my father's house on my first days back. But then I have started to evade it this summer too, escaping angry sunlight, heading for a purely nocturnal Villa Bougainvillea.

4

Paloma, in the *pueblo* again this year, sees the ghostly man a second time, from the lighted entrance of the villa.

He is still there, she thinks, and trembles – but not from a sea breeze on a summer evening. Though regardless of whether he is just several stone steps down there in the street, among dark bougainvillea, or if he has passed on, I feel him. He is a presence with me as I stand, hearing the piano. Not listening, now knowing he has gone, I find the music tying itself up in knots – as my parents do to each other in El Castillo.

I cannot bear the tensions between them. So I've told Heidi, asking her to arrange with her mother for me to have the key to the uninhabited villa whose absentee German owners always leave it with her.

You would not know from what my parents say just how they suffer with each other, even if they do not deliberately intend to be cruel. Yet I sense it. Oppressive as the atmosphere of days on which Saharan winds are blown here is the way my father maintains an invariably suave, dryly ironic exterior. It's a reclusive self-sufficiency from which he keeps my mother at arm's length with painfully long-suffering courtesy.

She is prickly, silently bearing a perpetual grudge as the older women in the *pueblo* do the bereavement that has them permanently dressed in black. Gone are the heydays in which her husband played Chopin's *Preludes* further down this coast in Marbella. My mother, ever the hostess, had excitedly welcomed friends to receptions after the concerts, implicitly celebrating the undoubted start of a brilliant concert career. Then came my father's affair. Although it was short-lived, not followed by others, the break with my mother simply remained.

It is as if the real reason for it had not been illicit passion but the need for a rupture. Why was it necessary? I don't know, and wonder if he does. In any case, it is something for which he seeks no pardon. Now they stand permanently in terms of each other, outside marriage.

My father, particularly, seems far from his sentimental self, though not only regarding my mother. He is outlawed from it just as he is from the country whose military junta made him an exile for decades, but to which he has never ceased mentally returning. And he and his ex-wife keep gravitating back to each other, yet not as spouses: without intimacy, barely cohabiting. They are passengers in adjoining cabins on a liner forever sailing with no known destination, walking endlessly around the deck, gazing at an ocean without landmarks. From its saloon, the sound of a piano floats out, as now, tonight.

But the *Last Prelude* is not what it was in harmonious times. It is having its recurrent trouble in this middle section. It is breaking up into that disorder into which it fell ever since his life went adrift.

The problem is how he might liberate it, so as to reach a conclusion. Although what, if anything, would really be concluded?

I have seen my father pause, finally, from his exhausting nightly effort of calling on what is lost; of straining to find it's there as it has been all along. Seeking respite through other music, he puts on a recording from a series titled *Great Instrumentalists* with Cortot, Schnabel, Fischer playing.

The piece ends. The music evaporates with the faintest reverberation. It's a memory. Silence, utter silence, opens up. My father has lost mobility and stares, unfocused. Something implicit looms heavily between us.

It does so, too, in the equally dangerous moment when he sometimes swings suddenly away from the piano stool, without putting on other music, to talk to me about whatever will take his mind off a frustrating session of practising. Either way, he wants to know what I am doing. Although, so far, my father has been good about not asking me more than if things are alright at the Madrid art gallery where I am working. But of course it is my frame of mind, my feelings, into which my father really enquires. The nearest he comes to broaching what is so disastrously near to my heart, or to showing direct interest in the current state of my feelings, is to say:

"I suppose nothing was ever mentioned about Speer and his interest in music." But the query, not quite daring to be asked as a direct question, remains unanswered. "I thought not."

He has taken refuge in the notion that a pretty girl cannot be expected to grasp such weighty things, just as he has hidden behind the idea that she must be shielded from all mention of hard emotional truth. Yet isn't the real truth that my father no more knows how to express empathy openly for his daughter than for his wife?

It is the sympathy my mother has shown on various occasions that most troubles me. I dread the intrusion into it of pessimism and nervousness derived from her own experience of love and life. It suffuses her outwardly encouraging tone, saying things surely have to get better for me now, after all I have been through; that I will doubtless feel better if I just give it enough time, attractive as I am; that all will be as it should when I finally let bygones be bygones and meet the right kind of man: one my own age, of a similar background.

Even when my mother manages to be quiet, I feel her heavy interest in me reverberate in her tense exercise of self-control. But I am not remotely ready to open up to her or to anyone else. I am hiding away in the dark villa.

Having to rely on Heidi for the key to the villa should, on the face of it, present no problem. I remember gratefully her quietly sympathetic understanding, listening to me that blazing morning last summer. It is this very solicitude that has allowed her to go on being close to me on my return now from the art gallery. For while her relief at Franz's abrupt departure may be less evident than my mother's, she is still seeking, through her compassion, to fill the great vacuum it leaves in my life. She is continuing, in other words, to press her emotional case with me. But the last thing I want is to shoulder the burden of Heidi's love.

If she came into my life before Franz, it was at her own insistence. Then again, who has Heidi to blame for my involvement with the man she herself suggested I care for? Did she really suppose her claim on me would survive it? The truth is that I barely have energy for myself now, let alone for someone else's feeling of abandonment. And despite her initial emotional tact, that feline strategic finesse, her true demands on me have inevitably surfaced in recent days – together with the full force of her disappointment at not finding them realised.

I cannot face the futility of those endless discussions, of that anger or sulky silence. Nothing can change the outcome for her. It must be as draining for her as for me. Particularly wearing is sensitivity so raw, so touchy, that virtually anything can set off a distressing scene.

She has been so upset that I had not let her know I would be coming this late to the *pueblo*. Couldn't I have called her? Even more hurtful than the time she wasted sitting around in her mother's *pensión* waiting for me, she has said in her dry, rapidly rising Germanic voice, was the discovery that I had been here for several days before my mother, no less, revealed on the phone that I had arrived but was not going out yet.

"Why are you trying to avoid me?"

I don't answer, except to say how exhausted the heat has made me, when she starts embracing. I am longing for her to leave El Castillo, where we are talking in the room in which I expect her to assume that I, repeatedly yawning, am going to bed the moment she can tear herself away. Once she has gone, I too make my way down the hill. I escape to the villa.

Everything is bringing me down to the villa. It is inevitable that I should be here tonight, every night, within the circumference of light cast by the hall lamp. I am drawn within the compass of my self, the cat brushing past my leg. It turns into bougainvillea where the man stands obscurely before me, twice now, inside the invisible circle described by this dark street girdling the *pueblo*.

We are mute beneath the moon, taking each other in again and again. We are here forever, without stopping; knowing it without knowing.

What must happen next, this evening that is every evening: tonight?

5

It is barely light. As if it is possible to cheat the morning, to deprive a blinding Villa Bougainvillea of its incendiary power to ignite memory, I am walking away towards my bed in El Castillo.

I retain, surely, the protective atmosphere of this other, nocturnal villa. It encircles what passes for me, myself, somewhere within my painful void. It is the invisible sheath that enabled me to transport whatever I am to Madrid, to hold it there among the dismal, barely human images of contemporary art, to bring it back here. Now it will keep me safe from unwanted interference by those meaning well, though made clumsy, insensitive, by their own fractured relationships, their unrealised love.

No one will see me evading the dawn – or so I think. For crossing the deserted plaza, I notice Bog Man getting up from one of the café's chairs, left out all night. There is no escape from him rising to his full Scandinavian height, the man who is awake latest and up earliest. Does he never sleep, this creature of barely exhumed passageways and burial chambers? Now he is kissing me with that stink of the rough local tobacco on breath preventing me from knowing if he smells more of coffee or wine, of this morning or last night.

"I'd heard you were back. What news of Franz?"

There is none, of course. There have been no police reports suggesting a disastrous end. The press has been silent. The *adios* of that farewell note in the kitchen was final. It has drawn a tight shutter over any idea of continued contact, let alone news.

Paloma's brow has knotted here on the dawning plaza as she unsuccessfully fights the realisation that Franz, unlike her, always conceived of each without the other. He had known from the start there must soon be a parting. It is incredible to Paloma that he can slip away from his identity as her lover as easily as he had out of a swimming costume left on a granite-veined stone the day he temporarily disappeared on an overcast beach. For she, having come into herself through him; she, now unable fully to *be* except with him; she, incapable of reverting to that faint prefigurement of who she is before knowing him; she, Paloma, Franz's lover, simply cannot detach herself from her identity as the man's lover – and so from Franz himself.

Trapped by her feelings, she is amazed at, resentful of, his. Doesn't she envy his very independence? It liberates him from having to be with – through – her. What has he to know, wherever, whoever he now is, of all she is having to suffer from uselessly but inescapably needing him? She cannot even imagine being able to free herself from the self-destructive burden of this unrequited love, or foresee a time when she might live outside it.

Bog Man's desire for news about Franz could not be more unwelcome. But more than tactlessness makes him request it, pulling on himself to ease his shorts, short at the crotch. This is schadenfreude at my loss of the winning contestant in the competition for me – which never existed. Yes, it is spleen, for he knows very well there is no news. And if he did not, he could have read it in the slight shrug of my shoulders. In fact, he pretends that is what answers him as he rubs the mosquito bites at the back of a leg with the other foot, saying:

"So he just disappeared, did he? After the innocent, beautiful girl that you *were* entrusted herself to his arms. What a pity! You could have done far better. He was so old and ragged. Such a dismal creature! I can't imagine what you could possibly see in him. It's a mystery."

Bog Man is, of course, wondering, like others, what I saw in him. But it had not been attraction. Looking after him, a man re-emerging, I found my undiscovered self surfacing too, like land rising from water around the Dutch dikes. He had been raising me with him, hadn't he, the one I was increasingly attaching to?

Though Bog Man should not be so surprised by *Beauty and the Beast*, a title he has implicitly coined for such a relationship. He would gladly have played Beast: he has been his constant understudy.

As for my mother, well, she has effectively leapt at the title. She has commented on every inch of my body since earliest infancy, remarking on who each feature takes after in the family; minutely assessing the development of my supposed attractiveness. And she made no secret of her view of Franz. So I could just see her mentally choreographing our relationship as one of her cruellest ballets.

Nevertheless, even if her company's most brilliant comic character dancer had performed the grotesque, wouldn't the performance have had to come to this: the transformation of Beast in Beauty's eyes – though into a Prince all-too-soon evaporating like a mirage, an illusion, pure fantasy, while continuing as the Beast he had always been as far as everybody else was concerned?

"It's a mystery," Bog Man continues, "like him. Did he ever really say what he'd learned from Speer? I doubt it. Such a man could never have confided in anyone, even supposing you, a poor girl, could have understood what he was talking about. That sort can hardly trust one enough to be frank when they've so much to hide."

So says this Norwegian rumoured to be self-exiled here for activities during the Quisling Regime.

"Or did he just want to create interest in himself, that no one who'd never recovered his memory properly, and who would have had next to nothing of importance to say for himself even if he had? But I doubt such a charming creature as you," Bog Man says, passing a long hand like a lizard across my cheek, pushing off hair behind my ear, "could have known what to look for, or understood what it was if you'd found it. And now he's left you high and dry. You badly need someone to take you in hand."

I have not uttered a word, waiting for Bog Man to play himself out. I know he never will. For it is all envy, undeclared bad conscience and the self-loathing of one only capable of coming to self-awareness at one remove.

The knowledge that he can go on like this forever draws my mind away no less than my footsteps. I simply leave Bog Man in his sandals and shorts, lighting one cigarette from the butt of the last while staring at the girl departing the deserted plaza. My consciousness of him is submerged by anticipation of arriving at El Castillo while it is still dawn, and getting into bed.

Are my parents aware that I have spent the night away? They never ask. Yet they are not fools – in this, at least. Still, they will act as if nothing has happened, as though my empty bed were filled, as if the absence that has passed for me there *is* me.

PART II

1

Frank receives a phone call from Magda inviting him to drinks at El Castillo.

"Ah! Thank you. But at what time?"

Yet the question is not simply for Frank to be certain of the hour, which turns out, surprisingly, to be six o'clock that evening – not the ritual, cooler time of sunset at eight. It is to recall him to the mundane, from which, over the last few evenings, he has found himself set disturbingly adrift by glimpsing a light on in Villa Bougainvillea, a light it took a panicked further circuit of the *pueblo* to confirm was more than the illusion he realises his entire time back here has been nourishing. Especially so with that further sight awaiting him of a young woman in the open doorway.

Odd, too, is Frank's discovery that it is not really Magda who is inviting him. For Bruno, abruptly suspending the irascible piano practice his guest hears on arriving, receives him in his studio. He continues sitting at the Steinway among piles of sheet music and recordings. A framed photograph of his teacher in wing collar, with the stern expression of a previous age, hangs by the piano.

An open door leads to the library. Frank glances at the rows of books, many on the war, and on Speer. He is uncomfortable, accepting this unexpected summons from a man who, when last they met, had abruptly broken off discussion in the plaza's dim café. Bruno, for his part, sits mutely here with Frank in the dusk. It is as if, nervously searching for a way to resume their conversation, he is again lost in that inner space he falls into when practising; unable to find himself at the point in the piece where he seems abandoned to an invisible, tightening labyrinth.

Then it has started, this subject of Speer's hollowness. And Frank finds it inevitable that Bruno should be picking up this theme. It is his apology, surely, for walking out not only on considering how empty Speer had felt in Spandau, but also on the worthlessness of his accomplishments even in triumphant days. Maybe Bruno has somehow overcome his initial sensitivity to the idea. Now he is perhaps implicitly accepting that he – Speer, actually – was always in a void, turning later to the issue of how he mastered such feelings.

"But did Speer ever *understand* his emptiness?" Frank asks as much himself as Bruno. The question has come naturally into his mind now after having reflected in his room, when Bruno had broken off their discussion in the café, on Speer's strange bond with Hitler, and on Trevor-Roper's assessment of his character. "Certainly he felt it when his elaborate Survival Techniques failed to distract him anymore. Though did he recognise it as more than flagging confidence in prison projects to prevent him from rousing himself for days, even months, to continue writing his *Secret Diaries*? Had he any idea of what really left those pages blank, what made life lose its appeal – even when he became so badly depressed that he required medical attention?

"And this isn't a matter of Speer simply being conscience-stricken for having lacked whatever ethical sense should have prevented him from colluding in the atrocities. It's one thing to want to atone, quite another to know what made you commit the crimes in the first place.

"Not that Speer failed to express regret. He cried, didn't he, seeing those films of the concentration camps at Nuremburg? He sought spiritual help from priests."

"If Magda were here," Bruno says gruffly, "she'd offer no quarter. She'd say his whole defence was based on actually denying responsibility, specific culpability, for the crimes. When he claimed that he had planned to kill Hitler by dropping a gas canister into an air intake in his bunker, the rest of the defendants in the courtroom simply laughed."

"Magda has a point," Frank says. "Because Speer, highly intelligent as he is, repeatedly claims to be the inevitable outcome of the twin personae available to him as a young German: the artist and the technocrat. They're both divorced from politics and moral judgements. So it's his environment, not he himself, that's to blame for what he has – or alleges he hasn't – done.

"Prisoner 5, later Speer the best-selling media personality, may even admit in the slow, careful way which gives an impression that he's wearily reading from a script, that his biggest regret is learning too late that humanity is life's most important value. But lip service aside, has he ever really plumbed his abyss?"

"I think he did try," Bruno says. "Remember that George Casalis, the French prison chaplain, called Speer the most tortured person he'd ever known. Speer asked him to help make him 'another man'. Casalis recommended the writings of Karl Barth, the theologian."

"Ah! Karl Barth," Frank says. "His *Commentary on the Epistles to the Romans* is supposed to be 'a special-delivery letter for the twentieth century'. Well, after reading nine hundred pages, Speer couldn't remember a word."

Then Frank thinks of the book Bruno lent him, with its devastating new research and unremittingly accusatory stance. "The fact remains," he continues, "that Speer was as empty spiritually as personally."

"Well, emptiness is what Spandau meant to him," Bruno says. "It was his challenge – as I've been saying."

"But *did* he ever fathom his void?" Frank says. "It's the question we keep coming back to. Did he at any point confront the personal hollowness that made his relationship with Adolf Hitler his ultimate reality? Because it wasn't just ambition, grandiose architectural commissions and immense power that laid Speer open to the great leader. It was a self unformed. Hitler's emotional blitzkrieg, his narcissistic adoration of the younger man, simply overwhelmed him. Speer colluded, with paroxysms of illusory self-value."

Frank pauses, only now taking in what he has been involuntarily acknowledging while talking: quite how easily a false sense of who one is can take hold. One might not even recognise it is happening. He had not exactly been aware of his own amorphousness all those years ago when the magisterial Professor Keller had easily drawn *him* in. Reverting to how Speer saw himself in terms of Hitler, from first to last, Frank recalls Trevor-Roper again:

"He asks Speer, if he could have his life again, and be, like his father, a respectable bourgeois architect in a provincial German town or become a minister for the most evil and destructive man in the history of Europe, if not the world, which would he choose?

"Speer takes time to consider. Then he says: 'You have to understand the irresistible fascination of power.'"

Intrigued, Frank and Bruno discuss exactly what the story means. Is it fascination with Hitler, the most powerful man in Europe, or his minister's thrill at his own power? But then Frank doubts that the two can be distinguished, in spite of what he has been reading recently.

As I talk, it again bears in on me that, just as Trevor-Roper is fascinated by Albert Speer, no one need feel constricted by Professor Keller's prescription for what ranks as a fit subject for historical study. Far from it. Finding the topic opening up in me more and more over these summer days here on Spain's southern coast, I feel myself increasingly freed of my mentor's views, his prejudices, my own deference to him. I recognise my newfound independence of mind has given me the self-confidence implicitly to take the lead, surely, in this discussion with Bruno by his piano.

It prompts an image of the man at this Steinway, late each evening, beside the framed photograph of his teacher. As if confirming, by contrast, my newfound capacity to see, at least, what has constrained me over the years, that walrus face, summoning up the other great pianists of the period, high priests of art such as Edwin Fischer and Artur Schnabel, is as stern as it has been throughout its years hanging at Bruno's side. How the pupil must have sought to impress him with early virtuosity! But such musical pyrotechnics had, alas, worn thin, breaking down before the Master's impossibly exacting standards. For Bruno had been expected, surely, to communicate new human depths.

Yet it is not to discover them that Bruno, turning in this break in our conversation, looks through the darkling plate glass window. It is to say, as light suddenly dazzles from the patio: "Ah! The others have arrived."

2

Paloma's mother has invited some people to meet her. Do my parents have any idea of how little I want to see Heidi, Paloma thinks, as Heidi kisses her in greeting as neighbours, mere neighbours, despite the strength of her embrace, the meaningful sternness of her expression? How little I want to see her, with that glowering resentment of hers, the claustrophobic intensity of her feelings, the unwelcome relationship she seeks to foist upon me!

We are joined by my father and a man who has been talking to him. Strangers, we are caught off guard, each coming unexpectedly like this on the shadow known from the entrance of Villa Bougainvillea for two nights now.

My father introduces the Englishman. He is in his mid-thirties, serious, academic, his face made youngish by the clarity of his features. He is courteous to the point of shyness. I take in the way he takes me in with those repeatedly averted eyes; glances, surely, at the beauty my parents harp on: an endless source of trouble to me. Tact prevents him from staring insistently with the obtrusive lecherousness I all too often encounter. But his glimpses indicate, too, a scrutinising presence underlying the mannerly person. It's a recessed creature conveying sadness, exchanging pleasantries as in a Kensington living room such as my mother's rather than among unacknowledged volcanoes.

Amalia, effusive Amalia, kisses Frank. Heidi, tense Heidi, says: "So tell us, have you finally found what you're looking for out here, now you've finished your book?"

"It's stirring," Frank says. *I feel it,* he thinks. *And that I am equal to whatever I am on the brink of knowing, doing, becoming ... Though something is still not quite there ... It's vague ...* "Though I mustn't bore you with it."

"You're not at all boring," Bruno says.

Retaliating against Magda, who, in her unending need for society, has foisted these guests on him, Bruno provokes the ladies by boasting: "I've finally found someone intelligent, Dr Ward here, to talk with in this human desert."

"What about?" Heidi says sharply.

"Guess," Magda says sniffing. She has contrived that the men's discussion of Speer is over and done with before drinks.

"Certainly not Speer's chauffeur," Bruno says.

But even this gruff dismissal has his daughter cringing. She fears the mere mention of Franz could lead in no time to her mother again dwelling on how unthinkable it had been for her own daughter to consort with an associate of Speer, a war criminal, especially one so much older than she. She dreads Heidi's stern, almost angry, reaction to how he had spirited her friend away from her. She simply cannot bear to think of all his parting has meant to her since morning sun annihilated the daytime Villa Bougainvillea.

"Oh, really!" Heidi says. "But what light *did* Franz shed on Speer?" Then, needling Paloma with a catch in her voice, she says: "I suppose he must have said something about him in all those hours you spent with him."

It is Heidi's eternal question to which Paloma simply shrugs, letting it come over as her incompetent stupidity. She has no intention of fuelling Heidi's envy of Franz, let alone that which she senses Heidi instinctively seeks to create in the Englishman.

"Come now," Bruno says protectively, the blasé bluntness of his earlier riposte having proved ineffective. "How on earth could a wartime driver know what his master went through *after* the war, when Speer finally had to face up to being – or not – in Spandau? And regardless of anything that may have happened up to now, this is the point where this story actually begins."

"Spare us your views, Bruno," Magda says, fearing he is hijacking her relaxed social gathering. "In any case, you're far too sympathetic to the man."

"Just put yourself in his place for an instant," Bruno continues, blithely ignoring what she has just said. "Think of him in his cell, remembering all he'd been, done – and lost. Though not only the big things," he adds, so caught up in his own thoughts that his eyes are lost, beyond the range of the patio's light, in the dark garden. "Moments when the piano was played to perfection: like Cortot's rendering of Debussy."

"I've no intention of paying him that compliment," Magda says as Bruno gets up without explanation. He heads, erect as a sleepwalker, across the grass to his studio. Frank, following him with his eyes while still mulling over Bruno's earlier point, muses:

"Obviously the driver couldn't, at the time he worked for Speer, have known what the man would go through. Besides, he couldn't then possess the human experience to understand what Speer was to face later. But has it stayed that way? What's become of him since leaving here? After coming back from Russia and recuperating in the *pueblo*, returning to himself in Villa Bougainvillea, has he gone on to face the challenge of actually becoming who he is – as Speer had to?"

Instants pass. Frank's mind has wandered, leaving, like debris on the beach, the image of a skeleton laid out on a trestle table, inexplicably – till he remembers Bog Man explaining to tourists on the plaza's *mirador* that it comprised the remains of more than one corpse. Suddenly Frank understands what is now obvious. Speer and his driver compose a single human in his thoughts.

For days, they have been doing so, the driver acquiring the capacity to exist knowingly; Speer, in continuation, always evidently existing, faced with the challenge of fully being. Between them, they are the single person increasingly drawing Frank, ever less an observer, into the epic of becoming oneself.

"Returning?" Paloma mutters. She has only half-heard, distractedly, Frank speak of the driver coming back to himself in Villa Bougainvillea. "Who? Franz?" she says.

Amalia's large hand squeezes hers consolingly.

"Who cares what's happened to him?" Magda snaps as a light appears in the music room.

Bruno is putting on a recording. In the electric hum before music begins, he calls out to Frank: "I've been meaning to play this for you."

It is *La Cathédrale Engloutie*. And Frank knows they are hearing exactly what Hitler's young protégé had: Cortot releasing Debussy's piece, chord by gentle, fluid chord. Those ghostly bells of Ys Cathedral, sunk off Brittany 1,500 years ago, still warn of storms. Cortot, employing Debussy's own sfumato technique, making everything tremble with mysticism and the supernatural, uses the long pedal to preserve the bass pedal notes. He is summoning up a fantastical edifice, fresh and intact, at the rise of an equally improbably resurgent sun.

This is one of the recordings Paloma has heard her father put on when dispiritedly breaking off from an unsuccessful practice session. She has sensed how, witnessing the rise of this Cathedral, in air filling with a perfect structure against all the odds, he finds the soothing of his anguished lack of fulfilment. And beholding the edifice again tonight, she all but feels something previously known, yet also surfacing invisibly here between herself and the stranger. She herself is thrilling at whatever it is that is palpable, but beyond the senses, as they sit taking each other in among strange chords.

The Cathedral subsides, fully submerged by the final, faintest reverberation. The piece ends in silence, utter silence – darkness, too. The Steinway is an obscure hulk. Magda, troubled by mosquitoes, has gestured to the maid, bringing out tapas and wine, to switch off the patio lights.

"Imagine Speer remembering *that* in Spandau," strangers hear Bruno's disembodied voice say.

The Englishman and Paloma have lost sight of each other while sitting there. They are blind shadows in this further mute moment for Bruno's thought to hover.

"But then," Bruno continues, "he'd soon find what he'd recalled from the depths of his memory engulfed: the Cathedral; dinner by the Seine; an impromptu concert in Cortot's apartment; the free, youthful decades; his power; all he'd been and built. They'd gone with the passage of time, the middle years, the lost years 'in place of a life', as he put it. Yes, it had all eluded him, empty-handed now, with useless memories like a cruel dream in the prison to where he'd somehow brought himself.

"That, surely, is when Speer relapsed into his abyss. It feels to him that he does not exist. Will he ever surface from that void? What could possibly draw him out of it?"

Will the Englishman answer? Paloma wonders. But perhaps stung by the poor reception Heidi gave his earlier remark, he has retired from conversation. The academic persona is fading. He is fast sinking into whatever part of himself underlies his intellectual buttresses, drawn into wordless vacancy opened up through these mentions of Speer's own emptiness. For a void extends through porous bodily boundaries: entered at a point in oneself, it sets one drifting into another's nothingness.

So Paloma herself does, through a moonlit eye she catches momentarily, admitting her to the Englishman's interior. Barely acknowledged, here is recognition nonetheless of what opens between them; of what is shared, in a look instant but timeless. For they have somehow always seen each other, taken one another in before this moment, faceless shadows unlimited to the present external nocturnal encounter.

Heidi may be noticing. Sullen, she says no more than Frank as Bruno rejoins the guests. He, too, sits in a moment of mute immobility following the sinking of the Cathedral. It is the plunging of a reality into illusion.

"And it rises again tomorrow," he sighs.

Mosquitoes feast, regardless of the dark. Magda scratches, telling the maid to bring the spray as her guests continue chattering. Except that her daughter has withdrawn from the whole ambit of conversation as much as the Englishman now seems to have done.

Paloma, inwardly recessed, is in the same place as the man gone still while the hour passes. No longer full-blooded but pale, a breathing statue in his moonlit chair outside time, he is not now the shy, intelligent, fine-featured historian. Another self is opening up in the space Paloma inhabits with him when Amalia finally gets up to leave. Moments afterwards, her daughter joins her, stiffly awaiting the remaining Englishman.

Faces, personae lost to the paring night, they continue sitting together, awaiting, unawares, how each will surface from this long minute more in all-encompassing dark.

3

Frank has finished reading Speer's biography. He will give it back to Bruno sometime before he leaves the *pueblo* in just over a week. Then again, he is inclined to do so immediately, although it means calling on the man so soon after the previous day, when they had sat on the patio with the ladies – and his daughter, a shadow he has been seeing outside Villa Bougainvillea. That scene in El Castillo's moonlit garden has held at the back of his mind all day. And it's evening once more as he returns to the house atop the hill, hearing, as every night, a fractured piano piece in the alleyways.

The maid opens the gate for Frank, whereupon, encountering Magda in the music-filled hall, he apologises for disturbing Bruno.

"Not at all," she says, too used to this practising to mind interruption. "You know your way." Magda lets Frank walk on his own into the music room for what, seeing the book in his hand, she dourly presumes will be another of their tedious conversations about Speer.

Bruno is unfazed, too. Abandoning the keyboard to take the biography, he puts it on top of the piano. Not leaving his seat, but gesturing to Frank to sit too, he says: "Give me your verdict, as a real historian."

"My 'verdict'? Well, there's a concept the author would understand. He simply damns his subject, casting him in an unflattering light wherever possible. This involves, for instance, unmasking him as a shallow fraud merely intent on satisfying his rampant ambition rather than on advancing a loyal commitment to Hitler and his ideology.

"Yet that's to misread the purpose of history, seeing it as an indictment. It results in overlooking what's crucial: the bond between the two men which Speer went on acknowledging long after it was prudent to do so. Though since an historian can't fully understand that relationship without more evidence – the historian's stock in trade – the temptation is just to ignore it, producing an entirely accusatory account instead, which is precisely what this biographer does."

Frank is happy to explain matters so trenchantly, with a clear understanding of his discipline – and its limitations. He is, moreover, gratified to engage with accomplished, even celebrated historians from higher-profile fields, especially on Speer. For the subject, denied any chance of Professor Keller's imprimatur, not only raises the issue of Speer's link to Hitler, but also underlines Frank's growing detachment from his own mentor.

So Frank thinks, beside Bruno even now at the Steinway. There, eternal wrestler with his *Last Prelude*, he nightly breaks up the piece to perfect the technique needed to render each section, although he can never reconnect the elements, launching a performance of the entire work.

Frank, for his part, is uncomfortably aware that newly incisive as he feels as an historian, this has not yet amounted to identifying a new project, nor to finding the decisiveness, even courage, to attack it. He has still to conquer an alarming new flicker of fear: despair almost at not feeling equal to fill the expanse of years lying open before him.

Frank takes a breath. Then he risks addressing the father of last night's young woman – now glimpsed again through the plate glass window where they were sitting yesterday evening. She is wandering into the garden over the dark grass, as Frank says: "Would you play something now?"

"Oh, no!" Bruno says wearily. "Go join Paloma. She could do with some civilised company. It may cheer her up. Listen to this with her instead."

Since her return to El Castillo, Paloma has been staring at her sketch pads and watercolours. They seem childish to her, with their limited subjects, dating from before Franz's arrival. She has not touched them since, distant as they now are from her – whoever, undefinably, she has become. How can she resume them, despite art being her supposed interest in life, without any idea of where to begin these days? They accumulate dust floating in her sunlit room, where she, too, hovers. And Paloma, lacking an awareness of time except during longueurs such as the previous night with her parents' guests and that Englishman, drifts into the evening. She is drawn back to the dark garden. She holds before that shimmering seaview, passing the time before she can steal away.

Shadows from Villa Bougainvillea, the strangers re-encounter each other without interrupting the music. Submitting to it, they again take their seats where a cathedral, something huge but immaterial as memories from the past, surfaced in a nocturnal present between them. Leaning back in their chairs, faces raised to take in a shaving of moon, a skein of stars, they appear as mediums. It is as if they transmit, in a trance, the lost, to each ghostly other in this darkness, as Rubinstein's performance of Chopin's *Last Prelude* is upon them. It courses through the warm night: subtle, sensitive, deep as life.

What Bruno so seeks is here: the *Prelude* in its streaming entirety. But the light has gone off in his room. And he continues within the bounds of El Castillo's fragrant, flower-covered adobe walls; in the tasteful, comfortable house whose music studio and library provide ample scope, surely, for the experience and exercise of personal fulfilment. But how can the man access the perfection he yearns for, now hovering tantalisingly in this his space? How, lost to inner darkness, can he reconnect with what he once had at his fingertips?

The two strangers continue sitting out in the dark silence. Faceless, they face each other. Beyond their lunar masks they are sightlessly taking one another in. Each knows it, feels it happening between them, through them, as surely but invisibly as the music reached each hearer on its intangible arc across the night air.

At last, finally, he gets up, that dense mass of him, saying: "I s'pose I should be going."

"Me too," she says surreptitiously.

Only night lights are on in the house. All others must be abed.

They walk down winding streets, through narrowing unlighted alleys. Continuous, the slope points the man all the way to his *pensión* – though, ever more shadows, they are first coming to a dark Villa Bougainvillea.

Slowing down, they are, in effacing moonlight, simultaneously themselves and conduits for each other to the other pair halted there: spectres of those departed haunting the place, evening upon evening, in the memories of this returning couple.

How long have closed, vacant rooms awaited encounters, each with each?

PART III

1

He, a shadow before Villa Bougainvillea, says he had met the original occupants. They built the place. "Did *you* know them?"

"No." She stands, holding open the front door.

"I wonder if there's any sign of someone who was once there," he says, now from the half-lit porch.

"Anyone who's ever occupied the villa has gone, who knows where? Nobody's here now, I can tell you."

"I notice those North African brass plates, matching the hall lamp with its coloured glass discs, are still on the wall. They're a link. They bring her back."

"Come in and see."

The shadow detaches from bougainvillea to enter and finds what will be seen in coming upon a woman haunting the half-light of an entrance she cannot fail to revisit.

Entering, what is this feeling? Surely that nothing could be more familiar than to be here. Why, then, does it sound foreign to be saying *I've always known I'd come back*? What is so strange about telling each other *Returning, as I'm doing with you, was inevitable* ? Is it that our dialogue is speech that we, featureless silhouettes, hardly appear to utter? Barely an echo, it seems to occur through us, without our intervention.

Porous, we are invaded by shadows from a place, a time, in a villa somehow awaiting us and seeping between the words and their syllables. They hover, dark in the intervals, on the brink of perception, reverberating in our odd sense of the present somehow displaced. For in the villa, of which this moment makes the two of us creatures, we, dense voids, are here to lend expression to what has been between these blank walls.

But pausing sufficiently to have a chance of recovering what is, who we are, we come upon ourselves; each self, Paloma and Frank, now in touch with the other, as words tremble through us in the nocturnal stillness of a vanishing summer.

It is an empty space, this villa, but hardly inert. As on the hills, the mountains nearby, there is a silent air of time past, of violence now endlessly becalmed, of patiently anticipated convulsions.

The floor is laid with local marble. Polished once, dusty and cracked where it is heavily veined, it feels cool in the August heat to toes unthinkingly released for a nervous moment from their sandal. It strikes the foot like the stone stage of some amphitheatre abandoned since dramas in classical times.

Bare it is, with shadows less than characters in a plot unborn, yet to unfold, still to implicate them – but that is already the very situation of these two, having found themselves in each other's presence one summer night that is also other summer nights, in a void that is the void for either, for both: the charged void of this deserted, expectant Villa Bougainvillea.

Beyond the hallway, ahead of dense, irrepressibly striving bougainvillea, we are together in the cool vacancy of the downstairs bedroom and bathroom, breathing in the mustiness of the stone quarries. There is a smell of drains in the parched *pueblo* with its primitive water and sewer systems.

What of this other odour, so slight, so unstable? Is it the trace of a burned-out candle, of an incense stick, of long-faded perfume? Is something here redolent of pre-existence? Is it awakening silent echoes? Or is it just the remains of a mothball, if not a paper strip once hanging from the ceiling to draw insects to their deaths? Together in this space, where we are being attracted into whatever it is, we now find ourselves. Here the night air carries up the heavy smell of the sea. It makes one light-headed. Throwing open the windows of the first-floor bedroom, we are invaded by the scent of jasmine from its wide veranda.

Heady, one is unconstrained, impressionable, pliant away from one's normal habitat: a capital with an urban self. What might one not succumb to in this place, this atmosphere that has no connection with the prosaic regularity of who one usually is?

We are fish out of water; shadows out of character – the character adopted as the self one has, without realising it, accumulated in the brusque world with which one necessarily rubs shoulders. Here, unconfined by work schedules, the need to know and keep one's place, we float: we, whatever selves we shall find we are to each other: we, undefined, stranger-beings in a shadowy, seemingly unbounded space. We have no bearings except each other in this situation taking us out of ourselves – the selves we have become, the situation to which we easily succumb as if it has a ghostly will of its own.

The hallway, the rooms, the veranda, even the kitchen and its terrace now strike one as smaller and larger than before. Their dimensions, it seems, are so variable as to be unconfined by what is supposed to have been previously. It both is and is not what it was. For here is not just the past contained, confined, trapped. This has become an unrestricted space, one not previously defined; one that is also existing here between us.

The boundaries, dim walls, are less lines than traces. It is dream geometry. There are elements from the waking day, yes: the years-long mornings, afternoons, nights with their dust around the hall's brass trays; on the sitting room's plastic-covered sofa in which the eye is sure, isn't it, that there are still depressions from those now interminably reverberating conversations? Yet here, too, is room for what is to come between us, to open up around us, obscure beings in this tensely awaiting vacancy.

It is eerie to be here. It is all so familiar and strange, moving through shadows. We are surefooted somnambulists, at home but vagrants, adrift. Ahead, in the patch of hall where the dining area leads to the kitchen, the moon catches an expanse of floor.

Now we are standing on that stretch of smooth, white stone before the dark mouth of the upper stairwell. Pale light blanches our bare legs – female calves shapely, male ones lank. Marble statues from the past might be animating as we, scarcely at arm's length from each other, hands at our sides, feel the warmth of each other's breath. Yet in sudden stillness, our hearing surprisingly acute, we notice beyond those steps – increasingly obliterated to view in their pitch-black shaft – the creak of latticework for plants to climb in a roof garden. It hides neighbouring roof terraces, lending cover to shadows where not a bark, not a purr, mutes breathing at an hour when everyone is a dreamer.

Hovering merely in this present, seeing with double vision what is and was, we take in that which we experienced beyond that musty door closed ahead. Then, all at once, its aching tenderness hurtles into our space: the space within. It is as if a soft, infinitely vulnerable, feathered creature were rushing through, but too fast to be distinct.

Now there is this sensation of queasiness, of inner melting. It unbalances, as though the usual laws governing equilibrium have themselves been caught off-guard. And the stairs, with steep, ill-maintained, narrow treads, promise only further unsteadiness. There is no question of entering their dim mouth only to find one's self rising into ever more disturbing nothingness.

So now there is an achingly static feeling here; a sense of oppression in the villa, on this upper floor, closed, shuttered, sealed against the summer night, over those yearlong days, an eternity, as if something inaccessible but undeniably there is weighing down the ceiling from a star-heavy terrace.

Bougainvillea, its mauve turned black by night, is dense, unimaginably heavy, surely, as on a distant star. Over the decades since it was planted, when the villa was built, it has not simply grown luxuriant with freedom but borne down increasingly on the roof it's invaded, driving all from the tiles, confronting even what is to come.

We have not put a foot forward. We are still in moonlit whiteness. We continue on the stone floor, not so much as making a move to open the door to the roof. Above our calves we are obscure, quite unclear to each other.

Now, finally, he sighs. It's deep, drawing him back from the brink of wherever his reverie led him. He is trembling, as if from a breeze.

"Thank you for making it possible for me to revisit." Why is he whispering? Who – what – is he afraid of awakening in this deserted villa, withdrawn behind his stilted English courtesy? "But I must go now."

Stiffly, he turns his back on her, there on white stone. He forsakes their motionless moment before stairs leading to a roof terrace.

Carefully, deliberately, as if to avoid displacing even the shadows, he steps out of Villa Bougainvillea.

2

It is almost seven o'clock and I am awake, although I came back to the *pensión* so late last night. I tossed and turned in those few hours of rest. My sleep was disturbed by a hyperreal sense of being in the villa. An almost nightmarish dream sprawled through it in repetitive, ill-aligned sequences. I am trying to get its mangled narrative straight now, still lying here. But despite eluding me, with its phantom hints of the past, it bears down.

Maybe I should turn my back on this false awakening and doze. I silence the radio before it starts. I don't need reminding how little time is left to squeeze through to a life beyond. And I do not want my thoughts to dwell on the time I have squandered in the *pueblo* since hearing that warning. For the past week is a blur amounting to hardly anything in particular: social gatherings, meals, musings, conversations about some driver and his master. I am marooned in this early morning haze with nothing solid to hold on to.

Or is it simply my memory that is to blame? It might well have atrophied in the dim decades since I was last in the *pueblo*. What was there for it to transport from my time in archives hunched over ill-lit parchment – that tiresomely repetitive image? But despite fearing my loss of such a faculty, I still seem to feel, here in bed, the unforgotten; all that is there but unclear and yet presses on me.

Frank senses it, staring at the closed shutters with cracks of sunlight struggling to enter. Whereupon last night's villa comes surging back to mind: that expectant space, a decades-old venue for shadows. But, on the verge of recovering all his dream brought him face to face with there, he finds it dissolve again.

It leaves him recalling intrusions in the shuttered room of a gloomy Edwardian house off the Gloucester Road. Its heavy door keeps him from the séance whose gasping spiritualist ushers in shades from a past while light strains through cracks in windows closed like this one facing Frank in his *pensión* bedroom.

I go to the terrace for breakfast. I will wake up once and for all with coffee, here at my table beside this low terracotta ledge filled with earth, cactus and geranium. Then I notice Heidi. Not for several days has she had breakfast here. Nor does she keep her distance as she used to, remaining at her table and joining me for coffee only later.

"So, has she been speaking to you about Speer?" she demands, approaching me directly.

"Who? Paloma?"

"Who else? I don't care what anyone else says. She was with the man's driver for weeks on end. But I can't get a word out of her about it. She's been sharing what he said with you, I'm sure – now that you're seeing her."

"Am I?" *Why am I flushing?*

"Aren't you?"

I am silent, considering this is just the latest in a series of things conspiring to make me feel involved with the stranger. Aren't we repeatedly being put together, not against our will exactly, but without conscious compliance, as though by something beyond ourselves? And I'm unexpectedly aware of whatever it was in me that fleetingly saw it as a possibility while I took her in, there in her father's garden.

Yes, I recognised it vaguely – *and her*, the young woman I have never seen before, do not know, imprinted on me as an ineradicable memory from a time we have never spent together.

"Well …" I say. "But I haven't discussed Speer with her – or anything, really. I barely know her."

"But there's something there … between you. I can tell."

I shrug, mouth downturned. I am not used to being spoken to so directly – or to anything direct for, well, since when? "Look, I really don't care about Speer."

"Perhaps another interest you're not quite admitting to, Professor?"

"Dr … Frank …"

"So, Dr Frank Ward, there turns out to be a lot more to you than appears on the surface."

Coolly analytic, the words turn instantly corrosive. She is suddenly an interrogator such as Speer himself often encountered. It makes me defensive, as if hiding dread secrets I must on no account give up, least of all to myself.

What am I to make of this shift from her professional, academically collegial self with me, a change to this other personality she has apparently had stored up in her all along? It is the one putting me on the defensive for crimes I can neither identify nor recall having committed. I am a defendant in a Stalinist show trial for which shadowy circumstances have contrived to make me feel inexplicably guilty.

Heidi leaves. I take a further sip of this bitter coffee. And I am rudely reminded that, regardless of Heidi, the real reason why I am here, by this terracotta ledge, in this *pueblo*, remains to discover the subject for my new book. All else is a distraction to which I have been too ready to succumb.

It would have been easier if Professor Keller were still alive. With him, I should have settled the matter long ago. But on my own I am finding it hard to summon up his enthusiasm for any historical topic other than the magnetic Albert Speer. Keller could no more have approved of my interest in Speer than Heidi seems to. I imagine the look of distaste on his face for a Nazi who, at best, is a case study in psychopathology.

"So, can anything of value possibly be learnt from Albert Speer?" I hear a disembodied voice ask.

I suppose I have been considering it repeatedly recently. Knowingly or not, I have been exploring whether or not he faced, then finally overcame, his inner emptiness. Did he ever find whatever freedom beckoned beyond, any more than had a man doubtless struggling to discover it in his time with a girl in Villa Bougainvillea – such as, it finally comes back to me here on the sunny terrace, I myself spent with her last night?

3

She, at the portal of the nocturnal villa; he, pacing up to it and halting by the dark bougainvillea: we join each other, shadows, again, tonight.

We enter rooms barely outlined by moonlight, recognising how little each is known. Should it be any different, chancing to find ourselves in the same place, a summer resort, with no more investment in one another than an unattached man and single woman are likely to feel, not least with this difference in our ages?

We remark on the heat, the night; comment on the way the *pueblo* seems to have changed; refer to this or that person the other never knew here. Words, as from purely social occasions, they conceal that we are hardly speaking to each other until, lapsing into some inner situation for a concentrated moment, we come upon each other at last. Yet what is there to know of ourselves by answering the question we now raise? *What brings you here?*

Is there a flicker of interest when she asks: "Are you visiting this place purely from nostalgia?"

"I'm an historian. I've just finished a book. I'm taking a break – and considering what comes next … You?"

"I'm visiting my father and mother. I've been working in a Madrid art gallery." But he wants to know if she will return to the gallery. What does the future hold?

She is asking if I shall write another book. About what?

Each pauses. Neither replies. Lightly worded, our same unanswerable basic question evokes heavy silence. It sweeps over us as we recognise that one can no more explain oneself to oneself than to another. What would it take to move the muting obstacle we apparently face?

Something indefinable, invisible, suddenly paralyses us, restricting our tongues, blocking our gullets. But what is shying away in me from what seeks, surely, to lure me on, but arrests me here? Isn't Paloma recoiling from stumbling again on her sudden isolation, abandoning her to blankness she is now undergoing?

The air does not stir. There is just this sense of oppression. It is as if, hanging over us, about to bear down with all its weight, were something outside this room, atop those stairs, beyond its rickety door. It is drawing its massive, obscure freight onto us from a roof terrace open to night sky filled with still-unseen dark matter.

Can anything release us from this constriction? What would it take to open oneself up to something that might loosen the immobilised shadows sitting apart on dusty plastic, setting free a pair to the balmy fragrance, to the thrilling promise of a Mediterranean summer night?

4

The following afternoon's heat is finally waning. People are in the plaza for a spectacular sunset. Some stand against the iron railings giving onto the landward side of the *pueblo*. They are dark, without depth, flickering in a Balinese puppet show from the other side of a screen – existent, but not of flesh and blood.

Those at tables in the open-air café drink apéritifs. Several look up, straining to hear what Bog Man is telling a growing group standing around him. It had started with the few tourists who succumbed to his attentions after he asked them for a light. Now they hear him distinguishing between the volcanic hills and other mounds.

The mounds have been partially excavated, revealing the range of cultures, of peoples, who were here. A surprising number, some now forgotten, left their impression. Even the dullest, sleepiest place has all the many traces of the past continuing within it. It is like radioactivity: although buried, it never dies. They were Copper and Bronze Age Iberians, Celts, Carthaginians, Romans, Berbers and Arabs, all before the supposed Christians of today. So were the Greeks and their trading ships, sailing the wine-dark seas crossed by their heroes, demigods and monsters, making landfall even on this rocky beach.

The number of listeners increases, facing that brightening glitter of a villa down there in the valley. Its white colonnade, set among orange groves, shows against imperceptibly darkening sky. Frank, coming into the plaza along a side street from Pensión Amalia, veers from his encircling walk. He joins the audience for the impromptu lecture.

Standing there, turning an instant from the railing, he glimpses Paloma leaving the small supermarket, plastic bag in hand, to cross the square. She gives a wide berth to Bog Man on her way back to El Castillo. But Frank, taking off his now-redundant sunglasses and straw hat to look at her, has done enough to suggest she join him to listen to a lecture delivered in that clear, organised and informed academic style which, he is all-too-aware, from his own professional experience, gives little clue at first to the personality and prejudices, and indeed passions, of the speaker.

They stand side by side, Paloma and Frank, hearing of a necropolis now in darkness that has fallen before them. It is situated down by the road, between the hill opposite, location of the original *pueblo* till its inhabitants abandoned it altogether in the Civil War and this, its new site. For Bog Man says most ancient civilisations buried their dead outside their towns in special places. Proper burial was so important that, where this had not occurred for some reason, the mortal remains of unquiet souls would be exhumed and placed in their correct resting place.

Bog Man excavates the necropolis, he says, as the lecture ends and the audience disbands. He mentions this for the benefit of an attractive young woman who has caught his eye: "Would you like to visit it?"

"Shall we?" she says, taking Frank's hand in self-defence so instinctively that she is barely aware of having done so.

"Oh, *do*!" Bog Man says in resentful mockery. "Tomorrow?"

We are standing, holding hands, scarcely realising it, in what's taken for a mute *yes*.

"Have you visited the necropolis before?"

We have walked back to Villa Bougainvillea, and are sitting on the plastic-covered sofas by moonlight.

"No. It never occurred to me. My mind was elsewhere."

"Weren't you curious, though?"

"It would have had no relevance."

"And now?"

"I have mixed feelings about accepting Bog Man's invitation to tour a burial site."

"But you're interested, aren't you? You're going after all."

"'Troubled' is more like it – at the idea of disturbing those graves. The thought's gruesome, indecent. The dead should be left to their own devices. Let bygones be bygones."

"Mm."

Though we agree that, of course, it is not as if old bones, clay shards, cold stone give one much sense of the past – of *who's* passed. Times gone by, those inhabiting them, who was, then: they are not attached to material remains. They float off invisibly – though sometimes they reattach to the old places in the minds of those suitably attuned, according to psychics."

"Eerie ..."

We lapse into silence-that-is-not-silent. There's a persistent rattling.

"I don't remember summer nights having been so windy here before. Something badly needs doing to the hinges on the roof door. It's very unsettling."

The noise continues, the door straining, on the point of bursting open.

"Well, it seems that we *are* going to the necropolis, finally."

The decision seems to have come upon us, without our conscious volition. It is as if it's inevitable that we, the pair of us, should come face to face with what is being exhumed in a *pueblo* finding us both here this summer.

It is late next afternoon. We are driving down from the *pueblo* in Bog Man's old SEAT. Air rushes through the open windows as he explains that this is where the El Argar culture originated. It flourished in the southeast of Spain between *c.* 1800 and 1300 BC. The previous Megalithic culture had collective burials; tombs are placed in a burial chamber reached by a passage. Sometimes a number of sub-chambers lead to the main one. But with the arrival of Bronze Age El Argar culture, our expert continues, there is a trend to small cists either under the homes or outside. This comes from the Eastern Mediterranean, specifically Mycenaean Greece. While in a later phase of El Argar civilisation, he says, expect to find increasingly frequent burial in large jars.

Thus informed, we descend all the way down from the *pueblo* to the crossroads at the foot of the hill. We rattle on through flat landward terrain. It is rocky, dry, with an occasional, now-silhouetted almond or carob tree. We pass a group of peasant houses, organised as a right angle around a well with a grapevine writhing up to a trellis. There is the heavy smell of pigs. Barely past, the car swerves off the road into more open land. It jerks to a halt.

"Here we are," says Bog Man, striding on the sandy soil.

"Are we?" Paloma says, looking dubiously at this mere continuation of the scrub vegetation we have been driving through. "Where's the burial site?"

"Beneath your feet," Bog Man says, flicking the match with which he has been lighting a a cigarette in the direction of her English companion's sandal.

"But I thought you said you were excavating it," Frank says, eyes naked now he has removed his sunglasses to cast this appraising look at the untouched surface.

"I am," the archaeologist says with insolently professional composure. He brazenly ignores the implied reproach. Or, possibly less shameless than simply thick-skinned, does he even recognise the implication that he had sought to lure an attractive young woman out to this desolate spot under false pretences – before realising she would be accompanied, by which time he could not withdraw his offer? "I'm studying the site first."

Bog Man, justifying the fact that he has made no start on excavating this burial ground, speaks of the irreparable damage a rank amateur such as Schliemann had done by blundering into the fabulous site of Troy, of the need to avoid over-hasty, harmful exhumation:

"There's no substitute for a scrupulous prior review of the terrain."

"There isn't much to see, is there?" Paloma says, wiping her nose.

"Not to the naked eye. But to those who have eyes to see …"

We are staring at the ground. Having anticipated coming upon the immemorially departed, finding ourselves brought into such close range of those we expected to encounter from their opened tombs, we are frowning away the anticlimax as if insisting, eyes downcast, on seeing beyond this surface.

Could just standing here together, holding still in thin, weakening light, could it clear the depleted, unexcavated ground on which there is scratched out what passes for life – a mess of splaying corn stalks, collapsed bamboo tomato frames, a mongrel nosing up to that sham human form, a scarecrow?

There is a bell. It is a church, Paloma supposes, remembering, while gazing down, a peasant man and woman pausing in a field to pray at the end of their day's work: "I saw them in the Madrid gallery's art encyclopaedia, reproducing *The Angelus* by Jean-François Millet. There is a basket of potatoes by the woman, and a wheelbarrow behind her. An upright pitchfork is stuck in the ground by the man. But the earth between them is more than a few feet of the painter's northwest France, according to the book. In his original plan for the canvas, I read, Millet sketched their dead baby's coffin."

Looking down though, soil is all they see, not the being beneath.

"Let's go," Bog Man says, as Paloma stands there. She does not respond, looking down in her reverie. Frank has not moved. "I can't stay here any longer," Bog Man says impatiently to the disconcertingly motionless, unresponsive beings on this necropolis he has yet to open up.

"Then go," Frank says.

We continue on the unworked field, watching sudden darkness engulf the Norwegian burying himself away, according to rumour, among skeletons in the cupboard of his war. The man is eclipsed, driving off with those blinking, diminishing lights.

We start walking on the road. Frogs belch loudly in the irrigation ditches. The fragrance of orange and lemon blossom reaches us from invisible groves as we make our way to the next *pueblo* with its gypsy encampment. I have been there before, but with Heidi, prior to meeting Paloma – just a few days earlier, though it feels strangely more distant. Yet there is no time to regret remembering the once-neutral academic who has resentfully accused me of having an affair with the younger woman. A car races towards us, pushing us to the side of the road, against each other. We hold to one another as it passes. We're arm in arm moments longer in this warm, enfolding breeze.

We walk into the village square with its war memorial. At the bar we are served mineral water and a beer by a talkative girl in pink plastic curlers. She is meeting her fiancé as soon as her sister comes to relieve her, she says, smiling with the angular face of an inbred peasant for all her glad rags, perfume and makeup.

"Where are you staying?" she asks us, obvious holiday-makers. We tell her. "Much better than being stuck in this *pueblo*. It's dead. Look through the door behind you, past the war memorial and to the other side of the plaza. That's right! Over the butcher's. That whole dark storey is the mayor's – the *ex*-mayor, Ricardo. It's been shut up ever since his son was killed in Barcelona. There's not been so much as a light in the window in all those ten years.

"It was in all the papers and on tele. They even had reporters from Madrid trying to interview the family. But Ricardo wouldn't talk. You see, Paco, his son, was murdered by what turned out to be his boyfriend. 'A crime of passion,' they call it. Ricardo hasn't set foot outside from that day to this. He won't even allow his son's name to be mentioned. People say he could go on up there like that with the blinds drawn for another ten years. And one hot summer, like this one, when the smell starts blowing into the plaza, someone will come across him in the dark as dead as his son."

Looking through the deserted plaza, drawn to that drear, dark place, Paloma finds her mind's eye momentarily superimposing another image: Cézanne's *House of the Hanged Man*. From that Madrid art encyclopaedia too, it pulses across her vision, this painting of what are actually parts of several cottages in Auvers-sur-Oise. They amount to a wall. The eye is blocked. The viewer is constricted, as was the man by the noose. And Paloma, suddenly feeling airless, faint, longs to leave this place, buried away inland, where someone dead for love may not be recalled by even so little as a name.

Yet Frank does not move. He is picturing the ex-mayor, hair now long and unkempt, at the other side of that monument to the dead. Unused to speaking, rocking in a rattan chair through stifling darkness, he has condemned himself to a life sentence. But Frank seeks to disentangle the verdict. He supposes he had not only suffered a body blow of shame, disinheriting his son. Nor had Ricardo merely undergone the ghastly realisation that he might have been responsible for nurturing the disposition in Paco, bringing him to his nightmarish end. Hadn't he also been stricken by a sudden, painful access of love for his own flesh and blood at precisely the time he was so achingly gone? Thus Ricardo, deadening himself through mourning, that response to impossible feeling, inwardly denies the now-unrecognised prodigal's return to his father's arms. It deprives him of any chance of releasing himself, that silent, unremembering man, from incarceration in a chair rocking through darkness over that butcher's shop.

They leave the bar and trail wordlessly across the plaza, walking towards the closed shops and the seemingly non-existent apartment opposite. Frank's footsteps draw them further on, leading up a hillock to the gypsy encampment.

It was over a fortnight earlier when he had visited it with Heidi, in the afternoon. They could see brilliant flowers growing in tins on the window ledges of these low shacks from which the gypsy had emerged to travel to their neighbouring *pueblo*, springing up wildly there for his woman, rising to his highest pitch of passion among glittering knives, reaching the fullest moment of his love, his life – then falling to his knees, dense fluid welling out of him in spasms, dead as next morning, laid out under a tarpaulin before the mayor's office.

One of the incurious gypsies Frank and Paloma are now passing must be the woman with her lover gone and buried forever. Having to continue with her daily chores, she cannot keep recalling a man who might not then have been.

For an hour longer the pair continue to move around in the *pueblo*. They show little interest in the historic monuments. Yet they seem to have no alternative purpose. Moving blindly, almost staggering around, they appear uncertain as to what there is for them to accomplish there. Are they even asking what has brought them to this point in a place of ruined loves?

The pair return to the darkening plaza to telephone for a taxi. They wait for it in the light of the bar behind them. There they will hover, spectres almost in this greenish neon glow, until transported.

Even in the taxi they continue mute, without contact. They are held back as if earth, still unbroken by Bog Man, is blocking access to what lies beneath, deep in unexhumed chambers. Yet, riding through the black night, they still somehow take in the necropolis with its entombed, unseen but felt. As unawares as drawing breath, or finding waking thoughts flooded by the previous night's dreams, some part of themselves is responding to an impulse to continue excavating. Efforts are imperceptibly afoot to liberate what is buried by the detritus of unlived time, as, in archaeological sites, archaic waste blocks access to rooms storing what is of beauty and value.

But in the taxi they sit vacantly, if tensely, minds blank, with a neighbour who is a virtual stranger. They glance at the destination, dark ahead. Either had known a sunnier moment there. Now, thinking an instant of the *pueblo*, each pictures the villa whose bougainvillea, with its once green shoots, sends wiry tendrils over windows, coiling thickly round the wrought iron railings of a bedroom balcony, and up to the roof.

There, on the terrace, feeling out over the tiles every trace of that once-peopled space, they reach, unthinkingly – like these hands discovering themselves touching on a plastic-covered taxi seat. They are fingers of shadow-beings staring ahead into obscurity seeming both to encompass the other.

Their hands tremble, clasp. For they are surprised, finally, to have found one another exactly as the pall pales. And what is instantly revealed is their *pueblo* atop its hill, as the driver turns to bring into range moonlight cast far across the Mediterranean.

Sky, sea: they are luminous, immense. Sudden visibility abruptly opens up intoxicating inner space too, with spasmodic thuds of breathing. Then their hands grip with pangs this instant releases on a summer evening odorous with earth, eucalyptus and brine. They are snatches of tenderness and bewildered pain; confusingly mixed emotions only now leaking out from being dammed up during lost time, since they were first felt in the *pueblo*.

The pair have, at last, come back to it together. They pass Pensión Amalia as if it never existed. They return here, to Villa Bougainvillea.

5

The piano does not reverberate in the evening air tonight: there is silence, though hardly absolute. It is, for these arrivals, like the held moment once a recording has been switched on and the music has yet to start; electronic muteness as when Cortot was about to play, taking up the murmur of sea storing Debussy's Ys Cathedral, making ready for its reappearance. Till then, in mere sound, the hearer, awaiting what is expected to emerge, is in the dark like these two, approaching the villa's front door.

We hold still together on the threshold for an instant that is, subliminally, its own image. Beheld, it is – like us – momentarily without history or intimation of what is to come.

"Watch your step."

We have now passed beyond the coloured hall lights, through the moonlit rooms with their stone floors, bare walls and high ceilings. In this narrow passage to the roof, smelling of the local mountain quarries, we reach for each other, advancing hand in hand to maintain balance with the vertiginous momentum of the climb. Our only way is up.

Beyond the door, once blocking on rattling hinges, we are surprised by an evening such as any that's awaited with a burst of stars. The sky is immense, filled with unjoined points of brilliance abbreviating mythological presences. Here, before the starscape, one can truly breathe, vastly widening the torso – *your* torso suddenly felt, at last, as I inevitably hold you, strange shadow.

We are in one another's arms on the roof of Villa Bougainvillea. I feel your full force against me, palpitating in this sudden wave of Saharan heat invading the balmy summer evening. But we are obscure beside a trellis dense with climbing plants. Dim precipitates of our todays, surviving a life gone to pieces, living over a faultline, the scene of prior disaster, with a misalliance of tectonic plates, each is a void, and yet this vortex with the power to attract.

I am in the dark with you. But I make you out better than during the blinding summer day, here in ghostly moonlight. I am seeing more and more of you. Unsighted, we are drawn to each other, with raging desire erupting within us again. It is back, the feverish yearning for a form that has been out of focus – till, with this arresting recognition, I see it's for *you*.

A body blow, it awakens me to your reality. My lips set about confirming, tracing it by grazing the lids of your absent eyes. Our tongues swim into caverns of each other. Though soon, still blindly searching out one another, they stall.

Stopped, we cannot fathom our depths. We have lost our bearings on a seaward roof before a dark continent. Our hands are moving aimlessly over eerily lit surfaces, perhaps our selves.

We're drifting …

6

Awakened, each is troubled by what survives from sleep. It is hard to evade this inexplicable mournfulness, to unmask the dream's distorting charade. Only gradually does the feeling, the focus, start to fade. Even so, it isn't possible to drive them entirely out of reach. A detached part of one never forgets anything, emerging in fraught moments – a car crash – to resume an entire life in an instant.

Nothing lapses. It steals up in the blink of an eye, the merest moment of drifting off again. But it is long enough to release, once more, the pain from that undeclared, muffled drama in sleep coming upon us after the long Mediterranean summer day through which we have shouldered so much up to this terrace.

It is happening, too, on the succeeding nights we now sleep together. We are dreaming that dream in this darkness between us, reducing us to these shadows of ours on a roof.

And yet, night after night, we are suddenly, violently almost, in each other's arms again, stretched out here on the roof. I am convulsed by yearning. Legs entwined, I feel painfully sharp desire for you, so distant. Barely known, *un*known, from your other country, it is you I nonetheless crave: you who have given me my taste of myself through being with you – but have now gone to pieces like me. For pressed to this shoulder, on which I had all but regained you time after time for a tormentingly brief second, I cannot see you. I can't make you out. No, I cannot find you; you are quite lost to me.

Everything is black. The stars are extinguished. It is a total eclipse.

What remains from our phantom embrace? What else could it be but that fatal emotional gravity pulling irresistibly down to darkness in this villa, in which I plummet eyeless, as if blinded by sun?

Out from the deadness of sleep, a hand reaches. I feel it, this warmth, through which I am once more finding you touching me this evening, every night, on a roof from whose densely overgrown trellis there is something irrepressible extending across the tiles. For your nervous system is set off too, surging alarmingly on the covers where we are lying and you caress me.

I am awakening to myself here, despite coming back to this situation with a stranger. But insistent as is the fugitive stare, of recognition almost, with which we have fixed each other over these last days, as acute as may be the somehow shamefully dangerous need we have discovered through the look each other has opened up, what is this I am now hearing?

A low, protesting moan, it seems. Perhaps it is wind soughing through a villa poorly built with local materials, here on the arid foothills of mountains where trees are scant. Misshapen beams buckle, barely able to bear the load of so many years.

It might be a sound of distress, releasing long, pent-up misery now limbs are thrashing about, though less from desire, sheer passion, but as if forced by something within oneself. For are we not using the sharp urgency of our arousal after so long without sex to buoy us over the troubling novelty of this present situation?

"I'm sorry …"

The words almost say themselves. But maybe it's only from the cramp of a misplaced limb as, gently, her head falls onto his shoulder, which is finding itself, again tonight, weighed with the heaviness of a woman who must eventually detach from being with him on the terrace.

"... sorry ..."

The word returns as he holds her, as if gesturing: *I don't want to hurt you.* He supports her in the crook of his arm, this virtual spectre with the warm, pulsing weight. He will remain there, cradling her, not letting her go, so he implicitly promises. They will continue on the moonlit terrace for as long as they need to catch up with themselves; with who each is.

Immobile, they await, holding shadows. There is a lightness in their arms instinctively stretching, touching, entwining. They may be rousing later tonight, or on another of the succession of evenings they now spend together. Though it cannot matter exactly when they emerge from sleep: for profound, recurrent sleep is already effectively underway during waking, with its increasingly dwindling focus.

Again and again, they may be awakening from sleep that is not planned, ushered in, but unobtrusively arises within them. It permeates as if with hovering droplets, so luminous and fine, that they are not felt as sudden rain but taken for granted as their very atmosphere. Surfacing from it refreshed, they gently hold with such as they invisibly carry from that slumber, aroused to each in the *pueblo's* inky darkness.

Time does not exist. There is no before or after, no sense of passing days: only this, to which life has always been leading them. They are lost to each other, to themselves: the self each is, that presents itself. Increasingly, they are one. But the other's body quivers to the touch, unused to it, almost fearful. The skin rises to this soft caress. Its tiniest hair follicles mount with deepening, increasingly resonant, breathing.

Her nipples grow as he fingers them, circles them with his tongue. She, touching his sex, draws out a silky thread and, turning to lick the dome, allows it to slide into her mouth, while he turns to her pubis, so short in this summer heat, to run his tongue down the smooth, salty seam, widening, opening, more luscious with her increased panting.

Now there is a deepening intake and release of breath; a speeding up of heartbeats. They thud. And with their painfully strong embrace, there's a fierceness to their kissing.

The entry is inevitable, forceful despite this startling return of a self-abandoning fury in their lovemaking. It is again the void to which they are lost, the void each represents for another, for one another: the void each is to their self.

Approaching the climax, striving for wave after exquisite wave, unexpected sensations flood in. They surface from amnesia, dissolving like sea haze. The perfume he smells is unlocalised, but as undeniable as visions people see. It is so pervasive, so real, that it causes a sudden melting in his torso. His breathing is almost ecstatic as his hands, arms, once more hold her on the dark terrace.

While he lifts and sinks, rising and falling to her breasts, so warm, so pert, she catches something indefinable in him. She absorbs more and more of his atmosphere of meaningful muteness, filling her, in this sudden, explosive discovery of him coming here with her.

It surges, the massive wave booming on. It crashes in our temples as we are thrown tumbling out, naked.

We have stopped moving. Our limbs are slack. We have subsided, feeling now only the pull of a Mediterranean tide. In and out it sweeps, with the synchronised pulsing of our heartbeats, our respiration – till our awareness of it fades for tonight. It leaves just the increasingly infrequent smell of the kilometre-distant sea with its secret coves, the odours of lovers.

Who knows how long we continue awaiting what is to become of us, taking ourselves in, finally stretched out once more beneath the stars, the pair of us on the roof tiles, the rag covers, of Villa Bougainvillea?

PART IV

1

It is not dawn. It never is. But, in the accumulated coolness of the night, they always glimpse, from beneath the rag cover they have pulled over themselves on the roof terrace, a thinning of the nocturnal sky.

Stretching, then reaching for those summer clothes flung off prior to all they have been drawn into during hours naked with each other, they dress slowly, deliberately, in silence total but for the pulsing in their temples.

They go down the stairwell towards the kitchen and dining room. Without needing to switch on the light, they tread beyond the bedrooms, into the hall. They hold mutely together as she, out on the front step with him, once more turns the key in the front door of Villa Bougainvillea.

On they walk together, never questioning why he is not turning back to his *pensión*. Arm in arm, they again go up the alley letting them out at the plaza. They cross its deserted flagstones dawn after dawn which, unnoticed, has only then started breaking. Continuing some way up a side street, past the mayor's office, their pace slackens. Wordlessly, they halt.

He takes her in his arms. She rests her face against his shoulder, warm on what she once more recognises as a chill early morning. He kisses her head, hugging her tightly. Releasing her, returning that still stare, barely flinching, he feels her diverge. He remains there without moving as she continues the steep, narrow climb.

He is still there when she looks back, with a near-wave. And turning a corner, she has gone on her way back to El Castillo.

Slowly, he paces back to the plaza. He always crosses over to the *mirador*. Holding the wrought-iron railing with both hands, he will take a deep breath of the early air with that great prospect opening up before him.

Again, over the valley, he sees dawn dissolve the last remnants of darkness. He almost feels the pall being lifted. It rises from the hills, the small farms, the orchards.

But today his shoulders tense. He has a sense of oppression.

"Hello my friend."

The voice has emerged from the shadows. Bog Man has been sitting there all along, on a chair taken from the stack by the locked door of the café. As if magically materialising from his ghostly form in the darkness, he appears this morning through a sulphurous cloud of cigarette smoke. "Still here, are you?"

It's a good question, having also been Frank's. For although the end of his month's vacation is approaching, he knows his deepening affair with Paloma means he shall not leave the *pueblo* as he had a decade ago. That had been an impulsive flight; now it is instinctive to stay – which is why he telephoned the archive in London yesterday to request a significant extension of his holiday. ("Well, you haven't taken a vacation in years," his dry old supervisor said, unexpectedly helpful. "I imagine our vellum and parchment can hold out another month for you.")

So Frank responds to Bog Man with: "Oh, yes! I'm here, alright."

"Must be worth it. What's the outcome with her?" Bog Man says, walking up onto the lookout as if onto a stage. There is something provocatively crude about his near-nakedness in those brief shorts, over-washed shirt and worn sandals. Surely he, too, feels the chill in air wafting in from a lightening view from which his very presence, his provocative tone, is an unwanted distraction. "Has she opened up her treasure trove to you, dear boy? I'm sure you've had a good chance by now to see what she's offering … Well? Haven't you?"

Frank moves down the railing, away from the cigarette smoke and odours of alcohol, stale sweat and bad breath. He looks searchingly into first sunlight warming the soft flanks of the hills, seeking to abandon himself to that view of the valley with its orange and lemon groves, pomegranate trees and rows of maize. No longer hearing the voice, won't he turn back to find the speaker, too, has vanished?

Not so.

"Come, now! You can't be spending all this time together without her telling you what that driver fellow of hers revealed about our war criminal."

Frank goes on staring out at the horizon.

"Everything emerges eventually."

"Indeed," Frank says, turning back. He walks off through the plaza.

Paloma is always back in El Castillo so early that the maid has not yet arrived. She goes straight to bed in a household she is sure still cannot know where she has been, or with whom. Later, the smell of freshly brewed coffee will awaken her again, this time from dozing in her room during the last few hours. She follows it into the kitchen.

On this particular morning she finds Amalia there, with produce she has brought them from the farm supplying her restaurant. Capers, rosemary, garlic and lemons lie out on crumpled pages from the local paper. The maid stands at the stone sink washing clots of blood from a skinned rabbit as Amalia kisses Paloma. Then the two women sit at the kitchen table nursing their mugs, waiting for Magda to stop issuing her audible instructions to the gardener outside.

Now, as the maid finishes at the sink and goes out to hang washing on the lines in the back yard, Amalia puts a hand on Paloma's arm. "You know, you're Heidi's best friend. And I can only imagine how much you must care for her. But these days she's so unhappy. D'you have any idea why?

"Because things appeared to be going so well. She's struck up a very nice friendship with that polite Englishman staying with us at the *pensión*. It really seemed to be taking her out of herself. She's so serious. She works much too hard – just like her father. Though it finally looked as if she might have the chance of a life like everybody else.

"But all of a sudden she seems to be on her own again. I'm sure you know what I mean. She appears to have given up. I'm afraid she may just take off and leave everything behind. I'd hate to think anything's happening to prevent matters developing as they should.

"I'm depending on you, Paloma, her best friend, to make sure she has every chance to be happy. Because I know that if you love Heidi as Heidi loves you – and you know how much she *does*" – Amalia squeezes her hand again – "you'll realise how important it is to make sure she can take full advantage of her opportunities."

2

It is mid-morning. We have reunited at the villa, and leave the noisy bustle of the *pueblo* for the beach. Getting out of the rickety bus, we track down from the road, across sand and quartz-veined rocks glittering with mica. Wordless, as if by homing instinct, we make straight for the secluded cove. There we install ourselves with our towels, our lunch, our clothes and abandoned swimming costumes. We settle in the unheard static of the sea's restless roar, inattentive to repeated surges of water in this haze.

Somewhere, on an extended blur that is the horizon, a boat gleams. A bird, maybe a kite, flickers: an illusion vanishing in painful brilliance overhead. Other people, way off on the beach, like someone in a straw hat, are stick figures whom I find you glimpsing featurelessly in annihilating sunlight.

You, anonymous, intimate, are far apart from that remote world beyond our noiseless bay. In the stillness we find here, we are separate, too, from echoes within this overhanging shell of rock musty from the intrusions, the remains, of untold tides.

It is a secret cove: secret from ourselves. I do not tell you of any such place as I have known before. I do not tell myself.

We don't talk. We do not need to. Nor should we. This moment together, here, in our innermost space, conveys everything. It is complete. We shall always remember it as this. We always have. We have never forgotten it, holding one another like this.

It is the siesta hour. Nothing stirs, not here in the bedroom in the villa, which we have penetrated again.

There is not a sound. We hear no noises. We are aware of nothing but our breathing, the virtually imperceptible thuds of heartbeats behind the half-drawn jalousies. Here we lie in protective shadow, a mere few earthenware tiles away from the pattern of glowing sticks cast on the floor.

I run a hand over your leg, your sex still moist.

Darkness has deepened by the time I turn and shudder, awakening from our long doze. Instants later, I know it's you who is rousing also, in my arms. Evening is settling in. The *pueblo* is astir outside the shutters, the veranda beyond. Boys shout in the street. Their cries are close, but distant from us lying sealed from that present, all pasts, in our waking dream.

We find ourselves on the roof as night unfolds. Pigeons, doves in their cotes hereabouts, noisily resist finally settling down for the hours ahead. How busily they whir beyond the high trellis dark with creepers! But in this, our space, heavy with the fragrance of unseen jasmine, it is a low hum from another dimension. It's a sound our ears edit out till we are lying alone, lost to the immensity of the starry night, to a lonely sense of the isolation of our constellation, our world.

Cold, we draw up the rag covers. We huddle, submitting to the blissful extinction of all beyond our embrace.

We return to the villa again this mid-morning. Once more we lounge here without having bothered yet to gather into a single raffia beach bag our swimming costumes and towels, mineral water and lunch. We continue lazing on the settee with its plastic cover, *alpargatas* abandoned to the marble floor. What is holding us in each other's arms, dazed by the shaft of sunlight pouring in through half-opened shutters from the blinding blue?

We are suspended in barely furnished space. What more than ourselves does it contain?

Will Frank even notice charred remains of the newspaper in a fireplace dark from wood he has never seen burn on either this occasion, or on his only other in the *pueblo*? He does not take in the date on the remains of a page, which therefore cannot prompt him to dwell on what might have been happening at this hearth since he was first here.

Paloma bypasses the brass plates on our way into the hall. She touches one so idly that she barely feels the metal's coolness on her fingertips. She even misses him overlooking the North African decoration she does not trouble to remember has been in the villa since before she knew it, holding still in their embrace.

I do not probe your memory.

You do not enquire into mine.

I don't open up my own to myself, either.

It would be too hazardous, given what has come upon us in these last Andalusian summer days. Long yearned for, unthought of, it has changed everything so suddenly that there has been no time to take stock, to measure the risk, to gamble on the outcome. So we have not had a chance to find ourselves in a fragile, a delicate, situation.

Our being together needs protecting against whatever might disturb it. Nothing can be allowed to evoke my past love, so dangerous for you, for me. There is no place for the past at all since it did not include ourselves; the ones that we are.

Disconnecting from all that – and yes, from precedent for failure – we secure ourselves with each other by sleight of hand: a held moment. Sun irradiates a villa where we are locked in kisses, mindless of the schedule for buses to the beach. Traffic plies the hill unbeknown to us.

Such legerdemain it takes to protect us in the villa, our secret cove, during a siesta, lying on the roof! No questioning disturbs the light and the lovemaking; the stars, and our sleeping. We do not talk. What could we add to our silence?

3

Somehow it yields, the vision of a couple together in a room flooded with light from opened windows. Scarcely perceptibly this mid-morning, with the two of us no more moving, no more expressing ourselves than through our bodies' moist arousals, the image is passing.

Something uncradles us from our settee. Feet forsake *alpargatas* to detach themselves, naked, pace by pace, from the salon's marble floor. For beyond the boundary of our brilliant moment, we seem beckoned past these luminous limits, our protective sheath, into dimness unseen, till finding myself in the kitchen with you, taking the coffee percolator from its shelf, bringing out the bowls.

Hands draw on knowledge at our fingertips we had not recognised, busy in the sitting room. Unthinkingly they reach out and find the gas lighter, the spoons. Then, well water seeping through the grounds, they undo the shutters, the French windows, to admit light from the small veranda with that unkempt bougainvillea reaching in.

"You certainly know your way around."

We see more here in the kitchen, now seated at the table across from each other.

Oh, yes! I might have said it to myself, amid this vapour rising from our coffee bowls. It is as comfortingly enfolding as the mid-morning sun had been in the sitting room minutes ago. Yet the aroma filling our nostrils seeps so deeply into us that it invades the part that oriented our footsteps, our hands, as an invisible compass into this unacknowledged periphery.

Once more in this kitchen, brought back to light, you have been making coffee without speaking. Silence is our element. It has been coiling out from you all along, though I have not sought to question it, to submit it to the test of words. Mute, too, in the face of it – of you – I barely realise that something in me is wondering what it means to you, what it contains for you, what, in consequence, it holds in wait for me.

It is Franz who takes down the percolator from the kitchen shelf this morning. You quietly go about making the coffee without explaining that you will be doing this from now on. It has just become part of our habitual stillness, Paloma thinks, as her bowl is refilled day after day.

How long will it go on?

It is by being with you that I have entered this late silence, Frank supposes, sitting again at the kitchen table before the bowl Esther wordlessly fills. She sets the sugar before him. He places one cube upon another like dominoes, motionlessly observing them. We are waiting to see how long the two can maintain their balance.

I wonder where this silent moment, drinking coffee together morning after morning, is taking us. What are you thinking?

I don't ask, seeing the vagueness just stolen across your eyes; that occluding of the clarity with which they had been so much a part of the present. Why should I? For I too know, don't I, such heaviness descends from distracting images simultaneously appearing in the mind?

I assume your thoughts from this sudden flicker on your face, stricken as if by an instant's quivering of the ground. It is detonated by some quaking deep within. You too are unexpectedly experiencing the mid-morning brilliance quite differently.

Warming, vivid till just now, sunspots draw me into blackness swarming with photisms. Sightlessness so annihilates wellbeing that one is transfixed once more by the moment, the instant, when I saw everything I had come to with you was razed, feeling again in stunned silence the lack of being at all.

Frank gets up to close the French windows. After their previous night on the roof, he is heavy with the image of walking in scalding light before a bougainvillea-wreathed villa in which, from this day on, a decade ago, he will never more sit with her over coffee bowls at the kitchen table where he is still trying to understand how he now finds himself back with a young woman in the sun.

He throws her into shadow, suddenly ageless, featureless, shapeless. It casts all into the darkness that – now, years later, finally and fully – he sees he enters on leaving her, Esther, to spend lost years among subterranean manuscripts, on the Underground burying him ever deeper in the suburbs. He loses her again and again, leaving work in the false light of catalogued documents, eyes strained, to meet her illicitly each time he comes upon another woman in London.

Eventually all alone, he is in solitary confinement for some undisclosed crime, this unacknowledged Bluebeard, serial exterminator of women, surviving, like other long-term offenders, a living death one day at a time. Yet do they, sleeping away the morning, the afternoon, no less than night in a continuous light doze, quite outwit the sensation of existing? Can they ever evade the raw feeling of non-existence? Or does the prisoner, like a suffocating man drinking in air more precious the longer he is denied it, clutch tenaciously in spite of so many wasted years at the surviving feeling of being alive?

Though, beneath the blanket under which he has buried himself so long, maybe he also fears what it will be like when he is released. What will remain, not least of himself? Will it be worth having? Does he not doubt his capacity to have a life at all? Can he so much as *be* in the open air; the bright sunlight?

Is life awaiting him, through thick and thin, wonders Frank back here in Villa Bougainvillea with the woman who, in an access of tenderness, he recognises his dark thoughts have cast into the kitchen's heavy shadow.

Paloma stares from her stool at the sink where she had found a single drained coffee cup that mid-morning, the scorching glare of which made her shun it for darkness such as this. Here, where there is nothing, no one, only shadow, the wild alarm flares up again, seeing you are gone.

I am realising, I finally know, you are gone, truly gone. Then there is simply the deadened dimness into which everything falls. It is the feeling of having lost the life force, as Franz put it.

I am answering your question to the woman who has been sitting over coffee at the kitchen table with a man striving to come to himself, to pull himself together through conversation with you after long in the shadows.

"What did he tell you during your hours together here in Villa Bougainvillea?"

Isn't that when we began to talk? For did it not start with this answering of the questions asking themselves through us?

Paloma comes out of the troubled vacuum her thoughts have been producing in her. Only now does she realise how tightly she has been holding her coffee bowl. Putting it down carefully, afraid of what might spill over, she is thinking aloud about the man emerging from his decades of collapse.

He might have been emerging from a dream. He still was not fully in control of his thoughts or sure of his memories. He just seemed to have moods floating past like clouds. I let him continue coming back to himself naturally. Although I was supposed to be there to look after him, the moods somehow invaded me too, like this aroma of coffee enveloping me again with the man alongside whom I am finding myself.

I never asked him anything, despite Heidi's insistence. I am not sure how much he would have remembered anyway, after all those lost years in the airless dimness of his Russian psychiatric prison hospital. I just let him speak whenever something in him was ready to emerge, surfacing like islands following a sub-oceanic eruption. Thereupon he relapsed into immense habitual silence. That is when he told me about losing the life force. It was like falling apart from a solar system. You're a random object shunted around – till halted in cold, damp vacancy.

What is this feeling? We are trying to come to terms with it, seeking now to disentangle together whether Franz was referring to the times when Speer took cover in copses, in roadside ditches, with his adjutants, apart from the drivers, during air raids. Or were these the dark hours, the endless nights, spent in the equal gloom of an institution on Russia's tundra, moist and dank?

Could this be the feeling of both, the dim woodland outside Berlin and the sub-Siberian gloom; something repeating itself, never overcome, dispelled, but invading any new situation, even this Andalusian villa in the glittering freshness of the Mediterranean, denying any chance of change, of renewal, of living free?

We want to know. And it is knowledge we seek in the case of Speer too, abandoned also to that wood, then to his prison cell – and maybe even on his release to his parents' home in Heidelberg.

So what *has* been revealed of Speer? Paloma does not know. No, she did not ask, and Franz did not tell. The most she can say, to Heidi's fury, is that he was in a carpool serving important people. Even so, did he disclose nothing – not in any way? Did he shed no light on Hitler's friend, here in this bougainvillea-wreathed villa where, despite the brilliant Andalusian sunlight, the Mediterranean's fresh salt breeze, he continued striving through dark Dutch images to recover submerged land, to reclaim sodden, black, heavy-smelling earth?

4

Bruno invites the Englishman for a drink. Paloma is not included – or apparent, now. Having skilfully stolen away to her room, she has evaded her father, abruptly suspending his irascible piano practice on recognising the older man accompanying his daughter again to El Castillo at dusk.

The mother holds back, too. Hovering by Bruno as he played in their expectant final minutes before the couple's recently customary arrival, Magda has just turned off the light in the music room. She has thrown it – herself – into gloom for the men to drink not by the piano this time, but on the patio. Still there, scarcely a shadow in the gathering darkness, she can overhear, oversee, from behind the blackness of the glass, a conversation she is enabling, promoting, not least with this illusion of her absence.

I am hardly inclined to drink wine in the day's accumulated heat, after hours of lovemaking in the shuttered villa. Not that I should be wary of conversation alone with a man whom I am surely only encountering coincidentally on delivering a friend – yes a friend – at twilight as a piano sounds; leaving her at a threshold where, as anyone can see, I never linger before returning downhill through the *pueblo* to my single room in the dark.

Who could suspect our rapidly tightening bonds, these feelings deepening as swiftly, as obscurely, as the night, I ask myself, witnessing in my mind's eye, as Bruno's proxy, a couple from without. It provides an instant's illusion of being detached from her, after all; of protecting myself from any possibility of claustrophobic closeness, from collapse into a permanent, suffocating embrace.

An emotional safety net, it somehow leads me to suspect, too, the authenticity of what has come upon us. Perhaps our attachment simply testifies to the primitive power of repetition; as if unfinished business were an objective entity with the capacity to manoeuvre me, a pawn, without will or consent, into a replay of my aborted affair with Esther.

It's a passing doubt. Haven't I come to Paloma older, more knowing, less a stranger to myself – my submerged self, which, rising to fuller stature on my return here, can, far from being overwhelmed again, respond fully to Paloma?

Despite which, instinctively certain that her father is not casually inviting me, her older, foreign lover, for a glass of wine, but issuing a summons that cannot be refused, I still teeter within, taking a wrought-iron chair on the patio. Regardless of my protective politeness and *savoir faire*, my very poise, I feel exposed without Paloma. My host has taken her absence so much in his stride that I cannot but presume the tenor of discussion he plans to have with me alone, obviously her lover.

Yes, I am in danger of losing my balance, my centre of gravity, for all my English, my academic, conversational skills. There is a plummeting in the pit of my stomach, tumbling into the void shared with the young woman – herself drawn to it by the long-term prisoner of war still coming to himself while looking with her at seventeenth-century Dutch paintings of lost land reclaimed.

Bruno sits mutely with Frank, eyes shifty. It is as if, searching for how to begin, he is again lost in that inner space he falls into when practising, unable to find himself in the piece where he is abandoned to an invisible, tightening labyrinth. He is seeking for a way to begin a conversation that somehow has to happen.

"So – o," Bruno says, as if his mind is actually on something other than raising the one subject they have shared throughout their brief, if hardly trivial, acquaintance. "You didn't think much of Speer's biography, did you?"

"It's perfectly good," Frank says dismissively of a work he read in that recent but now remote time before all that has been happening so swiftly, so totally, to him and Paloma. "Workman-like. But … are you reading it?"

"God, no! Least of all these days. Especially since you say it takes such a negative view of the man and whether he finally overcomes his darkness ... Though," Bruno goes on, drawing himself up, "let me ask you a question".

Frank is not certain whether he is actually voicing *yes*, alert as he is to what he expects his lover's father to start saying.

"You say you're an historian." Then, on another expiring, actually anti-climactic breath, Bruno goes on: "Haven't *you* considered writing a book about Speer? Devoting yourself to a *Life* would surely be a good way of spending your time."

This question, articulated now by my host, has actually been asking itself of me for some time. So although Bruno does not wait for an answer, complaining instead about another day without water in this damn *pueblo*, I respond inwardly.

I have recently suffered no constraint in thinking about Speer. I have joined the historians considering him, even identifying their limitations. And when speaking to others about the man, I found myself doing so with ease. Naturally, my insights have not been based on any archival research; it is as though I have received what I read in bargain basements and on the terrace clairvoyantly. I, its conduit, have had the sensation of living it.

I cannot, however, help regarding that continuous flow as recorded. Written by me, paragraph after clearly developed paragraph, it already contains the germ of an argument I have the illusion of advancing in the book I have just glimpsed I've always had in me. It is the very project I have been searching for by Pensión Amalia's potted jasmine and restless cockatoo, but which I am only now realising, sampling wine here with Bruno on his nocturnal patio, has actually lain in wait for me during my breakfasts, distracted midmornings, and evening tours of the *pueblo*, all a mere stone's throw from Villa Bougainvillea.

It has been growing in my mind throughout the decades of reading defunct late medieval records, preparing a monograph initiated – if not owned – by Professor Keller, Sir Emil, who, as I openly take up my secret subject (despised by him), cannot lay claim to.

Of course, no magic wand has suddenly endowed me with linguistic skills by whose lack I had barred myself long ago from undertaking the historical research for a volume on such a topic. It is, rather, that I have a dawning sense – a conviction, actually – of coming to terms at last with issues focused by Speer's life, his predicament, the man himself. And I find them recorded less in documents, which in any case I cannot read, or even in remaindered paperbacks I never bought, than at a fundamental level of who I am, as one's genetic characteristics are invisibly imprinted on the book that is oneself.

Not that I necessarily assume this can form the basis for writing and publishing an academic work, least of all conventional history. Though I am not dwelling, as I listen here with half an ear to Bruno beside me, on what specifically I might do. Yet what I know for certain is that I have myself emerged into clarity, freedom from whatever continues to trap Paloma's father. It gives me the advantage. And it makes me see, finally, that, while this is the second time I have encountered the father of a lover in the *pueblo*, it is the first in which, sitting here as conversation wanes while each of us quietly takes in the presence of an absent woman, I am neither sheepish nor intimidated.

Now, in the evening's darkness, comes the sound of a throat being cleared. Bruno has sipped from his glass to wash down some pill he has taken. Then Frank finds him coming finally to the point for which he has surely invited him to a drink.

"I want to talk to you about my daughter."

Not about *Paloma*: it is, rather, the possessive, releasing acid in Frank's stomach despite his previous moment of self-confidence and Bruno's quietly tentative tone.

Treading carefully, Bruno says he does not want to seem moralising, though, with an indicative backward movement of his shoulder, he supposes Paloma's mother might. But it's obviously not natural, he is sure Frank will agree, that a vulnerable young girl should have been drawn into an affair – if affair it was – with a man so much her senior. It could obviously never have come to anything. It was the height of irresponsibility. And despite Paloma's courage and appearance of having got over it, she is still in pain. So they, her parents, are anxious that nothing should impede her slow recovery. Which is why they are both asking Frank, whom they know has become trusted, and close to her lately, and must obviously have her best interests at heart, to shield her from … well, anything untoward.

There's a creak. Frank feels, not notices, a movement in the father's dark study.

Part V

1

The landward side of the *pueblo* is less developed than that facing the sea. It is the memory of what the rest has forgotten. Its carob trees, seeming to grow out of the mound on which the place is built, their roots protruding from the crumbling earth, dumbly recall a civil war in which famine forced the few remaining villagers to eat the overhanging seed pods, normally fed only to pigs.

The wretched, the "peeled", as they and their impoverished descendants are known, survived in these shacks that have remained barely changed since the '30s. They are not sought after by visitors wanting sea views in the houses they buy and restore. The unpaved track between them is deserted except by bored infants, mongrels and flies.

Only Heidi is walking through this abandoned quarter. She is avoiding crowds such as those in the plaza, with its café and *mirador*, avoiding people clogging the streets giving onto the Mediterranean. She can yield to her need to escape the close atmosphere of her mother's *pensión*, savouring her solitude at this equivocal hour, hovering between afternoon and evening, out on a path now ascending beyond these dwellings. It offers a glimpse, just here, of a road on the *pueblo's* other side leading up to what surmounts the village: El Castillo.

Paloma and that new older friend of hers, the English historian, tend to return there at dusk. But they are not who Heidi glimpses now. It is somebody more immediate, suddenly before her among the parched vegetation where goats clank and feed. He looms like a satyr on Greek vases she has seen with her father in Berlin's Altes Museum, the long, white neoclassical structure of which surely inspired Speer's more inflated architecture. Terracotta on black, with tail, hooves and rampant sexuality alarmingly exposed, the image is instantly imprinted by Heidi on Bog Man now halted in sandals and shorts to grimace as much as smile in greeting.

Taken aback, she then wonders if he, cigarette in hand, has just taken in the couple of whom she has been denied sight. For he says, without introduction: "I don't know how you can stand it. Coming here, well, it must be terrible punishment for you. Surely you're not putting up with it any longer."

Is he simply referring to the seasonal crowds she is evidently seeking to evade here in this neglected part of the *pueblo*, who make life much less pleasant than in a modern, civilised place like Germany? Or, having just seen Paloma and her friend arriving at El Castillo, is he – recognising Heidi's misery at their intensifying relationship – adding salt to the wound? Having known her summer after summer since infancy, Bog Man long ago intuited her nature, her love for Paloma.

Is it so evident? she asks herself, shying away from his – from anybody's – probing eye. She does not answer him. She walks away, leaving the satyr to take her in, probing lasciviously as he continues standing there, smoke coiling up from his cigarette.

Bog Man is a provocation. His words also provoke Heidi: she will leave. The thought has been in her mind for some time, but more as an intermittent, despairing mood. Now it's a decision, though not to depart early for Berlin. That would mean leaving Paloma altogether, not seeing her again until the following summer, if then. It is, rather, to spend a brief while apart; just a few days, regrouping as she has on previous summers, which she has even more need to do this year for reasons she will have time to ruminate on, driving off in her mother's car.

Amalia lends it willingly, doubting she will miss it. Most of her time is spent in the *pensión*. For the rest, she'll manage with lifts from neighbours of nearly a lifetime in the *pueblo*. After all, her daughter, always tense but more so than usual lately, would clearly benefit from a break – which, happily, does not involve leaving Spain prematurely. And she can stay with her sister, Heidi's aunt, in Granada.

This is something that Heidi has no intention of doing. She heads for somewhere not far from the city, though it might as well be a hundred miles away as far as her mother is concerned. It has nothing to do with the protective domesticity Amalia has in mind, which her daughter fears would be claustrophobic. It is where Heidi will meet Rebecca, despite her mother's reservations about this German friend, no less implicit than those she somehow discloses about Heidi herself.

Heidi's true destination need not, of itself, make Amalia suspicious, of course. The famously picturesque place for which she is actually heading is an undeniably desirable goal. All sight of the Mediterranean is left behind as she sets out across the arid plain, its riverbed dried up as on a planet where water existed only in an irrecoverably distant time.

Has life ever even been here? Heidi wonders passingly among the archaic remains.

Hardly realising it, I have begun an ascent. I go on climbing. The countryside grows greener. I breathe in air much fresher than in the desiccated desert *pueblo*. I make out a lingering white crest on that slope of the Sierra Nevada, whose winter snow melted through spring to create this high altitude oasis.

For clinging to this southern flank of that great range are mountain villages with terraced farmland. Driving up through their vineyards and flowering almond trees, between orange and lemon orchards, I pass the Berber-style houses running down in sheltered valleys with deep gorges all the way to the sea. They are clustered like grey-white boxes, produce set out to dry on their flat clay roofs with tall chimney pots. I take in the redness of tomatoes and peppers, drinking in the air – till jolted by an unevenness in the road. I am made aware again of what, despite losing myself in the verdant landscape, its balmy atmosphere, I am still carrying within me from before.

Or am I? Just think of what I have left behind. By the very act of coming here, haven't I shrugged off the agony of being denied by Paloma, of witnessing her increasing closeness to the Englishman?

What will be made of my departure? Will my courage in letting go of my impossible feeling, the unbearable situation, be recognised? Will my self-sacrifice on accepting such an unacceptable reality be appreciated? I will hardly be missed by those less clear-seeing, who must ultimately fare no better than me. Paloma is again throwing herself into an impossible relationship with an older man, someone on a mere month's vacation. He has embarked on a liaison at most with one too much younger for it to last. Don't they yet realise they're both bound to be hurt, that they should count their losses sooner rather than later?

Of course not! They are in the midst of their love. Nothing exists outside it for them. I doubt that they have even sensed the chill awaiting them on exiting one another's arms. How can they know they have been cursed with such a love? For love is a raging fever that never burns itself out. It eats one up, working beneath that imperturbable surface on which the rest of the world goes about its mundane business. The thought possesses me as I peer at the sunny view of where I am headed, for respite from what I know must always torment me.

Others cannot possibly appreciate how considerate I am being to Paloma by removing myself from the *pueblo* for these few days. Most won't even know of the love that I – being so private – would never dream of advertising. Nor could those suspecting it, including Paloma herself, understand how keenly, just how sharply, I feel it – and recognise my sacrifice on withdrawing.

But then they will not see my tenderness for the girl, either. How can they recognise my protectiveness in wanting to shield her from potentially hurtful situations such as that between her and the Englishman from whose periphery I am retreating? My concern, if Paloma were to feel it, might make her more appreciative of me, readier to embrace all the love I have to offer, instead of falling into a succession of fated amorous traps.

Yet such is the tenderness I have had to pack up in my weekend bag and take away not only from Paloma's latest liaison, but from the girl herself. To continue in her presence with such troubling feelings, regardless of whether she is alone or not at this particular moment, would be to hover awkwardly, making myself irritating, resented.

I could tell myself it is just a matter of dignity, a horror at making myself evidently vulnerable; a refusal to be humiliated. But the truth is far worse. This would be as much, if not more isolating than to leave altogether. For this is the very loneliness striking me as I drive through the now somehow melancholy tranquillity of the sunlit countryside. With whom can I share my feelings?

Well, at least there is Rebecca. She has known ever more about my predicament, Paloma, over the years – until it has reached these proportions, becoming this pain I am now carrying up to her, beyond those farmhouses into a cluster of public buildings. Here is the mayor's office, the bank, the police station. It is the town where my friend lives.

2

The town is dominated by a square tower. Erected in the late nineteenth century, it is in the style of the Alhambra. The adjoining building, also part of the spa hotel, is of the same period. It extends in a line down the sloping road, with a score of regular, room-size domed windows, each with its pantile roof and tree before the inclining balustrade.

People come year after year from Spain and abroad, for therapies making use of the health-giving water melted from the Sierra Nevada. It can be drunk from any of the fountains in the hotel's gardens. But for those wishing to walk in the pleasant year-round microclimate, it also gushes from five natural springs spread around the town. There the visitor can find equal refreshment for the soul, with a quotations on tiles from one of the nation's great poets.

Rebecca's family has owned the spa hotel for generations. But she studied in Germany, where she met Heidi. Fellow university students, they became close in the days before Heidi's mother divorced and came to the *pueblo* to open Pensión Amalia.

Heidi arrives in the late afternoon. She embraces Rebecca in the hotel foyer, with its smell of eggs from the spa water. Hans, an old German member of staff, holds her weekend bag beside them. Heidi knows him from her previous visits here, as well as from occasions when he has come up from the beach to her mother's *pueblo* during holidays of his own. Rebecca directs him with her eyes across Heidi's shoulder to a corridor. So she will stay in a room in the hotel, not in her friend's apartment.

Yet there is no chance for her to go there now. Kurt, Rebecca's husband, has just appeared. Tall and athletic in his track suit, as befits the proprietor of a "Wellness Centre", he greets their guest enthusiastically, inviting her to make full use of the health facilities. Clients enjoy them so much that they come season after season. Bookings have soared. They have even completed a highly successful extension to the hotel.

"I'm sure you'll be impressed", he says, leading Heidi off to have a look. "This is exactly the time of day to see it."

They cross the foyer, passing the marble staircase, and soon come out into the ballroom. Its glass chandeliers and gleaming floor bear testimony to an elegant previous époque. Then they walk alongside the large swimming pool, its walls decorated with mosaics and sculpted tritons. It grows more humid; the air is sulphurous. They have entered the treatment centre with its mud baths, hot tubs, steam-inhalation cabinets and electrotherapy rooms.

Kurt points it all out. And Heidi says "yes" to each in turn. But she has always disliked being informed, especially on guided tours, preferring to discover things for herself. Kurt, tall Kurt, friendly Kurt, is overbearing, claustrophobic – especially since Heidi is aching to be alone with Rebecca, opening up to her about her latest feelings.

Surely she could have averted the husband's intrusion, postponed their review of this clinically white modern extension into which she is being led. I would be just as pleased to find myself with Rebecca in the cramped student accomodation we once shared, she thinks, as in this suddenly spacious meeting room with its glass wall like those in other suites giving onto the dramatic view.

Heidi takes in the undeniably superb sunset over that southern flank of the Sierra Nevada. The mountain is tinged by the spectrum of the tentatively advancing evening. Yet it could not feel more external to her. It continues, separate, through coldly transparent plate glass, in a long moment of deepening shadow and silence that Kurt, evidently awed on everyone's behalf, might be content to go on and on despite his visitor's longing for it to end and to be alone with the presence she acutely senses rather than sees: his wife.

Darkness has engulfed the view. The window is eclipsed. There is the sound of breathing. Kurt moves away to turn on the light: painfully bright. "Well," he says, "I'll leave you two girls to each other."

Heidi has supper in the hotel restaurant with Rebecca and her eight-year-old son. He is on holiday from his boarding school in

Germany with a friend. The boys conduct an incomprehensible, giggling conversation during the adults' silence.

The meal over, they are left to their own devices as the women walk into the gardens. These, too, offer views beyond their ink-black hedges. Starry sky spreads widely all around; the farms below are scatterings of lights.

There is the sound of a fountain playing with the health-giving water that guests not only sample from beakers chained to the ceramic pedestal, but also submerge in. For Heidi is taking in the pair of marble baths standing on gravel, surrounded by rose bushes. They appear Roman even by moonlight, with their carvings and metal fittings.

It brings back sharing a bath with Rebecca when they were students: a closeness, she thinks, she badly needs with her here again.

It wells up in me once more. Our bodies float, weightless. Separation dissolves, transmitting all I have had to hold within me – although marble, I'm jolted into recognising, stands between us after all. It is no more porous than the cranium holding my emotions, my thoughts, all I am. Each of us is, at most, in her separate bath.

Though, no. We stand apart from them, aside from each other, hearing water that once enfolded us, drew us together, leak out of the fountain and waste itself, drip into the drain. Has Rebecca, I worry, unremembered our closeness? Has she, in marrying Kurt, in giving birth to their son, shut the door imperceptibly more and more each year on feelings we shared, but that have survived in me, at least, only with a new, painful focus – Paloma? And is this the summer in which, now I am finally resolved to withdraw from the girl for good and most need my friend's support, to be the one in which Rebecca has at last decided to turn her back on me?

Maybe coming here was a fiasco. Or is Rebecca still inclined to listen, to understand? Is she open to talking about unattainable love?

I wonder all this anxiously, drawing myself up to speak in the nocturnal hush, a calm so different from my turmoil. But I must settle on how, on where, to begin. I need to pluck up courage to risk Rebecca's indifference. Yet now, an instant later, I realise I have already done so, plunging in with: "Everything's the same as the last time I was here."

I sigh as if in deep relaxation at the changeless night view, the plashing fountain, the fragrant flowers – and being here together after all these years. Yes, everything is well between us, close as we remain, I mean, allowing time for the unspoken words to float and Rebecca to agree.

"The same?" she murmurs.

But in the pregnant pause for an answer to suggest itself, I recognise that sameness is also terrible for me. My love is an unending torment. It is the butt of another's perpetual refusal to acknowledge and accept, let alone return, it. This will never change. Never.

There's rustling; flowers rocked overhead; lights flickering in the valley.

Rebecca hugs her arms in the breeze, saying: "Things seem unchanged – on the surface. But nothing stays the same."

Her eye is on the fountain, rivulets gusted onto its marble base, never playing with the same water. Channels run from it, irrigating herbaceous boarders where even perennial plants are replaced in time. Boyish laughter erupts, somewhere in the dark gardens.

"You can't have children and fail to feel the changes time brings – in yourself as well as them."

The voices fade. Silence, utter silence, holds until the women's ears have time to adapt to the night's noises. Quite still, beside one another, Heidi and Rebecca are drawn in this eerie instant beyond tree-fringed gardens, up into the distance, eyes lost in utter obscurity.

The dark mountain's snow melts into a rapid river, watering the surrounding farms, making the whole area verdant. Racing down the valley, it empties into sea, flooding one of the world's oceans.

"Don't get stuck in your feelings," Rebecca warns, only too aware of the emotional preoccupations of someone who has become increasingly synonymous with them during the time they have known each other. "Let the tide of life carry you. Who knows what – or who – might lie in store? Move on."

"That's exactly what I'm trying to do. It's why I've come here."

"But make sure when you're closing the door on her that it's what you're really doing. You may think you're penalising her, angrily, but actually secretly slamming it on yourself as a punishment for failing in love. Listen, Heidi, if you lock yourself out of life everything really would stay the same – till the day you die."

I am taking the treatments offered by the spa during times I am left to myself. In the steam room, the hot tub, I keep returning to how I have eventually come to see an impossible love as just that, finding the strength of mind to turn away from it by joining Rebecca to escape what is taking place in the *pueblo*.

Yet submerging myself in a bath for my thoughts of her to go blank, I find instead they are still heavy with the long-standing strain of believing in what cannot be. And expecting to be free of it on surfacing from this amniotic sac, I am winded by a vertiginous sense of nothingness opening out – and within.

I breathe deeply, to come to myself. Then I wonder if Paloma and the Englishman will also renounce such a love. Can they discover what one needs to be in order to open oneself up to what's possible – assuming it is in one's nature?

Rebecca finally joins me in the afternoon. We sit together by the side of the swimming pool. She deftly manages to steer conversation away from anything personal to me. It is gossip, strange news – but through which I am now finding her unintentionally talking precisely about my morning's theme: whether or not people are ultimately able to go beyond the past.

3

Heidi drives back from the fertile enclave. Speeding through the parched plain, she heads up to the *pueblo* atop its mound of white houses. It holds there, the Moorish village, a frame from a film. Still, silent, it is caught in the brief unreal light between sunset and evening. Viewed this long, ever closer, the image reverberates with expectancy. It is the picture of a *pueblo* anxiously awaiting the intelligence Heidi is delivering at this very moment from her days with Rebecca at the spa.

Several people in the *pueblo* have heard what Heidi has come to know. Or they claim to have done so, sometimes even without Heidi's intervention. Take Bog Man. He has lived in the area, some say, since before, the end of the war. He hints darkly at Germans living in the near vicinity and of being aware through the grapevine of things that pass invisibly to others across his keenly monitored field of vision.

Amalia also hears what Rebecca reported; it has not taken long for her to learn what her daughter's friend has told her. Such is its impact on Heidi that she has shared it regardless of her mother's opinion of Rebecca.

Amalia, for her part, instantly feels morally obliged to pass it on to Magda. How could the mother of Paloma not want to know it? And Bruno himself is thereby informed, as he has signalled to Frank.

Indeed, Frank is the one who will hear the story most fully and clearly, although he is surely the last with whom one would expect Heidi to communicate. For Frank Ward is the friend, the older lover, surely, of Paloma, and thus *persona non grata*. But then he is also the polite English historian with whom Heidi has been able to have her most rational, professional conversations about Albert Speer and his driver, starting on Pensión Amalia's terrace.

Frank is having breakfast in bright sunlight, overlooking the sea. He has returned from seeing Paloma to El Castillo at dawn. So used is he to being with her nowadays, though it has been barely two weeks since they met, that he feels strangely weightless with only this squawking cockatoo for company. It is as if part of him is not here but with her, as if the remains are somehow exposed; that his movements, pouring coffee, are lighter, less substantial, lacking.

Not without regret, however, he now notices a neighbour after all. For she has reappeared on the terrace after an absence of several days. Politeness forces him to overcome his self-absorption and talk to the brittle, highly charged woman. He has to search within himself for a subject of conversation, needing to avoid the one topic they actually have in common but that most strains Heidi: Albert Speer, and what his chauffeur revealed about the master during his months at Villa Bougainvillea with Paloma.

"Good morning. Welcome back. And what a beautiful day it is. But of course every day is fine here, isn't it?"

Then Frank, chancing on his subject, says that with such perfect weather there's no wonder that British outposts developed along Spain's southern coast even before the war. The owners of mining, railway and electricity companies, all the way between Barcelona and Gibraltar congregated ritually at their golf clubs.

Is it patriotism that makes Heidi remark, almost as a correction, that German communities have existed since that time, too? But of course there was a significant further influx in the last days of the war and just after, given a nominally neutral Franco's actual sympathy for the Axis. By now they, together with their children, have spread out from Madrid and the Costa Brava. Yet there are still concentrations of them if one looks below the surface, as in the area Heidi says she has been visiting.

For Germans love spas such as that in the town where she stayed. The family have owned it for generations, just as their compatriots have had their farms and estates nearby for decades. The spa is so successful that people book from Germany seasons in advance. This was the case with someone whom Heidi goes on to explain to Frank her friend Rebecca told her about.

Frau Müller actually came from England for ten days the previous year. Still attractive in middle age, this reserved woman had a different name on her passport – although the hotel and the few Germans nearby visiting her continued to call her "Frau Müller".

She and her adult daughter spent their time silently taking the treatments. Then they rested for hours on extended chairs set out in the glass-fronted annex overlooking the mountains, or else in the gardens gazing down at the valley.

One day, a clerk at the hotel's registration desk came to see Rebecca in her office. He said a dishevelled workman was asking, in a mixture of broken Spanish and halting German, to see Frau Müller. Should he admit him?

Rebecca asked the woman, then in the spa. Frau Müller agreed. Dismissing her daughter, she sat in her bathrobe alone with the visitor. They were inaudible by the large, rumbling swimming pool, dazzling with its shifting surface of sunlight and blue. But then they hardly appeared to be talking during the entire time they spent together. How long might they have continued in silence, had the daughter not joined them after an hour?

The following morning, a car drove up to the hotel. It was an old black Mercedes, driven by Frau Müller's visitor. He opened the back door for her, then expertly circled round to open the opposite one for the daughter. Off he drove them, heading for the looming mountain. They did not return for lunch. Sunset was far advanced by the time they returned.

The driver held open the door for his passenger to get out of the Mercedes, followed by her daughter. He stood by the car, remaining there while she climbed the marble steps to the hotel. She halted at the entrance, looking back at the man. She nodded in acknowledgement as he inclined his head.

The journey over, the chauffeur's role complete, the man moved as the revolving door swept his passenger away. He got into the black car. It now finally conveyed him into darkness.

Frau Müller was also collected one day by a local resident known to Rebecca. He himself drove mother and daughter in a sports car for lunch at his villa, set among kilometres of trimmed olive trees. The estate was just as he had inherited it. His father was an aviation engineer who – having worked for the German Minister of Armaments – went on to establish himself successfully in Madrid in the '40s. He had once invited to this Andalusian retreat the man who, at that time in the 1970s, was a best-selling author and international celebrity. And the conservatively elegant, detached Frau Müller, visiting the villa with the son all these years later, had been the newly acquired lover once accompanying Albert Speer there.

This was rumoured, if not actually known, among the local German community. It included an oddjobs man, a gardener, an occasional driver, recently surfacing in the area. He had apparently learned of the woman's presence from a hotel employee, some ex-POW from Russia like him – although it was likely he had heard much earlier by bush telegraph in his *pueblo* that she had reserved her stay at the spa hotel.

Soon after Frau Müller left, her visitor, the occasional driver, left too. But not many noticed the absence of what had always in any case appeared a taciturn, vacant near-vagrant. Did people even give it a thought when, months later, a man was washed up on the Mediterranean beach into which this valley runs?

Only now, yet later, has he been tentatively identified as Franz.

Part VI

1

The villa is dark and silent. Drunken voices in some bar are less echoes from the further side of the *pueblo* than of another world. Within, a shadow searches bare marble walls drained by pale moonlight. He leaves their bedroom, once more a deserted space, returning to the entry hall where, flicking the switch, he releases sudden colours from the brass Arab lamp. For a while Frank waits there, standing at the front door, peering out from the tangled growth by the outside steps. Then he turns in and goes upstairs.

There is a creak much further within: the sound of ascending footsteps, a door being yanked open. He is moving on the roof. Seeking his ghostly counterpart, he comes to the side to search the road. But he is alone, except for barking he attracts from an adjoining roof terrace. Frank gazes intently, repeatedly looking up and down the street. It remains deserted. Eventually, arms held limply before him on the edge of the roof terrace, he stares vaguely, out to sea.

Later, the barking has ceased. The hall is dark again. Moonlight engulfs the entire villa as the front door opens for Frank to appear, empty-handed. He descends the stone steps, past the bougainvillea, and heads into the street.

Frank reverts to a recently abandoned habit of walking around the *pueblo*. Hardly deciding to, he cannot help travelling through the late evening, once more passing the villa where he has failed to encounter the woman: the villa where they make love, where he has made love since the start; the villa – *their* villa – from which he is actually as detached now as from the music in the wine bars he passes. He does not hear it, recognising instead that tonight he is missing the usual strivings on a piano.

He plucks up the courage to break away from circulating through these roads, continuing on the rising path to Paloma. She will be ensconced with her parents, won't she, in El Castillo? He has never visited there at such a late hour.

It is sudden resolve, firmness of character that he has been realising this summer he long wanted to possess; finally finding it, holding to a woman on terms he seemed incapable of, here in this *pueblo*, its villa, with that lover leaving him, decades ago.

Bog Man sidles up to Frank from the dark *mirador* as he makes his way again through the empty plaza.

"How's Paloma taking the news of Franz's death?"

Frank has to accept that his relationship with her is common knowledge as Bog Man wonders, his breath stale with tobacco and wine, if she is as distressed as when her first "mature" partner unexpectedly left her.

"Of course, I predicted it at the time. And I knew," he reveals with smug pride, "Franz was sure to disappear the moment I told him the once-young woman, in whose arms his master, Speer, had died in London, was expected at a spa hotel near Granada. I'd been tipped off by one of its old German porters holidaying here."

Frank does not answer. He has no response. He stares at the starlight over mute mounds. There are only his anxieties as to what the reply might be. Not that he would share it if he knew it, or that he needs to. Bog Man has evidently already shaped the answer he wants, and so has no need of the girl's lover before him, braving his breath. Having him here, with Bog Man all but saying Paloma feels a misery that is terminal for the Englishman's relationship, serves only to provide a welcome opportunity to inflict pain, Frank knows.

He walks away.

Even at this distance, Frank sees the lights are on in El Castillo. There is a brightness in the night over the garden, with its dark screen of pantiled walls and trees. A lamp glows by the front gate through which Frank now makes out voices. He hears Bruno arguing with Magda as he is about to ring. But pausing a moment for them to quieten, he finds the door opened by a youth.

"Ah!" Bruno says, "I was just about to send a servant to the *pensión*, asking you to come over."

"I told him it was too late," Magda tells Frank with a forced smile, gesturing for the boy to disappear. "One can't go around bothering people with one's family problems."

"Paloma knows," Bruno says flatly, ushering Frank through the illuminated garden into the house.

All the lights are on: everything is exposed. They gravitate to the music room. Chopin's *Last Prelude* is set out on the piano's reading stand. Bruno casually touches the keys. They make no sound, though he might be hearing whatever notes he has in mind in his sudden distraction. And Bruno, failing to suggest they all sit, leaves them hovering, the three of them, as unsettled as Paloma's parents have been all day.

From the time that Amalia had given news of the death of Paloma's German lover to her mother the previous day, it had been the intention of Magda and then Bruno to hide it from their daughter. After all, haven't they assumed it has been possible to keep her untouched by a lifetime of parental strife? But they are at a loss now Paloma knows too.

"She found out in the worst way," Magda says. "Amalia brought us *The Costa Times* this morning just as she always does, coming over for coffee. Paloma was there with us in the kitchen, having breakfast."

"It was on the front page," Bruno says. "And since Amalia – our dear, thoughtful Amalia – didn't want Paloma to hear about it from one of our *pueblo* gossips, she opened up the front page for her, complete with the man's photograph."

"And she didn't spare her the details," her mother says. "She told her everything that daughter of hers must have told her – and then some …

"She's taken it very hard," Magda says, suddenly trembling. "She hasn't eaten all day. And she's locked herself up in her room. She wouldn't come out for us, let alone when Amalia sent Heidi over to talk to her."

"That's why you must see her," Bruno says quietly, moving a pace closer to their visitor than Magda who, despite her tensely controlled exterior, her brittle resistance to the man, is on the verge of tears.

"If she'll see me," Frank murmurs.

It is an annihilating moment of self-doubt. Frank may just have lost everything he thought he had found with the now-absented girl who has, at last, raised him from years submerged by a failure to come to himself with the woman in Villa Bougainvillea.

"Why shouldn't she?" Bruno says. He has leapt over conventional qualms about Frank's difference in age, and not simply as a man of the world who has himself had affairs with younger women. He speaks from the pain of helpless tenderness for a stricken daughter lately in the hands of a man whom Bruno not only likes, but wants to trust. "She'll talk to you, if anyone," Bruno says.

Frank sighs. It sounds emptily in the strained silence in which the three of them continue wavering.

"Well ..." Bruno eventually breaks in, nodding the surely compassionate Englishman off in the direction of his daughter's bedroom.

"But how can a man of his age have been so irresponsible?" Magda says in a choked voice, turning away from Frank as he walks to Paloma's door. "What have we done to deserve a man like that coming into our life?"

He had to return. The news has shocked Paloma into realising she has known it all along. He always had to have surfaced even while she has seemed to have moved on, living and loving on the surface. And now that he, this bloated remnant of him, has emerged from the deep, there again shoots through her, here in El Castillo, the alarm she had felt at his sudden absence, in obliterating sunlight in Villa Bougainvillea a year ago.

She is still lying on her bed, as she was when the previous night stole upon sunlit slats escaping the drawn Venetian blinds. Against this dampened pillow, her eyes are closed.

I am in darkness, she thinks. It invades everything. It fills the villa, a place of shadows; vacant rooms to which I have not gone. For it is empty, now the man who rented it is dead. It was empty even when he was there with me, over our coffees, on the nocturnal roof terrace, in bed, since he was actually already dead. Just waiting to leave from the start, surely, he was committing himself not to me but to the sea, belatedly delivering him with the rest of the waves' wreckage to the foot of this hill.

It leaves the villa empty; me empty, unable to feel I'll find anything to live for, after all, among its cold, ghostly walls.

"Paloma?" Less than a knock, it is the tentative tapping of fingertips on the door. "It's me … I'm here."

Softly spoken, the words reach her in taut silence, conveying Frank's still presence there, without the repetitive persistence of her parents. And from that other world of external light showing below the door, his voice enters the scope of her feelings. So, mute moments later, stretched out through all these hours, a dark impress on the coverlet, she is raised to let him in.

Together we sit on the bed in light entering through the half-open door. I receive from Paloma's hand the photo of Franz she must have stared at again and again all day. Now, with stopped tears, she looks across from her crumpled image of a lover who had abandoned her to me.

I read the question implicit in her drawn features: "How can I trust another man not to leave me?"

Maybe she is also wondering if she can be sure that he had simply departed on impulse. Maybe he had planned his escape from the outset, lying all along, perhaps even to himself, about how deeply he had fallen in love with her.

Yet what has she heard of Franz's intentions to quit, alleged by Bog Man, I ask myself, while considering that – regardless of whether planned or impulsive – breaking away amounts to a lack of courage, an absence of self-confidence – of a self. And that is what a young man lost in Villa Bougainvillea decades ago had disastrously discovered he lacked to support a woman in a situation into which they had blindly flung themselves. Where had been the inner strength, the arms, to support her then, I wonder, feeling the soaked T-shirt on Paloma's back.

Finally, she draws herself up. The room where we have been hugging is stifling.

"Let's go out," I say. "It's cooler now."

The lights are off in El Castillo. There's free passage through the darkness. Only a small but intensely focused beam is on behind us, in the piano room.

The Master's picture beside him, Bruno sits squinting at music, not playing but lightly sketching a phrase on the keyboard. Repeated, it is halted midway as the latch sounds on the front door. Now Bruno stares again at the score. What will it take to get through the piece to the end?

This is the road we have often walked before. At dawn and dusk, it has brought us straight from Villa Bougainvillea to El Castillo; at midday and night, as now, the reverse. The *pueblo's* dark lanes also lost me with you, barely shadows to ourselves then, in that labyrinth now deep as the subterranean tunnels of a necropolis. Yet the path I – we – have travelled has always been this, judging by the destination we now instinctively pursue. Though this time, at this moment, we are no longer sleepwalkers. Awakened, we are moving apace to where we can fully be with each other.

This late at night, the plaza is so dark that there is no knowing if anyone is there. Only occasionally, dense clouds floating up from the sea separate, providing a crack for the moon to cast its ashen glow over mounds on the plain Bog Man views from the *mirador*.

Smoke from his eternal cigarette coils up as if from a medium receiving deathly secrets from a past buried in sites Bog Man has spent his life excavating since mutely escaping his War. Nothing has, of course, been revealed. And while the mounds serve as reminders of past cataclysms, he still wonders, glimpsing the couple entering the plaza, whether, despite their calm in this strange light, disaster is finally extinct, or might erupt in them again.

Uncharacteristically, Bog Man does not greet the pair now stopped in the centre of the square. For, having taken each other in their arms, they are just standing there, holding their embrace. No, there is no question of disturbing them. They are engrossed in this present they have found together.

Arriving at the villa, we do not speak. There is no need. Our footsteps lead straight ahead, past dark bougainvillea, without us having to put on the hall light. Heedlessly, we pass the empty rooms, the bed where we often lounge first upon meeting late in the evening. We pursue the creaking stairs right up onto the roof.

This has been our eventual destination throughout this past of ours, though the exact time we have spent together, time itself, is no more clear to us than each other's arms, legs, smoothed and stroked in this dark, than your sex, known to me now only by this moistening arousal to my touch; than these features: yours, mine, unseen.

Here is where I have always been with you; on this roof behind the bougainvillea-covered latticework where silent doves leave us to the unmarked sounds of our synchronised breathing. Yet you, this spectral you, my first you, re-emerging momentarily in the guise of one now embracing me: you were the one whose reason for making love to me I did not understand. I gave you solace, though without realising that either – you, whom I also did not know. But equally, I did not know myself, or my reason for being here; loving you, with whom I found myself too far into the night to be within any recognised dimension of time.

Shadow, Frank thinks, *seeking your* pied noir *lover murdered in the Bois de Boulogne, you have left the startled, wanting medium for your search as you flee your agony in Paris.*

Stranger from the steppes, Paloma feels, *you have used your late liberty in Villa Bougainvillea to prepare escape from the innocent who has striven to make you feel free here at last.*

Wraiths, you are woven with coloured rags into the coverlet protecting the sleep into which we are subsiding, passion now spent. You are straying into slumber, losing yourself in transformations, mystifying pursuits, spent dreams.

You are fading away, Frank finds. I am hardly aware of it. Rousing, I barely recognise my *déjà vu* in consoling – currently for a man's loss to the sea, endangering his girlfriend's capacity to love. Though more than solace, here is tender recognition of the one with whom I am emerging from sleep. And we find, you and I, here and now, that we are making of this moment a present that is us beneath the wide, starlit Mediterranean sky.

We continue drinking in our reality. We draw the cover further over our naked shoulders. There is a chill now night is edging on. Soon, the dark starts thinning. Dawn comes. The growing light cannot be denied. We are confronted, still abed, by what the day, a future, will be.

2

Not yet ready to pursue the path leading to El Castillo, it comes upon us that we shall go down to the sea. We take the first bus from the *pueblo*, its only passengers, descending through the warm salt breeze rushing in at us through open windows. We hurtle past century plants, cacti ripe with Barbary figs, and get off at the foot of the hill.

We step over the low wall separating pavement from beach, running parallel to the road. But instead of heading for some secluded stretch, our 'private cove', we continue, without needing to discuss it, in this exposed public bathing area. Silent, we approach a rock on which to view the sea in clear, early light not yet blurred by the daytime heat, settling where a man was carried out onto the sand.

We go on finding his body pulsed forward by the waves. It continues before our unseeing eyes. But soon it is just the rhythm of the tide, the sweeping wind, that we are absorbing. Aware that there is still no traffic on the highway behind us at this hour, we are now conscious of gazing at an entirely deserted shore. And knowing we have not spoken till this point, we find conversation about the departed man opening up.

"They say it was suicide," Paloma says flatly, gazing at the blank sand.

"Apparently." Frank does not further voice his thought that even if it had been an accident, such carelessness shows he had held his life so cheap that it qualifies as unintended suicide.

"But why?"

The question makes Frank dare to feel that Paloma, no longer submerged by distress at the drowning, having by now realised what a reliable foothold she has with him, is prepared to risk the two of them discussing it openly. Maybe, then, he too can be more forthcoming about the man. And having answered her, he will, in settling the matter for her, also allow both of them to pass beyond it.

Thus Frank finds himself recounting what Bog Man told him about Franz's summary departure from the *pueblo* to contact Speer's lover at the spa hotel. Paloma listens, barely flinching. Perhaps she has already heard this. Maybe it is one of those "details" Magda said Amalia had recounted to her, derived from her daughter or even just village gossip. In any case, such is the directness, the clarity, with which Paloma looks at me as I talk that I do not hesitate to spare her feelings.

"Franz might have felt he'd finally rounded out his life, fulfilling it, by re-encountering and driving his master, Speer, that last time in the person of his lover. She made his existence complete."

I say it despite knowing I am hurting this other competitor for him. She blinks with the realisation that, with such a rival, she could never have stood a chance of gaining more than his transient attachment. He was unavailable to her from the start, in the very paroxysm of her love, the man deceiving her even from the first moment to that when, I imply, he committed himself to the waters in celebration of a life finally achieved. What more need there have been to live for?

Yet if Paloma presumes to think it could ever have been her, the mere idea has surely been destroyed by what I am shocked to find is my own ruthlessness, no less than his. It stings – and not only her. For the next instant, witnessing her misery, I feel such a rush of tender remorse that I suffer the pain of my own whiplash.

Whereupon a visibly aggrieved Paloma proposes with sudden distaste: "Of course his life could equally well have been too empty to go on living."

Released, she is thinking that Franz, an historical afterthought from years lost in Russia, might actually have remained a being submerged despite all he had received at Villa Bougainvillea. Although she had felt at the time, she remembers, a knuckle wiping the side of her eye, that he showed signs of emerging as a person during their long hours taking in art books, drinking coffee, wandering the *pueblo*, making love on the roof terrace – in other words, *being* together. But maybe he had never come to himself at all. Did he simply end as he had started in the war, as a mere shadow driving the mighty minister, a servile transport for a godlike Speer?

Never finally himself perhaps, merely filling a role, the self surfacing from Russia might have seemed to him unachieved. Perhaps it felt neither worth having nor keeping, Paloma is considering when Frank says, eyes lost in the sea: "Maybe it's not death that he wanted specifically, but a chance to start all over again; to live properly. Suicide could have felt to him like the passport to a new – a *real* – life. That's assuming he didn't view it, as I've said, as the seal on a life fulfilled."

"How can you ever know," Paloma muses, "whether the one you meet, who becomes your lover and you give yourself to, is living a '*real*' life? And besides," she says, finding the man next to her taking off his clothes in the strengthening sunlight, "can even the person you fall for be certain?"

He lays his shirt on the rock slowly, lost in a long thought.

The man wanders naked over the still-deserted beach and stands at the water's edge. Pensive, he watches waves washing over his feet, each small retreat leaving a froth of bubbles on the glistening pebbles he feels pressing against his toes.

Suddenly, unaware of any instant of decision, he flings himself into the sea. He yields to the current, willing the coolness to engulf him. He submits to deep, dark soundlessness. Even the reverberations in his inner ears have submitted to insensibility he realises now the tide has turned him out onto the shore.

He lies on the wet sand, washed again and again by the waves. Getting up, turning inwards to the beach, he finds he is living as reality that dream of weeks ago: emerging from the sea, naked, free to be.

Then, seeing he has been watched all along, thrown out of the water, by the young woman next to the rock, he joins her. They are together.

She is squinting in the sunlight, playing with her hair, taking in what she has seen.

3

A family with young children trails onto the beach, far off. A car drives by, unseen, on the road behind Paloma and Frank. He is dressing, gazing at the sea. They walk over to the bus stop, holding hands.

Soon, from the window of the spluttering Peugeot, they take in a man leading goats across a sloping a field. A peasant woman jogs down on a donkey buttressed by earthenware water jars filled at the village well.

The couple find themselves holding each other tightly: morning is encroaching. Ford Madox Brown's painting *The Last of England* passes through Paloma's mind, its huddled pair tensely contemplating the immensity of their new life. She wonders what Frank is thinking, with the day and its demands on them.

Frank and Paloma get up as the bus swerves into the *pueblo*. They cannot put off going to El Castillo any longer.

We are making our way up the narrow street past Pensión Amalia. Glancing ahead from the strip of shade to the other side, we blink. Our eyes hurt. The light is fiery: it's a conflagration.

For all at once, scarcely knowing it, we are revisiting the moment of recognising in scorching sunshine that Villa Bougainvillea is voided. The one beside me is gone, forever. I am empty too, losing everything I feel you gave me but suddenly doubt that you ever have. So it comes to me in an instant of dread, as I shrink from the furnace morning makes of the place. With windows blazing, their frames dry as tinder, thorns on that briar-like plant by an equally flammable front door repel entry.

They draw back. Paloma almost stumbles, stooping to adjust her *alpargata*. She steadies herself on Frank's arm. Getting up, she walks scarcely a pace behind him. Then they stop again. They have discovered that the door to Villa Bougainvillea is wide open.

Justi, seconded from Amalia's staff, cleans for the absentee German owners. Short, fat and dressed in black, though livelier than most village women, she rises from the hallway she has been sluicing down to wave to the couple. She knows Paloma, who has been coming to the *pueblo* since infancy and took care of that strange, mute foreigner renting the villa. But now she is with this polite Englishman booked into the *pensión* where his room, which Justi also cleans, is so tidy that he might as well never have stayed there.

Straw hat in hand, he gazes with the younger woman past mauve bougainvillea into the luminous entrance. A wave of cleaning fluid smells of local lemon groves, its heady fragrance seemingly incorporating even orchards far off in Andalusia. Justi, amused, finds the pair continuing to hold still in the lane in one another's arms.

"Come in," her smile and open palms invite. But they can't – not till they have been to El Castillo.

Bruno and Magda avoid looking as if they are waiting for their daughter to return. But Bruno is not playing the piano or even studying a score. Magda has abandoned the nightgown she usually wears late into the morning. She is fully dressed, as if ready for an event – Paloma's appearance – despite her pretence of sitting casually with Bruno.

Actually, they are perched on the living room sofa. Bowls of shells, a pair of amphorae from an ancient Greek shipwreck, a vase of dried wildflowers from hereabouts, hardly make up for vacant spaces denied family photos by Bruno's early separation from Magda. Yet although he is now beyond all that philandering, through deep changes as unseen but as real as those within the local mounds, it is too late to do more than nervously await his daughter with her mother in the gloom of blinds half-drawn against the mounting sun.

The night has drained Paloma. She hates walking into this dim, heavily interrogative atmosphere. So, hovering before her parents with Frank, whose ongoing presence they silently register, she merely murmurs a soulful "*bye*" apparently intended not only for him.

Bruno, anxious to avoid awkward tension by downplaying the concern he and Paloma's fidgeting mother feel, says to Frank, gesturing to the girl seeking to escape to her room: "Thanks for looking after this one."

"There was no question of it – for me."

Whereupon Magda, at the end of her nerves, blurts out: "I wish you were just a friend – *our* friend. Or that you were younger."

"We all wish we were younger," Bruno says, to make light of the remark that's thrown Paloma into tears. Now she is fleeing to her bedroom, followed by her mother.

It leaves Frank alone with Bruno. A far-off door closes in the tense silence of this dim living room.

"I hope Magda didn't embarrass you," Bruno says, gesturing to Frank to take a seat. "She's highly strung. But then we're all worried about Paloma – including you, of course. It's just that, with no disrespect to you personally, whom we like even if we don't really know you, we've already had experience of my daughter being involved with someone older – though that was hardly the only problem.

"Yet men, as you and I must admit, tend to get giddy, easily losing their heads over a girl, and thinking it gives them a new lease of life, even if they soon leave her high and dry. Not that Franz was typical. He was a complicated character …

"Franz." Bruno repeats the name pensively. "You must have heard of him. It's about all Magda and I ever did. We didn't meet him socially, let alone talk to him. There was never an occasion when we could ask him about himself or get him to open up to us. Neither he nor Paloma ever encouraged it. They had a very private relationship.

"Franz was a closed book as far as we were concerned. Not that we didn't suspect at least something about his personality. We couldn't imagine he had any left after all his years as a POW in Russian psychiatric hospitals.

"What parents would want their daughter to be wasting herself on such a lover, for all her fondly naïve belief that simply by being with him she could help make him whole? Well, that was bad enough. Yet how could we have predicted that Franz, beneath his stunned exterior, was actually harbouring the even emptier person he'd always been?

"Far from ever having had serious intentions for Paloma, he was just biding his time with the poor girl, accepting all her love and devotion, until it was the right moment for him to expose his true, unreformed self at the spa hotel Heidi visited. For that stunted being of his still expressed itself through homage to its master of over half a century before by placing incense on the altar of Speer's own younger lover."

"That's right," Frank hears himself saying in the shadowy living room. It brings to his mind others, from the Siberian steppes: ice maidens, preserved unchanged in the permafrost, complete with tattoos, since the fifth century BC. "Paloma and I were talking about it earlier. Whether the man drowned himself, feeling the episode at the hotel had finally fulfilled his life, or because he thought his existence was empty and that self of his had never changed."

Facing Bruno, the image of another man passes through Frank's mind. He places it, before it vanishes, in the kitchen of Villa Bougainvillea: Esther's father, whom her young lover faces, tongue-tied – so unlike Frank now, speaking uninhibitedly to Paloma's father.

"No doubt," Bruno says tersely. "But the point isn't only that we didn't know who our daughter's lover really was. It's that we *couldn't*, because we never talked to him."

Magda has pursued Paloma to her bedroom. Yet, by the time they enter, the girl's reaction to her mother's attack on her lover has become so intense that it outdoes Magda's own emotion. The mother, remorseful in the face of the misery she has caused, sits at the foot of the bed where her daughter is lying.

"You obviously love him," Magda says gently. "And I've always known you'd fall hard."

She is skipping over the previously insuperable barrier of Frank's age, no less than across her abiding scepticism about the capacity of men for that "four-letter word" – *love* – as her ex-husband calls it. At least that is something they can agree on after their years of failed marriage.

Magda is also about to say: "But we've been here before, haven't we?" Yet she holds it back in a long pause during which Paloma, acknowledging her mother's unexpected sensitivity, hoists herself on an elbow, now finding Magda saying: "But what does he mean to you?"

"I've always been waiting for him ..."

Magda frowns, nonplussed by this tone she has never heard in her daughter before.

"And he's here," Paloma muses. She is re-experiencing him coming to her naked from the sea, holding still with her before the villa where she had been abandoned.

"What do you mean?"

"How can you explain love to someone else – or even to yourself?"

"So how can you be sure about it?"

"His or mine?"

"Either."

"You can't. It's a risk. It takes courage," Paloma says in this new way of hers.

"Not foolhardiness – if it's to last." Paloma doesn't answer: she's taking it in. "I know you have courage, darling – *too* much, considering you've barely even known each other for a summer. But does *he*?"

Again, Paloma does not answer. She gazes at her mother, on whose face the question remains.

PART VII

1

The women seem to have taken permanent flight to Paloma's bedroom. Conversation has lapsed between the men, still seated in the shuttered living room. It feels large and empty in this heavy silence among impersonal relics from the sea.

Then Bruno, swallowing one of the pills he is taking these days, says: "I think you must accept that my daughter is unlikely to appear for the rest of the morning. So, although I know you're exhausted, why don't you drive with me up to the vineyard I have in the hills? September is the best time to visit, and I should see my tenants. They'll be harvesting soon. It'll give us a chance to talk."

Actually, I am not tired at all; or, rather, I am beyond it. I am elated by Paloma's return to me, by knowing I am loved, that we love each other. I am fully myself at last. I am quite content to leave Paloma to El Castillo for now, sleeping. Then, when I return from the vineyard heavy with fruit for next year's wine, I shall awaken her with a kiss as the Prince that I, among her contending suitors, though seemingly conventional, will emerge as, from this excursion for which her father leads me to the garage.

Beside the old Mercedes and Magda's Renault eggbeater, there is a vehicle that Bruno is now uncovering: a BMW top-back sports car. It looks virtually unused.

"I haven't taken it – or myself – out for some time. Too much piano, you know," he adds almost mournfully.

Soon they are out of the *pueblo*, racing up inclines, lurching round bends. They glimpse sea, then the inland plain spreading vertiginously far below. And Frank is recalling that Arturo Benedetti Michelangeli, the pianist, with his famed technique, also loved flying and fast cars.

Suddenly they slow down. Why? They are on a stretch of clear road. Is it simply another instance of the uncertainty recurrently afflicting Bruno's own piano playing?

Deferential, almost cowed, he is considering von Karajan. "Maybe it was the adrenalin rush from speeding in a Porsche along the mountain roads behind his house near Salzburg that provided him with all that confident energy for conducting."

"One prefers to think the music supplied it," Frank says.

"Of course. Though is there any telling what's really driving someone?" Bruno says, ensuring the direction of his train of thought. "What are we to make of that late romance of Speer's? Was it just the thrill of adrenalin, like racing with the Führer in his Mercedes on the *autobahn* round Obersalzberg? Or had he finally overcome a lifetime of, well, nothing? Was he at last finding himself capable of love?"

At which Bruno pulls decisively into the vineyard. He has reached his destination.

Overcoming emptiness: it has been Bruno's focus of interest in Speer all along. But then Frank senses why Paloma's father seeks his views on an ex-Spandau inmate's late romance now in particular. He is judging obliquely the emotional depth, the dependability after such a short affair, of his daughter's lover.

As for Frank, he himself cannot help probing Speer's character as he supposes he has been doing intermittently since Heidi reported on her excursion over their breakfast tables at Pensión Amalia. Subterranean till now, his thoughts surface while Bruno's tenant, surprised by the owner's visit, sycophantically distracts him with promises of a bumper harvest thanks to the alleged care with which Señor's vines have been tended over the year.

So Frank, watching the tenant, finds himself assessing Speer for more than just Bruno's sake. He is not only judging the man's authenticity as a lover. He is sounding out his own fitness as one. More to the point, this surely is the long-awaited culmination of Frank's own interest in Speer; a preoccupation dating from long before this return to the *pueblo*, well prior to Heidi's recent revelations about a certain Frau Müller.

Speer, rivalling Professor Keller, had first attracted a trainee historian in London with his dazzlingly high profile under Hitler. Despite which an emptiness, undeniable in Spandau, always underlay it, as Frank has come to recognise – unlike that unobservant young researcher with a lostness of his own. Whether or not Speer, thrilled by his late discovery of sensual love, had ever overcome that void, finding an eventual wholeness, is for Frank to consider in this vineyard, implicitly taking a final human reckoning of him both on Bruno's account and, at last, his own.

All at once, I am aware of my tiredness. It sweeps over me in this midmorning sun as the tenant offers us stools at a table on the beaten-earth patio between his whitewashed shack and the vineyard. The equally garrulous wife is bringing us refreshments. But I am almost swooning among their seemingly distant chatter.

Yet I am content for Bruno to be distracted. I can continue to be sunk in my thoughts. This lightheadedness, my very exhaustion, gives me the sense of being transported, of straying into the dense heart of a dream where I am exploring whether there was – or could be – an awakening from emptiness with a young lover.

Eyes unfocused by the glare, then lost in the avenues of gloomy vines facing us, I re-enter Speer's void. I almost hallucinate the apocalyptic last days of the war when Franz was driving him. He no more exists than the buildings crashing down around him; whole cities reduced to firestorms by saturation bombing; the ghost of Dresden – "Florence on the Elbe", as Churchill called it.

I hear, once more, a reinstated Speer responding to Trevor-Roper's question about what he would do if he had his life again: "You have to understand the irresistible fascination of power". For it was the unquenchable fever of his attachment to Hitler, the flaw it amounted to in the man, that lasted throughout Speer's life. It earned him those twenty years in Spandau during which he wrote his *Secret Diaries*.

A young German woman reads it. I find her fervently turning the pages of the paperback edition I came upon one lunch hour in that London bookstore. And there courses through my mind what I suppose must have been Speer's relationship with her, while I weigh how much or how little of a person another can really know, as I had undressing on the beach with Paloma hours earlier.

The young woman is married with children, but she is lonely living abroad in postwar England. She feels it is prejudiced against her country. She sends Speer a letter saying his book made such an impact on her that she was moved to tears. Speer invites her to visit him in Heidelberg, as he has with many correspondents. She is attractive: they begin an affair, to the horror of his wife. He experiences the first truly erotic relationship of his life.

But how will the woman fare with this hollow man, equally lonely in his final years? By then Speer's relationship with his family had lapsed, Frank considers, deserted here in the vineyard by Bruno and the others. During the twenty years of his imprisonment, the children had grown up without a father. A stranger on his release, Speer was too distant and emotionally unskilled to establish easy communication. While his close friends from the old days, resenting his exhibitionist contrition for German wartime crimes and his disloyalty to the Führer along with high-handed personal slights, had disavowed him.

But did he not suffer an even greater isolation, Frank wonders: the loneliness of knowing an annihilating truth that could never be confessed? It was that he certainly had been aware of "the horrors" about which he had once sought to set his daughter's mind at rest by falsely promising her, in a letter from his Spandau cell, that he had known nothing.

Speer was fully conscious that Jews were being cleared out of their dwellings in Berlin to make way for his Germania project. Well, he might be! He had enriched himself from such construction. He also had a close association with Himmler and the SS, assisting in the construction of concentration camps, including building the crematoria at Auschwitz, and using their slave labour. Speer had even attended, with all the Reichleiters and Gauleiters, a terrible speech Himmler gave in Posen in October 1943. Bruno's book quotes the letter, surfacing only after Speer's death but that he wrote in 1971, to Hélène Jeanty, widow of the Belgian resistance leader. "There's no doubt," he says, "I was present as Himmler announced ... that all Jews would be killed."

It must mean, Frank supposes, that Speer knew full well at the time something he claimed in retrospect only to have suspected. It related to one of the situation conferences Speer attended at the Führer's headquarters earlier that year. Hitler went to stand at a window, opened to let in some air, and said, with his back to the military still present: "Gentlemen, the bridges behind us are burned."

It referred to what had been done to the Jews.

Yet Speer's knowledge became incontrovertible only after his death. For years, he could gather plaudits for his Nuremburg strategy of taking general, if not individual, responsibility for the crimes of the regime he served. It gave him a chance to seek a conscience; to grow into "another man". Of course, Speer had to continue to lie, Frank knows: he had no choice. But "he lied to me only about facts, not his inner life," Casalis, the chaplain, said. "He constructed for me a path on which he thought I could walk with him a while." And twenty years of imprisonment seemingly wiped his moral slate clean. Released from Spandau, he could begin again as that other man.

So Speer, back in Heidelberg, appeared to the few people ultimately visiting him to be finally withdrawing from the past. He was finding, he told them, if not quite "the happiness of forgetting", at least that of "being forgotten".

Despite which, all was not as it seemed. Speer was becoming increasingly preoccupied at this late point in his life by the surfacing of new documents that opened up potentially incriminating lines of enquiry. Full exposure of his personal knowledge of the worst atrocities of the Third Reich – and his direct involvement in them – was becoming a real possibility. He ran the risk of criminal action being taken against him by the Central Office of the State Justice Administration for the Investigation of National Socialist Crimes set up in the '60s.

Speer's surprising quasi-friend, Rabbi Robert Raphael Geis, once said that if Speer would not confess the truth, he would have to live with the consequences of suppressing it. This meant that his mental energies now had to be strictly focused on preventing the escape of what there could be no question of him admitting, if the very defence protecting him at Nuremberg – general rather particular guilt – was not to unravel. The consequences would be disastrous.

Albert Speer, having been released from twenty hard years in Spandau for using slave labour, was sentenced anew for life to living a lie. Was there no reprieve?

"Was there any way for the man to overcome himself – his lack of self – and to love?" Frank revives the question Bruno had asked before being led off, without touching his glass of wine, to marvel at how free the vines were from infection rife in the region. For Bruno, having reluctantly inspected the grapes, the leaves, in avenue after avenue, prior to receiving a wad of worn banknotes, is finally back at the table. Distractedly wiping his brow, unused to more exertion than practising the piano, he is still to focus finally on whether or not, as Frank puts it, there had been a further chance for Speer, with the prospect of damning new revelations, to nourish a nascent conscience, that fledgling being stirring during decades in which the question of his specific knowledge had perhaps become sufficiently dormant for him virtually to forget he had ever possessed it.

"Might there have been respite in the abbey of Maria Laach?" Frank says. Bruno looks at him questioningly. "Yes. It's the Benedictine abbey whose monks have been stigmatised for welcoming the Nazi seizure of power in 1933, and collaborating thereafter."

"Ah!"

"Speer explains his repeated visits there, saying it's where he finds the inner peace evading him outside. Whereas others on retreat stay only a couple of days in the guest wing, he spends up to five in the monastic area marked for total seclusion. It is the one place in which he can escape all the people visiting him in Heidelberg as if he were a freak in a deep cage. They expect to hear rote *mea culpas* for general criminal responsibility freeing him from individual blame.

"Maybe Speer's sly boast that he's an expert escapist amounts, in such a receptive environment, to smugness at shaking off his accusers. But perhaps the similarity between his monastery and Spandau cells, with their equally harsh regimes of food and study, amounts to nostalgia for simpler days unpreoccupied by unwelcome truths. And might those green shoots of a conscience appearing in prison have revived, if not survived, under such well-protected conditions?

"Yet could even Speer himself, so isolated now, distinguish between satisfaction at dodging pursuers and renewed striving for a moral self? Could he be sure that his new Spandau was a fortress protecting him against the truth and its consequences, or was it a cell that his finally ethical being sentences him to for personal knowledge of 'the horrors'? Either might be equally, simultaneously, so.

"Who – what – was he," asks Frank, "the man in the monastery receiving a letter out of the blue from an equally solitary, attractive young German mother in England?"

Having returned to the question about how Speer might overcome his personal emptiness, I feel Bruno's eyes on me. For Bruno, silent, sitting at the table with me beneath a dense canopy of vine, is not only recovering from exerting himself in the heat. He is also waiting for his daughter's older lover, the English historian, me, to come to the point of his question when commenting on the photograph of Speer on a sunlit terrace in Provence published in the book he lent me. Can I thereby show an understanding of a man's capacity to love?

"Speer is not," I say, "in uniform, as in the wartime and prison images of him. Nor is he wearing the sober business suits he wore for press conferences and television interviews. In that snapshot, seen by his publisher, he is in a white turtleneck sweater and slacks with a beautiful woman in a negligée. They're relaxed, laughing.

"How so?" I ask on Bruno's behalf. "The young woman need not view the old man seducing her with contempt. On the contrary, his *Secret Diaries* is the first time she has found a German of the war generation presented in such upright human terms. Far from being despised, he commands respect, indeed affection. For the *Secret Diaries*, carefully crafted once Speer left prison, omits even the slightest suggestion that their author knew of the 'horrors'. He was misled by Hitler: Hitler, who betrayed the Germans' idealism. And it is Hitler and his henchmen who have spoiled everything noble about the Nazi project. Germans, the entire German nation, are no longer incriminated. Speer has liberated them all from guilt. No wonder his attractive young reader sheds tears of joy!

"The woman's admiration for someone accustomed during the Reich to universal deference, as well as to virtual love by the Führer himself, frees Speer from his now-habitual strain. For she, at least, does not suspect him of having known of Nazi crimes at the time. With her, he is not the butt of accelerating probing into the exact extent of his direct involvement. The man in that photograph is relieved of the need for personal guilt and perhaps finally impossible moral reparation.

"While the young woman, badly wanting to hero-worship the man freeing her from having to think ill of herself as a German, unaware of growing rumours of evidence that will only incriminate him decisively after his death, allows Speer to appear as he wants to be seen. He is Hitler's great architect; the Führer's miracle-working Armaments Minister; a postwar, bestselling historian and reinstated public figure.

"Lovers' collusion!" Bruno hears his daughter's friend say it with a soft, even tender sigh on behalf of the man he is embodying, to judge by these explanations coming so easily to him; insights that Frank supposes some unknown self has been recording in a secret diary of his own, with invisible pages capturing what he now suspects had, in reality, been attracting him to Speer from the outset in London bookshops. "This enables Speer," he continues, "to disavow all that, from a profound inner well, has poisoned his whole life, rendering him, the unexpectedly intelligent, urbane Nazi, implausibly monstrous. His spoiled, humanly unachieved past is simply eclipsed."

Frank pauses for a deep intake of this summer air, fragrant from orchards his acclimatising eyes glimpse on surrounding hills from the end of this avenue of vines. Bruno, raising an arm to prevent the tenant's fussy wife from bringing out more bread and interrupting his attention to Frank, lowers his hand to the table. He taps his fingers, searching out an elusive *Prelude* as the Englishman continues:

"But is Speer only being duplicitous by consciously denying his knowledge of the atrocities or his active part in them? Short of publicly confessing his personal guilt – out of the question, as it would be a death sentence – the only way for this escape artist to connect with the being he wants to be, namely the person the infatuated woman sees, is simply to jump over the crimes; not merely through denying them, but by actually believing he really is the one on show. He has taken himself in – an artful dodge, though it adds up to rather more than a low trick. It's a longing for an ethical self, the painful yearning for personal authenticity, of a piece with the guilt and thus conscience he had guardedly disclosed to himself, at least in Maria Laach Abbey – all stemming from a moral being *au fond*."

Bruno abruptly halts his mock piano playing. "So you're saying he's finally faced himself: his abyss?"

"Yes."

The answer reverberates. "How do you know?"
"It rings true."

Bruno strikes the table with the palm of his hand: acknowledgement, I take it that I, his daughter's lover, have identified a grain of truthfulness in the man's approach to his affair; that I, the English historian Bruno likes and has already been edging dangerously near to trusting (my age notwithstanding), feel it is important to find at least a trace of human authenticity in Speer's relationship with the German woman.

"So Speer," I continue, "on a balcony overlooking this same Mediterranean out there with his young lover, is understandably full of high spirits and the joy of life. It's the exhilaration he'd felt in the *Wandervogel* movement, and when embarking on a career of unimaginable promise. The dark aspects of what he'll become don't exist for him now.

"Yet of course that's always been the issue, hasn't it?" I ask it rhetorically, Bruno continuing to listen in silence, his hand now motionless on the table. "Speer, in his attraction to Hitler, with all their friendship made possible for him in that genocidal regime, had simply ignored what was ethically inconvenient. He lived, triumphed, through less than everything that had actually become part of him.

"In the photograph, as in the rest of his life, Speer exists as a thin layer of himself. He is his innocent being before ever hearing Hitler or having been tainted by the Nazis' crimes. Hence such youthful gaiety. And implicitly added to that pristine persona, for the sake of his *amour propre* and the young woman's adoration, are his Reich offices, his recent media fame, all blamelessly presented. What alternative could he have?

"Had there ever been a chance of the man expressing his full self? Maybe he knows contrition achieves little. Repentance, whether for general responsibility in the media or secretly for personal guilt at Maria Laach Abbey, can never change a past that he was unable to confess without condemning himself to a lethal penalty. Rather than renewing him, it leaves him dissatisfied with himself; perpetually mournful. It does nothing, finally, to overcome the woeful sense that his regrets, his bygones, will always dog him like an incubus. Far from passed, the past may erupt at any time as Speer is starting to find.

"In fact, being forced by circumstances to hang silently on to that incriminating knowledge he can't reveal, perhaps the very impossibility of doing the one thing necessary for real forgiveness and becoming the new man he longs to be, public confession, is denied him.

"Did Speer, namely whatever part of himself was available to him, while making love with his attractive young German mistress in the Palm Court Hotel in London, consider even for a second, just before the massive heart attack killing him in St Mary's Hospital in Paddington, whether or not it is possible to return to the beginning?

"Can one revert to the point before the past has taken over?" I ask beside Bruno, his fingers flexing as if uncertain now whether or not to treat the table as a piano. "Can one reconnect with the moment before time spoils and sours, allowing a new start, a second chance?"

2

Bruno gets up from the table and conversation, if that is what it has been. Is it really just wishful thinking, I ask myself, to suppose he has heard enough for his purposes?

He leads us through vines, their broad leaves lending a greenish gloom to the avenue we are walking along as if down a cathedral aisle between luminous stained glass windows. We come out into blinding sunlight where the sloping vineyard suddenly halts at a precipitous drop. Eyes acclimatising, we take in the surrounding natural amphitheatre with its other patches of vineyard, although much of the encircling mountain is uncultivated, as it has been since the Arabs left with their system of irrigation. Will the rock face continue shrivelled forever?

The men look down at large mounds in the plain sweeping below them. It is silent, almost unnaturally so. Not a straw-like oregano stalk moves once an insect has passed. And it is impossible, as they hold their breath, involuntarily, to know whether this soundlessness is deadness or anticipation.

There is no telling if the mounds, with all they contain, those remnants of a life, time gone by, are extinct, forming at most a backdrop for whatever is to come. Or perhaps they are charged with the energy of all that is unresolved deep down, threatening havoc at any moment. One cannot be sure which, looking down. Maybe one must continue unsuspectingly in the eerie calm of an all-too-visible but unrevealing brilliance.

"How do *you* come to be so interested in Albert Speer of all people?" Bruno asks his daughter's lover, standing right beside him, also looking straight out at the view. "For us," he continues, "with that short-lived affair our daughter had with the man's driver, there could be no escape. But how on Earth have you, an historian – a medieval one – been drawn in?"

A polite, cultured Englishman such as me, I take the question to imply, could not be further removed in background and ethical standards, to judge by those implicit in my character assessment of Speer, from the Führer's closest friend in the most criminal regime of the twentieth century.

It is a good question. But I am no surer how to explain to myself what the man has meant to me than to Paloma's father. And I have a sudden inkling that he has a further, still more personal reason for asking. He wants to know why he, too, is so interested in Speer. What is it, I wonder, hearing his breathing as he waits for an answer, gazing beside me into the plain? How am I to convey the way this figure has come to loom so large in my thoughts, going on imperceptibly to infuse my most intimate feelings about myself? Too strange a matter to tell, I begin, as I must, at least by insisting that I *haven't* approached Speer as an historian.

"I was originally intrigued by my father's memories of the war. Then this became an antidote to the rigours of historical research. But I didn't realise how engaged I was, not just with the war generally but with Albert Speer in particular, till I returned here to the *pueblo* where I'd been years before starting work with my professor, Emil Keller."

Frank glances over to the mass of whitewashed houses atop a nearby hill.

"I was enthralled by the story Speer tells about himself in the newly published bestsellers I began reading as a relief from my work as a London archivist. But that was not all. How could it be, when a truer, more drastic tale began irresistibly opening up around him?

"He turned, didn't he, from one knowing nothing of the 'horrors', the Third Reich's most reliable insider (according to his bestsellers), the 'Good Nazi'? The so-called 'real' Speer emerges as a charlatan hoodwinking journalists; the grand deceiver only too well aware of the worst of the crimes, proven from lately available documents. They even show him, judging by the recent book you lent me, Bruno, taking an active role in them.

"Well, it was impossible for me not to be drawn into the constant discussions of a man whose devious afterlife I had been following as much as his life itself; not here of all places, where an ex-prisoner of war, his driver, was recuperating at Villa Bougainvillea."

"Yes," Bruno says, turning directly to Frank as if that were all there was to it. "There's no way we could ignore a stranger coming into our midst and involving himself with our daughter. And that includes me, an Argentine, used to ambiguous characters with submerged pasts washing up on the shore – even in U-boats."

Bruno turns decisively away from the precipice. Now he heads back into the sheltering vineyard, past the tenant and his wife, forcing baskets of grapes on him with an exaggerated *adiós*. He makes for the car.

Does he feel he has received his answer here?

Frank fastens his seat belt for the drive back to the *pueblo*. It occurs to him that despite its new arrival, Franz, who was soon to leave Paloma high and dry, the place has not changed since he was last here. It is as it was, at first and at last: Villa Bougainvillea, with a woman drawing him to her arms on that starlit roof.

It is a held image; a single frame. But suddenly Franz and so Speer, whilst having had no part in Frank's first visit to the *pueblo*, cast a long shadow back in his mind across his original moment with a young woman, now coming to him anew.

Then, with Bruno's reference to "submerged pasts" sticking in his thoughts, Frank recognises once more, in the wordless whir in which they speed round a hill, that he had never been exactly aware on solitary London days, abandoned to historical records, that he was not fully himself even while completing Professor Keller's book. No, he was not to realise these were lost years till his thoughts turned to Speer's Spandau, back in the *pueblo*.

Again the car turns, offering another glimpse of the mountain visible from the edge of the vineyard. Instantly, Frank suspects that both he and Bruno have left that precipice too soon. The view leads, doesn't it, to more of why he is so interested in Speer? It contains the caves in which local boys had fallen to their deaths when he was first in the *pueblo*; dark, deep caverns he would never have dared explore that summer when he lacked the nerve to accompany Esther into the unknown.

So now Frank sees, years afterwards, it is actually his thoughts about how Albert Speer's inner emptiness laid him open to Hitler that have been drawing him close to accepting that it was his own lack of self that not only failed to resist Professor Keller but also deprived him of the independence of will, the sheer courage, to take a leap into the dark, like those bad *pueblo* boys, and commit a folly – so sublime – with Esther.

Speer has been the route to recognising my own feelings, Frank thinks. No matter that what fascinated him in London was Hitler's brilliant protégé, then the man's intriguing changes of face in press revelations. What really drew Frank to him, if unknowingly, was the challenge to Speer of an inner vacuousness sensed vaguely, but from the start, as much in the Englishman as about the German. And he realises just how much he personally has been implicated by thoughts about Speer, finding him so ingrained that he might well wonder who he has actually been considering, this medium or himself.

Yet, Frank realises, driving in this silence, here is no obliterating alternative to him; not an oppressive shadow like Speer's Führer or even Professor Keller. It is where he is unexpectedly finding his intimate, most sensitive feelings. It is the alternative location from which he is telepathically receiving intimations of himself.

Has it not even brought Frank, headed back to the point – *this* point – of also seeing he has overcome his feelings? For, weak and unworthy, aren't they discarded, together with the irreparably guilty war criminal embodying them, in Frank's second chance of a life – with Paloma – denied Albert Speer?

"But I still don't see why anyone would want to be mixed up with somebody most people think should have been sentenced to hang at Nuremberg ..." Bruno, driving, turns from the wheel to look at Frank. It is a direct stare – for an instant; enough for Frank to suspect Bruno's mute train of thought.

"One can find one's strayed into an unmarked tunnel in oneself," Frank says as Bruno turns back to the wheel. "It lets out into unsuspected thoughts and feelings – anyone's" he adds.

Frank glimpses, it seems, the personal reason why Bruno finds Speer inescapable. It is a marriage-wrecker's fascination with Speer's impossible yearning for a whole self, despite his inability to confess the unforgiveable. Then Frank says, as they approach a hill surmounted by the white *pueblo*: "Speer struggled to be good, not just as a Nazi but as a man. And it's how he sought to present himself to his young lover."

"But he wasn't good."

"Who is? Though some try. Speer did, if in a twisted way, as deep within himself as a monk's cell in Maria Laach Abbey."

"Even so," Bruno says, "why ever choose to view goodness through a war criminal like Speer?"

They are skirting the sea shore, about to drive up the steep hill.

"The ancient Greek mariners lit sacrificial fires on that beach," Frank says. "But why did they venerate their gods? To appease them, yes. Yet more specifically, because the gods and other mythological figures expressed for them emotions, impulses, which, while part of them, they didn't experience directly in themselves.

"Not that Speer is a god, regardless of Franz's worship of him. And his recent status as confidence trickster makes him too shabby to rank as a mythic devil. He is merely part of whatever comes to us randomly from life: my respite from research drawn from bestsellers in the news; scandal in this *pueblo*. It has just attached itself, as any of the flotsam or jetsam of existence might, acting as one's means of seeing the things about oneself one doesn't relish taking in directly."

Frank speaks quietly, confirming to himself with slow clarity what he has only recently understood and can now tell Bruno. "Speer is a medium for thinking about what one shrinks from acknowledging in oneself: all that's spoiled and wasted, making life empty. He is the being one least wants to be. So what a relief to realise, at long last, one is essentially quite different from the one haunting one; that one can shrug him off like a coat that doesn't fit anymore!

"One isn't under any sentence, after all. Nor need one live an endless charade to escape even more terrible, final punishment. So emerging from Speer's shadow, no longer unwittingly inhabited by someone other than one is, one has the second chance denied him – except as his illusion of living free in his second relationship."

"And *do* you have that 'second chance'?" Bruno asks pointedly, driving into the *pueblo*. "Can my daughter expect the second to differ from the first – whatever it was for you?"

As Bruno's words tail off, Frank appreciates him not inspecting his past. Bruno, a retired philanderer, might assume Frank has just had a series of casual liaisons. Or, irksome as Frank finds the thought, isn't Bruno viewing him – the English historian – as too staid ever to have had a history himself, let alone a romantic one?

"I feel I'm having a new beginning," Frank says, Villa Bougainvillea visible from the narrow road.

"And why now?" Frank hears the question pose itself inwardly to him, as if on Bruno's behalf. *Because having finished my book, my servitude to Professor Keller,* the silent voice continues, *I am, in experiencing my freedom here of all places, not only closing that chapter of my life but opening this fresh page.*

"A new start for you is one thing," Bruno says driving into El Castillo. "But is it a future for my daughter?"

PART VIII

1

Paloma rouses, her still-dissolving dream detaining her in Villa Bougainvillea. She is alarmed that you are gone, that you'll never come back, abandoning her to invasions of light through these slats of jalousies only now becoming the Venetian blinds in El Castillo. It is here that her mother told her, earlier, that Frank had joined her father for a drive.

They are up in the vineyard where, she thinks, I had found myself when Franz disappeared. But more than just missing, he had become wrenchingly unavailable to me, collapsed in a dim avenue of grapes, unconsoled by our maid missing my father. I am waiting for Frank to return, as he must be doing with this sound of the approaching car that has been calling me out of sleep.

This is "Sleeping Beauty", for an instant. She is awakened by a kiss from her young prince as the one entering her bedroom becomes, defying appearances. The illusion lifts, leaving her the anxiety she has carried out of sleep. While he, holding her hand reflectively as she lies there, blinks, as if roused too from some inner swoon.

Sleepwalkers no longer, they continue sitting silently on the bed. They are serious, as if faced by an invisible obstacle. Eventually Paloma asks about Frank's conversation with her father.

"I think it was fine."

Does she doubt it? Or is something besides holding her mutely to the crumpled sheets? Maybe it is an awareness of heading into terrain wider, more uncertain, than can be contained in a single summer month exorcising ghosts in Villa Bougainvillea.

Doesn't he too feel uneasy, despite privately insisting that Bruno's reaction could never, in any case, have changed anything? They are still where they have been with each other – though finally leaving Paloma's bedroom to move on together from El Castillo.

They are talking, half-talking, not talking now as they cross the plaza and look down from the *mirador*. There Bog Man, that eternal reminder of gloom, tips his cigarette butt across the railing. It flares down the precipice. He is provoking the mounds, Frank imagines, to reveal that they, together with their skeletons from the past, are far from extinct.

Frank draws sharply back from the edge, suggesting that we have lunch in that small coastal town nearby. For although it feels so long since he joined me last night, while I was reacting to Franz's drowning, I find it is still only noon.

I nod, eager to dispel the atmosphere of recent hours. Besides, we have been so confined to the *pueblo* by our developing relationship that we are both suddenly quite ready to go further afield to enjoy the holiday each of us is supposed to have been having all along. Though isn't this, above all, to sample a prelude to our life to come?

We have found each other out in the nocturnal rooms, on the starlit roof of the villa swathed in bougainvillea. But do we yet know who we are, he and I? It will take a future surely to open us up, each to each; oneself to oneself.

Yet we feel it has started here even before it begins in London, as we saunter arm in arm along the marble *paseo* where locals drink apéritifs beneath overarching palms. Carefree, we all but tell one another how alive we feel, unencumbered for the first time; that life has finally begun.

Wandering by a low seaside wall running all the way down to the small port, we gaze across the blue expanse to an invisible dark continent, sharing ideas on where we might travel together in the future.

"To Paris," he ventures peering out – and back to me. He has always felt its pull, he tells me, but never ventured there except on a school trip. Not till we have lunch at one of the tables set outside the fish restaurant by the harbour does he explain that he had once had a lover who invited him there. He could not go at the time, he adds, using a spoon and fork to heap anchovies from our shared platter of fried fish onto my plate.

"I'll tell you why, sometime ..." He has taken my hand. I leave the squid. "Don't you like it?"

"I don't mind fish, if it isn't too fishy."

"You should have told me. I'd have ordered something else for us."

"But you can have fish."

We are making concessions, discovering just how much we don't know about each other. It affirms that we can be together. But later, when we have gone on to share details of our immediate lives, our work, and he reflects on going back alone the day after tomorrow, reappearing at his work desk on Monday, he becomes serious. Silence falls upon us.

It should not matter. We were alone, each of us, before we met. And it will only be an absence of weeks, a month or two at most. Yet the idea of days, nights, alone is suddenly heavy. It threatens to become unbearable till he seeks to summon the evasive waiter for the bill – a forlorn enterprise.

Now Frank says: "Look, as soon as I'm back I'll look into art colleges for you. Then you'll join me."

Isn't it to put a brave face on it that, when he eventually succeeds in paying and we leave, he impulsively accepts the gypsy's offer of a drive in the horse-drawn carriage parked directly outside the restaurant? *Don't fret. We're free as the birds,* Frank's gesture seems to say. And, as if to make the point, a flock of seagulls rises up from municipal geraniums around the statue of some bewhiskered nineteenth-century worthy in a rotunda. The sea breeze is fresh on our faces.

On and on the horse clops. Its ornamental brass hangings clank, the whip cracks, as we hug in the back, passing a Belle Époque apartment building. We no longer speak. And aren't we deep in thought, taking in that we have crossed the Rubicon with each other, reckoning quite what we have come to take on each from each, that there is no undoing it, no going back? Is it why, dismounting from a shorter ride than agreed, though actually quite sufficient, he accepts the offer by a waiting photographer?

We are fixed, the pair of us, together in a snapshot regardless of thoughts, fears, ghosts.

I stand here on the balcony, feeling the October sun warming me through my turtleneck pullover as I gaze out. It is still and blue in this perfect moment by what I now realise is the Mediterranean with you, so much younger and attractive. We are taking in the deliciously fresh air after our siesta's lovemaking.

I feel light, especially my shoulders. A burden weighing me so far down in the past has fallen away. I am fully myself with you: I, tall, distinguished, confident and accomplished with this new lease of life.

I awaken with you beside me. We are in bed in the villa. There was no question of taking our siesta on the roof in that fierce afternoon sun, after lunch in the harbour.

Parting the shutters to look out at the balcony, I try to hold onto my dream of Albert Speer. It is forsaking me, only leaving me wearing that smile I remember from his photograph in Provence, as I glance across our pillows at the scattering of hair that is you.

Later, beside each other on the roof of the villa that has become habitual for us even after what we must acknowledge have been relatively few nights, I unexpectedly feel again the impact of our first meeting. It is an emotional ambush: magnetism working through this abruptly revived idea, this feel, the atmosphere of you, all impossible in any other who does not have your exact pair of eyes, the shock of their glance, the heady scent that is you.

You are once more unknowingly mysterious to me, surprised at finding you: you, uniquely, so appealing. I am half-fascinated, half-bewildered, to know what being with you will be like. And spread out on the rag covers, you are apparently as content as I am to suspend our lovemaking and lie still, looking up at the stars, to reflect on our next steps. Though now, in this long-held moment in each other's arms, we neither feel nor fear the Earth moving beneath us.

2

"He'll be leaving now," my mother says.

"He" does not have a name. "He" is simply the one attached to me at this time, time running ever more freely through the hourglass of this *pueblo* where we have found each other, and which will be measured, experienced, quite differently in that unknown dimension of a life coming after this.

"He" is the man my parents would not wish for me, because of the discrepancy in our ages, to say nothing of the lightning speed with which we have bonded. "He", it is assumed, will hurt me when, judging from the past, he will leave me: "he" whom they know they cannot compel me to renounce now. It is why my mother is relying on that natural course of events, the final end of a summer from which "he", a mere holidaymaker after all, must return home.

He will of course be doing so alone, my mother's remark assumes. Yet, actually, it is a hope, a forlorn one about much more than just his movements, expressed in her implicit question.

I answer it to her evident disappointment: "For the moment".

Her crestfallen expression dissipates in the sigh with which she takes me in her arms. "We just want you to be happy, your father and I."

She is referencing conversations they have been having out of earshot; discussions in which I sense they exchanged impressions of the Englishman. My father, following his interview with him up in the vineyard, apparently concludes inconclusively that the relationship with his daughter is not stillborn, that it will continue in some form or other, that Magda and he must simply find a way of accepting it.

I draw back from my mother's arms. I walk away not only to my room but also into musings on the life we shall have once he returns, and I visit him. I am imagining what we shall make of a future together. Yet, surprisingly, I am overcome by the thought of the parents I have left behind. I see the pair sitting in silent acceptance of what they do not exactly want as it continues beyond their reach, outside their control. They continue holding their concern to themselves, growing muted, older.

Paloma is not deliberately distancing her parents, and no more does she wish hurtfully to shrug off Heidi. She has intermittently wanted to leave things well with her, though without knowing what Heidi – so easily hurt and difficult – would settle for. But events have a momentum of their own. So Magda, saying later that Amalia has just come to visit with her daughter, tells Paloma that Heidi is leaving and wants to wish her goodbye.

They sit together, Heidi and Paloma, in the garden overlooking the pampas grass and pantiled terracotta wall. Seeing the ribbon of sea and sky beyond, Paloma does not speak, dismissing clichés about regretting that things could never be other than they are, wishing Heidi well even so. Heidi's eyes are also on the distance as she says she wanted to come and say goodbye, that it would not be right to have left without doing so because she doubts that she will ever return – although she is not leaving in anger, but has finally found the courage to walk away from an impossible love; in other words, to come at last to herself and whatever life will bring.

She can say goodbye to Paloma, she knows, because she needs nothing further from her. For she has now realised Franz had nothing in the end to say about Speer. Or if he did, it was simply that the great *Reichsminister*, as he had always remained in his own mind, betrayed no more sign of coming to himself than had Franz.

Paloma frowns. She wonders if that is true. Maybe Franz drowned because of a life fulfilled.

No, Heidi says. Few people achieve that. Especially not an older man, embarking on a liaison with a younger woman, who breaks it off, as is inevitable with a relationship of this type. And Speer was essentially lying about himself in his late affair, obviously thereby fated even if death had not intervened.

It takes great resolve to move oneself – who or what one is – ahead in life, as Heidi is doing. And there is no looking back, except for Lot's wife. If one does, what disastrous breakups might one encounter in the *pueblo*?

Paloma receives an embrace, coldly chaste, perhaps to assert just how little she means to Heidi after all.

Frank's days in the *pueblo* have dwindled. In the interludes between nights with Paloma in Villa Bougainvillea and her return to El Castillo, he registers on the terrace of Pensión Amalia the oleander, the argumentative cockatoo, the seaview: images stored up for his return to London's reality.

His morning solitude now feels quite different from what he had experienced as a new arrival here. He had expected to lounge, enjoying a well-deserved rest on completing his book after the arduous effort of many years, so restricting him. But lingering over more coffee, eyes still attuned to Britain's grey skies, sensitive to early Mediterranean haze, he had actually been far from calm. More turbulent than he realised, he had nervously sought a new project: a search that, it has turned out, intersected with the pursuit of what he had lost in Villa Bougainvillea.

All the issues his emerging subject, Speer, faced in having any chance of a real relationship with that young German lover were challenges, modulated into a different key, that Frank feels he has overcome with Paloma. He can now wait for her in this new contentment on the terrace, enthusiastic about the prospect of their future.

Indeed, the very thought of Paloma, the sensation of her in his arms, comes forcefully to Frank. He is drinking it in – until such soft blankness is interrupted by another element of his daily hour here: Heidi.

She is not sitting with her books or lingering over coffee, prepared to talk as sometimes before. She is carrying a suitcase out of her room in the *pensión*, across the terrace to the entrance and the street. She loads the car that will take her to the airport. Noticing Frank, she pauses, letting the driver take the suitcase out. She comes over, wavering between uncertainty and defiance.

"So you're off," Frank says, gesturing to her to sit a moment.

"Of course," she says stiffly, still standing. But she relents and takes the chair, saying: "And you, what will you be doing now?"

"Good question," he answers, regretting that with Heidi there is little alternative but to be arch. "Coming here, I thought I would find the idea for my next book. But I'm not quite sure of the outcome."

"Really!" she says tartly.

"Do I actually need a project? I'm not certain. Maybe I should just give myself time to think, focusing on myself."

"But I had the distinct impression you'll be writing about Speer."

"Maybe," Frank says vaguely. "Though I'm an historian, and everything I've been thinking about him is personal."

"That's surprising," Heidi says. "I don't see how." But what she goes on to query is not, as Frank expects, what evidence is available for those kinds of thoughts. "It's unlikely, isn't it," she asks instead, "that a criminal impostor is capable of real human feeling? Not someone so cold-hearted."

"Oh! But I think some such impulse is in everybody, don't you?" says Frank. "Can't everyone come to life? Speer from Spandau, Franz from Russia – everyone? Though how far does one also have to travel to come to oneself, that's the question."

There's tense silence. It is broken by clattering in the kitchen.

"Talking of Franz," Heidi says, "we've heard nothing that he might have revealed of Speer. Or is it just me that hasn't been told ..."

"I doubt Paloma has anything she wanted to share with me but not you." Silence descends once more. "Because," Frank eventually goes on, "he obviously had nothing to reveal – except nothing. What he came back to was the identity he had lost in some Siberian psychiatric prison, as Speer's driver, chauffeuring the *Übermensch's* lover. He never progressed beyond it. He was nothing more than that.

"But his case does serve an important purpose. It put us in the right frame of mind to see the equal hollowness of the one he served, the man in whose shadow he existed – raising the issue of whether or not the Führer's beloved ever surmounted his own emptiness, with that young woman, say. It's the critical question to ask of Speer – but who, finally, can answer it?"

"So you're left empty-handed," Heidi says, flushed by an illusory moment of bitter triumph. "Not that it can matter now. It's water under the bridge. Everything is," she adds, voice faltering. "Nothing holds ... *Adieu* – not *Auf Wiedersehen*."

"We call it *The Last Prelude*. But it's not certain whether it's simply the one chancing to come at the end, or the culmination of the entire series."

"What do you think?" Frank asks.

They are in Bruno's study. The book he borrowed sits on the Steinway against which they lean, after having had lunch.

"I play it as the summation – dropping everything that's gone before into the abyss with that terrible series of runs. It's tragic, leaving nothing after it; just reverberation, nothing."

"*Last* indeed," Frank says. "Makes it hard to play, I'm sure. Not much chance of an encore."

Bruno does not react, which to Frank's mind *is* his reaction. Bruno merely swallows another of his pills while looking away, through the window at his daughter and her mother.

They have been talking of plans for Paloma to return to the Madrid art gallery for a few months until she begins studying art in London the following year.

"You'll stay with me while you visit him," Magda says.

Paloma does not answer. But her mother does not belabour the point. She knows the civilised older Englishman is the best deal she and Bruno are likely to get for their daughter – from Paloma.

Now they are sitting together for coffee, the four of them, making conversation with idle chatter about the *pueblo*. Amalia has reported that the German owners of that villa have been in touch about it.

"No, I don't know the details," Paloma hears her mother say.

But she is not listening. She is taking in the group: her parents together, with herself and Frank. Yet rather than summoning up another's painting of some such image, she finds herself portraying in her mind's eye this magic circle.

After lunch we wander down from El Castillo. We are not usually out together late in the afternoon. It makes us see everything in the light.

We slow down, entering the plaza and approach the *mirador* to take in the view this last time together. We are starting, though still together, to feel the melancholy tug of parting; of our tomorrow.

"So you're leaving." It is Bog Man, sidling up to Frank. There is no point in asking who told him. He knows everything, even to the extent of being aware, surely, by some process of emotional osmosis, of our apprehension at the idea of leaving each other, of each having to revert to being only partially without the other. "I hope you'll see him again," Bog Man says.

He is an insinuating smile, this odious Cheshire Cat now lost in a rank cloud of cigarette smoke dispersing below the metal railing. We move away, turning into an alley almost invisible to our blinded eyes, and walk down to the villa, hand in hand – to be brought up short.

A gardener is trimming the bougainvillea, radically. Its windows, walls, bared, it looks naked.

Clearly part of the refurbishment the German owners ordered, we feel it as an intrusion on what is ours. It is an indecent peering into what has allowed us to come to one another; to find ourselves there.

We enter, needing no key. Justi is here, filling the hallway with her lemon-scented cleaning fluid. But we go to the living room, sitting and agreeing a time to leave tomorrow for the farewell, the departure, at the provincial airport. We continue there as the light weakens. We hear Justi arguing with the gardener, barely agreeing that he, not she, should sweep away the mass of snipped creeper. Then the two locals go, leaving us to this silence and now darkness.

Mutely, we get up and climb the stairs to the roof. Night reverses all changes to our villa. The late summer air is fragrant with jasmine growing atop the surrounding houses. A piano makes its habitual nocturnal attempt to see a piece through. Somewhere, dogs bark.

We embrace. But, holding each other, we continue leaning against the wall of the roof terrace. For we are facing across the flat tops of moonlit houses, over the sloping hill with its cultivated kilometre, out to a silver sea and star-filled sky.

All is as it has always been and will be. We hold still, part of each other, here at our changeless vantage point: Villa Bougainvillea.

3

It is my last morning. Paloma gets into the taxi to accompany me to the provincial capital, where she will bid me farewell at the airport. Hurtling down the hill from *pueblo* to sea, with the early sun and salt breeze filling the car, we hold hands, listing everything we look forward to doing together in future.

We skirt the beach – deserted, I see, as we continue our animated exchanges. It is too early for families, holidaymakers. For it is October, and while you are talking now I already sense the coming coolness.

Despite inwardly seeing, feeling, the one emerging naked from the waves, regardless of the solitude that could be his at this hour, I suppose, as Paloma and I remind ourselves, that we shall soon be together again; that he could not long await there, alone, what his life will be. Not as a cold season closes in, freezing him out.

A shaft of warm sunlight drives away this premonition of winter together with the shuddering bather, as we see, through Paloma's enthusiastic eyes, ourselves wandering arm in arm through the richly endowed museums and galleries of London. We plan our visits to Kew, Windsor, Stonehenge – all to take place soon, in a few quickly passed weeks, surely; just a month or two, assuming we are safely reunited before the rain, cold and short days set in with their freezing restrictions.

Crossing this desert terrain, we barely take in the harsh moonscape from our taxi window. We are caught up in a sense of what our life together will be, though something is stealing up on us, deeper than our distracting chatter. It is the climate of an unaccustomed season without the August sun and its languorously long nights. Eerily deflating our thrill of loving, with its festive aura, isn't it leaving us fearful of finding oneself unaccompanied after all?

We peer mutely, unseeingly, at grey volcanic soil. It is too sterile to hold one's glance except for an occasional cactus turning to bark and a barely cultivated small holding smelling of pigs.

We had not expected to be so lost in thought, immersed in feelings, consumed by what comes upon us today. It is the prospect of that dangerous moment when, whether now or later in some drear future, divested of the other in a wrenching farewell, I have returned to all I am, less than myself, without you, now part of me.

Emptiness has appeared again, coming as an alarming instant of nausea; the trembling before an earthquake breaks open the surface. For we had never sought to imagine, whilst together in the *pueblo*, once so alone there, a painful prising apart; the anticipation of that final instant when, having entered the Departures Terminal, I am exiled to the wrong side of a gate that my inner eye sees closing inexorably between us.

Of course, we still have not arrived. Clinging to each other in the taxi, we claim a reprieve. But I am suddenly lurched away from your cheek as we turn towards the airport, a converted building in need of the modernisation urgently called for by those eager to continue developing the province's tourism.

Looking across each other's shoulders, we find dusty creeper extending across dirty whitewashed walls. What we see, our breath caught, is a dense façade of purple flower-like leaves. It encloses the place in which we shall find ourselves, as ever.

Part IX

1

Many years have passed since a mayor sought to attract outsiders to the *pueblo*. In those early days the newcomers, whether Spaniards or foreigners, were diplomats, businessmen, professionals. For a time the Queen's private secretary, during the monarch's annual retreat to Balmoral, summered in the villa built on land the mayor gave him.

Now tourism has invaded, as in the rest of the country. People come here on package tours, preferring the bars on the beach. Increasing numbers buy cheap bungalows in the urbanisations that speculators fast develop in the surrounding areas.

Nowadays it is again mainly locals who inhabit the *pueblo* in summer, though their youth increasingly join the foreigners on the beach. Or the tourists decide to come up to view its quaint alleys for the day, drinking in its cafés and bars for a night out. Vacationers owning property in the *pueblo* visit less frequently, and it is not as easy to rent out their houses as it once was.

The villa across from that small *pensión* overlooking the sea has remained largely unoccupied. Its German owners have not come here in years, leaving it in the care of the *pensión's* owner. But she, too, is less often in the *pueblo*. The *pensión* is open erratically, especially now the owner's daughter does not visit. Amalia spends more and more time with her sister in Granada.

It means she is less available to help rent the villa. Thus, despite its refurbishment a year or so earlier, leaving the windows cleaned, the shutters bright green, the walls white, it is shabby again. The bougainvillea is thickening once more, obscuring the façade. Cats have entered, overpowering the last traces of lemon detergent. Of a night, shrivelled jasmine from the roof trellis rustles like insects across the moonlit tiles.

On his first return after the August when he had met Paloma, Frank Ward stayed again at Pensión Amalia. But that was only for two nights, and well before Semana Santa. For he had joined Paloma, called back by her father's illness in March, and soon moved in with her, into El Castillo.

Bruno's condition had actually become serious earlier, before Christmas. Magda left her flat in Kensington to look after him, so there was no longer pressure on her daughter, who had arrived in London in October to view possible art colleges, to stay with her mother. She could at last move in with Frank – her true objective in travelling to England.

For Frank, this brought to a head what he had not fully faced till now, but nonetheless coloured even his keenest longing to join Paloma; his very need to be with her day and night, an anxiety about his capacity for domesticity. And this was just one aspect of his earlier, more profound fear that he might not have the courage, the force of personality, to launch such a relationship after all. It signalled concerns about giving up his single life, that daily solitude making him beholden, responsible – and responsive – to no other in bedsits with little more than a washbasin and electric kettle, a shared bathroom and kitchen.

Such facilities were plainly inadequate for living with Paloma. She was, after all, a girl who, regardless of her tendency to detach herself from her parents, had fully acquired their expectations for a civilised life, settled and comfortable.

Frank's parents had, however, died recently. Their only son, he had inherited their solidly middle-class house in Kent. So with few changes at this point, but many doubtless to come as Paloma cast her artist's eye over the dated sofa, carpets and curtains, they moved in. It was an orderly change of guard: one couple taking the place of another without ado – except when Paloma's mother telephoned to recall her daughter to her father's side.

March is cold in the *pueblo*. The Mediterranean is grey. Frank finds white-capped waves crashing on the beach. It is the first time he has witnessed it, only ever having been here previously in summer. Certainly, he has never worn an overcoat here before, leaving a *pensión* so deserted that he marvels it is still open to wander the streets up to El Castillo.

The place feels unnatural. The locals are restrained in bars it will take tourists and a few absentee homeowners to make rowdy in several months' time. Above all there is a noiselessness, a heavy vacancy, it seems to Frank, in place of a piano seeking, losing its way, beneath that cloud canopy blocking the stars.

Bruno is in bed, heavily medicated. His heart condition is worsening. The lamp beside him casts a parchment glow over the flask of water, ampoules, photographs of Paloma as a laughing child – and, can it be, of Magda? It renders him waxen, distant, almost unreal, the centre of attention for his daughter, her mother and, well, more than her mere lover by now, her fiancé, husband in all but name.

It is wearisome to spend time here. There is scant communication with the man. Does he fully recognise – or care – who is beside him? Certainly not me, Frank, a latecomer in his life, if one with whom he apparently appreciated exchanging views. I do not press the point even to myself, though Paloma and Magda perhaps concede it, exhaustedly leaving the man alone to me for a while.

I sit watching the hand on the crumpled fold of sheet against the blanket. It is blotched with liver spots. The nails would have been clipped, had he not been confined to bed. Otherwise they would have clinked against the piano keys. But even now, the fingers are mobile, tirelessly striking ivory for all the man's withdrawn inertness.

I am not there as he ascends and plunges down precipices of notes. But I cannot take my eyes off the intensity of his effort, the sheer certainty of the runs. Then, unexpectedly, almost violently, the hand reaches out. It clasps mine tightly, painfully. I'm known; acknowledged, in the instant that, grasping, he expires.

There's a smile on his face: Bruno has finally overcome all the obstacles to his *Last Prelude*.

Frank stays on at El Castillo. Neither Paloma nor Magda suggests it. It just happens in this sudden vacancy, the reverberating silence.

The funeral is the following day. Once over, Paloma, inheriting El Castillo, tells her mother, lingering in the piano room: "Of course, you'll use it".

"No. I couldn't."

Paloma leaves with Frank for London that evening. Magda remains.

2

Juan has not returned to the *pueblo* since he invited his undergraduate friend Frank Ward to spend a summer with him there. They meet again for the first time at a black-tie college reunion that Frank would never previously have attended. But now, with Paloma, to whom he is engaged, he has broken out of his shell, attending Sunday lunches with her mother's side of the family; going with her to sketch in Constable country; joining her for that weekend in Amsterdam with a group of her contemporaries at art school to whom Frank has a nagging, secretly shameful fear he might lose her, despite which they all became great friends.

Frank introduces Paloma to Juan over drinks in the honey glow of the Master's wood-panelled lodge. While she talks in Spanish to his wife, a soignée woman Frank's sleekly prosperous friend has presumably (and judiciously) settled on marrying only after many liaisons, the men reminisce. It is jovial, out of earshot of the women. They are recalling that far off summer in the *pueblo*.

"D'you remember *Maruja la Bruja* – especially those breasts? And have you kept in touch with the Frenchwoman you broke up with? You were so upset at the time. No? Well, I noticed her in some magazine a year or so ago, whilst in Paris on business. Of course she was older – aren't we all? Her hair was short and white in the way some middle-aged women consider stylish. But her features were still strong. And that dark, smouldering expression – we both remember, don't we? – was even more intense.

"Apparently she's a journalist, active as a feminist. Now she's written an autobiography describing growing up in Algeria and adapting to France as a young woman. It talks about how she finally found herself in Paris, living with her husband, an academic, and their two grown children.

"The magazine says the book will surely be of interest given the difficulty France's North African population has in finding an identity for itself in the country. But that's wishful thinking, isn't it? She's writing from a *pied noir*, not a Muslim, perspective."

Juan does not wait for his friend's answer. He fails to notice the inward look with which Frank wonders if she says anything about her time in Spain. Juan is telling him that his parents sold their house in the *pueblo* years ago. He himself has never felt inclined to return since that summer. He's heard it's lost its rustic charm. Apparently very different people go there now. Christine and he have a place in the Caribbean.

Frank says: "I went a couple of summers ago, to relax after finishing a book."

"You were always the scholar."

I don't feel complimented.

"And how did you find it, all those years later?"

"The same – and different." I say it vaguely, dismissing my impulse from minutes earlier to meet Esther again – not merely from commitment to Paloma, but because so unimaginably much has changed in both of us since we were together. What could such personal exhumations amount to? "We met in the *pueblo*," I say, looking over at Paloma in conversation with Christine.

"Ah! I see," Juan says, taking in the younger woman with his connoisseur's eye. "Nice!"

Then he asks: "So, are you writing another book now?"

I sigh, saying: "Who knows? Not on the same period, anyway."

"Which one, then?"

"The war."

I mention my interest in Speer, especially the discussions of him I had in the *pueblo* following his driver's convalescence in Villa Bougainvillea.

Juan tries to remember which villa that is. Of course, he can't. It has never been part of his experience, he who was missing from the *pueblo* in the hills, on the beach, in its abandoned coves with his girlfriend; he for whom it harbours no past, no resonance. But the villa beams into my mind with its luxuriant trails of purple flowers.

"Though I've yet to see if I'm up to writing an historical study of him. That's another reason why I'm here this weekend. As well as attending this reunion, I'm visiting Peter Freeman tomorrow."

Freeman, our contemporary, now a lecturer on modern Germany, is being interviewed by the BBC tonight.

"I hope it works out … But then, you could always write a novel about Speer."

Friendly words, they feel dismissive as I notice Juan's eyes tracking over my shoulder to our host, the Master. Juan, a successful businessman, sparing no thought for the years of application demanded by a serious writing project, treats it lightly.

"I don't know," I murmur, wondering what could come from such a book.

"Really? But with those recent revelations in the press about all he knew and contributed to Nazi crimes, there must be quite a story to tell."

"For journalists, perhaps. Though not as a novel, at least not along the lines Speer had in mind. He suggested putting *'À la recherche du temps perdu'* as a motto on the title page of his memoir. But his life is about forgetting, not remembering.

"Of course, early on in Spandau, Speer thinks of himself in terms of that hidden picture of Dorian Gray," I say, continuing this unexpected review of his fictional self-presentations. "Despite which, on the next page of his *Secret Diaries*, he reflects that Hitler, far from leading him from himself, actually led him *to* himself: what Speer calls his 'heightened identity'.

"That only refers to his architecture, of course, licensing him to design buildings that indulged his own romantic protest against modernity. Though Speer's mention of Dorian Gray applies more generally than he supposes. He colluded ethically, we now know, with Hitler and his henchmen. Which makes it equally impossible to portray his early years as a moral coming of age in some *Bildungsroman*."

"Ah!" Juan says, halting me, merely another guest at this cocktail reception, from arresting him with what should simply be a passing aspect of our small talk.

"There's simply too much Mephistopheles in Speer," I go on, undeterred. "Who can swallow his self-serving claim that he was the victim of an unwitting Faustian pact? He makes it responding to his daughter Hilde's birthday letter, asking how he could have worked for such an evil regime. He even goes on to liken himself to Oedipus.

But Speer is no Oedipus punished by destiny for sins he committed unknowingly.

"No, there's no novel to be written about Speer," I say, returning to Juan's suggestion. "At least no *standard* one," I add, surprised by thoughts continuing to come to me about how best to render him. "Not that the canons of tragedy and myth apply either – irrespective of his driver's veneration of him as one of the fallen Reich's *Übermensche*.

"What *is* relevant, though, is his inner recognition of a spoiled life: the issue of how he can continue leading it. With little enough left by Spandau and the unforgiving verdict of time, how could it be tragic or heroic? At most it leaves open whether there's still a chance of *un*spoiled living – before life's closing gate finally slams shut."

"'*Inner recognition?*'" Juan says sceptically, looking at me as if detained by the Ancient Mariner. "How do we know?"

"Ah! There's another question," I say. "For tomorrow."

3

Frank has a momentary vision of Villa Bougainvillea, its creeper blooming riotously despite all its years there. He is passing the bin with that plant still surviving cigarette butts, abundant despite a recent university 'no smoking' policy, set outside Professor Keller's office.

Frank walks on, ignoring the new incumbent. He has no new project to propose on the early modern state. Yet Keller is still at the back of his onetime student's mind, shaking hands with the contemporary he implicitly veered away from throughout the decades Freeman received plaudits for research that Frank himself failed to undertake. This pang is not only the humiliating sting of recognition of how much less he has achieved, with one lonely book, than the spate of works placing this self-confident, energetic, balding man securely in the public eye – as in a widely acclaimed television series. It is also a lingering sense of committing treason against the Master by now outlining fascination with Albert Speer.

Peter Freeman, for his part, is curious about the suggestion. But this is less a matter of cordially welcoming a resurfacing member of his generation. Rather, evading the need to show personal warmth, Freeman expresses interest in Frank as a curiosity: the protégé of someone so far removed from the kind of history he himself practises that Frank is unexpectedly hurt to hear Sir Emil referred to simply as "quite a character".

It surprises Freeman to find Frank contemplating such a radical change in his field of interest. It is all the odder as Frank confesses he knows next to no German and lacks familiarity with the German war archives in Koblenz.

As for the idea of a specifically biographical study of Speer, anathema to Keller, Peter Freeman wonders how Frank comes to be engaged by this kind of subject in particular. But he does not wait for an explanation. He says: "In my view, what's most valuable is research into structural matters like the nature of Germany's electorate, its political organisation, industrial potential and military capacity. That's the sort of thing I'm working on. Though I might be able to suggest someone who'd have more time to guide an, em, a –"

"Amateur," Frank supplies.

"In any case," Freeman continues, "the latest study of Speer leaves nothing more to say about the man – not after the way it's eviscerated him. All the evidence is finally in. The picture's complete. It would be well worth you taking a look at the book before making any further research plans. Let me lend – no, I'll give it to you."

But before Freeman can get up and find the volume in his crowded bookshelves, Frank says: "Please don't trouble yourself. I've read it."

All at once, Mediterranean sunlight floods Frank's mind, as it had the terrace where Bruno's book kept him company till happily superseded by Paloma. Now she is waiting for him, by the river flowing through the university, while he meets Peter Freeman. Even so, Frank ignores Freeman's cue to leave, saying of the book: "It's true that the author treats the evidence for Speer meticulously. And he certainly advances his argument with lethal efficiency. I'd even say he relishes doing so. Nevertheless, I personally find the book leaves much to be desired as a work of history."

Whereupon Frank, never having written an historical review, preferring to shirk controversy, now finds a critique composing in his mind.

Frank is finally being frank.

"The author is keen to give a full account of what Speer knew and did in the war. He shows beyond doubt that Speer was not only aware of Nazi outrages, but also that he contributed to them. But such is the author's enthusiasm for exposing the terrible truth that, far from simply revealing what was actually the case and letting the facts speak eloquently for themselves, his book acts at one and the same time as a prosecutor's brief and final verdict. It's obviously a misuse of history, which should restrict itself to presenting and then neutrally weighing evidence to achieve an unimpassioned, balanced view.

"Besides, the author is so determined to expose Speer's successive denials of what he had known and done, whether in Spandau or later, so eager to rip off the mask he had adopted to throw others off the scent of what would have become his death sentence, that he offers us a one- dimensional, cheap fraud whose attempt to come to terms with his massive guilt is simply dismissed with contempt. After all, the book effectively says, shouldn't one be more concerned for Speer's multitude of victims than with the belated pricking of his tender conscience?

"It results in ignoring the actual agony of conscience Speer underwent, according to Casalis, the Spandau chaplain – a witness too discerning to be duped. While Father Athanasius, Speer's guide on retreats at the Benedictine monastery of Maria Laach, said he had never known anyone so aware of his own deficiencies. Although when Athanasius himself also criticises him as an incomplete man, he is mistaken. He claims Speer is incapable of sensual love, whereas he turns out to have had an affair with a beautiful young German mistress right up to his dying moments. So, brutally enough, it's the mistress that tells Margarete, the wife, of his death – almost certainly in bed with her."

Peter Freeman has not reacted. Necessarily reconciling himself to hearing out his visitor, he continues waiting as Frank goes on:

"Yet this opens up questions the book hardly addresses: what might Speer have been doing inwardly to face his guilt? Did he tell defensive lies to live with himself – whomever that self *was*?

"Answering requires emotional, even ethical, sophistication the author lacks. Or, if he possesses it, he declines to use it, denying it to Speer, too, by advancing this exclusively as a criminal investigation. He won't admit that a person can simultaneously be characterised by two contradictory things: an evasive persona, and a sense of guilt.

"Only intuition, perceiving the man's condition, experiencing his inner state, allows one clairvoyant – *clair voyant* – insight into how he came to himself in the only way available in Spandau; in his retreats in Maria Laach Abbey; and then in the arms of a young German woman unaware of the truth."

All at once, Frank is overcome by the sensation of an embrace. He feels its soft blankness. And thinking of Paloma, he knows it is time to meet her.

Freeman has not stirred. He continues taking Frank in with unflinching eyes. Now he breaks the fraught stillness: "It appears you already have a definite sense of what you'll be writing. But it's along quite separate lines from my own work. It takes a very different approach to evidence – or the lack of it. And that, to be candid, I consider a fundamental weakness, as I do whenever my more tiresome critics kowtow to some fashionable notion that everything's relative with no such thing as fact or truth."

"But I'm not doubting facts," Frank says, taking in Freeman's air of irritated superiority. "It's just that whenever one comes to what's crucial, including Speer's bond with Hitler, the sources fall silent."

"Well, you can't ask history to provide what it's incapable of."

"What's most important. Namely that Speer did discover a conscience, although he was trapped into having to deny the truth, and that he only fully experienced himself humanly in an oblique way through an affair.

"True, his late love inflated his sense of self-worth, diminishing him again. He ultimately made a drunken call to Gitta Sereny, the journalist who interviewed him at length, saying: 'after all, I think I haven't done so badly. I *was* Hitler's architect. I *was* his Minister of

Armaments and Production. I *did* serve twenty years in Spandau and, coming out, *did* make another good career. Not bad after all, was it?'

"Even so," Frank says, "you can't take away from Albert Speer what, if one's perceptive, if one's alive to his story, one sees he did, for a time, become: another man."

"A journalist, eh?" Freeman says, sniffing. "Look, on the basis of what you've been telling me, I doubt that I would consider anything you produce on Speer as a work of history. Nor, to be honest, would I expect Emil Keller to have done so. Because you're throwing out the baby with the bathwater, rejecting not only him and his approach, but what is actually also the method of every reputable historian."

"Oh! But I respect him and his writing. And I'm very grateful to him."

"Are you?"

"Well, he was extremely kind. Paternal. He gave me important opportunities, opening up so much for me. But now I've realised there's nothing to keep me in his shadow – or that of all the other historians with their valuable studies, at least as far as the evidence allows.

"Because it's not a matter of seeing historical figures externally, piecing together what's available from the sources and leading one to deduce motivations and character traits. Rather, it's having a sense of who they are from within: experiencing it as a medium does. Which is very different from mere invention, well-aligned as it may be with all the rest the historian knows on a purely documentary basis; forgery, in other words, even when verging on art. On the contrary, it's a sense that draws on the unique reality of the particular figure, lying outside the range of history as a way of study. And it's certainly an aspiration for knowing all one cares about, as in a few novels that universalise the inner being of their characters."

There is a long pause. Then Freeman clears his throat to say: "In that case, I'm sure you won't need any guidance from me. And I doubt there's much point in troubling each other further."

Frank moves towards the indicated door.

4

Despite Peter Freeman's apparent coolness when talking to Frank, their discussion leaves him restless. He wanders over to the college common room. There he recognises Juan reading the paper while his wife is – inevitably – shopping. Although Freeman might not ordinarily have bothered to greet Juan, their lives having taken such different courses, he now goes over, coffee in hand.

"I've just been talking to a friend of yours … Frank Ward. There's an odd bird."

"I knew him in my final year. He stayed with me in Spain when we graduated. He had a catastrophic love affair that summer, and became a virtual recluse. It's taken him forever to get over it.'

"If he has," Freeman says dryly.

"Well, he's here with his very attractive young wife."

"Even so, he has some pretty strange ideas. Has he told you his views on Albert Speer?"

Juan raises his eyes. "At length!"

"He's just come to discuss them with me. Seems he has a chip on his shoulder about Emil Keller. I realise it must have been oppressive to be his student. And I certainly don't agree with the Great Man's approach to research. But Ward should at least recognise he was a major scholar. His documentary work is impeccable."

"I'm sure Frank knows that," Juan says protectively. "He did choose to study with him."

"In that case, he'd do well to admit with Keller and the rest of us that history can only set out the evidence. It necessarily falls silent when there isn't any, regardless of how much one would like to know a particular thing."

Namely, what is most important, Juan thinks to himself, comradely again in the face of Freeman's brusque defensiveness about the cut-and-dried approach that has secured him such early success.

"Historians," Freeman goes on, "can't rely on imagination, fictional reconstruction. And anyone who feels compelled to do so, in full awareness of the academic risks, must be shoring up some aspect of his inner world. Because it seeks meaning for the author, not understanding for historians. But meaning and understanding serve quite different purposes; two distinct approaches to being. Your friend Frank has simply confused them, hasn't he?"

"Maybe," Juan says shrugging his shoulders. He prefers it to replying that intuition is what generally convinces people. For he is relieved to find his wife walking in with her packages; it releases him from additional discussion with this other Ancient Mariner about matters unrelated to Juan's life in business.

5

Walking by the river, Paloma asks Frank about his discussion with Peter Freeman.

"'Discussion', you say? More an historian's last hurrah," he replies. Then pensive, he adds: "Maybe I'll write something called *History and the Human*, history meaning 'what actually happened to people in the past' versus 'what the historians say'. But I'm not sure. I need time to consider how. The idea's so much part of me."

Away from the archive, the studio, we are in the open air these days; out in the light. I am drawing sluggish fen streams; slow-moving barge canals; riverside meadows of motionless cows and wildflowers; blustery seaside heights; days so sunny it's barely possible to squint across grassy hillsides.

I had gone there on field days with other students. But having finished my course at school, seeing clearly what I want to paint, I go only with Frank. Just the two of us, him and me.

I am always able to accompany Paloma. I have extended a three-month sabbatical into a further year's leave of absence without pay. I can well afford it from my inheritance.

We sit on riverbanks with anglers beneath their wide green umbrellas. It is drizzling softly. My mind is drifting in the midmorning silence, untethered from the present situation; free of visible forms, thoughts. Lost in the passing stream, it is filled in this vacancy here with what, on coming to myself, I recognise is Paloma.

I see what she is drawing, painting. Increasingly it is non-representational – like the purely purple canvas on our bedroom wall. It doesn't require planting herself, or me with her, in a particular place.

Where is it growing from?

We are holding each other, drifting into slumber.

We emerge, held, from sleep, with barely a trace of what has joined us in that dreamed interval. There is scarcely a sign except for a sense of ragged thread, thickly woven; long, tough stems; diffusions of light.

We are back in the *pueblo*. It is summer. Magda, feeling Bruno's loss despite their long alienation, has joined us at El Castillo. She recognises, from some long-suppressed store of love in herself, the success of our once-disputed relationship.

"They're made for each other," she confides to Amalia.

Now Magda takes seriously her approaching role as grandmother of the boy soon to be born. The expectancy is infectious. Paloma's preparations for motherhood are absorbing us all, focusing on diet, sleep, exercise. Or is something more preventing me from making progress with the book I have come to the *pueblo* to write?

It isn't Speer's story. That is already available, fully worked out within me. And I myself am, by now, an open book, telling my tale of self-discovery through him. But a new title is announcing itself: *Another Man*. This is what is preventing me from starting *History and the Human*.

Who hasn't come upon another man, I wonder – one or more? Surely it is not only Hitler's protégé or Professor Keller's student who, each eclipsed by such a potent figure, has existed merely as his own shadow. Haven't others, too, reached unknowingly from dismal depths to their vital selves through the medium of a Casalis or Speer? While the person they long to become, to *be*, well, isn't that yet another man? Can anything less than a novel say?

I am keen to start it. I shall write all in a rush, on nights when Paloma is preoccupied with our child. The theme will sweep through me. And soon I will have finished my book – the true one that *is* me – ridding me of Speer no less than Keller. Then, voided, my mind will be empty at last, here in this *pueblo*.

Amalia has arrived this morning to have coffee with us in the kitchen. She tells us this is the last year she will run the *pensión*. We listen, both of us, each silently reacting.

"But *you're* here," Amalia says, breaking out of her woefulness. "You keep returning. Which reminds me, the German owners of Villa Bougainvillea have written to me again."

The place has been on the market for ages, and they are apparently eager to sell. So, having lost confidence even in the *pueblo's* German estate agent (who has clearly gone native), they are relying on Amalia to find a buyer, presumably for a commission.

"Why don't you make an offer?" she asks us. "You might get it for a knock-down price. The place is of great sentimental value, isn't it – for you both?"

Later, we go for a walk. We have had the sensible conversation about how much work and expense is needed to restore the villa; how complicated ownership would be during our absences, especially now that Amalia will not be available to manage the property; how little we need a second place in a *pueblo* we shall rarely visit.

Our footsteps pursue the narrow streets, circling the rows of tightly packed peasant houses, still white in the dusk. They are drawn to this heavily overgrown one, its creeper dense and dark among mute reverberations the expectant ear conjures up at this hour. The stillness is complete.

We stand there, unmoving, entered into the interior, passing its pale, moonlit walls, statically treading floors laid with locally quarried stone, heavy with the musty odour of subterranean watercourses. We head up worn steps to a now starlit roof – seen from down here, before the unopened front door.

We take in all we have been in possession of well before the door closed before us. How long do we continue standing, without needing to enter where we already are?

We hold there, in the embrace we have long come to, among the irrepressible purple flowers.

About the Author

Leslie Croxford is a British writer born in Alexandria, Egypt. He resides with his wife in Cairo, where he is Senior Vice-President of the British University in Egypt. He obtained a doctorate in History from Cambridge University and has written two novels, *Solomon's Folly* (Chatto & Windus, 1974) and *Deep Sahara* (The Momentum Publishing Company, 2017).